the proud man

ULSTER

The white section shows
Shane O'Neill's
inheritance;
the shaded areas are
lands later conquered
by him.   Names of
clans are in italics.

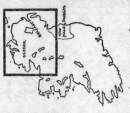

IRELAND

CANTYRE

NORTH CHANNEL

IRISH SEA

MacDonnell

ANTRIM

BELFAST

McArtle

O'Cahan

BANN RIVER

Lough
Neagh

O'Hagan

McGuinness

O'Donnelly

ARMAGH

BENBURB

McGuinness

BLACKWATER RIVER

english
PALE

DUNDALK

O'Reilly

O'Donnell

O'Donnell

T Y R C O N N E L L

Maguire

MacMahon

O'Connor

O'Rourke

Burke

ATLANTIC OCEAN

the
proud
man

a novel by
elizabeth linington

new york
the viking press

PRINTED IN U. S. A.

fOREWORÒ

Duilghe an t'uaibrreach do cheannsugadh.
It is difficult to tame the proud.

—GAELIC PROVERB

THE sixteenth century produced many colorful personalities. In what is now called the British Isles lived two queens—Elizabeth Tudor and Mary Stuart—and many stories have been written of them. But as there are more than two nations in those islands, there was a third ruler, and of that one no stories have been written. This is his story.

The only major fictitious characters in this novel are Rory McGuinness and Moyna. All the rest were real people; many of the scenes among them happened substantially as set down here. If chronology has not always been followed too strictly, it is because all this is long ago and far away and does not matter now. This is only a story for reading. But it is a true story.

contents

characters in this story

Shane, the O'Neill, chief of the clan O'Neill, Prince of Ulster
Hugh O'Neill, his brother and commander in his army
Dudley, Edmund, James, and Manus Donnelly, his foster brothers and
    commanders in his army
Cormac McArdle, chief of the clan McArdle and commander in O'Neill's
    army
Ferdoragh McGuinness and Terence O'Hagan, commanders in O'Neill's
    army
Rory McGuinness, nephew to Ferdoragh
Luke O'Givney, chief musician to O'Neill
John O'Hagan, chief secretary to O'Neill
Aidan Moran, another secretary
Manus McSweeney, constable (sergeant) in O'Neill's army
Moyna, a maidservant

Turlough Lynagh O'Neill, cousin to the chief
Sorley Boy MacDonnell, a Scot, kinsman to the chief MacDonnell,
    brother-in-law and friend to O'Neill
Liam Fleming, chief justice of the city of Armagh, counselor to O'Neill
Terence Daniel, Dean of Armagh Cathedral, counselor to O'Neill
Catherine MacDonnell, daughter to the chief MacDonnell, O'Neill's first
    wife
Mary O'Donnell, daughter to the chief O'Donnell, O'Neill's second wife
Catherine MacLean, widow of the Earl of Argyll and the chief O'Donnell,
    O'Neill's third wife
Calvagh, the O'Donnell, Lord of Tyrconnell, ancient enemy of O'Neill
Hugh, the Maguire, Anglophile in sympathy
O'Cahan, McGuinness, McMahon, O'Reilly, O'Rourk, O'Connor, etc.
Thady O'Brien, spy for O'Neill in Dublin

Hugh Ruadh (Red Hugh) O'Donnell, nephew to Calvagh and heir to the chiefhood

Gerald Fitzgerald, Earl of Kildare, second cousin to O'Neill, an Anglophile

Matthew Kelly, first Baron Dungannon, self-claimed illegitimate son to Con O'Neill (Shane O'Neill's father) and claimant to the chiefhood

Brian Kelly (O'Neill), second Baron Dungannon, Anglophile

The Scottish chief James, the MacDonnell, most powerful chief in Antrim and enemy to O'Neill

Aspuke MacDonnell, kinsman to the chief MacDonnell

The Scottish sept-chiefs Gilchrist and MacArthur

Elizabeth Tudor, Queen of England

Lord Robert Dudley, Earl of Leicester, friend to the queen

Sir William Cecil, Sir Nicholas Bacon, Sir Francis Walsingham, and the Earl of Pembroke, ministers to the queen

Mary Stuart, Queen of Scotland

Lord James Stuart, her illegitimate brother and advisor

Philip II of Spain

Pope Pius IV

John Knox, Protestant leader

Sir Thomas Cusack, Chancellor of the Pale

Lord Radcliffe, Earl of Sussex, military commander of the Pale

Sir Harry Sydney, political deputy to the Crown

Sir William Fitzwilliam and Sir Henry Radcliffe, other deputies

Sir Nicholas Arnold and Sir Nicholas Bagenal, special envoys to the Pale

Sir Thomas Stukeley, illegitimate son to Henry VIII, a pirate

Madam Rebecca Isham, mistress to Sir Harry Sydney

Colm McCaffrey, her servant

Mary O'Neill MacDonnell, sister to O'Neill, wife to Sorley Boy

PART ONE

IReLaNd

CHAPTER I

COLM McCAFFREY, that huge ogre of a man, watched the woman as she moved about the room, ordering the maidservant. "The Jerez wine, Nada—my lord Sussex is fond of it."

"Yes, madam."

McCaffrey wished he might talk with the woman, his employer; he admired Rebecca Isham. A bad woman she might be, mistress to Sir Harry Sydney, one of the deputies to the Crown. But she was also an attractive one—not tall, a fine full figure, a wealth of black hair, mirthful dark eyes, always so elegantly gowned. And she was not arrogant with her servants.

But this was Dublin in the Pale, the English-held land in Ireland, and he was an Irishman: native servants did not speak unless spoken to. Moreover, no one in this house knew McCaffrey could speak English; he had two jobs here, one of them acting as Madam Isham's doorman and the other, spying on the deputies.

Madam Isham turned at the sound of the knocker on the house door, and gave him a smile. "Colm."

He nodded, and went to admit the visitors. The two men brushed past him on the threshold, used to the hulking servant who knew no English, and he took their cloaks and hats. The lady came rustling out to greet them.

"Harry, my dear. My lord Sussex, always a pleasure to welcome you." Was there small irony in her tone on that? She knew why Sir Harry, the deputy, and Radcliffe, Earl of Sussex, met in her house to discuss. Sir Thomas Cusack, Chancellor of the Pale, was an honorable man who had no business in politics; Radcliffe, as military commander here for the new queen, Elizabeth, now and then fomented schemes the chancellor would disapprove.

Sydney kissed her cheek absently; his round pink-and-white face wore a worried expression. Sydney was Saxon English: short, stocky in his velvet diaper-trunks and hose wrinkled on his fat legs; he had pale blue eyes and thinning fair hair. McCaffrey spared him only a glance.

"Madam." Radcliffe gave her a short bow. He made no secret of his disapproval of Rebecca Isham on several counts: as an immoral woman, as mistress to a political deputy, and as a foreigner. McCaffrey had a notion Radcliffe amused Rebecca with his arrogance; he did not amuse McCaffrey, who was an Irishman and knew Radcliffe's military power in Ireland. He fingered Radcliffe's velvet hat, looking after the men as she led them into the little parlor. The earl's tall figure, spare even in padded velvet tunic and trunks, was silhouetted against the light; as he entered, turning, the arrogant profile was etched sharp for an instant— the jutting high Norman nose, the deep brow-ridge, the strong-thrusting jaw. A handsome ascetic, Thomas Radcliffe was, and his light cold eyes emotionless on everything they saw. A sudden involuntary shudder shook McCaffrey's big frame: something walking on his grave. He laid the cloaks and hats on a chair and went softly down to the half-closed parlor door.

". . . not disturb you important statesmen at your private talk." Rebecca, prettily gracious. "My lord, there is Jerez wine here, please to help yourself. If there is aught else you desire . . . ?"

"No, no, quite sufficient, my dear." Sydney sounded nervous.

"Then I excuse myself that you may make your discussion in peace, gentlemen." Little rattle of her heels on the bare floor. McCaffrey turned quickly and was ten paces away when she came out. She did not look at him, but glided down the dim hallway to enter the room behind the parlor. In a moment he drifted back to the parlor door, and with utmost care eased open the latch so that he might listen through the crack. His real employer, his reverence, the Dean of Armagh, was much interested in anything Radcliffe said.

"It might," said Sir Harry Sydney doubtfully, "have been street-thieves."

"Don't be a fool," said Radcliffe baldly. "Dungannon was murdered on his own doorstep, and not for his purse. It was a man of Shane O'Neill's put the knife in Dungannon—I can add two and two."

In the hallway McCaffrey whistled soundlessly to himself. So Dungannon was dead! Matthew Kelly, first Baron Dungannon—toady to the English—and a pawn in this game. Well, he was better dead than quick; and Radcliffe was probably right in his estimation of the killer.

"Con O'Neill was not cold in his coffin before that was planned. Not that Dungannon was much danger to Shane O'Neill," added Radcliffe bitterly. "Only a convenience to have him out of the way. I will always wonder if Dungannon really was Con's bastard. Con made that agreement naming Dungannon his heir willingly enough, but . . ."

Both of them bastards in one sense or the other, McCaffrey thought, listening. Con O'Neill! He had been a disgrace to a great clan. The English controlled three-quarters of Ireland—though officially occupying only this small area, the Pale—but Ulster they had never been able to take,

Ulster, the largest, wealthiest province in Ireland, Ulster of the O'Neills, ruled by O'Neills for a thousand years. And then Con, Prince of Ulster, had sold it to them—the black Anglophile traitor.

"God damn them both!" said Radcliffe. "Who took Ulster for the Crown? I did—with a little English earldom for Con and a pennyworth of ink on paper! And we lose it like that, for the lack of a few men and guns to put up a fight!"

"If we talk of past history," said Sydney with some asperity, "you had some aid in that from Con's second wife."

Radcliffe barked a short laugh. "True—I don't deny it. All the O'Neills are womanizers—and Con, being a weakling, was ruled by his women."

That Anglophile bitch, yes, thought McCaffrey darkly. But Con O'Neill's legitimate children had been by his own first cousin, Ailis O'Neill; it was after her death the other one beguiled him over to the English. And like any nobleman, Con would not raise his own sons, lest they grow vain of lineage; his eldest son, Shane, had been fostered on Cormac Donnelly, and Donnelly was a loyal Ulsterman, as was the sub-chief, O'Cahan, who took the second boy—the girl was no matter. That was one thing Con had done for Ulster—got his eldest legal son. If maybe too many illegal ones here and there.

"Past history!" Radcliffe was repeating now. "Very well, past history it is, but at least I can say I told you so, to you if not to those blind ministers of the queen in London! Fifteen years, always O'Neill—Shane O'Neill! I warned them—when he gathered that first motley army I warned them. Snapping puppies grow to biting hounds. But would they listen? Only a bragging little upstart, they said, let his father subdue him. Con! As well expect Con to halt a thunderstorm." He sounded bedeviled—as if he spoke with jaw clenched—and hadn't he reason? thought McCaffrey with a grin.

The ink was hardly dry on that pact Con had signed with the English, fifteen years ago, when his eldest legal son, Shane, only fifteen then, saved the clan's honor and Ulster. With an army of volunteers he did it, most of them scarcely older than himself; he was a genius born to war-leadership. If Radcliffe had had the reinforcement he begged for then, McCaffrey thought, Shane O'Neill would still have chased him and his English army out of Ulster like a pack of mongrel dogs. Radcliffe had challenged him twice, hoping to retake Ulster, and each time been soundly defeated.

McCaffrey, having heard some reminiscence from the Dean of Armagh, could appreciate the bitterness in Radcliffe's tone. From the first, there had been violent personal enmity between Radcliffe and Shane O'Neill: enmity beyond the reasons of loyalty. That first time they met, in the meeting-hall at Dundalk on the border of the Pale—the Dean said it flared like wildfire between them . . . O'Neill giving the deputies no time to open their mouths, only telling them plainly what would befall any Englishman who set foot across the border of Ulster. That was the only way to treat the Sassenachs, the only thing they understood: force. And never since that day twelve years ago had they got into Ulster again. A pity some of the other provinces had not such a strong leader to rescue them from English domination.

"The situation as it is," said Sydney from beyond the door, "Dungannon would have had no chance to claim the princedom of Ulster for himself, pact or no. He is small loss."

"Did I not just say so? He leaves a son, but that one is a weakling, too. Double dealing on Con's part, that agreement—he knew well enough in their Irish law such an official naming of his heir is not legal. The Ulster clans have always elected their princes, from candidates of the royal O'Neill line. Con's treaty with us outlawed such election—but that treaty has been scrap-paper these twelve years. It is not Ulster of itself I am thinking about now." There was a stir, sound of wine poured into a glass. Now Radcliffe's tone was harder. "There are graver aspects to this situation than a defiance of the Crown's power. O'Neill has been ruler of Ulster in all but name for twelve years. Con was terrified of him, you know as well as I, and never attempted to stand against him. Now Con is dead, the Ulster clansmen will hold their prince-election, and I don't need more than one guess as to what man they will choose. Essentially that will change nothing, only confirm him in his rank. I am thinking," said Radcliffe, "of some other treaties, Harry. The treaties Shane O'Neill has made with Philip of Spain—and Catherine de' Medici in France—and the treaty he will probably seek with this new queen of Scotland, Mary Stuart. They are not all trade-agreements, my friend—they are treaties of mutual military support, and with England's archenemies. O'Neill is not just a little provincial ruler, as some seem to think. He represents enormous potential danger to the Crown."

"It is not foregone," objected Sydney. "He is difficult to deal with, I grant, but a strong military leader like O'Neill is seldom subtle for diplomacies. A clever approach might win him over. I have sent a letter to him in the chancellor's name—"

"If I have learned anything in fifteen years," Radcliffe interrupted with a hint of contempt, "it is never to underestimate Shane O'Neill. Moreover, if he were only the simple warrior you seem to believe, he has shrewder advisors. Liam Fleming, the chief justice of Armagh, is one— and perhaps more dangerous than Fleming is the Dean of Armagh, Terence Daniel. Both are old hands at the game of politics. Lawyer and churchman—would they not be! You and the chancellor and every other man in the government appear to have learned nothing in the years we have had O'Neill to deal with. He is not Con or Dungannon—we cannot treat with him in any way. God, how I keep saying it, and none listening or believing me! How many raids into the Pale has he made these twelve years, Harry?" It was a violent question; a chair creaked as if Radcliffe flung himself back in resigned anger.

"It is not established that the raids—"

"—Are led by O'Neill? Oh, my God, yes, I have read the polite letters he sends to the chancellor, when we make some formal protest! Such destruction much to be regretted—bands of outlaws as yet uncaught doubtless responsible! Bands of his own army men and he at their head! The chancellor may swallow his lies—I do not. I tell you, Harry, the power of the Crown in Ireland is endangered every minute Shane O'Neill continues to live."

There was a short silence within the room. McCaffrey leaned closer to the door. He heard the sound of a glass set down on a table, a nervous cough from Sydney.

"We must be rid of O'Neill," said Radcliffe in a lower voice. "Rid of him once for all. When he is dead, whether or not we can occupy Ulster at once, we are in no danger from his present allies—or himself. The brother is not so strong a leader. Yes, yes, I know—how many attempts have there been to assassinate him! He has other enemies nearer than ourselves, and I have instigated a few attempts myself, as you know. But this time—and it must be done before the clan-election."

"When will they hold that?" asked Sydney uneasily.

"They may be gathering now, that is the devil of it. And as I told you, I sail for England tomorrow. I must have some personal discussion with William Cecil over the situation. Cecil is a shrewd man—the only one among the ministers. But I have a man hired to try for O'Neill." Radcliffe laughed. "I promised him five hundred for the job—and I'd pay it out of my own pocket and be glad to—but I doubt if he escapes to collect it, if he succeeds in putting a knife in O'Neill."

"Who is the man?"

"A Scot named Gray. And I hope to God—"

McCaffrey missed the next remarks, his thoughts running swiftly. The devil's luck he heard this only now. By the way Radcliffe spoke, there'd be no time to send a letter to the Dean, who would warn O'Neill. Someone must ride for Ulster at once to carry warning. Thady, he thought with a breath of relief: Thady O'Brien, who was in O'Neill's pay as a Dublin spy, and, being a street-peddler, could come and go unnoticed. He must see Thady tonight and send him north with the warning.

He was so intent the opening of the other door down the passage caught him unaware; a fraction of a minute too late, he stepped back as if only passing this door. But Rebecca Isham was startled too, seeing him—or she would not have rapped out the question in English, in a whisper: "Colm! What do you here?"

His startlement betrayed him to a hoarse whisper in return. "Nothing, madam, I only—" And then he felt cold sweat break on his forehead.

"Ah!" She came softly toward him; she glanced aside, noting the door eased open a crack. A hand on his arm, she motioned him silently down to the entrance-hall, where they might speak out of the deputies' hearing. "So you do understand English! I had wondered—at times you looked too intelligent when I spoke to others."

"I—a little I have picked up—listening, madam—"

"Listening to our important visitors?" she took him up. "This is not, I think, the first time you have done that."

He looked at her in silence. He could think of nothing to say, and expected her to denounce him to Sydney and Radcliffe at once. There was the vestige of a smile on her mouth as she stared back at him. Then, at sounds from the parlor, she half-turned.

"They are coming out—quiet!" She picked up her skirts and ran; when the deputies emerged into the passage, she was apparently just descending the stair, leisurely and graceful.

Radcliffe made her a formal farewell while McCaffrey produced the cloaks and hats. "My dear," said Sydney vaguely, patting her arm. "I will call tomorrow afternoon." In the midst of his anxiety McCaffrey reflected that she deserved a warmer lover. And why was she saying nothing to them of an eavesdropper?

The door thudded shut discreetly. A finger to her lip, she regarded him an instant in the dimness. "Come into the parlor."

He followed her in silence to the lighted room. A courtesan learned discretion; maybe she would only dismiss him and say nothing to the deputies. In any case, he must get to O'Brien tonight and send him to warn—

"Yes, I had wondered," she said, smiling. "You are not such a stupid hulk as you look, are you, Colm? So you listen to the deputies—perhaps just out of curiosity, yes?" She wandered to the table, poured herself a glass of wine. Holding it, not drinking: "But their talk is very monotonous, I find. Oh, yes, I too listen to them, now and then. From—another vantage-point, you comprehend."

He eyed her, wondering, cautious. Maybe this was a trick to make him reveal himself. He waited, not speaking. She turned and gave him a quick glance.

"Very monotonous," she repeated. "They talk of nothing but O'Neill, always O'Neill—of course, one hears talk of that man everywhere these days. Not so?"

"Yes—madam."

She took a sip of wine and set the glass down. "It is understandable that my lord Sussex—and others—regard O'Neill as dangerous. But also understandable that the Irish people look on him with admiration. Do you, Colm?" She shot the question at him.

"Well, madam—"

"Ah, yes, yes—you are a resident of the Pale, under English law! Forgive me, I should not ask." But he saw she still had something to say. And what was she getting at? To force him into self-betrayal, or—something else? "Many tales I have heard of Shane O'Neill," she said to her ringed hands. "He appears to be—what do you Irish say?—a man and a half, is it? Especially," and she laughed, "with the ladies!"

McCaffrey relaxed a trifle. If she only wanted to talk of O'Neill like that—"He's an Irishman, madam—and an O'Neill."

"He has wed two wives already, I have heard. One at a time, that is! Somewhere I heard an amusing story about his first marriage." And so you would, thought McCaffrey, if you heard it straight. "How one of his enemies made him drunken and married him to a wanton. A Scottish man, a—how is it?—a clan-chief. Was the name the MacDonnell? And the woman, she was one of his own illegal daughters he tricked O'Neill into wedding."

And by what the Dean said, O'Neill still held the grudge on James MacDonnell—would he not? The knot tied, he'd had to keep the girl; she bore him three sons before he found her in bed with one of his own army captains and packed her back to her father—after hanging the captain. No man played tricks on O'Neill without retribution; one day the MacDonnell would regret it, though O'Neill had bribed an annulment out of the Pope . . . But McCaffrey was more interested in this woman at the moment.

"It was most amusing," and she sipped daintily. "And now, I have heard, O'Neill is wed to the daughter of another of his enemies, an ugly woman no man would look at but for—political reasons."

You have heard the hell of a lot, my lady, thought McCaffrey uneasily. That marriage with the daughter of Calvagh the O'Donnell was not a year ago, and to McCaffrey's knowledge Radcliffe had not known of it last week—he had no spies in Ulster now. Perhaps the deputies had learned of it in the last few days, and she'd heard it from Sydney? That must be the way of it. It was true enough; but one thing he'd wager they didn't know, that O'Neill had been persuaded into the marriage by old Liam Fleming, in the hope of reconciling the clans O'Neill and O'Donnell, old archenemies.

"Indeed," he said noncommittally.

"Colm—" She turned to him directly, and he saw that the hand she lifted in habitual foreign gesture was trembling very slightly. "I take the chance with you. I said I had wondered about you—me, I notice little things—and now I will be open with you. If I am wrong—well, perhaps I leave Dublin very quickly! But I do not think so. I do not know who you are or why you spy on the deputies—but I make a guess: I think you are something to do with O'Neill of Ulster."

"Oh, madam—"

She silenced him impatiently, nervously. "I am—I am nobody," she said with quick bitterness. "An Italian Hebrew woman, maybe not so clever, who lives by selling favors. But since I am in Ireland with Harry, I—I have sympathy for your people, Colm. My people too, they suffer persecutions. . . . Colm. You heard what Radcliffe said tonight—about an assassin?"

McCaffrey drew a breath and stepped closer to her. "I heard him, madam, yes."

"You see, I find—from the stories I hear—I like this O'Neill better than Radcliffe, my lord Sussex." She was close to him now, all pretense dropped. She put her hands flat on his chest, looking up earnestly. "I will take a hand in this game myself. Colm, I want you to ride quick, quick, and warn O'Neill of the assassin!"

A grin widened McCaffrey's mouth. "There was a suspicion in me you are a right one—madam." And they both drew breaths of relief at understanding. "I was just reckoning how to get away and send warning. It's a poor excuse for a spy I must be when you see through me so easy—" There, she had it out of him; he damned himself for a fool, but at that could not feel much alarm. She had spoken from the heart, he'd swear it.

"Ah—" She relaxed more and smiled up at him almost flirtatiously. "My stupid big doorman. So we understand one another. You need not fear—I am very clever at keeping secrets. But you must go at once—tonight—"

"No fear," said McCaffrey. "The English won't be rid of him so easy."

CHAPTER II

Now at the beginning of this new year of 1559, Ulster stood rulerless, awaiting a new prince. Con the Lame was dead, his treachery done; and the chiefs and head-clansmen of Ulster were met as tradition demanded to elect his successor. So that man was an O'Neill of the royal line he need not be a son of Con's; but the name in men's mouths was that of the eldest legal son, as it had been in their mouths fifteen years.

At the house of old John O'Hagan, *rechtaire* to the O'Neills, they gathered for the ceremony of election that would be held on the Hill of Tullaghogue as it had been held for over a thousand years. This election meant freedom or slavery to Ulster; much talk and speculation about it there was, and the one name most often on all tongues—the name of Shane O'Neill.

Rory McGuinness surveyed himself with satisfaction in the square of polished bronze on the wall. "Will I do, uncle?"

It was hard work dragging words out of Ferdoragh McGuinness; Rory knew; he'd had practice. Ferdoragh only rumbled at him, "There'll be no eyes on you, cockerel." He stood naked after lacing his sandals, his great hairy bear's body dwarfing Rory; he pulled on a yellow wool tunic, draped a brown wool kilt athwart his thighs, reached for his stiff wide leather belt. No foppish dresser, Ferdoragh. Rory grinned at his uncle in exasperation. Much of his boyhood had gone to pulling stories out of Ferdoragh, who could tell them when he chose. He had fought in France and Spain against the English—and in Ireland.

Rory fidgeted with the collar lacing of his tunic; dressed, he would like to go down to the hall, but this day clansmen must stay together in group until the ceremony was done. He did not need Ferdoragh to tell him it was not his day, but in a measure it was his, too; for it would mark the beginning of his future in life and he was wild with impatience.

"My Christ, uncle, move! They'll all be before us."

"Two hours to noon, boy. O'Hagan will take—him up first."

"Yes—" wild with impatience for that as well, to lay eye on Shane O'Neill the first time. He knew all the stories—who did not in Ulster?

He had plagued Ferdoragh often enough for the little personal glimpses he could give.

"You can go to your father. I will be joining the retinue."

That he'd forgotten: Ferdoragh was not only a McGuinness this day, but one of O'Neill's army captains. He gave a last hasty look in the bronze. One of the red McGuinnesses—but not one of the big ones. A slim young blue-eyed fire-haired McGuinness, hot to fight and love and not unproven at either of them, twenty-one last month. He tugged the throat-lacings straighter to his blue tunic, settled the full blue kilt; he thrust the dagger more firmly in his belt and took up his cloak from the bed. He was pleased with himself, Rory; he was excited for this great day.

He went out to the dark stone passage and met the rest of the Mc-Guinnesses converging at the top of the nearest stair.

"I was about to send after you"—his father, Conan, grumbling.

"Is Ferdoragh still snoring?"—his brother Aidan, grinning. "I said to Fergus—"

Rory aimed an amiable blow at his brothers. "Your tongue off Ferdoragh. He is not." He gave a hasty salute to his grandfather, Michael, the chief McGuinness.

"A damned cold morning," complained his father. "Always awkward Con O'Neill was. He would die at the tail of the year—"

"As he lived at the tail of the English!" said the chief tartly. "I'm needing another cup before we set out."

"They'll be gathering in the hall," soothed his son.

They were, and the hall of O'Hagan's house crowded with them, the head-men of Ulster. Rory looked about, eager and curious, but the foremost group had already left with old John O'Hagan. They had come last night—the rest had been gathering for a week—but by custom kept to private chambers until after today's ceremony. There was an almost tangible tension about the press of men in the hall; they packed in clan-groups, talking low when they talked at all. A few servants ran about with cups and flagons; others besides the McGuinness felt the need of an extra dram of liquor this chill morning.

Ferdoragh came up behind Rory and rumbled vaguely at the chief, who eyed him sourly. "Ferdoragh," muttered Rory behind his hand—the atmosphere was contagious—"is it true O'Neill has said he will refuse be the election not unanimous?"

"True enough." Ferdoragh's hand swallowed a cup from a passing servant. He put down the contents at a gulp. "I heard him." At a touch on his arm he turned. Rory knew that man: it would be one of the four sons of Cormac Donnelly, who were foster brothers to Shane O'Neill and captains in his army. This one spoke no word, only nodded, and Ferdoragh turned to accompany him to men waiting at the door: more Donnellys. Any but a blind man would know those three for brothers, all slender, brown-haired, pale. Rory identified them from hearsay: Edmund, James, and Manus; the eldest, Dudley, would be—elsewhere.

And now the groups in the hall commenced to shift and move: it was time. Time they got on with the business. He thought old Michael would never start, but they came out at last; a bevy of grooms held the horses, and already a troop of riders straggled out the gate.

They rode out from O'Hagan's house toward the great Hill of Tullaghogue, and even Rory, perhaps the youngest man among them, felt that they did not ride alone: the ghosts of thirty years of history followed them—and how many years to come?

Men said of Shane O'Neill—what did they not say? He was more than a man. He had saved Ulster from the English, vindicated his clan when his father had betrayed it. And now the chiefs met to confirm a new prince, and what other choice could they make?

They gathered at the ceremonial clearing on the top of Tullaghogue, where the Stone of Destiny stood in the center. This January day was cold; every man was wrapped in a cloak, the bright crude colors making each man a bold apartness not to be blended to a whole—green, scarlet, purple, sky-blue. Here and there, even more of an apartness, showed the saffron that marked a clan-chief. The cloaks blew aside to show the short kilts and tunics beneath, the bare legs and high-laced sandals. Over all an iron cold sky, the sun somewhere behind high mountain fog, cast white light like the reflection in a warrior's shield: over the restless pack of men, the grooms holding horses at one side, the ceremonial stone and old John O'Hagan beside it, and the sudden sharper glint of color as a man moved and a jewel on finger or armband or belt caught the light. McMahon, Kelly, O'Connor, O'Cahan, O'Dogherty, McSweeney, McArdle, O'Hagan, Donnelly, McGuinness, O'Hanlon, O'Reilly, all were there—all the clans of Ulster represented.

But Rory searched the groups eager-eyed for the man who dominated this meeting, him they said was more than a man. He saw every man there before his eyes found the place. Near O'Hagan at the stone was the little cluster of four Donnellys. The other army captains stood apart —handsome Hugh O'Neill, tall, brown-haired, blue-eyed, very finely dressed: Ferdoragh the red bear: big Terence O'Hagan that was twin to Ferdoragh: and the little chief of the McArdles, Cormac. Rory had never seen him before, a small man but wide as a church door, with skin white as a girl's; he wore a full black beard but no mustache. There was Terence Daniel, Dean of Armagh Cathedral, erect and handsome still in middle age, and wizened old Liam Fleming, chief justice of the city of Armagh —both were counselors to O'Neill. There was Hughie Maguire the chief, who had been wed to Mary O'Neill, sister to Shane and Hugh (men said she was a wanton for any man's taking; she had run off from Maguire and was wed now to the Scot, Sorley Boy MacDonnell). There was Turlough Lynagh O'Neill, immense and stolid.

Rory might be fascinated as any man by the tales and deeds of Shane O'Neill, but he was aware of dangerous contentions among this crowd. There were four men of all these here who might hold back from casting their votes for O'Neill: and he had said, if the election was not unanimous, he would refuse the chiefhood. Rory cast a look at his grandfather, the old McGuinness, who was one of the four . . . "Well, I don't deny he is a strong man and no Anglophile, but impulsive he is and listens not to the counsel of elders . . ." The other three had better reasons. Maguire had taken chastisement at O'Neill's hands over a little treaty he made with the English. O'Reilly's land adjoined the English Pale; O'Reilly talked soft to the English. And Turlough Lynagh was first cousin, in line to claim the chiefhood if he had any backers.

But where—? Then Cormac McArdle moved, and a man rose from where he had sat on a boulder; Rory drew a deep breath, seeing him. He had known from Ferdoragh what to expect, but the word was a little thing beside the man. He stared. "Oh, by Christ," he breathed to his brother Fergus beside him, "that is a man—that is a man!" He was not the only man there who saw the legend in the flesh for the first time; a little mutter rose from the crowd. A small piece of melodrama: O'Neill had known the precise moment to stand and reveal himself, the moment before the ceremony began.

As John O'Hagan took one step forward from the great stone a few eyes transferred to the old McGuinness. There would be a certain influence exerted by the first to vote. The little rustle of the crowd hushed still as if at sharp command, though O'Hagan's voice was thin and high.

"Chiefs and men of Ulster! Hear the *rechtaire!* It is duly certified and witnessed that the prince over you, Con Baccagh of the O'Neill, is dead of a sickness at his Castle Dungannon. In due ceremony is he committed to the earth and Ulster stands under no prince. Therefore by rule and custom are you gathered to name and elect a new prince over you, all you who have a vote to cast. So the name be that of an O'Neill of the royal line it may be any name. Now I direct every man to disarm. We talk words, not blades." Part of the ritual: each man unsheathed his belt knife, dropped it on the ground before him. The tension was building to new height; there was a short pause before O'Hagan spoke again.

"By brehon law, by ancient custom, by all courtesy, the eldest of the chiefs among you has the right to name the first name and cast the first vote. Michael of the McGuinness, I call on you to speak!"

The portly old McGuinness took a step forward into the clearing; his round face was red as fire. He hitched up his kilt with a belligerent gesture. He took a breath and his voice was a bull's roar.

"I name Shane O'Neill of the O'Neill, and who in hell have we in Ulster to best him?"

The roar that went up broke the formality of ritual like a physical blow. No need to take individual count; the vote was unanimous. The hills rang with it, and O'Hagan's voice could not still it for a space.

"Men of Ulster! Men of Ulster! Silence for the *rechtaire!* You have chosen your prince." His voice could not carry above so many voices; but he turned, and bowed, and bent his knee, and then the thunder stilled, for the new Prince of Ulster lifted a hand and stood beside the stone.

O'Hagan was a tall man, there were other tall men about, but this man topped the tallest by a head. He was big of bone but not clumsily built, wide of shoulder, lean of waist and thigh; his shoulder-length hair was dark auburn, his eyes silver-gray in a dark lean face. Of all men there, he was the finest clad, in a bright emerald-green kilt and tunic; a scarlet cloak hung to his heels, but he had flung that back from his shoulders. Jewels blazed in his four-inch-wide belt, the hilts of four daggers thrust there, and more jewels on his fingers, the twin shoulder brooches, the three armbands. His sandals were gilded and the laces tipped with emeralds. He moved a hand and the crowd stilled instantly; his voice was rough bass thunder to their louder thunder.

"Chiefs and men of Ulster! Your new prince you choose—I swear to you my honor to abide by the law and rule of Ulster." There would have been another roar but he hushed it. His eyes traveled over them, bright, excited. "Now, by God, come and bend the knee before the O'Neill!"

They needed no second invitation. There was a scramble to line before him. Rory's heart was pounding; he pressed up behind his grandfather. "Grandser—you'll not forget? You said—"

"Sst, boy, no. Bide your time."

One by one every man present stood before the prince to swear allegiance. He stood, hands on thighs, thumbs hooked in his belt, head back, the aura of triumph nearly tangible about him. His foster brothers the four Donnellys were lined beside him, his brother Hugh and his other captains.

When the McGuinness knelt before him he laughed and struck the old chief a light blow on the chest with the back of his hand. "My thanks for the send-off, oldster! But not you, some other man giving that." This close, Rory felt the tremendous hot power of him, like physical heat. He nudged his grandfather urgently in the spine.

"Let be, boy—stand back! Precedence! My heir—my grandsons, my lord. I beg a moment. I'd be the first to offer you a gift suitable to princes."

· "Gracious man—I accept it."

"Only if you choose, O'Neill." The McGuinness hauled Rory before him. "Plaguing me to it he is. The third grandson—but, I remind you, nephew to your Ferdoragh, for all its lack of size. If you've a use for it—"

The O'Neill laughed again, eyes on Rory, who stammered, "To serve you, O'Neill—I swear fealty—"

"You would do that anyway, my red one." The silver stare raked him head to foot. "Can you handle an ax?"

"I am the hell of an axman, you can ask any—"

"What makes a good horse?"

Rory knew the answer to that and gave it promptly. "Four sound legs and a willing temper."

"Tell me, do you like the Sassenachs at all?"

He answered that promptly too and obscenely; the men in hearing laughed. O'Neill grinned and clapped him on the shoulder, heavy-handed. "Behind me, chief's man! The gift I take. You I'll find a place for."

Obeying, Rory nearly had to lean on Ferdoragh. Upborne with pride, he never realized the irreverence of his thought: meeting this man was like meeting God. And he'd be serving him, one of his army men, fighting for him. "Oh, by God," he whispered to Ferdoragh, "by God, but you never told me—" what? A more eloquent man than Ferdoragh might try to describe him, but coming face to face—it was a different thing.

"Hold up, cockerel," muttered Ferdoragh with a grin. "Am I knowing how you feel? I am. But don't go getting above yourself—you're not that much of an axman, and I'll see to your training myself. Be quiet and stand straight."

But nothing could damp Rory's spirit that moment. He was of O'Neill's army—what matter if they put him in the troops, the most junior officer? He did not care, so he was with O'Neill. That moment, if O'Neill had ordered him, he'd have charged the whole English army singlehanded. As in a dream he watched the rest of the ceremony, O'Neill seated on the stone, ivory wand in hand, while O'Hagan fitted the right shoe of gold to his foot, tossed the left over his left shoulder, and the chiefs murmured the invocation that confirmed a new prince of the O'Neills.

Ferdoragh prodded him in the stomach. "Move, boy, move." Rory sat up and moaned, clutching his head.

"Dying I am. Go away, uncle."

"Here is a hoof of the horse kicked you. Put out your hand." He did; a cup was placed in it. He swallowed and shuddered, opened his eyes and moaned again. "Up!" said Ferdoragh. "We ride in an hour."

"My Christ, I could not mount to save my life." But he threw off the blanket and sat on the edge of the bed, head in hands. "Give me another drink and I'm with you."

"Not until you dress yourself. Come, up now, fine you'll be."

"Gah!" said Rory. "I will not." He reached blindly for his clothes, the morning sunlight stabbing his temples.

There had been a great feast the night before, in celebration of the election; Ulstermen being Ulstermen, the flagons had made the rounds thrice often enough to give every man his fill and the house rolled to bed well and truly drunken—in degree. There were hard heads among the army men; Ferdoragh looked exactly as usual. He hurried Rory into his clothes, condescended to give him another mouthful of liquor; Rory began to feel slightly more alive. "He's hot to get home to Benburb now this is over; he'll be riding at once and all of us with him."

Rory yawned. "But I'll be going home, to collect the rest of my clothes —a couple of horses—"

Ferdoragh pulled him up. "You are O'Neill's man now. He provides for you, and you stay by him. You'll ride with us—I want to break you in to your new duties."

"Right with me!" He was nothing loath, save that he would like to say a better farewell to his mother; but he would be visiting home at intervals, of course. He had his ax and daggers with him, his best horse Fionn. He shook his head to clear it further. "Right with me, I'll just go and tell the others—say farewell."

"The courtyard in half an hour," Ferdoragh called after him.

O'Hagan and the other chiefs pressed the new O'Neill to stay for a more ceremonial visit; but, as Ferdoragh said, he was impatient to return to his castle. Rory was to learn of O'Neill that once he was finished with a thing he forgot it entirely. He had wed Mary O'Donnell eight and a half months ago, and when he left his castle to come to this meeting she was in premature labor of his child; he was hot to get back and discover if it was a son. "At least," Ferdoragh had said, "this one is sure as death his. Those first three might be any man's—it was an easy woman, that female bastard of the MacDonnell's."

"And you finding out the way Cathal O'Toole did?" hinted his brother Conan with a grin.

"Listen, brother, I've more sense than to cheat Shane O'Neill with the prettiest woman in the world—I've a fondness for living. The hell of a man, Cathal, but a fool. Six months he hung at the gate of Benburb and the crows picking his bones. She was not worth it."

So perhaps if this was a son O'Neill would name him the legal heir to the chiefhood. The other three—Eanruig, Con, and Turlough—were at fosterage with his own foster father, Cormac Donnelly; and there were plenty more to choose from by all accounts. The heir need not be legitimate, and they said he'd got his first bastard at sixteen. At any rate, he had forgotten yesterday as if it were ten years back, as if he had had no doubt in the world of the election—and maybe he had not. He ordered his personal retinue to assemble to ride in midmorning; when Rory came down with his saddlebag packed, having exchanged hasty farewells with his father and brothers, the little party was already mounting, O'Hagan and other chiefs in line to clasp the new prince's hand, reiterate congratulation. O'Neill had come with but a small escort, his high army commanders and ten troopmen; they were lined to ride, and Rory took his horse from the groom to mount beside Ferdoragh. With the shouts of the clansmen following, they turned out of the gate and rode southwest across the open rolling country.

The cold air revived Rory further, and he commenced to plague Ferdoragh with more questions, about O'Neill's castle and household. Ferdoragh—and Hugh O'Neill. He would have expected more formality among the commanders, and to himself as one strange and younger. But when Ferdoragh introduced them they were friendly—all but Dudley Donnelly, and Dudley, he had heard, was odd man out among all men; he believed it, meeting him. He was to know all these men well; that morning he thought only that McArdle was overserious, Terence O'Hagan another Ferdoragh in his size and redness, and the other three Donnellys silent. Hugh, however, rode abreast with him, careless and easy—Hugh, the man all men loved, who had most of the O'Neill virtues and few of the vices. Hugh he knew in five minutes; he was that kind of man. Ferdoragh had said once, "Put Hugh down in the middle of a desert and he'd be making friends of the ravens for something to talk at." Hugh had another foster father than the chief; the subchief O'Cahan had raised him. But he had ridden with O'Neill's army ten years. He was five years the younger, which put him only four years over Rory. Rory read him as a woman's man too, but it was never vice in Hugh—a kind heart only: they flocked at him, cats around cream, and, being an O'Neill, he had no impulse to back away.

He laughed at Rory's admission of inexperience at war. "You may not be as big as our Ferdoragh, but if you've half his spirit, you'll do, Rory!"

"He's half again too much," growled Ferdoragh. "Always getting himself into trouble. For ten years he's been agitating at me to get him into O'Neill's army—he'll make a bad officer, no understanding of discipline in him."

"You'll eat your words, uncle! What's discipline? I'll outfight you any day, half as much weight to carry!"

"Good man," said Hugh with a grin.

"But you were telling about the castle—" O'Neill had built his own fortress in south Tyrone, half a day's ride from O'Hagan's house.

"You'll be seeing it, what use to waste words? But you'll never see another like it."

The chief rode ahead of the party, the Donnellys about him. When they halted past midday for a meal, he sat apart with Dudley Donnelly, served by troopmen. Again, it surprised Rory that the others should be so informal; but they were professional military men and had grown away from social conventions. He noticed that none gave McArdle the respect due even a subchief. In that army—well, anywhere in Ulster now—when a man said "the chief," there was only one in his mind.

"We'll be in before dusk," said Hugh, lying back on the turf, careless of his fine clothes. "Not bad weather—cold, but dry. Who's any liquor left?"

"You filled your flask at O'Hagan's; if it's empty you can go without. Not bad," agreed Edmund Donnelly. "If the weather stays open we may make a few winter raids."

As Ferdoragh said, Rory was never shy; even among these important men, he spoke up promptly. "That's for me, I've heard of the raids on the Pale." They laughed at him, unoffended by his brashness.

"Good sport," said Terence O'Hagan with a wink. "When we burn enough of the corn they must send to England for more, and the queen complaining on them. That soft fool of a chancellor, Cusack—such polite letters he sends, protesting the destruction. And Shane's just as polite in apology—a few wild ruffians still uncaught, and much to be regretted. The English know well enough who leads the raids, but they've no army at all in the Pale. Radcliffe has been asking men and arms for years."

"He may get them under this new queen, Elizabeth." Edmund rubbed his nose thoughtfully.

"Small danger, by what old Liam Fleming thinks. Elizabeth Tudor wears a crown not uncontested. She's worried for that Stuart woman, not O'Neill."

The McGuinness land was just east of the River Bann, near the south end of Lough Neagh, that largest inland water in all Ireland, so Rory was familiar with south Tyrone, though he'd never been as far into it as O'Neill's castle. John O'Hagan's house lay north in flatter land; when, in the afternoon, they drew into mountains Rory felt more at home. Plaguing Ferdoragh again: "Is it near now?" They rode along the west shore of Lough Neagh for several hours; when they turned west away from it along the river the land rose under them to taller mountains, and presently Hugh pulled up, touched Rory's arm, and pointed.

"There is Benburb. An hour's ride now."

Rory stared. Ahead rose a range of rugged hills, and the highest was faced this side with a sheer steep cliff. At its summit was a wall, seeming almost a continuation of the rock, and beyond it, Benburb—the castle of the bold cliff—defiant above the precipice it was named for. It was not a castle in the English or even the Scot meaning, nothing Norman to it, no turrets or towers or guardwalks; it was a great gray solid stone pile of a noble house, and looking so inaccessible that Rory wondered how one ever reached it, or, having got there, came off again. But now they followed a path that wound among hills along the river until it turned sharp left and began to climb. It spiraled up between cliff-walls, so narrow that they must ride single-file; at places Rory's heel scraped the rock at a turn. "No force could ever take Benburb," said Ferdoragh, and Rory said he believed him. Toward the top the path widened and finally opened out where the wall ended it and a great oaken gate. A dozen guards were on duty there. The news of the election had covered Ulster like wildfire overnight; they snapped to attention and raised a great shout of welcome for the chief.

O'Neill lifted a hand, laughing, in acknowledgment; they rode through the gate to a wide walled courtyard. "Well, here is Benburb you were so curious about," grunted Ferdoragh. "Wake up, boy, will I pull you off your horse?" Rory saw a boy was waiting to take the bridle, and dropped to the ground hastily.

CHAPTER III

EVER since he could remember he had wanted to be one of O'Neill's army men; but he had never expected what happened once he was.

They came into the fore-passage of the house behind the chief, and he needed six pairs of eyes for all his looking. The large square passage gave a glimpse of the great hall through wide doors to the left, the trestle tables already set out there and laid for the meal; the walls were hung with axes, shields, and knives. Half a dozen servants came scurrying up, along with a dozen hounds that pawed at their masters; there was a babble of respectful greeting and congratulation.

"Let be, let be, for Christ's sake, let me get a word in! What of the child—is it a son?"

"It is a son, O'Neill—"

"Well, God be thanked for it, at least the woman knows her duty! Fetch me a drink—we'll dine at once." O'Neill turned for the hall, turned back casually. "The woman?"

"The Lady Mary is unwell, O'Neill—and—"

The chief shrugged; he said to the captains, "It is a weak female full of notions and humors—why did I let Liam persuade me to it? Politics! Rulers must sacrifice much to politics. I said liquor—at once!" A brimming cup was thrust into his hand; and a man appeared in the doorway of the hall, a man not a servant or of the house. He wore the kilt and tunic awkwardly as if used to other dress, and his eyes went to O'Neill in instant fascination.

"My lord O'Neill—"

The chief swung about and raked the man with a careless stare.

The fellow wet his lips nervously. "I am—from Dublin, lord, with news for your ear only. If we might speak private—" His Gaelic was Scots, not Irish, and flavored with English as well.

O'Neill laughed in little contempt. "I do not talk private with any man out of the Pale, stranger. Get you out of my house."

"No—O'Neill, if you'd listen—" The man edged closer. "It is important, a thing you must know, if you'd only step aside with me, so, I can—I will—" He sidled up to the chief as if to force him to a corner of the passage by the open house-door; he shot a quick look at that door and his eyes flickered. Involuntarily, the fellow so close, O'Neill stepped back away from the other men; they were doffing cloaks, calling for liquor. Rory chanced to be the only for a moment watching the chief; and he saw the stranger's hand at his belt.

He covered the distance between in one leap and got the man by the elbows from behind, and the drawn dagger flew wide. Then all exploded around him into outcry, the Donnellys crowding up, Hugh pushing between the chief and the rest, Ferdoragh loud with curses. "By God, the bastard—" "Are you right, Shane?" "Get his knife—" Rory held the man strongly; the fellow struggled and babbled wild English.

"Well, before God," said O'Neill mildly. "An assassin—another assassin." He stilled exclamation with a gesture, came up to Rory and the captive. "And a brash one. Quick work, boy. . . . What is your name? Who sent you here to dagger me?"

The man shook under Rory's hands, knowing death near. Failing to be alone with the chief, he had thought to stab and run; he gasped now, "O'Neill—mercy—I would not, but for the gold—I—"

O'Neill surveyed him dispassionately. "Hold him so," and he struck the man once with clenched fist on the jaw-point. It knocked him from Rory's grip six feet backward; he never made a sound but stretched flat as a corpse against the wall. "The little men," said the chief. "The little men who think to destroy O'Neill! You were quick, my bold one," to Rory.

Hugh threw an arm about Rory impulsively. "A bit less so and that dagger might have found you! Good man, Rory."

He took a breath to say modestly it was nothing at all, but at that moment hooves clattered in the courtyard, there was a shout from the guards, and another man tumbled out of the saddle at the doorstep and flung into the passage. All the captains surged forward, O'Neill swung round, drawing a knife; but the man stopped short. "My lord O'Neill—God be thanked I'm in time!"

"We are having visitors indeed," said the chief. The newcomer was a man to see: tall as O'Neill and broader, the ogre of all nursery tales come to life; he was a youngish man, swarthy, rudely dressed, and with no knife in his belt. "You I should know—who are you?"

"McCaffrey, lord—Colm McCaffrey. I came to warn—" He saw the assassin then, relaxed and grinned. "A fool's errand, I am thinking. I might know O'Neill and his men are not to be tricked so easy. We were unsure when he left Dublin."

"McCaffrey, my Christ, yes, you are the Dean's spy in the Pale. I'll make a little talk with you. Dudley, Hugh—the council room at once." But the chief turned back as if recalling a small errand, prodded the assassin with one foot. "Take this out and hang it."

Rory had never hanged a man but if O'Neill gave the order he was willing to try. He hauled the limp figure up and started for the door. The chief stayed him, hand on his shoulder.

"No task for a gentleman—give him to the guards." They were crowding up to the door after McCaffrey; the chief beckoned and pointed, and two men seized the captive from Rory and dragged him off.

McCaffrey said amusedly, "They were thinking myself an assassin and would not admit me. God be thanked he missed you, lord. A renegade Scot he is—Radcliffe sent him."

"As I could have guessed." Now the chief was looking at Rory, eyes bright with amusement. "My Christ, you know a little idea comes to me. How many attempts on my life these last five years? No counting. All too likely more to come. No man will ever dagger me from before, but I've no eyes behind. An important man like me, a monarch, needs a bodyguard for dignity. Quick on your feet you are—Rory, is it?"

"Yes, O'Neill."

"Good. You may have the job. A kinsman of Ferdoragh I can trust, and you proved yourself just now."

"Nothing about the man you know!"—Dudley Donnelly, quick, resentful. "You are overtrustful, Shane—"

The chief hit him a careless, friendly blow on the back. "My suspicious Dudley! No matter, we'll talk it over later—now I want speech with McCaffrey. Seosamh! Fetch liquor to the council room at once." He strode off down the passage with Dudley, Hugh and McCaffrey following. The others drew long breaths.

"That was a close thing," said Terence O'Hagan. He grinned at Rory, stroking his great red mustache. "I'm thinking it's lucky Ferdoragh brought you to us, youngster."

Ferdoragh, as usual, exhibited no emotion. "Come along, I'll find a chamber for you—and you'll want a drink."

The chamber Rory was given was large, fully ten feet square and well appointed, with two good beds, a table bearing several metal basins, a square of bronze as mirror, and two chests. He would have it to himself to start, but might acquire a chambermate; most of the unmarried officers shared chambers, for not even Benburb was large enough to afford all separate rooms. The army leaders, some fifty or sixty of them, occupied two wings of the house, one for those with wives and families. The McGuinness' house was crowded, his household large; Rory had grown up among twenty kinsmen and their families, who lived there. But Benburb was five times the size and sheltered a household of nearly three hundred, counting all the servants. The army made permanent camp in the hills behind. There were fifty home-farms about, supplying the house and soldiers; down the slope to the west side lay the chief's extensive stables and kennels. He rode nothing but Arabs, and bred some fine ones; there were over two hundred in his private stable, and twice that many half- and quarter-breds in the stable supplying the officers.

Rory paced the chamber when Ferdoragh left him, unable to keep still. Had O'Neill meant it? Personal bodyguard to the chief! By God, that would be something to tell his family! Ferdoragh sent a servant to him; he order heated water and bathed and changed his clothes. Unhealthy as it was to bathe often, he disliked the feel of fresh clothes over dusty, sweaty flesh and did so perhaps oftener than was advisable. The man gave him his name without asking; as in all large houses, there was a subtle communication line among the servants. When he came for the used water, he said, "The house gathers for the meal, McGuinness."

Having got back to the hall, not without a few false turns, he found upwards of two hundred people gathered; he could not remember half the names of those he was introduced to. There were some pretty girls here and there, he saw. A number of hounds wandered about, two guards stood stiffly at the door, and servants hurried about with platters and cups. He engaged in conversation with the prettiest of the girls he met, daughter to one McFee, an army officer. She was flirtatious and ordinarily he'd have put all his attention on her, but he was watching for the chief.

When O'Neill entered, he was flanked by Dudley Donnelly and Hugh. He had changed his garments for a saffron silk tunic without sleeves, a black kilt, and wore different jewels as well. He glanced about the hall; something appeared to displease him, and he beckoned a servant.

"You told my wife I expect her to the table?"

"Yes, my lord, but—" the man looked nervous—"the lady says she is not well enough."

"My Christ, women! She is quite well; she is notional is all. Her duty it is to welcome me on return. Go up and tell her to come to me at once." The man bowed and went off unhappily. The chief collected a full cup from another servant and strolled over to Rory. "Well, chief's man? Kin to Ferdoragh you are but different where women are concerned, picking the prettiest to be seen!" True enough, Ferdoragh was awkward with women. The girl blushed, and O'Neill gave her a little push and pat. "Get off, leave him to me."

"O'Neill, I wanted to ask—a great honor it would be—" He was not yet used to the close presence of the chief, the very force of personality creating a wave of almost tangible heat about him.

"Yes, yes," said O'Neill. "It is decided. For my dignity I must have a personal guard. I should have thought of it before, and you'll do well enough." Used to winning life-worship with a word, a touch, he knew when another man came under his spell. He grinned down at Rory pleasedly. "Here at Benburb it's not needful, but elsewhere you may trail me hound to master—and see you keep your eye on myself and not the girls!"

"Indeed, O'Neill! I never expected, I—"

O'Neill shrugged. "Not strictly needful. Hugh and Cormac seized on the notion—I said it in jest—but it may be just as well at that, who knows? I am an important man to Ulster, and I've enemies enough here and there." Glancing up to the door, he frowned. "The O'Donnells not the least of them. Christ, why did I marry an O'Donnell woman? I must have been in liquor when Liam persuaded me!"

The woman advancing up the hall on the arm of a manservant was scarcely one to look at twice, Rory thought. Tall and too thin, she was pale, raven-haired, and her long, big-featured face wore an expression of gloomy discontent he suspected was chronic, not only for her present illness. A length from the chief, she paused. O'Neill said harshly, "I see you were gowned and not too far off to obey my summons prompt. Whyfor do you ignore me?"

"I am ill," she said fretfully. "It is cruel in you to make me rise. I am dressed to receive my confessor, not to share a meal with you, you devil. Nothing I share with you again."

"You are impudent! I had it in mind to make you a present for that you bear me a son—"

"The son you may take—a son of yours I never wanted and have nothing but hate for!" If he was oblivious to the crowd listening, she was not; she looked about, spiteful, bitter. "They forced me into marriage with you— away from my God—you have damned my immortal soul, to take me in sin when you are still wed to that illegal MacDonnell woman—"

The chief went white with fury. He roared, "I am not wed to her—I never was! The Pope granted annulment—for a stiff price, damn his Italian arrogance! How dare you say that to me? By God—"

"It is true! What is the annulment? I—"

Temporarily beyond speech with anger, O'Neill lifted an arm and pointed; she retreated gladly. "Black bitch of an O'Donnell," he choked as she reached the door, "by Christ—by Christ—"

"Come, sit down and eat." And Hugh took his arm. "You're snappish with hunger."

"I'll be rid of her—by God, I will! A fool to listen to Liam—reconcile the clans, he says! By Christ—"

"Yes, yes, after dinner you can think about it." Hugh winked at Terence O'Hagan on the chief's other side. They got him up to the table, still swearing, and the company hastened to join him. Rory was wondering where he should be seated, if there was any order observed, when suddenly the chief reared up and roared his name imperiously.

"Rory McGuinness, to me! If I'm to have a guard he will guard me proper! With that O'Donnell woman in the house, no telling when danger might come—poison me as soon as look at me, she would." He made a savage gesture. "Behind me! Seosamh, see he is waited on." Rory hastened to obey; he took a position to the left of the chief, behind, the servant setting a stool for him, and there had his first meal at Benburb where he would have so many more in years to come.

He saw there was indeed formality in the seating arrangements. The chief sat alone in a high-backed armed chair at the head of a small square table raised on a platform above the first of two long main tables. Ranged at either side of him down two sides of the table sat his high officers: his brother Hugh at his right, Dudley at his left with the other three Donnellys, beyond Hugh, Terence O'Hagan, Ferdoragh, and Cormac McArdle. On the fourth side of the table, facing O'Neill, were chairs for the important guests of the moment; this night, Colm McCaffrey sat there, obviously overwhelmed at his welcome and awkward in noble company. At the first main table sat all the other gentle-born men of the house, the army officers and the gentlewomen; the house servants not engaged in serving the meal occupied the second table. In the midst of all this nicety, however, Rory noted that no table knives were laid save for the women, the men using their belt knives as if in the open on a hunt or journey; O'Neill, indeed, seldom used his knife at all, taking up the bones in his hands. The venison was excellent, barely seared on the fire, and tender.

The edge a bit off his hunger—there was little talk the first few minutes—Hugh observed, "Thanks to God the lady does not join us. A nuisance, having a gentlewoman at the table and needing to be so careful with one's tongue. Women I like, but not to talk with."

"And why we trouble to behave like gentlemen, God knows," said Edmund Donnelly, "Shane saying whatever comes into his head whether or not a lady is present."

The chief was amused at that and put down his cup to laugh. "Conventions! It is men foster the legend that ladies are all so delicate to swoon at a rough word. I notice they always seem to know the meaning." He reached to the platter for another marrowbone and called over his right shoulder, "Luke, music!"

Rory had heard of the chief's famous harpist, Luke O'Givney; he glanced that way curiously. O'Givney, a little brown man in clothes of the plainest, sat apart, his harp across his knees as he ate. "Before God, O'Neill, give me a minute to take a mouthful!" Only a musician, in brehon law unanswerable for any crime or necessary respect to any man would dare address O'Neill in that tone. The chief only laughed and turned to McCaffrey.

"Talking of women, I'm interested in that one you serve—the Dean was telling me of her."

"She has great admiration for you, my lord O'Neill. As I told, it was her said I must come—she listens to the deputies talk—"

"Who is this, or do I ask secrets?" asked McArdle in his musical bass. The chief smiled, pushing a chunk of bread round the dark deer-blood on his plate.

"I forgot, the Dean and I were talking private about that. Sir Harry Sydney's mistress, Cormac—it is a foreign woman, French, Italian, I forget—and what is her name, now?"

"She is of Milan, lord, and a Hebrew. Madam Rebecca Isham."

"Ah! And beautiful?"

McCaffrey, easier now among them, was bold to answer that. "Maybe not as you'd call it, but a woman a man would always be drawn to. Yes, I think beautiful."

"And conceives loyalty to myself. She must have a gift for sending to warn me, though it was not needful. I'll give you something to carry to her."

"That's kind; she will be pleased, my lord. Too good for Sydney she is. An honest woman, and spirit in her."

"So I collect. You will give her my thanks and good wishes. Luke! In Christ's name, earn your living!"

"Shout at me like that, I will leave you," grumbled the harpist, but took up his instrument and began to play softly. The chief cast a look over his shoulder at Rory.

"You I'd forgot. See you keep a still tongue in your head on what you hear of private talk." This table was out of earshot of the rest of the hall. "Not that I suspect you'd go haring off to Dublin to betray me to the English, the way you jumped that bastard today. . . . Radcliffe is in England, did you say, Colm?"

"He will be, my lord, by tomorrow," said McCaffrey. "He left Dublin yesterday, for a meeting with the queen's ministers."

"Which means Sir William Cecil—he is the bear master. By Christ," said the chief suddenly, thrusting a hand inside his tunic. "I'd forgot, I had a letter, come while I was north, and in talking to you I overlooked it. Out of the Pale—" He pulled it out, glanced at the inscription. "Sydney's seal. Now what is he writing to me about?" He slit the seal with his thumbnail, scanned the clerkly black lines of English with a growing grin, passed the letter to Hugh. Refilling his cup: "English! Such reasonable little men they are, always fancying talk will settle any argument! What does he say? He says the chancellor is concerned to hear that the Ulster clansmen violate their agreement with Her Majesty, Elizabeth of England, to hold the prince-electing outlawed by signed treaty. Will the new O'Neill not consider a formal meeting to discuss terms and renew that treaty as made by Con, the O'Neill? The chancellor and the deputies would be pleased if O'Neill will name a time and place—Aughh! How many times must they hear me say No?"

"Sydney is a Saxon man," said McCaffrey, "and no understanding in him of anything not to be seen in black and white. My lord Sussex—Radcliffe—is Norman Sassenach and a very shrewd man."

"And he does not like Sydney too well," said O'Neill, leaning back and drinking deep. "Not so?"

"Ah—" McCaffrey shrugged. "He is impatient with him, is all, the way they talk together. Madam gives them the little parlor to sit in"—he grinned—"all so gracious and respectful, and a door in it they don't know exists, a tapestry over it on their side. I've only just learned she listens to them, too. Very convenient, it is."

"Indeed," said the chief absently. Suddenly he began to laugh. "Oh, by God, I am going to play a trick on Radcliffe! Split the ranks—split the ranks. Furious he'll be—"

"What is in your mind now?" asked Hugh suspiciously.

"Oh, an innocent little trick! Here is Sydney in Dundalk, waiting for an answer to his letter—his it is, though it is sent in the chancellor's name. . . . Radcliffe and Cecil, the bear leaders, yes. The chancellor, the other deputies, they're bumbling old fools—and it is always no quarter with Radcliffe, a pleasure to fight him, open or otherwise. Sydney will take any word at face value. I'll tell you what I'll do. I'll write Sydney, so polite and respectful, and ask him to visit Benburb—I have a new son, and would have the honorable Sir Harry stand godfather if he will condescend—"

"Have you lost your wits? Godfather! Good Christ, not a year gone we burned his country mansion to a shell!"

"Yes, he'd never—"

"Oh, but he will!" O'Neill's eyes danced mischief. "Sydney I know. A good honest solid Saxon, as McCaffrey says. He will be flattered, he will think at last he makes progress with O'Neill, and north he'll come, all anxious and eager—with a fine present for the godson—and won't I be cordial to him! And the christening over, back he'll trot to Dublin, all pleased with himself, and meet Radcliffe just returned, likely, and tell him. And, my Christ, but Radcliffe will explode on him! You know Radcliffe—any concession to native Irish, any courtesy to us, any seeming favors asked, nothing infuriates him more. He will be wild with Sydney for accepting the invitation. And it's not unlikely I'll get some useful information out of Sydney while he's here."

"Well, it's a notion," said Hugh; he began to grin, too. "I take the point—Radcliffe would have an apoplexy!" There was laughter, agreement for the plan among all the captains.

"But to stand godfather—it's scarce decent, Shane—an Englishman."

The chief shrugged. "The son is half O'Donnell and deserves no better. By Christ, that woman I'll be rid of before I'm a year older."

When Rory went up to his chamber at the end of the evening, it was in company with new friends, several young officers who shared rooms not far off from his—the brother of the McFee girl, O'Hanlon, Kelly, Burke. The latter hailed a passing servant in the corridor. "Here, man, fetch me Meriel if she's not occupied elsewhere."

"Yes, Burke. Gentlemen? Will I fetch any other a woman?"

"You will," said Rory, "myself." It was the traditional custom in all noble houses to keep concubines for visitors and unmarried men of the household, but he had never visited a castle wealthy enough to hold by that custom, and he was curious. The woman the servant brought up to him was a dark, pretty girl, only a few years his senior; her name was Ena. He asked questions, and she told him some of the servant women earned a little extra wage this way, being quartered apart from the decent women of the house. She was curious, too, about a new member of the household, and had his life history out of him in five minutes.

"But you're an important man, then, personal guard to the chief!" Friendly, flattering: "I'm lucky to meet you first. Mind you ask for Ena when you want, McGuinness, none of the others!"

"And they all as pretty as you, *alannah?*"

"Oooh, no, I'm much the prettiest!"

"And the cleverest at wangling presents out of poor young officers, maybe?"

"You wrong me," she said demurely, making eyes. "But as you are new at Benburb, McGuinness, I'd best be warning you—the lord O'Neill is very particular, there are strict house rules. There are but a couple of dozen of us; all the other servant women are respectable, and he makes bad punishment for any who offers insult to them. It is a moral house. So you just look to who you talk to in dark corners; one little kiss stole from a decent girl and you are maybe put in the dungeon a day or so."

"Do you tell me! Well, I'll be careful," he promised gravely.

CHAPTER IV

M cCaffrey watched Rebecca covertly as she glanced about the room, wandering toward the gilt-framed mirror on one wall, smoothing her hair, idly admiring her reflection. He admired it, too. Since he'd discovered her sympathy for O'Neill, and she'd coaxed out of him his position as spy for O'Neill's advisors, he had not concealed interest in her. Breeding she had, but none of the snobbishness of English, and never reprimanded him for boldness—maybe because she was bored with Sydney, and no wonder.

"Have you filled the decanter, Colm?"

"I have. The brown Spanish wine Radcliffe is so fond of, right? Maybe out of caution the English drink wine—you'd want a gallon of it for any lift it gives you."

Her black eyes laughed at him. "But you Irish have no palates. . . . I wonder what they will discuss tonight. I daresay you'll put your ear to the door in the passage, as I to the inner panel. A fine pair of conspirators we are!"

"At least I've an excuse—paid for it, I am," said McCaffrey. "With you it's only curiosity, but then you're female." Wasn't she indeed, and the feeling growing in him he'd like to investigate it a bit.

She laughed and would have answered that, but the clap of knocker on door interrupted. "There they are—straighten your collar, Colm, wretch of a doorman that you are. Go and fetch them in."

He came out to the passage and opened the house-door; against the darkness outside, he noticed that more snow had fallen on Dublin, and the air was icy. As he had so many times before, he admitted the deputies, watched Rebecca usher them to the parlor, gracious on welcome. When she came out, she cast him a wickedly demure glance before retreating to her own listening-post.

Smiling to himself, he put his ear to the panel.

Sydney cleared his throat nervously, eying Radcliffe. "Really, you know, I think he is not beyond reaching—ah—diplomatically, Thomas. He was most cordial, it seemed to me a gesture of goodwill, and so I accepted it."

"God help us!" ejaculated Radcliffe with a barked laugh. "O'Neill, cordial to an Englishman! Do you think he executed the hired killer I sent without questioning him? O'Neill understands how we feel for him—and returns the feeling threefold! And God damn that blunderer, too—I made sure he would succeed, but that is how the dice fall. You are a fool, Harry, but you needn't prove yourself a damned fool. O'Neill inveigled you to his castle to annoy me and coax information out of you—"

"I gave no information! I—we talked for the most part of the queen, her possible choice of consort—"

"He does not trick me," said Radcliffe. "Well as I know you, I am surprised he tricked you—godfather to his new son!"

"Most cordial," repeated Sydney vaguely. He sipped his wine, not tasting it, uneasy in his mind as he had been since returning from the north. He wished he had not gone, but he'd not say so to Radcliffe.

They were a barbarous people, and it had been a surprise to hear an Irishman like O'Neill speak such cultivated English. It was said he was fluent in Latin also, but that was hardly credible. He had been cordial, yes —flatteringly so; Sydney tried desperately to recall all that had been said, the two days of his visit. No, he had not let slip any relevant information about military supplies, or— They had talked of the queen, the state of trade: other generalities. And O'Neill so polite . . . Barbarians, the Irish, but those with a little education had learned to conceal their crudities, on the surface. Only once had the mask slipped and the real man looked through. Sydney slid a hand over his mouth, remembering that.

The christening was almost finished—and a poor, weak infant it looked, on the enormous scarlet cushion; he had felt uneasy then, holding it, listening to the old priest's sonorous Latin. And then at the last, as the priest scattered holy water, intoning, "I baptize thee Shane Oge O'Neill of the O'Neill," the chief started like a restless bull at Sydney's side. The invocation was not complete when he pounced on the priest, his face contorted with fury.

"Whyfor do you give such a name to this sickly brat of an O'Donnell woman? I told you the name would be Manus! My name—my name on a thing half O'Donnell and looking to be a weakling anyway!"

The Romanist had faced him down safe enough. "Temper, temper, my son. It is well to name one son for yourself—"

"It is rank bad luck, old fool! By God, that was one time Liam was wrong all the way, coaxing me to wed that black bitch! Here, woman"—to the nurse in the background—"pack this up with anything it needs and take it into Fedan to Cormac Donnelly—no O'Donnell blood I keep in my house!"

Barbarians, yes: it showed then. And an hour later, velvet-voiced at the dinner table, smiling, flattering . . .

"—to mock you only!" Radcliffe was saying contemptuously. "Have you no wit to see it?"

"The chancellor said—"

"Oh, Cusack! He is as slow as yourself for seeing tricks!"

"You might credit me with some sense," said Sydney mildly. "I made a few observations of my own at O'Neill's castle, and I'd discuss them with you. There was a Scot also visiting O'Neill, and they seemed friendly —one Sorley Boy MacDonnell."

"That man is wed to O'Neill's sister. I have it on authority, however, that O'Neill and his brother are estranged from her, for her divorce from the Maguire and—certain immoral behavior." Radcliffe's tone was fastidious. "Sorley MacDonnell is a high clansman of that clan. He keeps a small mercenary army and has hired soldiers to O'Neill in the past."

"Which I was about to mention. A pact with the MacDonnell clan in Antrim—"

Radcliffe smiled. "One thing we need not worry for. The chief Mac-Donnell and O'Neill are old and strong enemies. It's not unlikely O'Neill's Scot brother-in-law is in no great favor with his own chief for his friendship with the Ulsterman. No, no, that hare does not run." He refilled his glass with the amber wine, stared at it.

"I really do not see the reason for your concern," said Sydney hesitantly. "True, the situation might be easier—"

"Easier!" said Radcliffe. He looked up, cold and grim. "God damn O'Neill. . . . Did I not warn them all! Give me men and arms to finish him now, I begged—and all of them telling me his little rebellion amounted to nothing! And now see where we are." He took a breath, swallowed wine. "Do you think he is done, Harry? Do you think he will sit quiet in Ulster now and make no more trouble? I know him better than that."

"The raids into the Pale, certainly—"

"Don't talk to me of raids on the Pale! My hands tied—it is insupportable! God, for an army to challenge him!"

"Sir William—ah—gave you no hope of immediate reinforcement to the military establishment?"

Radcliffe did not reply for a moment; he took up his glass and drank. "I cannot hold Cecil altogether responsible. He is a shrewd man, and he was frank with me. He is not always certain of Her Majesty's temper, shall we say. The queen scoffs at any danger of rebellion within the Irish colony."

"I see, I see. As I was about to say, certainly, the raids on the Pale show no disposition on O'Neill's part to—ah—entertain diplomatic overture." Sydney was remembering other things about his visit to Benburb—doubt and more unease rising in his mind. A veiled smile in O'Neill's eyes, a small inflection in his tone . . . yes. He said with unaccustomed asperity to the earl, "It accomplishes a great deal that you sit there and repeat, 'God damn O'Neill!'"

"Ultimately He will," said Radcliffe dryly. "But meanwhile? But meanwhile!"

Armagh, February 1559

In the hall of his house in Armagh, old Liam Fleming stared to a low-leaping fire and stroked his blue terrier. He said, "There is Jerez wine on the table—I know you are fond of it."

Terence Daniel filled a glass with a murmur of thanks. Handsome, suave, silver-haired, elegantly clad as always, he looked more courtier than high churchman. "Might I ask, by the way—this long after the event your conscience should be settled—how much did it cost you, that influential first vote of the old McGuinness?"

Fleming smiled. "He is land-hungry. A few acres adjoining his holding. No matter. It was necessary only because he had the first vote. The smallest dissension would have been fatal."

"As you say. So we go to king-making, you and I."

Fleming shook his head slowly. "I am a conniving man, Terrence—"

"You are a lawyer."

"And you a cunning one—as a churchman must be. But it is not chess we play; that is a false analogy. In chess the king does move but little, whereas in this game—I would not dare to say of myself, king-maker, for him. He needs none. I have served the O'Neills for sixty years, I have seen the great ones and the little ones. Before he was through his boyhood lessons I knew he would be one of the greatest. The election was but a formality bringing him to his heritage. There could be no power behind his throne, that you know as well as I. . . . I am wishing there were twenty years less on me."

"Why?"

"He will not be guided, he will not be controlled, he will not be hindered. Men do well to name him Shane the Proud. But me he trusts—on occasion he will listen to me. The word compromise is not in his vocabulary, and if you are thinking he will sit in his castle and rule Ulster strong and be satisfied at it, you can think twice. Trouble—trouble!"

It is a synonym for him," said Daniel amusedly.

"Among others, yes. He is a great man. I love him—I fear him—I fear for him."

Daniel said seriously, "I know what you'd say. I would do my best for him, Liam, if you are not there."

"Ah, no pretense, little priest. You and I are pawns on the board. But do that, Terence—do what you can for him, for he trusts you, too." Fleming roused himself and turned his keen old gaze on his visitor. "You came to give me news, you said?"

Daniel emptied his glass. "I was at Benburb yesterday. Sorley Boy MacDonnell is visiting Shane—"

"A good man, that, and a good friend to Shane."

"Which his chief, James MacDonnell, deplores. And for all the friendship Shane has for him," added Daniel, digressing, "he's not yet reconciled Shane and Hugh with the Lady Mary, his wife. I would like to know—"

"The truth behind her reputation? That is the curse of the clan O'Neill —the flesh is strong in them. The Lady Mary is no less an O'Neill because she is female." Fleming cast a look at Daniel, and added softly, "If she is not a good woman, I daresay it might be said you, as a priest, are not—"

The Dean of Armagh gave him his charming smile. "Oh, Liam! Were we talking of myself?"

"We might. No matter—you know I'm not narrow-minded." Fleming might have reflected that if Daniel was venal as a churchman, it had been none of his choosing that he belonged to the church. Found as a nameless infant on the doorstep of a monastery in Fedan, he had been raised for a priest to the glory of God. He was too handsome a man and too aware of his charm to shut himself away from the world entirely; and that, God knew, he had never done. "What of Sorley Boy?" asked Fleming abruptly.

"Why, he rode from Antrim purposely to tell Shane the MacDonnell is adding to his army and ordering arms from Scotland. Last month the MacDonnell had a guest in his house—Calvagh, the chief O'Donnell out of Tyrconnell." Daniel laughed. "Two fathers-in-law to Shane—and the both of them with strong hate for him, as we know. Sorley Boy thinks those two may be hatching some devilment. What lies between Antrim and Tyrconnell on the map? Ulster."

Fleming rubbed the terrier's head absently. "Indeed. No, neither of those two has any love for Shane, as you say. Calvagh O'Donnell"—he shrugged—"is another pawn on the board, but the MacDonnell is something else. What does Shane say?"

"He says the longest day in the year will never see hare and stag bedding together, even to get back at the hound. He thanked Sorley for the warning but said it was meaningless, and that in the unlikely event Sorley was right and those two chiefs think to challenge him, he could smash them both with his bridle-arm tied behind him." Daniel grinned. "I wouldn't doubt it."

"Eventually, they would regret it, yes. Unless between them they acquire more men and arms than is at all likely. I will tell you another thing that bears on that, and on Sorley MacDonnell's dislike of his chief. This is not the first time the MacDonnell has dealt with old Calvagh. Did Sorley Boy speak of his niece, the Lady Catherine MacLean?"

"Not to me."

"Ah. Well, Shane said he was much upset, and I can share his indignation over it. She is great-niece to the MacDonnell, and of good family.

Her father arranged a betrothal with the Earl of Argyll in Scotland, and she was wed to him at sixteen, but Argyll was in middle age and died a year or so later. By then, her father was dead also and she came under the guardianship of the MacDonnell. I daresay Sorley—and the lady herself—expected he would arrange a suitable marriage for her, but scarcely the one he did. Calvagh the O'Donnell wanted her, and the MacDonnell was willing."

"O'Donnell!" exclaimed Daniel. "Are you telling me they married a girl not yet twenty to that senile old lecher?"

"The MacDonnell was evidently pleased to oblige him, though Sorley argued against it. I understand she is a pretty and personable young woman, and though there was no dower, it should not have been difficult to marry her elsewhere, more—um—happily. She was Argyll's second wife, you understand, and all he left went to his grown sons. No one," said Fleming, "appears to have had much sympathy for the lady except Sorley Boy—and he is powerless to aid her."

Daniel grimaced. "Good God, old Calvagh must be rising eighty! That's a shameful thing."

"As you say. I wondered last year when it happened, why James Mac-Donnell was so anxious to oblige the lord of Tyrconnell. Calvagh is anything but wealthy or influential, and what use he might be to the MacDonnell in Antrim, I didn't see. But if they plot to join their armies against Ulster—"

"Well, we must wait and see what occurs for that. The lady has my sympathy, but her penance will not be long, likely—Calvagh cannot live forever."

"But so rude, Terence," murmured the chief justice. "I'm not far off eighty myself."

Daniel begged his pardon suavely.

"I do not think we need worry too much about the O'Donnell," said the chief justice.

"That is what Shane said."

"He is usually right. Is he not!" Suddenly Fleming laughed. "I had a letter today from my own niece in France—you've not met, I believe?"

"It would be my pleasure," said Daniel politely.

"Um—yes." Daphne Fleming, that lovely and ambitious woman, had gone far from her birth in the gray city of Armagh; resident of the French court, she was the latest of the French king's paramours. "She writes that the de' Medici woman is furious at her own stupidity at being coerced into that treaty with Ulster." That had been one of O'Neill's shrewdest strokes, that trade agreement committing France to such costly importation of Ulster's goods. "It is not often a de' Medici comes out the wrong end of a bargain."

"Especially Catherine de' Medici," agreed Daniel, pouring more wine.

"There are times I wonder, Liam—in Shane O'Neill have we got a bear by the tail?" He laughed, lifting his glass.

Rath O'Donnell, March 1559

Hugh Ruadh O'Donnell said to his uncle, "You are a great damned fool, old man."

Calvagh the O'Donnell eyed him, distrustful and moody. He was chief of his clan in name, and he had made this young red bull his official heir; he was afraid of Red Hugh, and an old weak man, and he knew it—and tried desperately to deny it. And there was more than the chiefhood between them, too, for Hugh Ruadh coveted his uncle's lovely young wife. And Hugh Ruadh was young and strong, if not exactly handsome. "Respect for your elders, puppy! Whyfor?"

"MacDonnell, the chief, is a breaker of bargains, being a Scot."

"Listen, my ignorant one," said Calvagh hardly. "The MacDonnell has no more reason to love the Ulsterman than myself or yourself. Together, we may break him, and for that reason the MacDonnell keeps his bargain with me."

"Reason!" said Red Hugh with a laugh. "The MacDonnell has the hell of a reason for his grudge on O'Neill. Just because he palmed off that wanton female bastard of his on O'Neill and got her returned to him for his pains! For once I say O'Neill can't be held to blame. A man likes to be sure of his sons. Speaking of that, O'Neill's marriage to cousin Mary scarcely seems to have reconciled our clans!"

"It would need more than that to reconcile O'Neill and O'Donnell," retorted Calvagh. His very slightly shaky hands played vaguely with his beard.

"The MacDonnell talks large—we'll see how he backs up his talk. There's no man in Ireland who'd be more pleased than myself to see O'Neill's power broken; you needn't say I'm crying off or a coward for fight. But I can see us getting into some trouble harder to get out of than into."

"Risk nothing, gain nothing," said Calvagh shortly.

Hugh Ruadh shrugged. "You are also a damned fool for the woman. You'd no need for a new wife. You outlived three of them and if you've any manhood left I'm a damned fool myself—which I'm not. Not that I don't share your"—he grinned—"appreciation for a beautiful woman."

"You are impudent—leave me," quavered Calvagh.

"Oh, no, uncle! I think I make you an extended visit this time. You're damned slow dying, but I don't give you more than five years more. I might marry her myself then—only fair to let her grow acquainted with me now, not so?" He went off, laughing.

CHAPTER V

IN THE week since Sydney's visit, Rory had begun to settle and feel at home at Benburb. Even in this short while, he was accepted by everyone as a fixture attached to the chief, as it were. He had looked forward to army life; he had not expected his service under O'Neill would be of this sort, but he was quick to see the advantages he enjoyed. Though he'd denied it to Ferdoragh he knew the discipline of regular rank would fret him, and the highest he might have held at first was troop leader at five pounds of gold a year. The chief woud pay him ten as bodyguard, but that was the least of it. Being always near O'Neill, he overheard much talk among the captains, and that was interesting.

Of all the captains, only Dudley Donnelly appeared disapproving of him; but Dudley was always suspicious. The other three Donnellys were friendly when one knew them: Edmund the sound professional soldier, James a light-hearted dreamer, Manus an eternal player of practical jokes. But Dudley—

Perhaps Dudley Donnelly was the strangest man he ever knew. The chief's exact age, Dudley had grown at O'Neill's side from infancy. He held aloof from liquor, women, all the pleasures of the body; O'Neill was his god. If O'Neill had ordered him to leap from the cliff wall at Benburb, he would have obeyed without hesitation; and he was standoffish withal, as if, having O'Neill, he needed no other, man or woman. Perhaps it was something to do with his health; for Rory learned Dudley had been slow-dying for five years, with the wasting sickness that made a man turn pale and cough blood.

Rory had been somewhat surprised, too, at Sorley Boy MacDonnell, who had arrived with a small guard of troops ten days back. There was no love lost between the Scots in Antrim and the North Irish, and to see O'Neill embracing this Scot, all the captains according him a loud welcome, was strange. But there was reason for it.

"You'd look long for as sound a man as Sorley," Ferdoragh confirmed. "We've all fought alongside him and that's a way to know men." But he cautioned Rory never to mention Sorley's wife to her brothers, O'Neill and Hugh. "The less said about it, the better, but I'll tell you to satisfy curiosity. She'd a different foster family, Lady Mary, and the chief and Hugh never knew her till after she wed the Maguire. She is older than the chief by five years, see. Then she sends and asks rescue from her brute of a husband, and so O'Neill rides down and chastises Maguire. Only he found then it was Maguire had cause for complaint—the lady had run off with another man. And by all accounts, her bed wasn't cold until she married Sorley Boy some while after she'd got a divorce. She's given Sorley two sons, but he's too good a man to be saddled with such a wife. But he won't hear a word against her, and the chief and Hugh haven't a good word for her, so she's never mentioned among them, see you?"

Sorley Boy was a man like Hugh, Rory thought: impossible to dislike. He was solider and quieter, a big, broad sandy-fair man a few years elder to O'Neill, with a round, good-humored countenance and steady blue eyes.

But O'Neill's visitors did not occupy him wholly; he was bored soon after Sydney rode south. The weather had stayed dry and clear, and the chief proposed a raid on the Pale. None of the captains demurred; after the excitement of the election, they were suffering boredom, too. They set off a few days after Sydney left, two hundred troopmen and all but two commanders left in charge of the home guard. Rory went along as a matter of course, and Sorley and his Scots joined.

They left Benburb in early morning, rode down to the border of Ulster by dusk, and circumvented the town of Dundalk to cross the border away from guards. In full dark, after a rest, they rode on into English territory at a fast trot, and attacked the first large house they chanced on. O'Neill made his own rules of war: he allowed his men no looting on English, though he took plunder with the best against Irish or Scot enemy; he said it made them appear common thieves to Sassenachs, who had some over-nice notions about war. The Scots with them took a good deal of valuable loot, and the Ulster troops were furious at the lost chance, but they dared not disobey the order.

Rory had been full of excited anticipation for his first experience of mass fight, but it all happened so fast he had time to feel little in the moment. It was a clear, cloudless night. Whey they came on the house, O'Neill, heading the party, spurred to a gallop, shouting the clan-cry at the top of his voice: "I am O'Neill! I am O'Neill!" The Scots and half the Ulstermen flung off their horses and commenced to batter in the doors and windows, broke into the house. The rest scattered to fire the nearest fields. The household, roused from sleep, came out to repel invasion, and they had a warm time for a few minutes, amid a great din of belligerent servants, outraged householders, looting Scots, and the rest of them only accomplishing what destruction they might. When the long yell that was signal for retreat sounded, the lower floor of the house and all the home-fields were blazing flame to the night sky. The men scrambled out to collect their horses. Rory, who had been dismounted scarcely five minutes,

and done little but set a few curtains alight and enjoy a brief fight with a
burly English servant, tumbled into the saddle, loosening his ax in its
sheath in anticipation of the next fight. The whole party streamed up the
road, horses jostling one another, men shouting and cursing.

He heard the chief's powerful deep voice roaring somewhere ahead, "A
torch! In God's name, fetch me a torch—we will leave every field burning
behind us!" At each side of the road, men plunged their horses across the
ditch into the fields, waving flaring torches to set the thin winter wheat
afire.

A mile or so on they came past one of the home farmhouses, a poor
wooden hut off the road. The silver light of the moon and the ruddy light
of the torches showed a little group of people at the door to watch the
troops' passing. One of them shouted out in a loud voice, "O'Neill!
O'Neill! Burn it all—it is Sassenach corn!" Then they were riding furiously
into English troops, warned and rushing down from the border. It was a
lively fight for a few minutes. There were not more than a hundred of
them and O'Neill's men scattered them off the road by sheer weight; but
some wounds were given and taken. The fight was a running one. The
Ulstermen never paused to give battle, and once they fled past the first
guard station and were out of the Pale, the English troops fell away behind. They never pursued over the border—that would constitute an act of
war—and the English authorities were walking soft and talking discreet
to O'Neill these days, knowing full well his army was twice the size of
theirs, in Ireland.

Safe over the border, the party dropped to a trot, a walk, laughing, excited, re-forming some order, the Scots comparing the loot they'd taken
while the Ulstermen voiced their grievance on that, men who had taken
wounds bandaging them with the help of comrades. Rory was still regaining breath and looking about for the chief to take up his lost post, when
Hugh O'Neill clattered up beside him in high spirits for the action.

"Well, Rory, man! How do you like your first time fighting Sassenachs?"

"For a start, not bad—when do we make the next raid?"

Hugh laughed and clapped him on the shoulder. "I knew I'd not mis-
judged you! You will do to ride with the clan."

The little company arrived back at Benburb in late afternoon of the
next day. As they came to the gate, Sorley Boy MacDonnell looked up at
the corpse of the assassin hanging in its chains on the permanent gallows
there, remarked that it was growing a bit high of odor; but by next week
the birds would have stripped the bones. The already plundered eyesockets
gazed down gloomily on the merry troops passing.

But the chief's mood changed when he saw the horses held waiting before the house-door. There were two grooms—and in English servants' livery, at Benburb!—and one horse bore a lady's saddle.

"Who in Christ's name—" he began in loud anger, and then stopped short. A lady was coming out the open door, daintily holding her skirt from the ground: a lady in English fashion of dress, wide-paneled brocade gown, bead-sewn from breast to waist, a pointed cap covering her hair, curly-toed shoes showing under the skirt. "Jesus and Mary!" exclaimed the chief furiously, and then let out a second curse as he saw the man trailing the woman: a tall, handsome young man, curled, whiskered, padded, perfumed in English style, all very elegant—the fop. O'Neill leaped from his saddle and strode up to the pair, who stopped to face him; Sorley thought they both looked a trifle taken aback for one moment, but concealed it instantly. He identified them with interest: the man was second cousin to O'Neill, Gerald Fitzgerald, Earl of Kildare; and the lady would be none other than old Con's widow, the Anglophile stepmother to the chief. What were they doing here?

"You bastardly Anglophile, what are you up to at Benburb? A Fitzgerald in my house—I have told you before—"

The young man said coolly, "You're inhospitable, cousin. Would I let a lady travel alone?"

"Lady!" ejaculated O'Neill with a contemptuous laugh. "Less than accurate you are. You will both be off my land at once, but not before you tell me why you have come here."

The woman, not young, never beautiful, a haughty-faced one and aging unlovely, looked back at him contempt for contempt. "If it is aught of your concern, I have paid a visit to your wife—stepson! And do not think it was my own notion to visit your house—I was duly invited."

"When I should be from home! O'Donnells—Christ! Get off," ordered the chief in rage, "get gone from my land!"

"The same O'Neill," said Fitzgerald with a conscious smirk. "Don't fret, cousin, we are but now leaving." Gallantly he assisted the woman to mount, took his bridle from the groom without haste; he doffed his velvet cap, bowed to the chief mockingly from the saddle: "Farewell, and our thanks for your hospitality, however unwitting!"

The chief gave a violent command when they were out of the gate, and the guards hastened to shut it. "Christ, the moment my back is turned! And whyfor should she want to see those two? This I'll know a bit more of!" exclaimed O'Neill. He strode into the house; servants hurried up for orders. He flung his cloak to one, loosed his war ax from its belt sheath and handed it to another to be polished free of the bloodstains marking the blade, said, "Liquor to the hall, now," and turned to the seneschal of the castle servants, Seosamh. "Fetch me those who've been waiting on my wife in her apartments."

"No need, O'Neill." Little Luke O'Givney strolled up, his harp cradled in his arms. "Come and sit down private. I can tell you what you want to know—and more than you will like to hear."

"Oh?" said the chief. He took Luke's arm, led him up the hall to the leaping hearth-fire, cast himself into a chair. The others grouped about him, and a servant came with a jug and cups. The musician leaned on the side of the stone hearth, striking idle soft chords from the harp.

"A great nuisance it was on me, and I in the middle of composing a new song about you." A plaintive minor chord. "And did I not tell you at the time you were a fool to take an O'Donnell woman under your roof?" A compelling arpeggio.

"Very well, so you did. Forget the song. When did they come and why?"

"Yesterday midday," said Luke. Casually he took the cup from the hand of the chief, who only surveyed him resignedly as he drank. O'Neill had strong respect for tradition, and where he would fell a man who did that to him otherwise, he held a musician inviolate of any punishment. And Luke, like all musicians, took advantage of tradition, sometimes in mischief, sometimes in contrariness. "It made a little confusion for Seosamh —knowing how you feel for the pair, but could he turn them away when your lady wife was welcoming them in, all effusive? I said to him, 'Leave it to me.'"

"Well? Get to the point."

"Finish your liquor," said Luke with a grin. "It may mellow you a bit for bad news. They talked late in the lady's chamber—myself with an ear at the door. I understand Con's widow is close as bitch to hound with that old whoreson, Sir William Fitzwilliam, one of the English queen's deputies in the Pale."

"She is that."

"Well, O'Neill, some precise information about your army and military equipment will presently be reaching the deputies. The Fitzgerald traitor wrote some of it down nice and neat so not to forget it."

All the captains began swearing, furious; Sorley cursed in sympathy; but the chief was silent. A white line grew round his mouth; his eyes darkened with anger. In a low, cold tone, he said, "Do you say. And a thing I might have expected at that. It is no matter at all—what good will it do Radcliffe to know the number of cannon, the number of men? Afford him more nightmares is all, and he with half of what I hold and no prospect of more to be sent him! No, I've no care for that. But treachery under my own roof, that is something else again. I will be rid of that woman before the day is over. Back she goes to her father and there is an end to Liam's fanciful schemes to reconcile O'Neill and O'Donnell." He finished his liquor and rose, grim-faced. "I'll give her an hour to be out of my house."

They watched him out of the hall. "And good riddance," said Hugh.

"A Friday-faced female she is, atop all else. I wonder did O'Donnell put her up to that."

"Spite is all," opined Terence O'Hagan bitterly. "He'll be well rid of her—but whether the Pope will grant a divorce is another thing."

Hugh laughed. "The Pope will grant a divorce for sufficient payment. Gold buys much denied to poor folk."

"True."

"Very true," agreed Sorley Boy, struck by the truism. "By God it does." Hugh looked at him inquiringly; he smiled. "I was not thinking of Shane. No matter, no matter." He thought, Catherine: somehow he must save her. Between the lines of her letters he read her unhappiness. She was like a daughter to him, Catriona—so he called her, the old name instead of its Anglicization, to mark the depth of his affection. Shut away with that old lecher, the O'Donnell, and now (he suspected from a word or two in her latest letter) O'Donnell's nephew, Red Hugh, after her, a disgraceful thing. It was true enough, gold would buy favors; he had not sufficient to bribe His Holiness in Rome, but he had land and could sell some acreage to have the gold, and that he would do.

The Lady Mary, all in a hurry, after a session with the chief, packed up her belongings and left Benburb. "And joy may her father take of her," commented Hugh. But it was understood that she did not get as far as Rath O'Donnell; she stopped at a religious house, where she would enter into orders as had been her intention before she was wed to O'Neill.

The chief, in better humor for being rid of her, yet was abstracted for some reason these days; Rory noted that and the captains were frank to speak of it. Several times that week O'Neill rode alone into Armagh to see Liam Fleming and the Dean, and would answer no questions about that. He sent north for young John O'Hagan, appointing him official secretary. "A ruler, an important man, he needs a confidential clerk!" But he already had two. "Not enough confidential for this business," he retorted to Hugh's reminder, and to the question, "Wait and see!" He commissioned the castle saddlery to build him two new saddles, and ordered new jewels from craftsmen in Armagh. He shut himself up in the council room long hours; and when John O'Hagan came, he spent most of each day closeted with him there.

"He is up to something," said Hugh. "Deviling us he is to keep it secret." But when, for the dozenth time, that night at the table, he questioned the chief, O'Neill answered openly enough.

"What am I busy at? Well, among other things, this day I sent a letter to Calvagh O'Donnell, reminding him he owes me the yearly tribute. The old fox, every twelvemonth it is later. He might be a Scot, he's so jealous of his gold!—present company excused," with a grin at Sorley.

He shrugged. "No reason to keep it secret from you. I have a little scheme in mind, is all."

"Your little schemes I know," said Hugh resignedly.

"Or maybe a big one," said the chief. He lifted his cup. "I give you an excuse for a drink—"

"A thing you never need."

"Defeat to Her Majesty Elizabeth of England!"

"That I'll drink to," said Sorley Boy, "but do not tell me you are going to press Elizabeth for tribute?"

O'Neill laughed, leaning back in his chair. "Something better than tribute, brother!"

"What? Shane, you don't mean—" Hugh was incredulous. The chief hit him carelessly on the shoulder.

"Unflattering you are. Why not—why not? By all accounts, and what Sydney said, she is playing the unbroke colt with her ministers. A year on the throne now, and she was no shy miss when she was crowned. They are harrying her to pick a suitable husband, which means suitable politically . . . but she is a woman, my friends." He was smiling, impish, pleased.

"But, my Christ, Shane—"

"Are they not coming at her right and left! I've heard. Suitors from every province in Europe. But I'll be the one to take her. They will see —you will all see."

"Elizabeth!" exclaimed Sorley. "Well, right enough, Shane, we have all seen you accomplish the impossible, but—"

"It is not in that category," denied O'Neill. "It will be easy—easy! Have you ever known me to lay suit to a woman without success?" All the men laughed and shook their heads. Rory, so surprised and interested he forgot the contents of his plate, was listening avidly.

"Her ministers would scarce receive your suit kindly," objected Dudley. "You have been at odds with the Sassenachs all your life."

O'Neill grinned at him, the sudden charming one-sided grin that betrayed the blood-tie with Hugh. "I'm not planning to marry her ministers. I have the whole plan in mind—you'll see. No woman withstands O'Neill. Once I am face to face with her in England—"

All the captains exclaimed in one voice, rose in a body to stare at him. "To England! Shane, you'd never consider—" "Go to England! Christ, they would have you in chains the moment you set foot—" "You cannot make such a reckless plan!" "Shane, you cannot—"

"Silence!" roared the chief. He banged his empty cup on the board in sudden violent gesture. "All of you with me how long and still you do not learn I am O'Neill! My plans do not go wrong—none can defeat me! Do I go into this plot without thought? I will wed Elizabeth, I said, and

I do not mean by proxy! Can I lay suit to a woman with five hundred miles between us?"

"But—to go to England!"

"It will be quite safe." Abruptly the chief regained his temper, filled his cup, laughed around at the concerned, disturbed expressions. "For the love of God, sit down, cease looking at me so mournful! It is no new idea; I thought of it a bit last year. A proud, haughty woman it is and doubtless coldhearted, and a Sassenach. But rulers must make sacrifices for their lands. I must obtain a divorce from the O'Donnell bitch—I have written to His Holiness in Rome already—there'll be delay, but it affords time to lay the groundwork. Do you ask how it will go? I'll tell you. I have every move of this planned. I will approach her by letter concerning a possible trade treaty—will they not be pleased!—and ask to send an ambassador to make discussion with her. Letters, many letters, and masterpieces every one—little said of the treaty, only enough to keep them interested, more about her beauty and charm and wisdom. And the ambassador I send her is the Dean. He is a smooth talker, my cunning Terence, and he tells a bawdy story well—he is a handsome man, he will keep her amused. But he does not go to England to discuss a treaty. He goes to tell the queen of O'Neill. He will spend all his time telling her. He will tell her that O'Neill is the greatest chief and prince in Ireland, that he is the best war leader of this or any century, that no man can beat him at personal fight, that he has forgotten how many beautiful women he has loved, that there never was such a strong, bold, handsome, accomplished, powerful, courageous chief anywhere in the world any time before as the great O'Neill of Ulster. In short—in short, my friends, he will tell her the truth." He drank with enjoyment. "Would not any woman want to meet this wonderful chief? She will send me invitation to visit her court. But do I leap at the first invitation, or the second, or the third? I do not. Tell a woman she cannot have a thing and straightway her passion is hot to have it, that is the second rule about women. She will be mad with impatience to meet this great chief—you will see! And eventually I will accept, and visit her."

"Shane, you cannot, no! A trick it would be, a trap for you—" Dudley shook his shoulder vehemently, almost tearful. "I beg you, no—" A paroxysm of coughing racked his thin body; he raised the back of one hand to his mouth and Rory saw the dark viscous splatter of blood on his wrist before he slid his other hand over it.

"You think I'm so easy tricked by English? That is part of the plan too. We will handle it between us, Terence in London, I in my letters. The ministers might think to do that—but the woman, by then, will be too fascinated. We will say—" He raised his glance to the ceiling, reflective, sardonic—"the queen will have heard infamous lies about O'Neill, slander spread by those who are jealous of him, how he is no friend to England or England's queen. He hopes devoutly the queen is too astute to believe such lies. But she will understand that rulers must think for their lands and people, and O'Neill is important to Ulster—he cannot take personal risks. Although he knows it is but a formal gesture he would have a signed guarantee of safe entry into English territory and safe return, under the queen's own hand, before he consents to visit her. . . . And," relapsing into his ordinary voice, "that she will give. Terence will bring it with him when he returns."

"A piece of paper," said McArdle. "Since when do English scruple to break agreements when it benefits them?"

"Listen, my shortsighted insular little men. The queen and her ministers know what Radcliffe and the chancellor know—who dare lay a hand on O'Neill? I have a large army, the largest in Ireland, well equipped and experienced, but that is not all they have to fear. The day O'Neill is harmed and England goes to war with Ulster, that army is quadrupled in size, and it is not only in Ireland the English would be fighting. I have treaties with the Pope, who would be glad of any excuse to see the English Protestants chastised; and Philip of Spain, who would rather dethrone Elizabeth than marry her; and the de' Medici in France, who wants to do business with England, but not with Protestants. And in the meantime, I will make a treaty with Mary Stuart, who has an eye on Elizabeth's throne. The Pope would be almighty pleased to see a Catholic Stuart over England, and she has a legitimate claim, which is more than Elizabeth has. Would England dare risk all those? It was a disordered, quarreling government Elizabeth inherited last year, and an empty treasury. England cannot afford even a little war, and that would not be a little war. It will be quite safe to go. I cannot court a woman at a distance."

"You must approach the ministers first, in any event," said Ferdoragh doubtfully.

"Oh, my innocent one!" O'Neill laughed. "I will do no such thing. All these anxious princelings and nobles and fortune-hunters who hope to become her consort, that is what they do—very timidly offer themselves and argue at the ministers! Is O'Neill an untried stud to beg a woman's favor? Rather should the woman plead with him! I will direct my charm at her personally and before I am in England two weeks she'll be blind in love with me. Once I've captured the woman, her ministers will have nothing to say for it."

"Well, by God," said Hugh thoughtfully, "I'll not doubt you, Shane. You might do it—you might."

"Might! My fainthearts! You'll see. . . . Shane, the O'Neill, chief of the Clan O'Neill, Lord of the Red Hand, Prince of Ulster—and King of England! Who dares doubt me?"

CHAPTER VI

Dublin, July 1559

COLM! Do you fasten this for me. . . . Most certainly my maid did so, but it is forever coming undone. I must have a jeweler see to the clasp."

"There's nothing wrong with the clasp," said McCaffrey severely. "An excuse only to complain how clumsy I am." His big hands strove with the necklet's fastening; he was aware of her musky perfume, the warm curve of her breast. "There, it is tight."

"Thank you, my clumsy one." Rebecca moved to the mirror in the passage by the house-door, examining herself critically. "I will do, you think?"

He surveyed her exotic full-blown charm, the rich brocade gown, the demure neck-ruff, the ringed hands, black hair in elaborate curls, the skillful cosmetic art: a practiced, clever, exquisite woman, Rebecca Isham, and knowing it, but amused with herself for vanity. "You will do—to entertain English," he told her. "And how came you ever to take an Englishman for lover, madam?"

"Oh, now you have asked me something!" She shrugged and laughed. "One must live, and he is rich. It is not that Englishmen are less passionate, that depends on the man, but so dull in between the passions! But Harry I like, a nice little man he is. But so are you—a nice big one."

He grinned at her. "Shocked he would be, you talking so to a servant-man."

"Oh, yes, they are arrogant people indeed. You may join me in the little room to listen, if you like."

"I do like. It is a deal more comfortable than the passage."

"Not that there will be anything of import to hear. They talk round and round at the same things! They are children frightened by the—what is it in English?—the bogeyman! O'Neill, always O'Neill, it is with them. Except that now Harry is convinced he has only peaceful intentions, and Radcliffe calling him a fool seven different ways—"

"I have heard them. And here they are"—as the knocker crashed on the panel. "Get into the parlor and prepare to act the lady, chatterer."

She made a grimace at him. "I should dismiss a servant who talks so to me." He grinned after her, waited a moment, straightened his features to stolidity, and opened the door.

Westminster, August 1559

In the council hall at Westminster, Sir William Cecil leaned back in his chair and regarded the rafters dreamily. Small, balding, his brown beard clipped fine, Elizabeth's chief minister might look insignificant, but his domed brow hid much cunning. "What I believe and what I would like to believe are two different things," he said in his soft, precise voice. "When enemies make peace overtures, that is the time to suspect them." He looked at Sir Francis Walsingham, suave, handsome, and another shrewd man. "You see what Radcliffe says."

"He has been saying it half a year," said stout Sir Nicholas Bacon fretfully. "It's a piece of absurdity, Cecil—you are both seeing ghosts. A barbarous Irish chieftain thinking to lay court to Her Majesty! Even he could not conceive—"

"Now mark," interrupted Cecil without apology, "there is no more dangerous thing to do than underestimate enemies. I do not. I know Radcliffe for a perspicacious man. I take what he says as fact—and I am not wholly ignorant of facts from other sources. We are not dealing with a barbarous chieftain, gentlemen. The Ulster prince may obey different social tradition, but because he wears a kilt and feeds himself with a dagger, he is no savage. He is an educated, brilliant man and a strong leader. And for some reason, he is, Radcliffe says, fascinating to women —all women."

There was a short silence; he looked round at them blandly: Sir Francis Walsingham noncommittal, Bacon unhappy, the tall, gray Earl of Pembroke half-smiling. Loud in the council chamber sounded what none of them would say: *but is she a woman—in that sense?* Walsingham cleared his throat.

"That priest, Daniel, is a clever man."

"And another dangerous man. It is to be seen what he is at, nought to do with a treaty. He fills Her Majesty's mind with all the legends about O'Neill, subtly capturing her interest for the man. Do not tell me O'Neill has not started elaborate suit for her. The Pope has just granted him an annulment of his second marriage."

"And so?" said the earl, vague and gentle as always. "We cannot suppose that Her Majesty would take him serious."

Cecil gestured impatiently. "Will you rid your minds of insularity for him! Neither a savage nor a fool could have accomplished what he has this fifteen years. Radcliffe is a shrewd general, and he had an army to command, but he never administered one defeat to O'Neill. I—"

"I never could understand it." Bacon sounded still bewildered. "How might they stand to an English army, savages like that? It was superior numbers only, man for man they could never— A disgraceful affair, but Her Majesty, Queen Mary, always refused to allow men and arms to war on a Catholic, it was—"

For a moment it seemed Cecil would curse him roundly. He only compressed his lips to a narrow line. After silence: "My friends, let us shelve ancient history; we are all too well aware what has occurred in Ulster." It passed through his mind briefly, grimly . . .

The revenue from Ireland was considerable. In the four hundred years since Henry Plantagenet and his Normans had invaded there, England had gained control of three-fourths of the country, all of it but the north, though officially occupying only the Pale. They had taken control in different ways, now subtly, now by force, but mostly by fomenting jealousy among the clan chiefs, to set those men quarreling and prevent united rebellion. While two hounds fight, a third may make off with the bone.

Ireland was kept from trading with any nation but England, and must take the price offered for her produce. If any landholder protested, joined rebellion against the system, very modestly the English withdrew into the Pale; one foot over the border, and those rebels were taken for invasion—the rope, the ax, or the rack ended their protests. It was good trading for the Crown—the seller tied at the cannon's mouth and the buyer holding the fuse to light the charge. Cecil, the statesman and cynic, put it that way to himself, flat and plain. He thought for England, not for ideals.

But the north—especially Ulster! Ulster under the strong ruler, O'Neill, traded at will with the Continent, and resisted all attempts at English intervention. Yes, and that foreign trade was making O'Neill a richer man every month.

He said decisively, "I speak plain fact to you. O'Neill is not only a wealthy man in his own right—as matters stand, he's doubtless more ready gold to call his own than Her Majesty—but he has a number of potential allies, all of whom would need small excuse to open hostilities with England. He has treaties of mutual military support with both France and Spain. If you persist in underestimating O'Neill, I trust you will not disregard that aspect of this business."

"By no means, but I cannot see what danger—"

"Let us not be so shortsighted for O'Neill again. That was what everyone said fifteen years back. But, gentlemen, we've not only O'Neill to consider. This day Her Majesty has sent him cordial invitation to visit her court."

Walsingham sat up with a jerk. "You cannot mean it appears she would believe him, or—? Ridiculous, Cecil! We all know the—ah—certain difficulties of dealing with Her Majesty, but facts are facts. Taking into account the overt hostilities upon the Pale—any pretense is farce, about that—for the last fifteen years it has been one trouble after another with him, his enmity is quite open. Her Majesty could not take as serious any overture of friendship, that I'll never believe."

"Nevertheless, she has invited him to come to England."

There was another silence. Walsingham stared blankly at the ceiling; Bacon twiddled his thumbs; Pembroke admired the large gold seal ring on his right forefinger. At last Sir Francis coughed uneasily.

"It is awkward . . . awkward. If Her Majesty would say definitely what is in her mind—"

Cecil laughed. "Gentlemen, who ever knows what may be in a woman's mind?—even the woman herself!"

Antrim, September 1559

In September of that year, before the weather made roads impassable, Sorley Boy MacDonnell rode across the top of Ireland, from his Castle Dunluce in Antrim to Tyrconnell, to visit his niece, Catherine. He was not welcomed at Rath O'Donnell save by her; he felt it a breach of courtesy to stay even two days. He was much grieved at the news he must tell her—that Pope Pius IV had denied an annulment for her.

"It is this new Pope—I fear he would always be adamant. A pious man, they say, and a reformer. Shane was the lucky one. I believe near the last dispensation granted by His Holiness, Paul, before his death was Shane's divorce from Mary O'Donnell. If there'd not been that delay in converting some of my land to gold to send— But the new man is unapproachable. I do not know what to say to you, Catherine, I'd hoped so much—"

"You need say nothing. I'm only sorry you went to expense for me, Sorley. I—you know I am grateful." He thought she had matured considerably this year, grown even prettier: her white skin almost translucent, her deep blue eyes gentle and withdrawn. He noted that she no longer troubled to arrange her red-brown hair in curls or braids, but let it lie across her shoulders carelessly. A sad, quiet, lovely lady, a lost lady, and his heart was wrung for her whom he loved. Trying to smile at him: "No one can do more. Don't trouble for me, please. I am—well, Calvagh may not live long." And then what of Hugh Ruadh, he wondered grimly. There was nothing he could do for her but say what he had said before.

"You can leave him, Catriona. You know you're welcome at Dunluce always, to live under my protection."

"And if I should do that, you know what would happen. Uncle James would chastise you for encouraging it—it was his choice for me—and perhaps Calvagh would send his army. I wouldn't do that to you, uncle." A brave lady, too.

On his ride back across Ulster with his escort of fifty troopmen, he stopped a night at the O'Dogherty's house, knowing that chief from the campaigns both had made with O'Neill's army. And what he heard from O'Dogherty sent him on swiftly past his own castle, southeast in Antrim to the Red Bay House in Red Bay, the home of his chief. The MacDonnell was in residence, and greeted him with his usual cold courtesy, bade him into the hall, gave him liquor.

"This is a little surprise, Sorley."

"I have come to get a plain answer to a question or two, James." Sorley eyed him grimly, his chief but a man he disliked and distrusted. The MacDonnell was middle-sized, wiry, pale, even nondescript, but for his cold light eyes; the character of the man was in his emotionless voice.

The western Highland clans in Scotland had held Antrim in north Ireland for three hundred years, and the coastal islands between Ireland and Cantyre; as the clan MacDonnell was most powerful of these clans, the chief MacDonnell was traditionally Lord of the Isles. Scots and Irish were cousins in race, with the same tongue and customs; for the most part, they tolerated one another here. But now and then a quarrel would arise. . . . "I'll make this short," said Sorley. "The O'Dogherty, who lives near The Foyle you'll recall, tells me certain ships have been landing arms there to parties of riders who collect them secret. He complained of the trespass and was told the cargoes were destined for the chief O'Donnell. The ships were out of Cantyre."

"Do you say. And what has that to do with myself?"

"You commissioned those arms. You and Calvagh O'Donnell are plotting war on O'Neill."

"And if so," said the MacDonnell expressionlessly, "what is it to do with you, save that you owe me loyalty and support as your chief? You are too close with the Ulsterman—one day you may be sorry you trusted him so far."

"I am warning you, James. You should know better. You will never defeat O'Neill with support or without it."

The MacDonnell smiled mirthlessly. "Will you take a wager on it, Sorley? One thing I know of you. Whatever your opinion, you pay me lip service, if only of fear—you'll not rush off to warn him."

"No need. He will know."

"Oh, will he? Mark it, Sorley. The day will come we both see him dead and done—maybe not far off. And myself taking a hand in that. I have sworn it."

Sorley smiled, too, leaned back, refilled his cup without permission. "I think not, James. The chief of the clan O'Neill you might conceivably challenge—and even the Prince of Ulster—but the King of England?"

MacDonnell sat motionless one moment. "So he seeks a marriage with the bastard queen."

"You have said it."

"Seeking is not finding."

"You speak without thought. What has O'Neill ever attempted and not won? Think back, James. Remember the Ulster of fifteen years ago—the English overrunning it like a plague—the Fitzgeralds with their fine influential friends out of the Pale—Radcliffe's armies of 'forty-nine and 'fifty-two—the meeting-hall at Dundalk—and the campaigns along the Boyne? Remember Matthew Kelly—Dungannon—the English gave an army to, he claiming the chiefhood as Con's eldest illegal son? The English are no longer in Ulster; the Fitzgeralds are broken and fled; and where is Kelly? In hell, and most of his army with him, and Radcliffe's armies too. Do not tell me anything is impossible to O'Neill."

The MacDonnell made a gesture of contempt. "He puts a spell on men—he is not invincible. It is a little disloyalty in you to own friendship for an Ulster chief, Sorley. A little more and I might take steps to correct it in you."

Sorley Boy showed no qualm for the veiled threat. He stood. "I have said what I came to say. Think twice, James, or you'll be the sorry one, not I. And the next time you are at your prayers, offer up thanks that there is a Shane O'Neill in Ulster. How long do you think the English would have stayed west of the River Bann if he had not chased them out?" He made the chief a deliberately careless salute and turned on his heel.

The MacDonnell waited until he heard Sorley Boy's escort clatter out of the courtyard. He rose, crossed the passage to his council chamber. The man who stood respectfully at his entrance was only his third cousin, but there was much resemblance between them—Aspuke MacDonnell also was lean, gray-cold of countenance, with pale eyes and tight mouth; and he was the same stamp of man as his chief: shrewd, secretive, and ambitious.

"He is gone?"

"He is. One day he will regret his impudence to me."

"Fortunate," observed Aspuke innocently, "he is too distant kin ever to claim the chiefhood." The MacDonnell glanced at him sharply and gave a short laugh.

"I've no intention of dying yet. And when I name an heir, it will be a man younger than I." All his sons were dead; he must choose among cousins for an heir; that was for Aspuke, who coveted the chiefhood and was near the MacDonnell's own age. Aspuke's fixed smile did not change. "You were telling me?"

"Gilchrist is more than willing—he hates O'Neill. Buchan has nothing to send, only fifty men—or MacLachlane. Ferguson will contribute a hundred. MacArthur—"

"Well?"

Aspuke's mouth tightened. "He is a young fool of a hothead. He has built a useful little army, he's even a pair of guns—and that clan breeds

strong war leaders. But as a war leader himself, he admires generalship—
and I remind you he is a friend of Sorley Boy. He refuses to join war on
the Ulsterman."

"Indeed."

"Quite definite," said Aspuke, a faint trace of remembered anger in
his eyes. "He used some forceful language. And ran myself and my escort
out of the yard with his hounds."

MacDonnell laughed, pleased, softly, for some time, and the look in
Aspuke's eyes changed to hate; but he dropped them quickly when his
chief turned back to him.

Rath O'Donnell, January 1560

The large chamber in the south wing of Rath O'Donnell was dim with
only a wall torch, the low flame in the little hearth that could never warm
the whole room. As the girl slid in quietly, shut the door, the figure curled
in the one cushioned chair, leaning to the fire, started as if in fright, and
turned. "Oh—Moyna—"

"It is all right, my lady. The chief was a little displeased that you are
ill, but he excuses you from joining the company."

Lady Catherine sank back with a sigh. "Thank you, Moyna. What
would I do here without you? Come and sit with me a little."

The maidservant obeyed, disposing herself comfortably on the deerskin
spread before the hearth, hands clasped round her knees. She was very
sorry for her lady, and loved her; she said, "Presently I'll go to the kitchens and fetch us some dinner. You needn't fear, I told him you are very ill
with your time of the moon, he will not come."

"Oh, I am a coward!" said Lady Catherine. "But how can I run away?
It would bring danger to Sorley if I went to him—and there is no one
else."

"The chief is an old man," Moyna reminded her. "After he's dead
no one could blame you for running from that red devil his nephew.
That daughter of the chief's is with them tonight; she came today for a
last visit. She takes her permanent vows at the convent soon."

"Oh, the Lady Mary, her that was wed to—? But what a great fool she
is."

"Mhmm," said Moyna, nodding. "Maybe it is the devil talking to me
but I think whatever life brings you, it is better than being walled up in
a religious house. Of course, they are very good, pious women," but
she spoiled that by a giggle. "She looks like a great black crow in her
habit."

"I did not mean she's a fool for that. I have some strange new thoughts
these two years, Moyna. They say young girls have no sense to choose
husbands for themselves, and I thought it true, but I wonder. My father
said Argyll would be good to me, and he was wealthy, and an earl, so I

should be safe. Well, so he was—kind. But—" She sighed. "There must be something other than that. I want something more than that. My mother and father, they had love for each other." After a silence: "With a man one loved, it would be— Moyna. Have you ever taken a lover?"

The maidservant shook her head vigorously. "No, my lady, and I don't mean to. There was a man or two at the Red Bay wanted me to, afore the MacDonnell gave me to you, but I was only fourteen then, they were thinking I was shy. I'm not off to be like my mother—kind she was, too kind, and to so many, she was never knowing for sure what man was my father. I mean to stay respectable, and I'll not wed until I find a man I love or at least feel liking and respect for."

"And that you can do, no kinsmen pulling and pushing at you. Times I wish I had never been born a noblewoman. Yes, I envy you that. What kind of man must he be, Moyna—if you could choose from all in the world?"

The maidservant smiled to herself. She leaned back against Catherine's chair, lifting an arm to smooth her black hair, polished in the firelight; her pretty round young face took on a dreaming look. "Oh—if I could choose? Well, I wouldn't want him handsome; handsome men are vain. But he must be kindhearted, and honorable, and—and—oh, I would not care, my lady, so he understood, so we had that thing between us—it must not be just for the love-making, but—loving—too."

"How did you grow so wise in sixteen years? I was a little fool then. I did not learn that until much later—that there is more, and the marriage-vow nothing to do with it at all. You have been great comfort to me, Moyna."

"My lady. If—if you could choose, what kind of man would you want for yourself?"

Catherine did not answer for a moment. The firelight struck red-brown glints in her hair as she leaned to it; her young, soft profile seemed to harden in the little silence. Then she said with sudden intensity, "I would not care what kind of man, so he was a strong man—the strongest in the world! I am so sick to death of weak men! I know it now; my father was weak, and Argyll a soft weakling who'd never done aught worth remembering, and Calvagh, the chief, is weak, too, and for all his loud talk so is Red Hugh, because he is a braggart and a bully. I would want the strongest man in the world, to keep me against any harm or unhappiness —and I would give him big, strong sons, would I not! And all the love I've learned there must be somewhere, somehow—learning it wed to men I never loved. I wish—I wish—"

"What, my lady?"

"Oh—I don't know." And that was a lie. "We are great fools, too, talking wishes, I think."

"Perhaps there are no men like that at all," agreed Moyna, "and we making them up out of our own heads."

Catherine smiled a secret smile into the fire. Presently she said, "Do you go down and bring us some dinner—and we'll have more light, and I shall give you another lesson in your letters to pass the evening."

CHAPTER VII

Rory felt his spirits lift to see the bulk of Benburb twenty minutes' ride off; he had been away, visiting home, only a week this time, but it was good to return. In one sense, it was hard to realize that he had been O'Neill's man nearly fifteen months; yet, in another, it seemed he had never known any different life. It was good to see his family again, but he was the youngest son and they still thought of him as a boy, which was a little irksome. He was glad he'd not mentioned the McFee girl to them; they'd have teased him about it. McFee had offered the marriage flatteringly, but Rory said frankly he was not ready to settle down to a wife, though he liked Lileas well enough.

He had made good time from the McGuinness' house; it was just on dusk when he rode into the courtyard at Benburb, shouted for a groom, dismounted, and carried in his bag. A servant took it from him with greeting; he strolled into the hall and found Hugh O'Neill there alone. Hugh had O'Givney's little harp across his knees and was improvising a tune. "Rory, man! Good to see you home again. I'm dying of boredom—we all are. Sit and talk to me."

Rory laughed, filling himself a cup from the jug on the table. By now he was on friendly terms with all the captains. "You mean, sit and listen to you. Where's the chief?"

"Shut up in the council room dictating another letter to Elizabeth. I've just composed a song. If I'd not been born noble, I should have been a musician; it's as good as Luke could do any day." Rory listened and told him it was outright theft from a song long composed, at which Hugh was offended and put the harp aside. Filling a cup for himself, he said, "I wonder if even Shane can take that woman. By all accounts, she's a cold one."

"He's heard again from his reverence, the Dean, in England?"

"Oh, yes. Terence is to come home in a month or so, I believe—he's done his work well. But Shane says he's in no haste, he must"—Hugh grinned—"whet the woman's appetite some still. I warn you, he's like a bad-tempered hound. Don't go provoking him."

There was reason for that. This last year, while the chief pretended diplomatic friendship to England, it had been needful that he cease his raids on the Pale. For ten years, at the onset of boredom or when he was otherwise unoccupied, he could always ride south for a little raid to lift his spirits; now he must stay home and write cunning letters to the queen. A full hunting season had kept him fairly content, but this was the end of April and for the past month he had been restless.

"What he needs is a little love affair to keep him occupied," opined Hugh. "Shane likes women beautiful, willing, and often—and if he is balked long in the latter, he's not particular about the first two. By the way, speaking of that, Meriel's child was born yesterday—a son."

"Did she decide whose?"

Hugh shrugged. "Shane claimed it because it's a son. A girl he'd have pushed off on me or Terence. No matter, so it's provided for honorably. Sorley is here, did I tell you?" He was strumming the harp again; he put it down as a door crashed open down the passage. "There's Shane, and in a temper again by the sound."

The chief was in a temper sure enough. He had no outlet for his eternal restless energy, and the plot against England's queen moved slowly. Any small thing was sufficient to set him off, these days. When the house gathered for the meal that evening, he was bitterly cursing McArdle, who had ridden to Armagh with a message for Liam Fleming and delayed return.

"He'll be coming, Shane, don't fret," Hugh soothed. "Likely he's got himself into a long dice-game or found a pretty tavern girl."

"More likely he's run across a new design of cannon and is trying to copy the plan," said Edmund Donnelly amusedly. McArdle was a lover of the big guns. "He'll be coming in with a demand for more money to buy the latest model."

"He will not get it," said O'Neill. "My Christ, I should have gone myself."

Sorley Boy changed the subject to ease his temper. "Have you had any reply from the Stuarts yet?"

It was an unfortunate choice. The chief banged his cup down in fury. "I have not! That bastardly James Stuart, ignoring O'Neill—as if O'Neill were any little provincial subchief begging favors! It is not to be borne! He is not even legal-bred—"

"He's the nominal power in Scotland until his sister comes from France to take her throne. Stuarts are always arrogant. It is an upstart of a clan, and untrustworthy."

"By God," began O'Neill, but was interrupted by a commotion at the front of the hall. A couple of hounds were fighting over a bone by the door, and Rory thought that was all the noise; but in a moment one of

the door-guards on duty came up the hall and begged the chief's pardon
for the disturbance.

O'Neill frowned. "So you make a second one by apologizing! What is
it?"

"Naught of import, O'Neill." The man bowed and turned away.

"And that he calls an apology, to whet my curiosity and leave it un-
satisfied! Aidan!" thundered the chief, and the man stopped as if shot.
"Come here! Now, what was the disturbance?"

"A boy, my lord. He slipped past the gate-guards and into the house.
He was wanting to see you."

"I know I am a handsome man, but is that the only reason this child
wishes to see me?"

"I wouldn't be knowing, lord. He said he had a message for you—fancy,
an urchin like him. Of course he was lying."

"How do you know he is lying?"

"My lord, he's a thief."

"Must I drag it from you word by word? What has he stolen?"

"A horse, O'Neill. It's a fine horse, at least half Arab-bred, and no such
boy could own a horse like that. The guards stopped him, but he ran
between and left the horse—it is a bay—"

"What in the name of God does it signify? You are a fool. Where is
the boy?"

"I told the guards to put him out the gate. But I thought you would
want to keep the horse—"

"Christ send me patience. Go, bring the boy back, search him, and,
if he has a message, bring it to me." The man bowed and went off.
Several minutes later he returned and, stepping up to the platform, ten-
dered a small folded page to the chief.

"O'Neill, there was a message."

The chief split the seal with his knife edge and scanned the contents
of the paper. He sat quite still one moment, then looked down at the
man waiting. "Bring the boy to my council room. Sorley, I have a fancy
to hear a bit more about this niece of yours. You have talked of her often
enough but I never troubled to listen. Who is she, and what kind of
woman?"

Interrupted in the middle of telling a story, Sorley stared at him.
"Catherine? A fine girl she is. Whyfor?"

"Trustworthy—at least as far as any woman can be?"

"She is that. What has brought all this on?"

Rory was straining his eyes to read the message held carelessly in
O'Neill's hand. The paper was stained and crumpled from being carried;
a few black lines of agitated script ran crookedly across the center. He
spelled out the words over the chief's shoulder.

O'Neill: O'Donnell the chief and James the MacDonnell join to lay you ambush-attack in thirty days. Their armies gather now at Kill O'Donnell by Lough Swilly, and O'Donnell is here. Come to the monastery gate at midnight on the Wednesday and I will admit you to take him. You may trust me, I will not fail you.—Catherine MacLean

O'Neill proffered the letter to Sorley Boy. "Is this the lady's hand?"

Sorley read, let out an expletive. "Well, it is Catherine's hand, yes— a brave woman she is to do this. Is it not what I've suspected? I told you, Shane, I told you those two were plotting. At least we know the time of attack now." Sorley frowned over the note. "A brave girl indeed, if James or the O'Donnell should find out about this—Shane? You'll be starting war in Tyrconnell. If you'd delay three days, let me go and bring Catherine away—"

"War?" said O'Neill. He was smiling, pleased, excited. "Who said a word about war?" The note was passing among the captains, who exclaimed grimly; O'Hagan and Hugh rose, breathing vengeance; Ferdoragh thoughtfully polished his dagger; the Donnellys were dark and silent. "You see what the woman says. I'll trust her on your word; the chance is too good to be missed."

Dudley seized his arm. "Shane—no! It is a trap, the wife is a tool for the husband—you'll ride into their axes!"

"Let us see the lady's messenger." Ignoring all the protest and exclamation, O'Neill rose. The others followed in a body, Rory at the chief's shoulder, out of the hall, down the passage to the bare council chamber smoky with new-lit torches, where two guards waited at either side of a very small, very dirty, and very frightened boy of ten or eleven years. As the crowd of big men came in, headed by the tall chief, the boy shrank back; the guards jerked him upright.

"No need to be frightened," O'Neill told him impatiently. "What is your name?"

"M-Malcolm, lord."

"Where have you come from?"

"Lough Swilly." The boy gulped, took a step forward, and burst into rapid speech. "The lady it was, the Scot lady, lord, you will help her? She said I was to ride fast—late it was when she came and said I must help her and the Lord O'Neill would reward me. I was to take a horse and ride very fast to the O'Neill's castle in Tyrone and bring the message. The chief will have me killed for the horse if he finds me, lord. I was frightened too, but the lady said I must come—"

Sorley Boy squatted down the better to see him. "Now, nought to fear, lad," he said kindly. "This is the Lady Catherine, wife to the O'Donnell?"

"Yes, lord—"

"I am not lord and you need not be frightened, I tell you. I am the lady's uncle and wish to help her. She gave you that letter herself?"

"Yes, lord. Please, you will help the lady? She is a beautiful lady—"

"Yes, yes," the chief cut him off. "Honest enough, you think, Sorley?" He looked at the note again; his eyes lit with mischief, and he threw his head back to laugh. "Too good a chance to miss. Those two little men, thinking to take O'Neill! It will end it as it should be ended—one contemptuous move, to show them what children they are!"

"Surprise attack," nodded Edmund Donnelly. "We'll alert the troops at once—"

"Why would I need my army? The lady says she will unbar the gate for me. I ride for Lough Swilly alone, and I'll whisk O'Donnell out from under the noses of his entire army. A jest it will be, and put these impudent upstarts in their rightful places." The prospect of a little action had brought him suddenly into excellent humor.

"Jesus and Mary," said Hugh, "have you lost all sense? No guarantee this is not a trap set by O'Donnell—"

"No," objected Sorley, "Catherine would not be a party to that. She admires you greatly, Shane, that I know, from what she told—I'll swear this letter is honest. But—"

"Send me, let me go," urged Dudley. "If it is a trap, captain is not chief."

"How often must I tell you, Dudley, I order no man to action I would not undertake myself! But I'll take you, and Rory as guard. We ride now, at once, to make the journey by night and lie in cover near Lough Swilly tomorrow. Go and order the horses."

"Shane, I beg—"

"I'll ride with you," said Hugh. The chief swore at him.

"Fool! Chief and both high commanders absent at once? You will not. I will be back day after tomorrow." He turned on his heel, unheeding the storm of protest from all his men except Hugh, who eyed him resignedly.

"You do not ride without me," said Sorley. "It's not that I think you're riding into a trap—you can trust Catherine. But if you kill O'Donnell there she will not be safe a moment. Hugh Ruadh—James—they would know she betrayed—"

"Talk, talk, talk about the woman!" exclaimed O'Neill. "What the hell does the woman matter? And I am not going to kill O'Donnell—his foxblood would stain my ax. You are staying here also. MacDonnell may be at Lough Swilly and I will not involve you in treachery to your chief. Dudley, you heard the order. The horses in ten minutes at the door, emergency rations." Dudley made a resigned gesture and went out.

"Your pardon, my lord, what shall we do with the boy?"

"My Christ, what matter? Take him off to the kitchens and feed him; we can always use another stableboy."

Sorley shook his arm insistently. "Shane, listen—bring her with you. She'll be in danger if you take O'Donnell and leave her. Listen, Shane, I—"

"Before God, burden myself with a female on a journey?" The chief shook him off, strode out. Sorley seized hold of Rory as he followed.

"For the love of God, try to persuade him—any price you name if you rescue her from there—"

Rory was unoffended at the insult, offer of pay to a gentleman. He liked Sorley Boy; he felt casual sympathy for this lady from what Sorley had said. "Well, I'll do my best, MacDonnell, but you know how he is." He ran up the stair to his chamber, got a cloak, his ax; when he came down to the fore-passage O'Neill was already there, cloak slung about him, swearing at delay. But in a moment grooms came up at a trot with horses, to the house door; the captains made a crowd on the step as the chief mounted.

"Shane—" Hugh wore a troubled look in the light of the one torch held by a groom. He laid hand on bridle to stay the chief a moment. "Shane, for God's love, use caution—"

"Caution is for fools and women!" said O'Neill, and wheeled his horse for the gate.

That was a wild ride and Rory had already ridden thirty miles that day; but he kept up, wondering how Dudley managed it. Once down off the cliff road, the chief set a furious pace across open country northwest. It was a clear moonless night; they stopped thrice to breathe the horses, but not long. When a gray dawn broke, it found them riding across dreary, rolling land, Rory would estimate sixty miles from Benburb, the horses worn and dragging. "Near enough," pronounced the chief, glancing round to identify their position. At the first stand of trees, he located a copse partially concealed by low branches, dismounted. "We'll lie here until dark." He unsaddled the Arab, unbitted the bridle to let the horse graze, tethered it long; Dudley and Rory, the latter ready to drop with exhaustion, did the same. "Rory, on guard for two hours. I'll wake to relieve you." The chief lay down on the wet bare ground, pillowed his head on the saddle, and was instantly asleep, and Dudley likewise.

Rory contrived to stay awake, after a little meal of the preserved venison in his saddlebag, until the chief woke. He slept heavily past noon, woke again to take turn at guard duty; it would have been a boring wait, save that he was glad of the rest. The chief was impatient, pacing the covert restlessly; Dudley watched him with brooding eyes and spoke little. Near dusk they shared a meal. As soon as it was full dark, they saddled and rode on, still northwest, but more slowly; and Rory, this country strange to him, soon saw why.

Some six or eight miles on from their resting place, the land opened out below and north to meet the sea, and here was a great sea-lake, shining clear in the first starlight. Bare little knobs of hills surrounded it; at the top of one was a dark pile of masonry which would be the monastery, Kill O'Donnell. And camped all about the hills and hollows was a great army of soldiers—from the number of fires, there must be well over two thousand. The nearest were not far off, and O'Neill ordered in a low voice, "No talking—and hold the bridle from shaking."

They rode on cautiously, making a wide circle about the sprawling camp, up the north slope of the hill where the monastery lay. There was a high wall enclosing the building; they rode along it single file, the chief in the lead, to a place where pillars against the night sky showed a gate. "Wait here. I will—"

A dark figure detached itself from the shadow by the gate and a woman's tremulous voice whispered, "O'Neill?"

"I am O'Neill." Instinctively Rory reached a hand to his ax. The brazenness of that admission! If this were a trap—

But nothing happened save that the woman moved closer. "Thank God you have come! I feared you might think it a trap—so worried and frightened I have been! O'Neill—"

The chief swung off his horse. "Women, wasting words. Where is O'Donnell?"

"Yes—if you will come—"

"Dudley, keep the horses. Rory, with me." Rory made haste to follow as the woman opened the gate and O'Neill started up toward the monastery. She had to run to keep up with his long stride, but after the fashion of women, she could still talk.

"God be thanked you're here—I did not know what to do! I have drugged his wine, O'Neill—a dreadful thing, Uncle James will kill me if he finds out, but I could not see such treachery. You are Sorley's friend. And I would not have known of this but that my—my husband is jealous and would not leave me alone at Rath O'Donnell while he came here. There was a ship, new weapons for the army, and some of Uncle James' army—there are more to come, I think—"

"Quiet in God's name!" said the chief. She slipped past him, leading the way round a corner of the building.

"This way—here, O'Neill—"

They came in through a narrow door to what was evidently one of the guest chambers of the monastery; there were hides on the floor, wall-brackets, a few chairs, a large couch. One torch flared smokily in a bracket. O'Neill paid no attention to the woman or anything else but the man lying on that couch in drugged sleep. He made two long strides to stand over him, hands on thighs.

"So I come up with you at last, you son of the family of traitors!" he said softly.

Calvagh O'Donnell, sprawled senseless on the couch, was not an attractive sight. O'Neill's description of him as a fox was appropriate, Rory thought—a small, bald, narrow-faced old fellow with a weak jaw and a thin white beard.

"Oh, O'Neill—" The woman gasped and moved behind them; Rory turned to see her, but O'Neill was absorbed in his enemy. Rory found Lady Catherine more interesting. She was a tall, slender young woman with brown hair lying loose on her shoulders, a fine white complexion, large blue eyes. Her voice was soft, with a little accent on the Gaelic, and he recalled hearing Sorley say she had been partially educated in France. With a dark red cloak caught round her over a gown of sea-blue, she made a charming sight even in her agitation. "You—are going—to kill him?" she asked faintly.

"I am not," said O'Neill without looking at her. "My thanks to you for delivering him." He bent, heaved the unconscious man up across his shoulder, and turned to the door. As if vaguely aware he should say more to her, he added, "My thanks indeed; it is very helpful." He was evidently about to walk off with O'Donnell and leave her to cope with the consequences. Rory had no hope of changing his mind, but he felt sympathy for the woman, and he touched O'Neill's arm.

"Your pardon, O'Neill, but Sorley Boy asked that you bring Lady Catherine away to him—"

"Oh!" she gasped again. "Oh, yes, please, if you would take me to Sorley—if you would wait—"

"Christ!" exclaimed O'Neill. He stood in the open door, the other chief's body draped across one shoulder, seeming quite unconscious of the weight. "Damn Sorley and his everlasting sentimentalities!" But that time he saw her. He gave her a long, thoughtful, appraising look, and then his sudden charming grin. "But Sorley never told me you are a beautiful woman. I would have made war on O'Donnell two years ago if I'd known it. No hardship at all to take you along, if you'll not mind sharing my saddle. Ten minutes—Rory, wait and bring the lady on with her gear." He turned, turned back and gave her another look. "Fifteen minutes. She is worth waiting for." He vanished into the dark with O'Donnell.

Lady Catherine stared after him, a queer little smile on her mouth. Rory remembered Sorley saying she had great admiration for O'Neill. Now, meeting him for the first time, she seemed half dazed—but she had been under great strain, of course.

"My pardon, Lady Catherine, if you'd make haste—"

She started, glanced at him. "Oh, yes—yes, I will." She went out of the room by its inner door. Rory waited in a little trepidation, knowing O'Neill would not delay long—or would he? But in a commendably short time she returned, accompanied by a cloaked figure carrying a bag. "It is right to bring my maid? I cannot travel without escort—"

There was no help for it, but not for the first time Rory was impatient for the awkward conventionalities of women. What would O'Neill say? He hurried them out, down to the gate. O'Neill was already mounted and O'Donnell was bound, face down, across the front of Dudley's saddle. "Name of God!" ejaculated the chief, but his tone was half-humorous. "Why am I such a fool as to offer to travel with a woman?" Then he saw there were two women. "My Christ!"

"But my maid," said Lady Catherine breathlessly. Even in that moment, with potential danger all about from the near army camp, there was a note of laughter in her voice. "You'd not have me endanger my reputation, and I traveling alone with three men?"

For once O'Neill was temporarily beyond words, perhaps taken aback at her self-possession when she had recently been agitated. "Come here," he ordered roughly, and, bending, lifted her to sit before him on the saddle, his right arm firm about her. Rory had no choice but to mount the maidservant before himself. "Now for the love of God, let us get off! No talking. Dudley, watch the traitor lest he come to life."

"He is bound fast," said Dudley indifferently. They rode down the hill the way they had come up and circumvented the camp again; a safe distance out of earshot the chief set a faster pace. The maid had ridden silent before Rory, but he was conscious of the warm roundness of her, of her hand clutching his shoulder; now it clutched tighter and he said, "Don't fear, I won't let you fall."

"Oh, I am not frightened of that," she told him in a remarkably unexcited tone. I am only a little feared Hugh Ruadh will come after us when he finds out. That one there, he is only an old weak man—Red Hugh is the real chief."

"So I hear." She sounded a self-possessed little creature, and was certainly a comfortable armful; he held her a bit tighter and said, "But he'd never dare attack O'Neill. Don't you know O'Neill is the greatest prince in Ireland, girl, and has the strongest army? You'll be safe enough." A pity, he thought, Sorley would likely take the Lady Catherine to his own castle and the maid with her. Of course, she might not be pretty at all in the light, but somehow she sounded it. He took the chance, bent, and kissed her soundly. She gave a small, outraged shriek and slapped him hard.

"Now, for God's sake, be quiet—I meant only to comfort you—"

"Comfort! Oh, yes, I've heard tales of O'Neill's army men! Your hands to yourself!"

"I am not a soldier"—he was annoyed—"but O'Neill's personal bodyguard and a gentleman, grandson to a chief, and I'll thank you—"

"Oh, a gentleman, is it?" she said crossly. "I would not know, you not telling me. I see I've no choice but to ride with you, but you mind the horse and not myself. I may be only a maidservant but I'm a respectable woman."

"Well, I ask pardon," he said stiffly, "but no harm I meant. Never a girl died of a kiss yet."

"That," she retorted, "is what you think about it. Next time I might bite as well as slap, so mind it."

"Women! Very well, very well, I have apologized—now be quiet."

CHAPTER VIII

Rory groaned, opened his eyes, shut them, and groaned louder. In that one glimpse, he saw that Ena was with him, and informed her in a weak voice that he was dying.

"Oh, you're awake, McGuinness. A head you'll have and no wonder. Lie quiet a minute and I'll bring you something for it." He lay and suffered until she came back with a tall mug, urged him to sit up and drink; he did so feebly. "Jesus and Mary"—hoping at least to die with a prayer in his mouth—"are you off to poison me now?"

"Hold it. I am not indeed. It's strong but it will make you better directly." In a few minutes the potion reached him; he shook his head, sat up on the edge of the bed. "A bout you all had indeed," said Ena.

"It was," he agreed, portions of the evening returned to him. All the army men, the entire household, had been so overjoyed to see O'Neill safe home again, they had joined a celebration lasting long past midnight. He had dim recollections of O'Neill emptying cup after cup without showing any signs of being affected at all, calling down ceremonial curses on MacDonnell, O'Donnell, James Stuart, Elizabeth, and Radcliffe; of O'Hagan, Ferdoragh, and Sorley Boy staging a knife-throwing contest, and Ferdoragh on winning it exuberantly drenching his opponents with a full jug of liquor; of Luke O'Givney accompanying Hugh's sweet high tenor on soulful renditions of many love ballads; of a fist fight between Manus Donnelly and McFee over some fancied insult.

She sat down beside him companionably. "But the chief was not drunken," she said regretfully. "Is it better you are now, McGuinness?"

"A bit. In fifteen months I have never seen him drunken—is he ever?"

"Oh, once in three years or so. When the liquor reaches him first he wants to fight and then he wants to make love—grand it was the last time, you should have seen it. He made a wager with Hugh he could heft a bull-calf ten paces, and they all went out to the barns at midnight to prove it, and he did, and then he wrestled O'Hagan and threw him head-down into the dung-pile, and then he came roaring into the house after a woman and I was the first one he saw so he took me then and there in the fore-passage and I was near lame for a week, a great man he is, in or out of liquor, I tell you."

"I believe you," said Rory. He still felt sick and had a dull headache, but knew from experience food and drink would help—especially the latter; he dressed himself with effort and staggered down to the hall, where his respect for the captains increased. Hugh, the three younger Donnellys, Ferdoragh, and Sorley Boy were sharing a large breakfast of cold beef and liquor, conversing brightly over it.

"You've not got a head after a little bout like that?" asked Hugh. Rory collapsed into a chair, reached for a cup, and cut himself a slice of beef he did not want.

"Do not tell me, I know—a soft weakling I am beside you! Where is the chief?"

"Behind you, weakling," said O'Neill amiably. He strode into the hall, no marks on him of a late wet night, elegantly dressed as always; Dudley was at his side. He went round behind Sorley and dropped a sealed packet into his lap.

"What is this?"

"A little errand for you. It is a letter to the MacDonnell you will carry. It underlines the insult that his kinsman brings it." O'Neill pulled up a chair, sat astride it, filled a cup.

"Well, I was riding for Antrim this week in any case," said Sorley Boy humorously. "He is at the Red Bay?"

"He is—waiting for the rest of the army Gilchrist and a few other chiefs pledged him, the bastards. For once I take a second thought for a war."

"They all deserve annihilation for such treachery," said Dudley violently. The chief smiled round the board.

"Nothing I'd like better than a lively little war, and all of you knowing it. That it would be. MacDonnell and Calvagh—and the Scots who joined —have three thousand or so, by what the one traitor we captured tells me. Oh, yes, I've been questioning O'Donnell while you snored." His teeth gleamed on an ugly grin; Dudley looked pleased. "But they will not attack now. Not because I hold Calvagh prisoner—Red Hugh would be all too pleased if he died under torture, and MacDonnell does not give a curse for him either—but because now they know I am warned. A pity it is I cannot claim a little retribution, but I took two thoughts as I said. I am busy with this matter of Elizabeth, and then," he laughed, "if I lay Tyrconnell waste in vengeance, how would Calvagh pay me tribute? Hugh Ruadh would cause me more trouble as chief than Calvagh—I'll take care to keep the old bastard alive, but he'll not enjoy his stay! And I'll lay a heavy fine on him for the treachery. They know my strength—I have no need to prove it to them." He rubbed his jaw thoughtfully. "Now listen, Sorley—"

"What have you written James?" Sorley weighed the letter curiously.

"Nothing he will like reading! I have told him he will be safe—if he stays his side of the Bann. And my opinion of his honor, to plan ambush attack. But, look you, Sorley. You know nothing of any of it. He will wonder who betrayed—let him. You only happened to be passing and I asked you to carry the letter. I'd not have him lay the blame on you."

"I would rather he thought it was myself than Catherine." Sorley's eyes softened a little as he spoke her name.

"More fool you. He could make you more harm than the woman."

"Well, I will take it, Shane—he'll be furious, but I agree, he would not attack alone, and Red Hugh will never join him now, he's too canny a man. They will march their armies home and sulk in silence—until the next time."

"Exactly. One day I'll give them both a little lesson in war—but not now. I've this scheme to play on Elizabeth Tudor first."

Sorley rose. "Well, I may as well ride today. I think I will take Catherine, though she'll be weary—I want to see her settled at Dunluce as soon as possible. She need not return to O'Donnell even when you release him."

The chief set his cup down, frowning. "Take the woman? You will not!" And then he checked himself, shrugged at Sorley's curious stare.

"I'll ask the loan of a horse for her—"

"None of my horses are so gentle for a lady to ride," said the chief brusquely. "Oh, get on, do what you will!" Suddenly he was in impatient mood. Sorley went off to collect his escort and see Lady Catherine; the others, eying the chief covertly, proceeded with breakfast, mainly in silence.

Rory filled his cup again, feeling a trifle more alive by now, and ruminated idly on the ride home yesterday and the maidservant, Moyna. His instinct had been quite right; she was a pretty one, seen in the light—a quantity of black hair, black-fringed green eyes, and a provocative plump figure. But an irritating female and snappish. He wanted nothing to do with her. Just as well she would be leaving Benburb with her lady. For if she was about—well, no denying she was an attractive girl . . . and most definitely respectable, not to say prim.

Presently, sounds in the courtyard indicated that the escort of Scot troopmen gathered to ride, and the captains came out to the passage for farewell. Rory followed—not, he told himself, for a last look at the maid. O'Neill was finishing the platter of beef and stayed where he was.

When Sorley came down, cloaked to ride, Lady Catherine was at his side. Rory thought she looked faintly unhappy; he wondered about that. Very likely she was sorry to be going away from O'Neill, and not the first woman to be that either. Women had no sense to choose their own husbands, but even if she'd been allowed to, she could scarcely have picked two worse ones than had her father and her chief: a middle-aged nonentity and a lecherous old fool like O'Donnell. She would never have known a young, vigorous man, for she was obviously a good, decent lady, and it would be no wonder if she liked O'Neill, or a bit more than that. The maid, Moyna—no denying at all she was a pretty girl—stood beside her mistress, impossibly demure. When he caught her eye, she put her nose in the air and looked away.

"Hugh—all of you, good to have seen you again." Sorley embraced Hugh; the others clasped Rory's hand. "Tell Shane I will write him as to how James takes his medicine. I have begged a horse for the lady. I'll send it back. Catriona, girl"—he gave her an affectionate hug—"God be thanked I have you away from those two at last! You know you are welcome always at Dunluce. You'll be warm enough? Sorry I am to ask you to make another journey so soon—"

"It is all right, uncle, you know I'm grateful." Her voice was low and soft; she was unsmiling. "But are we not to—that is, I should like to thank our host—"

"Sorley has already done so," said O'Neill. She started and turned. He stood in the door of the hall, hands on thighs; her eyes fastened on him eagerly. "No need for thanks, lady—the other way about. You have done me a favor, and"—his smile broadened—"yourself a favor as well, in my opinion."

She flushed very faintly. "It was wrong, he is my husband, but—"

"Now forget all that, girl," said Sorley, taking her arm. "Of course you were not wrong; it was O'Donnell's treachery. Come along; if we're to make any time today, we must be leaving."

"Oh, it is early," said the chief, strolling toward her. "A pity to rob my castle of such beauty."

Sorley raised his brows on him, said, "I'll let you know about James, Shane. Come along, Catherine," and turned to the door. Lady Catherine never moved, but stood looking up at the chief.

This was an O'Neill Rory had seen a few times before—whenever he was with a woman he wanted. A smiling, handsome man, all the famous clan charm, an aura about him: he was watching Lady Catherine boldly, mirthful mischief in his eyes. He saw—he could not help seeing—how he fascinated her: he was used to that look; it was his due from women. But mingled with the laughter in his expression was admiration. She made a charming sight, color in her cheeks, her red mouth a little tremulous: a lovely woman. He said in a drawling tone, "That whoreson O'Donnell, to think to keep you all to himself! Punishment he deserves for that. Has he turned you against the breed of men entirely, lady?"

"N-no, O'Neill."

"Good—good." He extended his stare from her face down the length of her slim figure, appraising and approving, and her flush deepened. "Some man will be fortunate for that. A great pity it is you are a noblewoman." He was telling her bluntly that had she not been a lady he would have no hesitation in seeking her as his mistress.

She took a breath and lifted her head to look him in the eyes. "Much of my misfortune, O'Neill, has come from my gentle birth. I might be pleased to forget—that I am a noblewoman."

"Catherine!" exclaimed Sorley sharply, but she seemed not to hear him. The chief was smiling wider.

"Do you tell me? Very well then, make your choice now. Go with Sorley—or stay here with me."

There was a short, rather embarrassed silence. Sorley Boy took a step toward Lady Catherine and hesitated. She had not looked away from the chief.

"I will stay, O'Neill. I will stay."

"That is my good girl," said O'Neill. He gave her a push in the direction of the stair. "Off with you now— You may have anything here you desire except my best horse or my favorite ax. And I shall send to Armagh for my tailors to come and make a new wardrobe of fine gowns for a beautiful lady."

"Catherine," said Sorley quietly, "you should think for this. Your honor —your entire life—"

Still she was looking at the chief, her gaze blind and blank. "I—will— stay. Do not press me, Sorley. He will look to me."

"Get off, get off," said O'Neill. "Why are you still hanging about? Do you not hear the lady, brother? I will look to her well, now and afterward." Yes, thought Rory, he would tire of a woman soon. Sorley made a gesture of resignation; he went to Lady Catherine and kissed her cheek.

"If he does not, you know I would. Your own choice is this. Good-by, girl. I will see you in a month or so."

"Yes. Good-by, Sorley." As they went out to the yard, her eyes followed O'Neill.

Sorley took his bridle, turned, and offered his hand to the chief. "Mark, Shane—you will treat her well if you value me as a friend." His tone was serious. "I would have been pleased at a legal match between you. This, I don't know."

"I am always kind to lovely women," said the chief. "You remember what I said and give MacDonnell no grievance on you." He watched the party out of the gate, smiling, and turned for the house; Rory started to follow him and he gave him a rough, playful push. "I'm not wanting you!"

Hugh had been right, Rory thought; the chief was soothed to temporary amiability by a new love affair, and one provocatively different. A woman was a woman to O'Neill; if he had leisure and choice, he would exercise some discrimination. Otherwise, he took the nearest to hand. He had never taken a mistress on permanent basis; he took now an un-

usual one—a lady, wife to a chief, a decent woman. She kept him occupied and pleased with himself.

His apartments were abovestairs in the west wing of Benburb, three
large chambers in a row. He gave one to Lady Catherine, and busied himself furnishing it as he considered proper for a lady. He haled a corps
of tailors from Armagh with selections of stuffs for her approval. The
lady seemed bewildered at his munificence, the dozens of gowns he insisted she order, the jewels he pressed on her; O'Neill never went halfway
in anything. That she was utterly under his spell was obvious. Probably
O'Neill took her mind entirely from her old husband in the dungeons
below Benburb. That was not the least irony of it, but to do the chief
justice, that aspect of the matter never occurred to him.

The O'Donnell had brought his troubles on himself. The woman had
nothing to do with that in O'Neill's mind. Some men (like Dudley, Rory
thought) would have taken great sensual pleasure in imagining the tortures
practiced on the husband while he enjoyed the charms of the wife under
the same roof. O'Neill had O'Donnell chained naked in a cell, and went
down a few times to see the ankle screws tightened and hear him groan;
but as entertainment it palled on him, and within a week he ordered the
tortures ceased. For the moment, his whole interest concentrated on the
woman.

Ferdoragh said philosophically, "He'll not keep her long. A month
or two, and he'll tire of her. He always does with a woman."

"Aye, so," agreed Terence O'Hagan to that. "But he'll treat her well
for it. I am a little sorry for the lady, a sweet lady she is and an innocent,
and deep in love with him. She will grieve when he turns her away. But
he's a strong sense of honor, he will give her a large dower for her next
husband." Rory expressed doubt that any man would offer for Lady
Catherine were she free. O'Hagan laughed and shook his head. "Many
men eager to acquire a woman O'Neill has approved, especially with the
gold he will give her." The others agreed. The lady was well liked at
Benburb. Despite her high birth, she had never been in a position to
grow arrogant; she was friendly and anxious to please. Even the other
ladies of the house soon thawed and grew friendly in return. Rory thought
it would have irked the captains that she shared the chief's table every
night, but (save for Dudley, who never spoke with a woman when he
could avoid it) they all seemed fond of her, vying with one another to
offer her the choicest morsels, telling innocent jests to bring her rare,
pretty laugh.

And all of them—including Sorley Boy, who returned a month later
to give the chief the latest news of MacDonnell's actions, and somewhat
regretfully expressed the view that O'Neill would soon have his fill of a
mistress and dismiss her—all of them were wrong. A month after that, the
chief at last released old O'Donnell moldering in his cell, deciding he

had enough vengeance, and sent him home to Tyrconnell to lick his wounds. But the O'Donnell's lady-wife he kept, with no sign that he grew bored with her. And in that time subtle changes came about in their apparent relationship, and in the Lady Catherine.

When she came to Benburb she was a girl, despite her two marriages. After the first half-year with O'Neill, she was a woman, and a charming one. There was no longer that blind worship in her eyes on him, but sometimes laughter; her tone with him was easy and affectionate, no longer timid. Perhaps the most astonishing thing was that he was never angered with her. No other man or woman around him was not now and then target for his temper that flared at a word, but never Lady Catherine. Several times, when the chief lashed out over this or that in company, they all saw how she quieted him—a hand on his arm, a whisper in his ear.

He was never a man for the courtesies with a lady—by reason of his position they owed him the courtesies. But he turned strangely polite to Lady Catherine, and there was a note in his voice, speaking to her, a look in his eyes on her, different from before.

Rory, as curious about it as anyone else at Benburb, got nowhere even about that with Moyna. That girl—she'd little right to be so uppish, only a maidservant!

He had sought her out and apologized cunningly, and at first she thawed a little to him. "Well, gentlemen are still men, McGuinness, I forgive you. Only see it does not occur again." She was friendly enough when he made opportunity to meet her, as he did.

He met her one afternoon on the hillside beyond the castle; having seen her leave the house, he followed. She said she was bound only for a walk, having no work and the chief being with Lady Catherine. Without enthusiasm she agreed he might accompany her.

"Everyone is surprised he keeps her as mistress this long. What do you think, you seeing them together?"

"So does everyone see them together, McGuinness. Only her maid I am. Is he in love with her, you say? That's a long word or a short one. Only, I think he is beginning to understand."

"Understand what?"

"Oh, a thing I can't explain to you, that women know about, but not so many men"—her smile that time a little shy. "I—I do not really know much about it myself, only that it is something very good."

"Then neither of us knows what you are talking about. Do you like living at Benburb?"

"Oh, yes, a friendly castle it is, not like the Red Bay House or Rath O'Donnell. Also, there are strict house rules as you very well know," and she slipped away the arm he slipped around her, "and a respectable girl is quite safe."

"Very set you are on respectability," he grinned at her, "and it a dull virtue."

"I daresay," said Moyna. "I will keep it—and all my virtues."

"Very well, very well!"

"You always say that, and then coming at me next time the same—"

"You don't know McGuinnesses! We never acknowledge defeat."

He met her coming down the narrowest, darkest part of the stair from the west wing, and, a little liquor being in him, he caught her up tight and kissed her hard against her struggling; her mouth was soft and ignorant under his. "Oh!" she said, and did not strike him.

"Sorry I am, girl—excuse it, it was the *uisgebaugh*, not myself." And on that she did strike him, and no ladylike blow either, and ran past away from him. Well, women—oddnesses in the best of them.

He met her on the west side of the courtyard in late dusk, leaning on the wall, dreaming at the stars, and he thought she wore a new gown, its deep green matching her eyes, and close-cut to show the swell of her breast. "Are you waiting for a lover maybe?"—coming up behind her.

She did not start. "Maybe I was waiting for you, McGuinness."

"Oh, now it's a little sense you're getting!" He reached for her confidently and she wrenched away.

"Holy mother, are you the stallion your master is, forever the one thing in your mind? It is all you want of me, ever."

"All!" He laughed. "And I showing you how pleasant it is—"

"Well, you will not. Leave me go." But backing off, she half-smiled at him before she turned and ran. He shrugged after her, smiling at himself. A fool he was to tease the girl. He had a decent raising; no gentleman would seduce a virgin against her will—there were plenty of easy women to hand. But a maddening female she was, and damnably pretty, and he had a notion she knew more about the situation between the chief and his mistress than she would say.

CHAPTER IX

IT was in that September of 1560 the unprecedented quarrel broke out between O'Neill and Hugh. Quarrel was the wrong word, for Hugh never quarreled with anyone in his life; but easy, amiable, soft Hugh was yet an O'Neill, as his brother and other men were sometimes reminded in no soft way.

O'Neill had, for six months, been making diplomatic overtures to the Stuarts in Scotland. The response had been cold, and that was puzzling; but that month he had a more cordial letter from Lord James. The messenger came one evening; the letter was brought to him at the table and he read it between mouthfuls, laughed, thrust it carelessly into his tunic.

"Is the man hedging? I wonder. Stuart," to Dudley's question. "Queen Mary arrived in Scotland last month. It must await her decision, he keeps saying"—with a shrug. "Damn the lot of them! I want that treaty before I go to England. Of all her enemies, Elizabeth has most hate for Mary Stuart." Suddenly his gaze turned ruminative; he put down his knife, leaned back in the tall chair. "By Christ," he said to himself, "there is a notion, yes. A great political victory it will be." He was fired with new idea, swung on Hugh abruptly. "You are going to Scotland—"

"Oh, am I now?" said Hugh, slicing more deer meat.

"Ostensibly with messages from me to the new queen, and gifts, and overtures for treaty. This bastard brother of hers I've heard of, but you are the man to get round him. You will do so—you will lay suit to her and get her to wife. That—"

"Oh, will I?" said Hugh with his mouth full.

"You will. You are very near as clever as myself at coercing women, and Mary Stuart will likely give you no trouble, a frivolous female of nineteen—that Frenchman was a poor excuse for a husband to her and he is long enough dead. A stroke of luck her French relations did not tie her up in a betrothal before she came home. You'll please her, an honest, upstanding man after all those foreigners. You will—"

"I will not," said Hugh. "If you are set on wedding a queen, I am not. I'll have nothing to do with Mary Stuart."

"By God, you will! It's the exact moment, when she is just returned to Scotland, and this long a widow. She will take to you, and we claim distant cousinship you can play on also. The political advantage—"

"To hell with the political advantage. I will not wed Mary Stuart."

The chief stood and thundered at him, dark with rage. "By Christ and all the apostles, you will do as I say! My orders are not to be disobeyed!"

Hugh smiled at him. "Roar all you want, Shane, I'll never marry the Stuart for you." The chief laid hold of him, pulled him upright, shook him violently back and forth. Hugh was no small man, and any other putting hands on him like that would discover he was no weakling either, but he did not resist and his smile was fixed. "No, Shane," he said.

Lady Catherine laid a gentle hand on the chief's arm; he let Hugh go at once. She murmured, "No way that is, Shane."

Hugh laughed. "My thanks, Catherine—bring the stallion to stand a minute while I soothe him down. Now look, Shane, would you be liking it, some man ordering you— Bed with such-and-such a woman? My own bedmates I choose, and a wife I'm not choosing at all, now or henceforth."

"What is it to do with me, fool? O'Neill takes orders from no man— he gives orders, and I am giving you one now!"

"Give it all you please," said Hugh calmly. "I'll not wed Mary Stuart if she'd have me, and that's the last word I'll say."

"It will not be the last you hear!" promised the chief grimly. It was not. For the next month the argument went on whenever the two were in talking distance, and privately the captains laid wagers on the outcome; only Ferdoragh and O'Hagan put money on the chief.

"Our Hugh I know," said McArdle, chuckling. "Never a harsh word out of him, but God Himself could not push him a road he was not wanting to travel." They got Rory to hold the stakes pending some outcome. The chief had deepest love for two men, Hugh and Dudley; the latter would never conceive of going against him, but this was not the first time Hugh had done so and always it roused fury in him that such insubordination should set them apart.

In the end no man won any money on it, for the outcome was stalemate. O'Neill argued as long about the necessity of a military pact with Scotland as about the marital alliance. Hugh said from the start he was willing to act as ambassador. "Well, by God," said the chief, "something I'll get out of you at any rate! You will go to Scotland and get me that treaty."

"I'm agreeable to that, if I must. I would not think there would be any trouble about it. Whatever you can say of Stuarts, they're not Anglophile."

"About that I don't know—this Lord James writes long words and not a definite Yea or Nay in a page of them. But they are not fools and know well enough what advantage a treaty with me will give them. You will leave at once."

Hugh said amiably, "I'll do that for you. The sooner I leave, the sooner I return."

He left Benburb with a small escort, carrying some elegant gifts for Scotland's queen, early in December; the expectation was that he would be absent a couple of months. McArdle wondered, "How will we manage without Hugh all that time?"

O'Neill grinned. "Maybe longer, Cormac. He may take the Stuart woman yet, who knows?"

During this time there were changes at Benburb none of them could understand, all duly ordered by the chief, but surely not his own notions; it was puzzling. Rory cross-questioned Moyna once or twice, but there was no getting anything out of her; she looked demure and said she was only a maidservant, how should she know anything of the privacies between the chief and Lady Catherine?

"You could say if you wanted. Secretive like all women you are."

Her head on one side of him—"Well, McGuinness, maybe we find it's best to keep some things secret."

"You never succeed too far—what woman ever kept a secret? Come and go a walk with me on the hill."

"I will not. It's not to walk you're wanting, I know that."

"Oh, grown to a woman it is—beginning to see through the machinations of men!"

Moyna giggled. "No standard that is. We begin to do that when we step out of the cradle."

But she condescended to walk with him now and then, and even to talk about the Lady Catherine. It was one of those times she said a good deal indeed, but that only exasperated and puzzled him further . . .

"We can go back this way," said Moyna, indicating the branching track.

"We will not."

"Oh? Very masterful you are." Her eyes laughed at him. She knew well enough why they would not take that path. It led toward Benburb through the permanent army camp and passed the settlement of camp-followers, the common women of the soldiers. They were goodhearted souls, but disreputable, and Moyna was a decent girl. "Men are peculiar," she added. "Black and white only they see, and a nice neat line down the center. Trying to make love to me all the time, and you turn so careful for where I walk!"

"Now have I said one wrong word to you the last hour?"

"You have not, all very nice at arm's length. I had you promise it afore I said I'd come with you."

"Very well then, sit down here and finish what you were saying."

"Was I saying anything?"

"An insubordinate female you are," and he scowled at her to suppress a smile. She seated herself on a boulder by the path and he took up a stance before her. "We were speaking of your lady. I'll never believe she's responsible, but go on and tell me."

"Oh, McGuinness, you are funny. I'm not sure I should."

"I'll shake you in a moment." Rory was exasperated. He would never believe the lady was behind it all. Changes at Benburb? It was only in the last month they realized how many there were, all come so gradually.

There had not, since Rory first lived here, been much observance of careful manners among the men of the household; they were all professional soldiers and gave little thought to social graces. O'Neill demanded attentive service but never noticed his surroundings particularly. The hall had generally been littered with flung bones and the dung of the hounds; now it was cleaned daily. Hugh was fastidious; it was his custom to be shaved twice a week and he kept his body-servant busy cleaning stains from his clothes, but the chief, and the other captains, were usually lax for such matters. These days, O'Neill was changed; his tunics were clean, his hair trimmed neatly at the shoulders, and at the table each evening a line above his wrists indicated he had washed his hands before meat. At the Benburb of six months ago, the servants had left the chamber-utensils unemptied sometimes several days; now it was done twice a day. The hounds were no longer allowed abovestairs. Rory had seen O'Neill clean his knife of grease from the meat before returning it to his belt; and the plates at the table were washed after each meal. These were all things a man would never think of: there was a woman's hand in it somewhere. But O'Neill letting a woman dictate to him?

Moyna was regarding him doubtfully. "I really should not answer you, McGuinness. It's explaining to a man how women rule men. You will all be ruled but you never like to know about it. But maybe it will do no harm to give you a little lesson. I'll confess to you, it has been an interesting lesson to myself. But then, Lady Catherine is near five years older than me, and that much wiser for men. I think I will tell you. He was at a disadvantage to start with—"

"O'Neill?"

"O'Neill. He is a man. There was the matter of his clothes. Always very elegant, but he cares nothing are they free of stains or no. Lady Catherine is a woman and she knew better than to say to him, 'Shane, my dear, will you not have your servant clean your garments?' He would roar out that only fops and women pay notice to such things. No, she says to him, 'Shane, my dearest, you are an important statesman, and it is not fitting you should wear dirty clothes. You should keep the servants up to mark.' He puts it down to a woman's foible and says 'Very well,' and of course, forgets all about it, but the first wedge is driven. So she has Seumas—his body-servant—fetch out all O'Neill's clothes, and she orders a whole barrel of bran from Armagh to clean the silk and wool. And when the chief complains she is stealing his things, whyfor all this nonsense of cleaning, she says he need not think of it, it is all looked to for him. And so it is, he is used to it now, only Seumas was complaining of all the work, and Lady Catherine smiles at him and says, 'But, Seumas, you serve a very important man, you should be proud to keep him looking his best!' And Seumas is persuaded. So now O'Neill is always in clean garments."

"Hmmm," said Rory. "Well, go on."

"There were all sorts of matters." Moyna leaned back, arms braced; he admired the slender line of her throat while she stared reflectively at the sky. "All the guards on duty had a habit of relieving themselves in the yard over the cliff wall, just under her windows, and she said to me it was like living in a city street—she has very nice notions about such things, maybe of being educated. So she says to the chief, 'It is not myself I think of, or the married women, but there are many respectable young girls here, and it is offensive to their modesty and may endanger their virtue.' Well, he was not going to have it said no decent young woman can stay at Benburb without being offended, was he now? He issued orders, and now they all go to the one place, round the other side of the yard where it is more private."

"Just a word or two from her? I don't believe it."

"She's a very lovely woman," said Moyna. "But I don't deny there was a bit more trouble over his shaving. She knew it would be no use at all to say, 'My darling, your beard pricks me when we embrace, it looks very uncouth, will you not cut it oftener than once or twice a month?' He would not be shaved for a year, to show his superiority. No, she says, 'My darling, an important man like you, a prince, should show himself to advantage! The smooth chin or the full beard, and you would look a prince! But this rough stubble, neither one thing nor the other, it is not seemly for a man in your position.' Well, he was not so easy to convince —it is a great nuisance to him, being barbered. So she says, 'But, my dear, you are so handsome when you've been newly shaven! I am foolish indeed to urge it on you, for if you appeared so most of the time you would have all the women of the house in love with you!' And of course, he was pleased and went off to be shaved. But every two or three days there was the same thing all over again, and she pressed him to make it definite, the barber ordered to shave him twice a week. Nonsense, he was no city fop, she was trying to make an effeminate idiot of him! What is it in a battle you call the second line of attack, McGuinness?"

"Well, in an engagement of mixed troops it would be the ax-ranks, the gallowglass."

"Yes, well, it was then she brought out her—her ax-ranks. It will usually end the battle, not always, but usually."

"What did she do?"

"Why, she put her arms about him and kissed him, and said, 'My heart's darling, only to please me?' And he agreed. And for five or six weeks there was a dreadful scene every time the barber appeared, but she soothed him very well and after a bit he grew used to it and now it is all settled and he is shaved twice a week and has even ordered all his high officers to do likewise."

"Are you telling me anything?" retorted Rory bitterly, a hand at his jaw. "Speak of nuisances!"

"Yes, there was an outcry about it, was there not?" She laughed. "Then there was the drink. Lady Catherine does not like *uisgebaugh*, it is too strong, and there was nought else to drink at any meal. Well, he is very generous with her, you know. She has but to say she desires a new gown or a jewel or anything at all, and he sees she has it. So she never thought there would be difficulty, and asked that he order some wine for her and some thin glasses to drink it from because the metal cups are rough and leave a taste in the mouth. Ooh, he was in a fury! This is a Gaelic household and no such effete foreign things should be brought into it. She would drink our own liquor or none at all. It is admitting foreigners and foreign things has brought to Ireland all her present troubles, and no money of his would be paid out for French wines or Italian glassware! Well, Lady Catherine was surprised, you know, but she did not give up. Oh, no. She smiled and leaned against him and said soft, 'Only to please me, my dearest?' But it did no good that time. He swore most frightful and said No! So—what is it that would be the very heaviest attack possible? Would it be the cannon?"

"Some men would say so."

"Well, then she brought out her cannon."

"What did she do?"

"She wept," said Moyna succinctly. "That is all. So the next day O'Neill sent a rider to Armagh and ordered a thousand bottles of French wine and four dozen crystal glasses."

Rory digested all that and said with conviction, "Women are underhanded and sly." Moyna threw her head back and laughed.

"Oh, McGuinness! The jest is, in your time you'll be ruled the same way by some woman and never know it more than the chief. No, of course, he has no idea he is influenced by her—I can hear him roar if any suggested it! It has all come about so gradual, a little here and a little there, you see. But she could never manage him so except that he loves her. Maybe he does not know it yet, but he loves her."

"Romantic, you mean?"

Moyna regarded him, her smile a little sad. "No, not like that. Did you ever stop to think, McGuinness, she is the only good woman who has ever loved him for himself?"

"You're sentimental," he jeered. "Who could count the women have been in love with O'Neill?"

"Except his wives," said Moyna with asperity. "Not like that. His first wife was a wanton, and his second a cold fool of a woman, what I saw of her at Rath O'Donnell. And all the other women he's had, they've been common, it was a thing like eating a meal when he was hungered, no meaning in it at all. Lady Catherine is a respectable woman—like me!—and she gave up her honor to love him, and has gone on loving him, and will until she dies. Are you knowing why?"

"I could make a guess. Why?"

"Because she thinks he is the strongest man in the world."

"And so he is," said Rory, "so he is. Come along, we'll be late for the meal. I think you think you have told the truth, but it's not so. I know O'Neill, and none will ever rule him, man or woman."

Moyna said nothing more, only rose to accompany him, laughing. He discussed it at length with the captains later, and all agreed with him except James and Manus Donnelly. As it happened, they were the only high commanders who were married men, not that that had anything to do with it. If O'Neill gave in to the lady's whims it was of his own volition; he would never be managed that way or any other. Very likely it was just that he settled down a little as he grew older.

Hugh O'Neill returned to Benburb in the last week of January, without the treaty the chief expected him to bring. He arrived in early evening, when the house was just joined for the meal, and had loud welcome from everyone as he came up the hall. O'Neill and the captains embraced him and on the same breath with greeting, the chief demanded his news. Hugh inclined to Lady Catherine and kissed her hand.

"There's a foreign custom I picked up on my travels, lady—a pleasant one." Taking his accustomed chair, reaching to the platter, he added, "I have not got what you sent me for, Shane—don't swear. You could not have got it yourself."

"Blundering fool," began O'Neill furiously. Hugh laid a hand on his arm.

"Now calm down and listen, Shane." He talked tersely as he ate, and on his tale some of the anger faded from O'Neill's expression. "It's a queer situation in Scotland now. James Stuart is the power behind that throne. Queen Mary Stuart"—Hugh grimaced—"is a spoiled charmer with an empty head, for politics at least. She has not lived in Scotland for years, she knows nothing of domestic feuds and loyalties. Because she is uninterested in anything but her own comfort and flirtations, she leaves all political business to Stuart." Hugh paused to empty his mouth.

"Well? Go on."

"Knox," said Hugh indistinctly through another mouthful. "That's the main trouble, that rabble-rouser with his Protestant horde. He's won over most of the Lowlanders to be Conformists, and they hate our church even worse than the Anglicans. It has split Scotland down the middle—religion. You run across some dirty Conformist on every street corner in Edinburgh, shouting about the scarlet woman of Rome—I never heard the like. And all that rabble nurses a deep distrust of the new queen because she's a Catholic and French-bred."

"Natural," said the chief. "So?"

Hugh pushed aside his empty plate, filled his cup, and sat back. "So the queen, by which you can take it I mean her bastard brother, James Stuart, must walk soft in ruling Scotland. The whole court and most of the gentry remain Catholic. But Knox's Conformists are not a force to be dismissed—thousands in number. If the queen, through Stuart, should make any political move the Conformists disapproved, they would rise in overt rebellion."

"Do you tell me. Yes, I see."

"And I'll tell you something else." Hugh lowered his voice. "This is only speculation on my part, but I flatter myself I'm no fool. James Stuart is no fool either, and the only loyalty in him is to James Stuart. He knows the danger from the Protestants, and he knows Mary Stuart, who is also dangerous—to Scotland. For she's the kind of woman who can be ruled by any strong man for a little; there is no thought in her head for to-morrow—yet she's willful. And Stuart is trying to drive sheep and goats together."

"What do you mean by that?"

"I swear it, he's conspiring with Knox. To try and hold the Conformists at bay while he develops some scheme. Maybe he's thinking to press the queen's claim to the English throne. I don't know about that. But as matters stand, he would never dare involve Scotland in a pact with a Catholic nation—it would precipitate revolution. He will keep Scotland neutral at all costs." He added with a grin, "In the unlikely event that Stuart or any other bear leader succeeds in ousting Elizabeth and putting Mary Stuart on her throne, you need not build any more deep plots against the English. A Stuart on England's throne would finish what you begin!"

O'Neill laughed. "I'd not say you are far wrong." He frowned and shrugged. "Well, the devil with the lot of them! I do not need a pact with Scotland. Elizabeth knows the temper of the Stuarts safe enough. And why should I let her know I have not got a treaty with Mary Stuart? Never mind, Hugh, I forgive your blundering." And he took up his knife again.

Hugh dropped an eyelid at Edmund across the table. "My thanks,

Shane. A well-known blunderer I am; you should have sent some other."

O'Neill had then been in correspondence with Elizabeth of England some eighteen months. It was a careful campaign and a leisured one; the gambit was cat-and-mouse. The replies to his first overtures had been cautious; the ministers, it was evident, were skeptical of any soft talk from O'Neill and had no intention of committing themselves. After the visit of Terence Daniel to Elizabeth's court, the letters the chief had from England were no longer signed by any minister, but in the neat, penurious script of Elizabeth herself; and they were cordial letters. The queen, having heard much of the Prince of Ulster, would be pleased to have him visit her court. And O'Neill said, confident and contemptuous, "Terence has snared her—she is all excited for me! We will let her curiosity feed on itself a bit."

He kept his secretary-clerk occupied with letter-writing from his dictation. Striding up and down the council-chamber, he dictated in rough Latin, breaking off to swear in his own tongue. The Prince of Ulster thanked Her Gracious Majesty for the invitation. She would understand that rulers of land have responsibilities not lightly to be abandoned, and would excuse him from naming any definite time for a visit in the near future. The letters in reply pressed him urgently, anxiously, to come to England; he was delighted with them. He had her agog to meet him, the proud chieftain, the great lover; she told him so, obliquely, in what she wrote.

Then he conceived another little trick to play on Elizabeth. "Why should I spend my money on a journey to England? She is hot to see me —let her pay for it." That letter was a little gem of Latin prose. Her Gracious Majesty was kind to renew her invitation. But she would know, although the prince must be forgiven to mention so mundane a matter, that Ulster was not so large a nation as her own, and not so rich. The prince much feared he could not undertake the great expense of a long journey at this time, or for some months to come. It was with great regret he must make his excuses. He had heard many tales of England's beautiful and clever young queen and was anxious to meet with her.

"Now this time you go too far," said Hugh. "No one would swallow a tale like that! You, too poor to afford a journey? The wealthiest prince in these islands you are and who does not know it?"

O'Neill grinned. "And why else do they want Ulster?" Trade revenues had risen threefold under his rulership, under the agreements he made with France and Spain. Always the richest province in Ireland in produce and manufacture, Ulster was now richer than ever. "It's no matter what the ministers believe or do not believe. It's the woman I'm after, and she will swallow it, brother—what do women know about money? She's so impatient to meet O'Neill, she sees nothing but her desire. It's a little gamble, but I think it will come off."

Nothing had been heard of Calvagh O'Donnell after he made a journey to Dublin, swore allegiance to the Crown, and asked help for vengeance on O'Neill—which he did not get. The deputies, probably mindful of orders from England to keep hands off the Ulsterman until it was evident which way the fox ran, were polite and noncommittal. O'Donnell sulked at home over the loss of his lovely young wife, and Red Hugh undoubtedly sulked too, wondering how long the old man would take to die.

O'Neill whiled away that spring and summer of 1561 with a series of visits to his subchiefs. He took his mistress with him, perhaps to display her to his subjects. The Lady Catherine grieved secretly to her maid that she did not conceive a son for the chief, even after this long while; and she was growing no younger. Twenty-two she was now, and past the best age to bear a first child.

The chief returned to his castle in August, and there found a letter waiting him which sent his spirits soaring. "Did I not tell you? Liam said she would never take the bait, but I knew, and O'Neill is never wrong! This shows I have her in leash secure, and that leash I'll shorten tight! All you doubters, you'll see. I will wed Elizabeth, it's foregone. I will hold England in my hand, in the palm of my hand. I'll be King of England before another year is out!"

CHAPTER X

McCAFFREY had kept his eye on Rebecca for some time and judged she was not averse to him. When he opened the door of her small retiring-room, slid quietly into semidarkness, it was with no thought of eavesdropping on the three English deputies he had just admitted to the house. She had welcomed them graciously, seen them into the comfortable room ready with cushioned chairs, dishes of sweetmeats and wine set out, and, murmuring her conventional excuses, left them. And what did Radcliffe think of her—was he suspicious? No matter. He could not connect Rebecca Isham with a castle in Ulster, there was no link. Her lover, Sydney, the trustful fool, was no danger at all. And certainly, a woman with old Sydney as lover would not say "no" to a hotter bedmate.

She stood by the hidden door, her flame-colored gown plain in the dimness; he came up behind her softly and she half-turned, a hand at her lips. He gathered her up tight against him and kissed her long, tongue moving on hers, and after the first moment, she did not resist him, but did not respond. Their mouths apart, she whispered, "You are impudent to me."

"I wager Sydney never was so—madam." Two breaths close in the intimate dimness: both were mindful of the deputies ten feet off beyond the door. Rebecca muffled a laugh in his shoulder. He kissed her again and that time her mouth opened willingly, her fine, full body pressing on his.

"Oh, it is a man—after the Englishman. How pleasant . . . Colm." And that was one time neither of them heard a word the deputies spoke in the next room.

"This is what comes of a woman on the throne," said Radcliffe coldly. "Good God, it is not to be borne, his arrogance! You see what Cecil writes."

Sir Harry Sydney looked again at the letter in his hand, while Sir William Fitzwilliam, that old crow playing falcon, sulked in silence. "Yes, but surely it is conceivable that O'Neill is sincere. No, no, I agree, it would be the worst alliance she might contract, but I cannot believe she would consider it. Or that the ministers would allow her to do so."

"The one fact increasingly apparent is that the ministers have little control over the queen. How many eligible suitors have they offered her? A dozen! And she continues to refuse. Now, this."

Sydney read the letter for the third time, his round, pink face worried, bewildered; he offered it to Fitzwilliam, who waved it away impatiently. Sir William Cecil had penned the letter himself for privacy, and the uneven script showed his agitation of mind, as he wrote. "I have done my utmost—I cannot understand her incredible folly. I have given her all the facts; she appears to dismiss them. Be sure I am in agreement with you, the day O'Neill instigates a peace treaty with the Crown we shall never see; it is only a ruse to come near the queen and lay suit for her hand. I read between the lines of his letters plain enough. We have dealt with O'Neill long; we know his cunning and hate for England; but for all I can say to Her Majesty, she smiles and expresses desire to meet him. . . . That smooth-tongued priest . . . and she is, after all, a woman. I am mindful of what you say about O'Neill and women! But this new enormity! I would not doubt that he has more gold in his coffers than Her Majesty, yet she makes no demur. Eight thousand pounds—"

"Eight thousand pounds!" exclaimed Radcliffe in agony, thumping the arm of his chair in emphasis. "It passes belief! So wild to meet him she sends him the gold to pay for his journey, a new wardrobe, jewels to impress her with! We will be the laughingstock of Europe if it is known. With a few letters and a clever ambassador, he has her making the overtures to him."

"If you had all listened to me ten years ago," began old Fitzwilliam, and Radcliffe almost snarled at him.

"I am deputy to the queen, not a gravedigger!" Fitzwilliam and his mad scheme for destroying the Irish population wholesale! He had been arguing it for years, how headsmen might take so many a day, herding the natives into the larger towns for convenience; with the corpses carried out to sea, in three months the land might be emptied and left free for the English to populate. No loss and much gain. An old madman, Fitzwilliam: the cost would be prohibitive, aside from other considerations.

"But the queen could never entertain the notion—a wild Gael chieftain! It is curiosity only," decided Sydney, satisfied.

"You are a fool," said Radcliffe baldly. "I do not underestimate him— nor does Cecil. O'Neill draws women as the moon draws the tide. Once he is in the queen's company, who knows what might occur? Oh, God, O'Neill! Always O'Neill to be reckoned with, this arrogant bastard—oh, God," and it was genuine supplication, "let me be the man to bring him down and see him dead and done!"

Elizabeth Tudor appeared more concerned with the nice arrangement of the large pearl-set ring on her left hand than for what her chief minister said; she held out her hand, admiring it, smiling.

"Your Majesty will allow that I have had some experience in diplomacies—"

"Ah," she interrupted him softly, "you would say that I have not?"

"I do not mean to imply aught, believe me. I speak only facts. The Prince of Ulster—"

"I hear many facts about the Prince of Ulster, which is the reason I am interested to meet with him myself. To judge what is fact and what fancy."

"If Your Majesty would allow me—"

"Oh, I think not any more today," she murmured. Rising, she suppressed a yawn; her glance was indulgent, amused, on Cecil. "I am weary with all this talk of politics. If I am to play adequate part in the dancing this evening, I must rest—and I have a last fitting for a new gown. You will excuse me, Sir William. Oh, while we speak of the Ulster prince, here is the latest letter I received from him. You may find it of interest. He turns a very pretty phrase in thanking me for my generosity." She smiled round gently on her advisors, rustled lightly from the room.

The little silence was eloquent. Sir William Cecil laid the letter on the table before them. The four ministers looked at the clerkly, even, flourishing script, the bold black signature, one arrogant name, running up crooked at the bottom of the page. Cecil said bitterly, "Fact! I will tell you the one big fact I am thinking of. Radcliffe there in Dublin with eighteen hundred troops, twelve cannon, no arquebusiers whatever—and O'Neill two days' ride north with four thousand soldiers, thirty guns, five hundred mounted arquebusiers, and fifteen years' experience of war—an army that has never been defeated. That is the fact before us."

The Earl of Pembroke said, in his usual vague tone, "And quite as unpalatable as certain other facts. . . . Of course, once he is in England—Accidents occur each day. Bricks fall from old buildings, horses stumble at over-high hedges . . ."

"Have I not considered it! But we dare not take the risk. His people would not accept an accident meekly, and there are capable military leaders with him to take up the fight. And once Ulster is at war, he has pacts with rulers who command more armies, I remind you. No, no, it could not be chanced." Cecil added thoughtfully, "I should even be willing to accept Leicester as consort, if it came to a choice between him and the Ulsterman. An alliance with O'Neill—"

"Absurd, mad," said Pembroke. It was monstrous understatement. Alliance with a Catholic, friend to all England's enemies, and not a man to be managed: if the queen took him, she would be under his rule.

Perhaps the whole history of England would be changed if that happened. There was no adequate word for such calamity.

"Er—" said Bacon, "as you say, anything preferable to that. If she was wed before he arrived— There is no indication of her serious interest in any suitor except Leicester. If we—"

"Easy settled!" said Cecil sarcastically. "Run and fetch a churchman, let us have the wedding over before dinnertime. Do you care to suggest it to Her Gracious Majesty?" Bacon subsided, looking uneasy.

"At times, and this is one of them," said Sir Francis Walsingham, "I wonder whatever possessed Henry Plantagenet to invade Ireland. Any profit England has from the cursed country we turn back and twice as much with it, to put down rebellion and maintain our hold." All the rest sighed, and there fell a silence while four pairs of eyes fastened gloomily on the letter before them.

Rath O'Donnell, August 1561

"My wife was not enough for him," grumbled Calvagh O'Donnell resentfully. "He must go out for a queen. I wish him joy of her, the cold Sassenach bitch."

"You're premature," said his nephew, Red Hugh. He had more cause to be resentful than Calvagh. To hell with the English queen—O'Neill would never manage that. The other woman—he had wanted that one, and he would have taken her had events gone a bit differently. This damned senile old fool, years at his dying! He did not trouble to veil the hate in his eyes on Calvagh. Calvagh the canny, so careful to see his food tasted, to guard himself from tempting situations—tempting to a man thinking about little accidents that can happen to old men.

"His Holiness in Rome has reprimanded him severe for the kidnaping of a lawful wife."

"His Holiness is some distance off," said Hugh Ruadh. Calvagh was finished; he would never go against O'Neill again. When Hugh Ruadh was chief, the tale would have a different ending, and he the one to write it . . . He owed O'Neill retribution for the woman.

Rome, September 1561

"His impudence a little amuses me," said His Holiness, Pope Pius IV, regarding the letter. "An arrogant and impatient man, this Ulster prince. I announce my displeasure for him at his impiety in stealing another man's wife—and he mentions that not at all, but demands that I confer the See of Armagh upon his own chosen man!" He smiled, shaking his head, and tossed the letter to his secretary. "I will compose a reply next month when I have had time to mediate on it." He had no intention of bestowing an archbishopric title on Terence Daniel. There was much corruption in the church; he would not add to it. Daniel's birth was unknown, therefore probably illegitimate.

But he had no intention either of condemning O'Neill openly until it was apparent what would come of O'Neill's political ambition. Venal or not, O'Neill was Catholic. If he wed the English Queen, that might mean a great reconquest for the church. A most arrogant man, but—!

Antrim, October 1561

Sorley Boy had been away for a week overseeing land he owned southeast. As he rode home, up to the gate of Dunluce, he knew the half-joy, half-pain that always greeted him on return these nine years. Dunluce, the third strongest fortress in Antrim, a solid, gray house with its back to the sea wall, its gate opening to the bare plain before: a friendly house, the place he had brought that first shy young wife from Scotland, so long ago he scarcely remembered her eyes, her touch—the wife who had wanted so much to give him a son, and died in the trying, and the son with her. All so long ago, it barely touched his mind as he rode in the gate.

He was welcomed loudly by all his household; he was a well-loved man, Sorley, by all who knew him. He went first to see his sons but gave them, young Hector and younger John, no more affectionate embraces than he gave the other children of the house, those of his army officers, for he was a man with great love for children and all helpless things. The hound puppies in his kennel, the blind kittens soft in the stable straw, all things like that loved and trusted him. His castle seneschal brought him a letter arrived while he was absent, and he read it as he went up to his own apartments to see his wife. He smiled as he read, but when he came into the chamber and saw her, his smile faded a little. He put the letter aside and she came with a rush to his arms, the tall, dark, beautiful woman.

"Why did you stay so long? Too long—oh, Sorley, Sorley, forgive me —I meant to be so strong, I meant not to—"

He held her tightly, quietly, the sorrow in him no longer bitter because he loved her beyond pettiness. "You must not ask forgiveness, Mary, love —it is not sin in you, but sickness. Maybe one day the physicians will learn that and find a help for it. Do not weep now, it is all right." What difference what man it had been this time, after so many before?

He talked quietly to her until the wildness of her grief died.

She slept presently, clinging tight to his hand. He took out his letter and read it again, again smiling. "Come and bid me farewell, brother— it is arranged, I will be in England before Christ-tide. The fearful little men about me are saying I will never return. Still they do not learn that O'Neill is never wrong and never fails—especially with a woman! A little insult that they doubt my prowess that direction . . ."

He looked at the sleeping woman, sleep smoothing the little lines of beginning age from the white features on the pillow. He thought, adjusting the blanket about her—and what else might she be, my love, my darling? She is an O'Neill, also.

CHAPTER XI

"D ANGER?" repeated O'Neill, and laughed. He glanced round the group of his captains where they sat lounging before the great hearth of the hall this chill day. "Since when have O'Neills turned back from the face of danger? And in this case, there is none at all."

"You will never set foot in Ulster again," said Dudley.

O'Neill only shrugged impatiently at this continued expression of fear for him. McArdle, grave as always, said, "We are not doubting you, Shane. But wise stags do not run into valleys with only one entrance. There should be a plan, in case you are restrained in any way."

"I have already made it," said O'Neill. His gaze went up the hall and his smile broadened. "And here it comes, punctual as I summoned." All eyes followed his. The door-wards were just bowing an arrival in: a man they all recognized, that big red man, Turlough Lynagh O'Neill. He was alone. He came up the hall and made the chief a formal salute.

Most of the captains eyed him distrustfully. There had been rumor, Rory remembered, that Turlough would challenge for the chiefhood, being legal first cousin to O'Neill. Now, seeing him at closer quarters, he thought it incredible the man should be near kin to O'Neill, or challenge for anything. He looked more farmer than nobleman, and mindless as a stone wall.

His voice was slow and deep. "You sent for me, Shane."

"I did." O'Neill regarded him between amusement and affection. "Some use you may be to me, and I will explain it to you private. The Dean and Liam and I. If each of us repeats it to you maybe it will penetrate that thick skull of yours, and you will keep it inside to yourself. One thing I say of you, cousin, you are not talkative."

"I do not think swift, true," acknowledged Turlough humbly. "If I may serve you any way I will do it."

"Meanwhile sit down and have a drink. I expect Terence and Liam this evening."

Turlough Lynagh remained at Benburb three days, and the reason for his coming the chief was pleased to keep a mystery. The captains wondered to each other—What can he want with this stupid farmer—but

O'Neill put off all questions humorously. He shut himself up with Turlough, the Dean, and the justice long hours in the council chamber. The rest of the time Turlough sat, a stolid lump, speaking when spoken to. At the end of three days he rode away as solemn and silent as he had come.

Some of O'Neill's preparation for his meeting with Elizabeth was more apparent. He had a corps of tailors busy on a new wardrobe, not only for himself, but for the men he took with him to England. No one, at that time, knew what personal retinue would accompany him, but he had chosen the escort guard. He took no mounted troops, but fifty picked men from his gallowglass ranks, the heaviest-armed foot-soldiers in the army. He chose the men on basis of age, appearance, and proven loyalty; they made an impressive guard. Not a man was under six feet in height, and a few approached O'Neill's own stature of four inches over that. He was supplying these with new garments and weapons.

He would take three of his finest Arab mounts, which were being conditioned for the journey. The new saddles he had ordered, inlaid with silver and jewels, were delivered and approved. Nothing was neglected which would add to the impression he would make on Elizabeth.

For himself, Rory had even more personal reason for curiosity about the retinue the chief would take. But O'Neill did not announce his selection, though Dudley plagued him often to say definitely that he might go. An air of unease hovered about Benburb those days, felt by everyone. from the lowest kitchen boy to the high officers.

Rory identified Moyna down the passage and lengthened his stride to catch her; he had not seen her for several days. "Here, girl, have you not a minute to give a friend good day?" He followed her into the little chamber, took her arm that was so smooth-white and rounded.

"Oh—McGuinness. Good day," she said, "does that satisfy you? I am very busy, now don't keep me."

"The very thing I would like to do." He grinned at her.

"Don't I know it!" This time her look was unsmiling. "Turn me into one of these wantons here—like that Ena."

He did not know that he would want that. It flashed across his mind —suppose he might summon Moyna to his bed so casual—and he was disturbed by a queer feeling, indefinable. No matter; only light talk. "Now, don't snap before I open my mouth! Very pretty you're looking; is it a new gown?"

"No—one of Lady Catherine's old ones, but it is nice, is it not? McGuinness—are you going to England with the chief, would you think? He will not tell even Lady Catherine who he takes."

"Then how would I know? I wish I did."

"Would you want to?"

He said frankly, "I wish I knew that, too. Not like a day's ride into Armagh. But I'm thinking I might be earning my wage as bodyguard to him there, anyway."

She agreed in a thoughtful tone, turned away to the shelves; this was the library room. O'Neill kept a large library, though he seldom looked at it; it had been acquired for its value. There were over a hundred books, only twenty or so printed, the majority being ancient, hand-scripted histories, religious and otherwise. Moyna studied the shelves absorbedly. She said over her shoulder, "The Lady Catherine sent me for somewhat to read. . . . You need not jeer, she has taught me my letters, I can read as good as you—better, likely! You and that Ena." She sniffed. "She wants a book about lives of the saints. There must be one here, would you think? She paints her face, you know."

"Who?" he asked, bewildered.

"Ena, stupid. It is an immoral foreign thing to do, the chief says. Only harlots and Englishwomen do so. Here is one." She took the book down, weighing it carefully in both hands, a massive volume bound in leather.

"Why are we talking about Ena? Speak of morals, it is not decent for you to mention such a matter at all."

"Oh, Holy Mother, men! The nice neat line only. Are respectable women all fools, not to see what is under their noses?" But she laughed; she leaned on the half-shut door and was suddenly disposed to talk. "Can you keep a secret, McGuinness? It will not be a secret long. The Lady Catherine is very happy for that she's to bear a child to him in June next. She feared she was barren, all this time—I've never seen her so happy."

"Does O'Neill know?"

"Of course, and he's pleased, too." Moyna looked at the book in her hands. "Such a queer thing she said, that reading of saints might help her to feel wicked—that she is not wed to him, you know. She said to me once, she feels more truly married to the chief than to either of those others."

Rory shrugged. "Women are peculiar."

"Yes," said Moyna. "Yes, we are that." She watched him moving in to her, she laid down the book and lifted her mouth, and he was very surprised, and kissed her hard; her arms were warm round his neck, her mouth not willing only but eager. And against his mouth she whispered, "What do you want of me, Rory McGuinness?"

"Do you need telling, *agrah?*" But she put her hand between their mouths quickly, and pushed him away.

"Not that telling. The gentleman—an idle hour with a maidservant, and forget it. I am not Ena." She slid a hand up his cheek. "You stupid, careless, dear men, making us so much trouble, and what would we do without you at all?" And then she slapped him, not hard or gentle, and took up her book, and whisked out. He looked after her, a hand to his cheek, rueful, exasperated. No denying it, women were peculiar indeed.

It was that evening O'Neill announced at last what men would accompany him to England. The meal was ended, the main tables carried away, but the chief dallied at his table over more liquor, his officers about him, the Lady Catherine at his side, smiling dreamily to herself. Dudley was again demanding that he be allowed to journey with him; O'Neill reached a careless hand to cuff him playfully.

"You are one man who does not come. You could not pretend friendship for the Sassenachs to save your life—or even mine! I will tell you all now who is to come. Three men only—"

"Only—but, Shane—"

"Now wait! It is not exactly bravado." He was serious now. "You have all made long talk about the perfidy of English, and on that subject I cannot argue. I do not believe there is any danger to myself—they know too well what wrath would fall on them if I am harmed—but there is always the chance with English. But the most they might try is to hold me hostage. So mark!" He pointed his knife commandingly round at them. "Damned high ransom could they ask for O'Neill, but how much more if many of his high captains were with him! And in that event, who is left to lead my army? Even if that is not in their minds now, if I arrive with all my captains, would they not seize the chance! An army without officers is no danger at all. I want every man of you here in Ulster as a safeguard —and if any difficulty arises, there is a plan for you to carry out that Liam will tell you."

They digested that and all reluctantly agreed, save Dudley, who would have argued. The chief silenced him with a gesture, and Dudley received a few impatient glances. The eldest Donnelly was suffered but not much liked by any man; even his two younger brothers were short with him; it was Edmund guided him out of quarrels. Rory had the notion, which was to prove justified, that Dudley was anything but an accomplished war leader; it was perhaps the only weakness in O'Neill, and understandable, that he kept Dudley in high military rank. All their lives Dudley had been his shadow, fanatic in his worship, and O'Neill had too much vanity by nature to judge impartially a man to whom he was God. Thinking that, Rory begged Dudley's pardon to himself for naming him heretic: and thought further that Dudley would not care greatly whether he went to heaven so long as he was with Shane O'Neill.

"I will take the minimum of personal retinue," O'Neill was continuing. "Luke—"

The musician said in a shocked tone, "You had not considered going without me!"

"No. And Aidan Moran—" one of his under-secretaries. "I will not even take John O'Hagan, for that he is of noble family and might be considered material for hostage. And," he grinned over his shoulder, "my faithful bodyguard, who may earn his keep for a change."

Rory's heart gave an extra thud. He said, prompt and bold, "I'll be sharpening my dagger, O'Neill."

The chief laughed. "You'll be doing more than that. All the men I take must have fine clothes and jewels to show the English. My expense —go into Armagh to my tailors; they'll outfit you. The same for you, Luke."

"New burial garments," said the musician, fingering a minor chord. "Nothing I have said before—not my place—but we will never return from England. A great pity it is, and I still a young man, but it cannot be helped."

O'Neill only laughed at him. "Not burial clothes, doubter—wedding garments!" He refilled his cup; his unoccupied hand was absently stroking Lady Catherine's arm. Rory wondered suddenly what she felt, loving him and his child growing in her, hearing this talk of his wedding another woman. Of course, love had little to do with marriage, especially a political alliance; she would know that well, being of high breeding herself. All the same, it must be a little sorrow to her, that the sons she hoped to give O'Neill must remain bastards. Her look was the same on him, loving, gentle—perhaps a little sad? O'Neill drank; new mischief and triumph came to his eyes, and he added, "You insubordinate doubters, maybe you are thinking I should be naming my legal heir before I leave? Well, I will accommodate you." His hand tightened on Lady Catherine's arm. "I name as heir, the child in Catherine's body now—if it be not son, then my heir is Hugh or his heir—but I am thinking it is a son."

She smiled at him slowly. "I, too, Shane. I feel it. A big handsome son it is."

"Well," said Hugh, staring into his cup. "And that is a good choice, Shane—the first, anyway." He smiled at the lady. "Let us hope the big handsome son is getting sons of his own before he comes to the chiefhood."

"Oh, yes—yes." But her eyes were on the chief, naked fear in them now she tried to conceal.

That last twenty days there was almost tangible gloom hanging like fog over Benburb. The very hounds seemed restless with anxiety for the thought of O'Neill going virtually alone among English. Since the start of the hunting season, the weather had been dry and cold, excellent for sport, but all the men stayed close to the castle, as if to guard against some evil fate hovering over the chief. Lady Catherine seemed to grow paler and quieter each day, a lovely ghost haunting Benburb. Rory did not escape the general uneasiness, even in the excitement of preparation. And then, the week before their scheduled departure in the middle of December, by common consent, the air of gloom lifted and false gaiety took its place, as if on the superstitious principle that evils are nonexistent if ignored. The officers vied with each other in suggesting ways to capture the English queen's interest, most of the suggestions obscene. Luke played nothing but gay tunes all through each meal. The servants hovered over the chief, assiduous to his slightest whim, and if Lady Catherine's smiles were forced, no one appeared to notice.

Rory took the trouble to pursue acquaintance with young Moran, the secretary. Since they would be much together, it seemed politic. Moran was a dark, serious man near Rory's age. If he had any qualms about the future he concealed them, as Rory did his; but O'Givney was openly nervous. It was not only his loyalty to O'Neill that made him go, or the chief's command, but his respect for tradition: in Celtic custom a chief went nowhere without a musician, so as O'Neill's harpist, Luke must accompany him, though he was convinced they would all be hanged and quartered the day they set foot in England.

On the morning they would ride from Benburb the whole household collected in the courtyard to see them depart. Rory had his bags down early. The guard was forming in the yard: those fifty big ax-men, at their head the mounted line leader, Manus McSweeney, a great barrel of a man with a magnificent head of copper hair and a flowing red beard down to his belt. He held O'Neill's two extra horses. The saddled black stallion was in charge of a groom, and others had brought up Rory's horse, a mount for Moran, and a sleek brown mule for Luke, who stood clutching his little harp in one arm and his pretty young wife in the other.

When the chief came out with his lady, all the captains made a circle about him. The Dean and old Fleming had come from Armagh yesterday for last consultation and were there to see him off also. Rory had not seen Moyna privately since that day she kissed him so willingly; she was there now, a pace behind the Lady Catherine, and he stepped closer. He thought she flushed a little, seeing him, and then lifted her chin a trifle and looked away. Everyone else was pressing last-minute luck and advice on the chief. Rory took her arm, drew her aside a step.

"Will you spare a prayer or so for me, out alone among Sassenachs, Moyna?"

"I might, now and then. Or for the Sassenach girls, a red McGuinness loose on them." But her smile was friendly, and she touched his arm. "I will that. God with you—all of you. And guard him well, for my lady's sake."

"I'll do that, for more sakes than Lady Catherine's." She stepped away then and he had no chance to snatch a kiss. Well, all this crowd, but—

O'Neill had one arm about Lady Catherine and that was the first time any had seen him display such open affection. But he looked to be in an impatient, tempestuous mood. He was all in dark saffron for the journey, and not much jeweled. He was exclaiming now, "Let us get off, no tedious farewells!"

"You will write," said the Dean. "Do not let the key of our code out of your hand. Tell me the exact situation as it develops—"

"And for the love of God, use caution," urged Hugh. "One wrong move—"

"All our prayers with you, Shane. If you'd reconsider and let me come —I can be ready—" And no need to look for who said that.

"Keep your temper with them and give no excuse for violence on you," rumbled Terence O'Hagan.

"And stay away from English harlots," advised Ferdoragh earnestly. "All of them have the French sickness, I've heard."

"Remember what I have told you—" That was Fleming.

O'Neill flung off all hands reaching for him. "My Christ, who is chief here? You no longer amuse me with your worry—it is childish. I will be back in eight or ten weeks." He took the bridle offered him. But Lady Catherine's hands went out to him as his arm dropped. He added brusquely, "And no clinging women!" But his eyes sought Hugh's. "Hugh —you will look to the woman—and—"

"I'll do that, Shane. Look to yourself." Their hands clasped; O'Neill swung up to the saddle. Rory mounted, clasped Ferdoragh's hand, made his own farewells to the captains, who, in a body, threatened him dire punishment if he took his eye off the chief a minute. The chief reined at once for the gate; McSweeney shouted and the foot-guard wheeled to follow. Before they reached the gate the crowd raised a confident cheer to wish him Godspeed.

O'Neill set a hard pace down the narrow cliff road, a pace Rory might have found hair-raising except that he was occupied, now it was too late, wishing he had kissed Moyna after all, crowd or no. When the three followers reached the bottom of the path, the chief was waiting at a stand, facing south down the main road. "Ride up!" he exclaimed impatiently. "We do not want to take a year on the way, and the foot-ranks will slow us as it is."

Neither Rory nor Aidan could retort, but Luke said, "It is no use bringing me at all, O'Neill, if I'm to ride at a gallop and endanger the harp! Are you so anxious for the company of English?"

O'Neill laughed. "One to you, man—I am not indeed."

When the guard was re-formed in its ranks of eight abreast, they set off at a slower pace. But before they came into forest O'Neill rose in his stirrups and turned for a last long look at Benburb standing solid and gray and defiant at the top of the cliff.

PART TWO

england

CHAPTER XII

O'NEILL was to suffer a good many annoyances, petty and otherwise, on this journey and the visit in England; some of them he expected, others he had not. The first was the necessity for accepting the formal escort of his despised cousin, Gerald Fitzgerald, Earl of Kildare. Fitzgerald and another Anglophile noble, the Earl of Ormond, had been detailed to escort him officially to the queen's court. Their party met his a day's journey above the border of the Pale, and the combined guards made a leisurely ride south, coming into the Pale the third day after the chief left Benburb. By then, O'Neill was in grim mood for the company of Anglophiles.

As the hour approached when they would pass into English territory, oppression lay on Rory, and he thought on Moran as well—and possibly on O'Neill, who bore himself with haughty confidence. But none mentioned it. Even Luke O'Givney, too proud to exhibit nervousness before Kildare and Ormond, only relapsed into gloomy silence. They came up to the border in late afternoon; Moran fingered the long scroll of the safety guarantee, which he had been given to carry, and expressed doubt of its meaning anything.

"A piece of paper," he said. It was an impressive document, with its Latin script and gold seals and the neat signature of the queen at its bottom, but—honor in English? The first time Moran had to tender it was then, as they crossed the border. A captain of guards came out to the detail standing sentry at the border station outside Dundalk, and examined the official passes the two earls carried, as well as the queen's guarantee. As the sentries opened order to let the party pass, Rory felt many eyes on them and reflected that very likely these same soldiers had given battle to O'Neill's troops many times in the past, on his raids of the Pale.

Luke rode up beside him and Moran. "Freedom, I have loved thee." He sighed. "We are now in England."

"No one is going to hang you at the moment," said Moran.

"No—likely they will do that with great celebration in London." And neither Moran nor Rory had the heart to contradict the prophecy.

It was a leisured journey; what with halting to meet the earls' parties, they took four days to come down to Dublin, whereas a man on a fast horse might ride the distance in a matter of hours. In Dublin they stopped the night at an inn, and the following morning boarded the ship specially hired for the voyage. Ormond and Kildare would sail with them, but not their escorts; O'Neill's retinue crowded the ship. The chief had been remotely courteous and amenable thus far, but that morning he flew into sudden fury at the roughness of the sailors in taking the horses aboard. It required the efforts of Rory, Moran, the earls, and the ship captain to soothe him.

"Arabs are not ordinary horses, they need much care! If there is any injury I will personally hang every man aboard this ship!" He was mollified when the captain escorted him below to see the six horses and Luke's mule comfortably tethered in deep straw.

That little awkwardness was scarcely past when another rose. They sailed on the midday tide, and all Luke's control vanished when he saw the strip of gray-green water widening between ship and dock. With a tenor wail, he rushed to the stern. "Oh, my woe, my grief, they are taking me off to die among Sassenachs in a foreign land! My beloved country, I will never see you again! Queen of heaven, have mercy on a poor sinner—" The earls, the ship officers, and all the sailors were vastly amused at his agitation, and O'Neill was furious again for such a display of weakness before foreigners. He stalked off to the cabin he had been given, leaving Rory and Moran to quiet Luke.

"Control yourself, man," Rory bade him bracingly. "The case isn't so bad; we'll be returning safe in a few short weeks." He wished he were as sure of it as he sounded. Luke heaved a sigh and stared mournfully at the receding shoreline.

"No help now, I must have courage and face whatever fate sends. I think I will make a song about it, McGuinness. You'd not happen to have a drop to spare from your belt flask?" He sat down where he was on the deck and fingered his harp. Musicians—they must be allowed latitude, they had unstable temperaments by nature, as Moran was explaining carefully to the Englishmen.

In that season they encountered rough weather on the channel crossing. They did not land on the west coast but ran up the channel between England and France to the River Thames and thus up to the city of London. With heavy seas and adverse winds, it was a voyage of five days, and most of the passengers, including Rory, were miserable with seasickness—but not O'Neill, though this was his first time off land. He would not have tolerated his body to suffer such ignominious illness, Rory thought, convinced that pride was all that kept him from sickness. They came into London after dark, and it was impossible to see much of it as they disembarked. O'Neill let the two earls arrange that, waiting in remote silence on the wharf.

It was Kildare who ventured to tell him, as horses were led up (English horses, those they brought being still too stiff from the voyage for riding), "We escort you now to the city house of Sir Nicholas Bacon, cousin—in the event you are interested. Lord Keeper to the queen he is, and will host you overnight." O'Neill inclined in acknowledgment, making no comment on that.

With the guard marching behind, they rode some distance, making many turns in the narrow, refuse-littered streets, until the earls signified the destination was reached when they came to a large city house facing on the roadway with only a small yard. "Your—er—escort will be looked to," said Ormond, and the chief nodded austerely. Rory wondered what accommodations would be found for the ax-men; McSweeney seemed ready to weep at being left behind, but there was nothing to do about it. Rory followed the chief up the steps of the house, Moran and Luke at his either side.

In the fore-passage, several servants came to take their cloaks and bags. O'Neill started back with a frown at having English hands on him; Rory took his cloak and handed it on to Luke, who tossed it to a servant. A door was opened down the passage; Ormond indicated the direction politely, and, flanked by the earls, the chief went forward to meet his host.

Standing in the center of the room they entered, lest the common courtesy of rising to greet a guest should imply deference to a foreign ruler, waited three men. Rory, Moran, and Luke stopped just inside the door, and Luke, after one look at the three waiting to receive the chief, whispered, "In no danger we are at all. Are these the highest Sassenachs? I've seen handsomer creatures pulled out of the Boyne with rod and line."

"Be quiet, jester," Rory whispered back. "We must not be seen to laugh at them."

"My lords—a pleasure to see you again." Kildare was very much the Anglophile gentleman, suave, assured. "It is my honor"—and something like a wink on that—"to introduce to you the chieftain, O'Neill." And he made an easy gesture to draw the chief forward. "Sir William Cecil—Sir Nicholas Bacon—his Lordship, Pembroke. O'Neill." The chief made no move, but turned a bleak accusing stare on Kildare. Like all Anglophiles, arrogant among his own people, Kildare yet felt inferior among English. He was nervous, and under the chief's eyes his fine English manners suddenly fell from him like rags. He paled and stammered, "I—that is —the Lord O'Neill of the O'Neill, Prince of Ulster—my lords—"

"Gentlemen," said O'Neill in his clear, unaccented English, "my pleasure to meet you." He looked at them one by one. Their expressions were noncommittal as they returned formal greeting, but Rory thought they concealed surprise and interest for the chief's appearance. Cecil—

small, slight, stooped, with a high dome of a forehead and a silky brown
beard, his smile tight; Bacon—corpulent, genial, uneasy; Pembroke—tall,
vague-eyed. What were they thinking as they met O'Neill?

"That little brown villain," whispered Luke, "I would not trust him as
far as a mother-in-law's affection." Again Rory hushed him while agreeing.

"It is to be hoped you had a good journey, gentlemen"—Bacon, heartily
polite.

"For the season, quite," said Kildare, regaining some of his poise.

"And the voyage, not too rough? Oh, it was, eh? Then we must not
keep our honored guest from rest, since he will be received by Her
Majesty tomorrow. If you allow me, O'Neill, I will conduct you to your
chamber." Bacon edged past the chief, beckoned a servant. "Your attendants also, of course." He stared twice at the little harp in Luke's arms.
O'Neill made the briefest inclination to Cecil and Pembroke and stalked
out, Rory and the others following.

The three of them were quartered in one chamber. To Rory's relief, it
connected with an inner one which the chief was given, and he and Moran
spelled each other at guard that night. In the morning silent servants
fetched in breakfast.

Eight hours alone, even asleep, were sufficient to bring O'Neill into
their chamber to share the meal, about which he complained loudly. Considering that his usual morning meal consisted of a platter of venison
and several cups of liquor, his complaint was justified.

"They are being subtle; they will starve us to death," said Luke.

O'Neill, who had wandered about the room naked as he ate, returned
to his chamber to be barbered by his servant and dress himself. Some
swearing drifted from beyond the door; he hated to be shaved. In the
midst of their own dressing, Rory and Moran used all their persuasion
on Luke to get him to dress decently. He sat on the bed, fingering his
harp and saying indifferently, "Why take such pains to meet a crowd of
English?" And when they argued, he commenced to sing, but stilled the
harp as the connecting door opened and the chief strode in.

"Are you all ready? My Christ, Luke, you cannot come like that. You
have finer clothes with you, get into them at once!"

"Oh, very well," said Luke sulkily, "but I do not know why I am going
at all. It is not likely I will be asked to sing. The English have no appreciation for music."

"Will I take her eye?" demanded O'Neill, strolling over to survey himself in the mirror. He needed no answer to that. Wherever he went and
however dressed, he took the eye—and especially the female eye—but that
day he surpassed even his usual appearance. He was fresh-shaven, his hair
brushed to shining smoothness, his magnificent body clad in a kilt of rich
dark green wool and a loose, sleeveless tunic of emerald-green silk, a gift

of Lady Catherine's craftsmanship. He wore three rings on each hand, a gold armlet on each arm, and a great silver brooch set with emeralds on his left shoulder; the thongs of his sandals bore emeralds at their tips. He was all afire for his meeting with the queen, the test of his long plan to win her to him: in high confident spirits, his eyes alight with the consciousness of his own magnificence. Inspecting Rory and Moran critically, the latter in subdued rich brown head to foot, Rory in black kilt, pure white tunic, he was satisfied, and with Luke in monk-gray and crimson. This was a personal retinue to do him justice.

They came down the stair to find Sir Nicholas, Ormond, and Kildare waiting. "Your guard is formed," their host informed the chief. "I would not hasten you, but we have some way to go and Her Majesty has set a formal hour for audience."

"By no means must we keep Her Majesty waiting," returned O'Neill smilingly. He cast an appraising glance at the guard as he descended the steps to the grooms holding the Irish horses; evidently it satisfied him, for he gave McSweeney a curt nod as he took the bridle. McSweeney's face brightened to see the chief alive and unharmed.

In the narrow streets they might ride two abreast only; Bacon and Ormond led, Kildare rode with O'Neill, and Rory followed beside the guard constable, Moran and Luke behind. All were aware of curious stares from the crowds they passed. "My soul," said McSweeney, "I am relieved to see you all again! I kept watch posted all night, among these English." He added gloomily, "They gave us beer for breakfast."

"My sympathy," said Rory, meaning it. "We had sweet wine."

"Oh, saints," said McSweeney, "I trust we do not stay long!"

They rode some distance, now in city streets, now through open fields. Presently they turned into a wide gate and a path leading, between hedges bare now with winter, toward a large country house. As they dismounted in the yard, a liveried servant opened the door, and grooms came to take the horses. Bacon made a gesture of ushering the chief up to the door, but O'Neill turned a shoulder on him and nodded at McSweeney.

"You remember the order?"

"Yes, O'Neill." The constable shouted and the guard wheeled smartly to make for the door. Moran and Luke fell in behind the men, and Rory too, reluctantly—he disliked to leave the chief alone, but could not disobey the order. The attendants drew back in a hurry at the solid front of men marching toward them, and only one, evidently the major-domo, retained enough presence of mind to scurry down the passage, leading the way, opening wide double doors at the far end. A hum of talk, lights, a flash of colored garments, a little rise of laughter, came from beyond the doors. With McSweeney at their head, the ranks of gallowglass marched in, and then, except for the tramp of feet, all sounds were stilled as the crowd in the queen's audience chamber stared and made way.

It was a long high-ceilinged room with wall torches and many windows. Perhaps fifty people, all very elegantly dressed, stood about a small platform at the upper end of the room, on which a woman sat in a high-backed chair like a throne. There were stares and murmurs now. Those nearest drew back to let the guard pass, opening a path toward the platform. There McSweeney halted and barked another order, and the men fell back to even ranks on each side, lining that path like sentries on duty. Rory and his two companions stepped to the opposite side from McSweeney, at the fore of the line of men. And then there was a little pause.

Rory saw these nobles and ladies of the English court studying the ax-men with awe, and pride rose hot in his throat. There was not an Englishman in the room to match any of them. All large men, clad in their fine new clothes, the heavy iron breastplates and leg guards of gallowglass ranks, armed with short hand-axes and the six-foot double-edged Irish battle ax that was lance, spear, club, and hatchet combined, they were a force to impress any foreigner—and they impressed these English. He saw that most of the men present looked to be typical courtiers, but here and there was a man who turned the professional appraisal of the soldier on the ranks of ax-men, and it was a thoughtful appraisal.

Luke beside him gave him a nudge with his elbow, and Rory's eyes followed his to the woman on the platform. This would be Elizabeth of England, on whom so much depended. He thought, Not a pretty one; and then he thought, But— No, not pretty, though still fairly young; a long, narrow face with narrow green eyes, a sallow complexion artifically tinted, a thin flat mouth, pale red hair arranged pretentiously. But there was something about the woman: with a little shock he found himself thinking it was like something in O'Neill, a quality of power almost tangible. To compare O'Neill with a Sassenach, a woman, even in the mind! All the same, there was something about her.

Now a growing mutter of comment rose from the crowd, but the queen paid no attention to that. She had seen what she wanted of the guard, and gave the other three only a passing glance. She leaned a little forward in her chair, her eyes on the door at the far end of the room. In a moment O'Neill appeared in that doorway and halted there. His cloak was still slung about his shoulders, an ankle-length cloak of dead-black wool, but he had flung back one side of it as if carelessly, to display the scarlet silk lining and the brooch on his shoulder. He was an arresting figure, black and emerald and scarlet, standing motionless between the two doorguards he dwarfed. For a long minute he remained so; then, when he was sure all eyes were fastened on him, he came pacing slowly up the room between the lines of his men, never taking his steady gaze from the queen. When he halted below the platform, his height brought his eyes level with hers. She leaned more forward, and Rory saw her ringed hands tighten on the arms of her chair.

And Luke muttered, "It is a woman after all—look at her. She is his any hour he cares to take her."

Slowly the queen rose. Her voice was thin and metallic and precise. "We are pleased to welcome the Prince O'Neill of Ulster to our court. We hope his visit will prove both pleasant and profitable." She extended her hand. O'Neill would not conform to any such Continental convention as hand-kissing, or bow the head to a woman, but he took her hand as he replied. His voice was even deeper than usual in his excellent English.

"The O'Neill is pleased to meet with Her Majesty of England in her own place, as she invited so warmly. Let us hope this meeting will indeed be profitable—to both." The easy, erect carriage of his shoulders mirrored the expression Rory could guess he turned on her—an expression of confident arrogance, the famous charm that had never failed him with women. It was impossible to read the expression in her eyes on him, but Rory thought he saw something kin to amusement as well as admiration, and as always in any woman's eyes on him, an awareness of him as a man, of the sheer animal size and strength of him.

"It has long been our wish to entertain the Prince of Ulster as is fitting to his achievements. As we expect his stay in England may be of some little duration, we are happy to present him to some of our friends." She made a slight gesture, not looking away from the chief, and a man stepped out of the crowd to her side. "We would present first—our very good friend, my Lord Leicester."

This time it was Rory who nudged Luke. Robert Dudley, Earl of Leicester: the gossip of him everyone knew. He hoped to wed the queen and, rumor had it, had murdered his own wife to be free for Elizabeth. Now at her word he offered his hand with obvious reluctance, making no attempt to conceal hostility for O'Neill. He was handsome too, with the stocky regular good looks of the Saxon English.

"My honor, O'Neill."

"And mine, my Lord Leicester." Their glances locked.

"What were you saying?" Rory whispered to Luke. "Two hounds, one bitch. And possession is nine points of the law. Look at her."

In the brief pause before she beckoned other court nobles forward to be introduced, Elizabeth watched the two men before her. O'Neill had assumed his favorite stance, head back, hands on thighs, thumbs hooked in his belt, and was looking down at Leicester from his superior height, smiling. Leicester's eyes were hot and hard on him, in return. Whatever the queen and her ministers thought O'Neill's mission to be, Leicester knew the real reason he had come. And the spark of hatred between them struck a like spark in the woman. Looking at them, her eyes held laughter, excitement, and more than a hint of malice.

CHAPTER XIII

Rory repressed a shiver at the cold rain, eying O'Neill's eloquently grim back in the saddle ahead. God be thanked, here was the house. They splashed up to the door in the wet, dingy street. The chief dismounted and barked at the grooms who came running, "See they are rubbed down and given bran at once!" He flung up the steps, pushed past the servants who opened the door. It was not a great deal warmer in the house. He strode into the little hall to the right of the passage, where a feeble fire burned dispiritedly on the miniature hearth. English houses! In silence he went across and stood with his back to it, his expression remote. Luke and Moran at either side eyed him cautiously, looked at Rory, who shook his head slightly. It was Luke ventured to speak first.

"Did you see the queen?"

"I did not see the queen," said O'Neill in a cold, precise tone.

"You annoyed the ministers considerable," said Rory in soothing congratulation, pouring himself wine; the liquor they had brought was drunk now and they must make do with what was available. "Will you have a glass of wine?"

"I will not." Another minute of silence brought the chief to exploding point; he loosed a stream of violent oaths and began to pace the room with long strides. "By Christ, this red Sassenach bitch! Is it her own doing? No, no, I'll never believe it—the ministers, it is, Christ damn them and their blandishments! How can I lay suit to a woman while they babble at me of political treaties? If I could get her to myself an hour—"

"You have," said Luke, "several times."

"In a crowd of court nobles at formal dinners! But I swear it, she is taken with me, as I knew she would be—why does she let them monopolize my time? If I could—"

"O'Neill," said the musician, "admit it to yourself now. You will never take Elizabeth." If any but O'Givney said that, the chief would have drawn his knife; he only shouted more oaths at Luke, who picked up his harp, unmoved, and stroked its carven body.

"Fool! I will take her, she cannot resist me—no woman! It is Cecil and that bastard, Walsingham—"

"It is the queen," said Luke. "Yes, she is a woman and she is drawn to you, but she is also the one woman in ten thousand who thinks of many other things before her own desire. However passionate she loved you, she still would never wed you, because it would be disadvantageous politically. Other men said that to you, but you would not listen. Am I a statesman? No, so I kept my mouth shut."

"Then continue to do so," said O'Neill furiously. "Mercy, heaven! Since when do politicians need to explain the rudiments of their craft to each other? They knew all my talk of a treaty was but an excuse! And now they waste my time and their own offering one—making solemn discussion of it!" He strode to the door, "One of you, for God's love, try to see they give us a decent meal! I must get a letter off to Terence. No, you stay where you are"—to Rory. "I have enough company for one day!" They heard him mount the stair and his chamber door slammed.

Moran sighed and took the glass Rory offered. "I am thinking we'll be in England longer than he planned."

"I have been thinking the same thing," said Rory. "He will never sign a treaty with the Crown. It has not gone exactly as he expected."

The chief had been in England five weeks, and since that initial meeting with the queen his frustration had grown daily. He had expected to be welcomed as the queen's guest; instead, Bacon had blandly suggested that O'Neill might find it convenient to rent a city house during his stay. Such abuse of courtesy by a Gaelic noble would have led to war: it was barbarous. But in a foreign country the chief had no recourse but to abide by its customs, however rude. He took a house in London, and not the least of their troubles resulted from that. Rory and Moran (Luke, of course, refused to stir himself) managed to collect some servants. Half of them were insolent and lazy at serving foreigners, and the other half scuttled about the house as if they believed the Ulsterman planned to butcher and devour them any minute. It proved impossible to prevent an English cook from overroasting meat, and the only drink obtainable was wine or the bitter English beer.

Living apart as a private visitor, the chief must await formal invitations from the queen, and these were not so frequent nor were the audiences so private as he had expected. But he had invitations—oh, yes!—from the ministers.

"They are wasting their time," said Rory.

"But keeping him from the queen," Moran pointed out.

"Does she need to be kept from him?" rejoined Luke. "When I see a brace of hounds guarding a door I assume their master has set them there —not likely it's their own idea. I saw all the arguments against his coming and capturing her, but I thought he outweighed them. In all the years I know him, I never knew him to lay his eye on a woman and fail to take her. With him it is as natural as breathing—a lift of his hand and they fall over themselves to reach him. I still believe he might do it, but he cannot exercise his charm on a woman he never sees."

"The Dean said from the start," added Moran to that, "that the one serious obstacle is her hatred for our church, for it looks on her as illegal-bred. What happened today, Rory?"

"What happened last Thursday or the Monday before that or the Friday before that? He met with the ministers, all formal and solemn in the queen's council chamber—but she was not there. Cecil smiled and smiled, and Bacon told some very old jokes and laughed at them fit to burst, and Pembroke stared out the window, and Walsingham purred like a cat. They offered him the two pacts again, all drawn up and copied—all they lack is his signature and Elizabeth's. He refused both, and they argued back and forth—all very polite, you understand, nothing vulgar about it—and then we came away."

"The documents already drawn," said Luke thoughtfully, running an arpeggio. "Suspicious it looks to me."

Rory laughed and agreed. "Since his arrival, they say, but I've a notion the ink is drier than that. He will never sign either—and it would mean nothing if he did; pacts signed under duress are not legal—if you can imagine anyone but God forcing him to a thing he was not wanting to do!"

The two documents the ministers offered O'Neill were both short, but significant. The first related to his legal heir. His father, Con, had signed an agreement with the old king to name as his heir his alleged eldest illegitimate son, Matthew Kelly, Baron Dungannon; Kelly was dead, but he left a son, the present Dungannon, and the ministers pressed O'Neill to recognize the claim and appoint Dungannon his heir. Dungannon was Anglophile, a fawner on the English—would they want him in as chief if he was not? But even if O'Neill signed that agreement, which he never would, it would mean nothing. In Brehon Law, a chief might name his successor, but the clan was not bound to accept that choice if they disapproved, and the O'Neill clansmen would never accept an Anglophile.

The second document was a small gem of composition, probably by Cecil: an agreement to keep the peace between Ulster and England, and Ulster and the Pale, for twenty years, during which time there should be free trade over the borders and free shipping. With that in force, the English would pour into Ulster, attempt to take over all trade ownership and manufacture, and set at their eternal game of splitting the clan chiefs, trouble-making to prevent any united rebellion. The fact that O'Neill signed a treaty with England would outlaw all his treaties of mutual support with Spain and France, with other Catholic rulers in Europe, which treaties specified military aid were Ulster attacked—not if Ulster itself instigated war.

"They never believed he wanted a treaty," said Moran now. "They knew why he came."

"We will stay in England," said Luke mournfully, "until I grow a long gray beard."

And for a while it appeared his prophecy was correct.

On the afternoon following this latest meeting with the ministers, O'Neill was bidden to a formal reception at the court, and Rory, as usual, shadowed him. It was a small gathering of court nobles, ladies of the chamber, a few ambassadors from France, Spain, Italy, even Germany, who were all in England to urge various husbands on Elizabeth. The Earl of Leicester was there, never far from her side, and, of her ministers, Cecil and Walsingham.

O'Neill would not demean himself to dress in English fashion; it would make him appear Anglophile, pay them compliment. His dress was probably the occasion for mirth among the English, but nothing could make O'Neill look ridiculous even to Sassenachs. That day he was dramatic, all in dead black, with gilded sandals and many jewels. Rory thought the queen's eyes held admiration as they greeted formally; she was obviously fond of elaborate decoration herself—with far less reason.

He thought other things about Elizabeth Tudor. Today, as when he had seen her before, she wore much artificial color on her complexion; her gown was sewn with pearls and gem-set buttons, her stiff ruffed collar so wide she could scarcely turn her head. Like many plain women (well, like all women!) she was greatly concerned with her appearance. There were many reports of the time and money she spent on lotions, face paint, concoctions to whiten the skin and brighten the eyes. It was a well-known fact that she kept a female attendant for the sole duty of "washing the queen all over once each month, or oftener, if she required it," which showed her extraordinary nicety of grooming. But with all her care, she could never make herself beautiful. Rory heard O'Neill say once, and believed it, that Elizabeth Tudor's lifelong enmity for that other queen, Mary Stuart, was not all fear for her throne, but female jealousy of the Stuart's feminine charm, the faculty she had of snaring men to her. For all her life Elizabeth would know that men who professed love for her did so of personal ambition; and that might be bitter knowledge for a woman. There were some said Leicester loved her truly. Rory wondered; he thought maybe she wondered herself.

There was a crowd about the queen, but O'Neill managed to keep himself at the fore, disregarding hot glances from Leicester, the attempted interruptions of the dignified old Spanish bishop who was in London ostensibly on church business but actually, as everyone knew, to urge another suit on Elizabeth. The queen appeared more interested in O'Neill at the moment.

"You enjoy your visit to England, O'Neill?"

"Very much." The chief smiled down at her easily. "Who would not? It is a pleasant land and the people charming. But then," and he bent a little nearer, "we have a saying, subjects take their temper from rulers—and with such a lovely young queen, how could the English be otherwise than kind and hospitable?"

"You flatter me," she returned to that with a laugh. "But then," and she flashed him a mischievous look, "we hear that Celts are all flatterers and charmers."

"Indeed no, quite serious I am—"

"I would like to believe that"—she laid a hand on his arm lightly, and Leicester's eyes were twin daggers directed at the chief—"but I must reserve judgment." And Leicester smiled.

"I should be happy to make the attempt to convince you." O'Neill moved closer.

"I am sure I should be at a disadvantage. Very likely O'Neill has much practice at convincing hesitant ladies." It was a neat little display of two word-fencers exhibiting their skill to each other. Rory had the strange notion that he watched two mummers masked on a stage. He could guess what the chief's true feeling was—but the woman? Perhaps there was a second mask under the one she showed the world, and a third under that; perhaps she wore a mask before herself.

"Can anyone doubt that after meeting O'Neill?" put in Leicester suavely. "More likely he convinces them before they are quite ready to be—convinced." A subtle insult, slyly terming the chief not above rape. The queen's high metallic laugh rang out, but she kept her hand on O'Neill's arm.

"Oh, I feel sure the prince is always indulgent with ladies, Robert. And the ladies"—a long, intimate look up at the chief—"with him."

Leicester's face darkened; he dallied with the court sword at his side. "Other peoples own different codes of honor from the English," he muttered.

"That is unfortunately true," said O'Neill, smiling. "It is for you English to be patient and educate other races."

"And you would advocate feminine tutors?" asked the queen provocatively.

"Why not? They would show their pupils greater—affection."

Talk like that might go on all day and get nowhere. It was any clever woman with two men. Little wonder, after an hour of it, that O'Neill was looking grim as he made conventional farewells. When they reclaimed their horses in the courtyard and rode out, he commenced to swear in a low, vicious tone.

"That red bitch, damn her—damn her! What am I doing here? Nothing! Before God, she put out that eight thousand pounds easy enough—

does she want no return from the investment? Six times I meet her in five weeks—six! And none of those long or private. Christ, if I could—"

Rory ventured to comment, "It's those treaties they're after."

O'Neill told him what they could do with the treaties. "Are they thinking I'm a child, to sign political agreements for the satisfaction of showing them I know how to write? This is knight against bishop in chess—equal advantage in different gambits." He rode the rest of the way to the house in frowning silence.

When they came into the hall, they found McSweeney building up the fire while Luke drowsed in one chair and Moran, who had taken cold from the dismal English weather, sneezed in another, a blanket round his shoulders. The constable straightened respectfully, and the chief seized on the excuse for a display of temper. "What am I paying English servants for when you do all the work?"

"Your pardon, O'Neill, but that Hawkins is gone out somewhere and with Moran as he is, the fire must be kept up. I only thought—"

"Christ," said the chief, "they are not even good servants!" Moran and Luke eyed him; behind his back Rory shook his head, grimacing at them, and they forbore to ask questions about his meeting with the queen. "For the love of God, someone pour me a drink—if I get enough of this wine down maybe it will affect me a bit!" Moran sneezed again and announced that if anyone was interested he was feeling better. The chief, glancing at him disdainfully, said, "God be thanked. If there is one thing I cannot abide it is this weak submission to petty illness, like a woman! And if you must succumb—I am a reasonable man, I realize not all men are so strong as myself—at least you might keep yourself decently out of sight until you are recovered." He swallowed wine and cursed again. "Jesus and Mary, I would as soon drink the stale of the troop-horses!" McSweeney, keeping one eye on him, began to edge toward the door.

"Oh, Christ," exclaimed the chief; he had been pacing the room, now stopped dead. "Is it any wonder I am near mad? I need a woman—six weeks and no woman; am I saint or eunuch? I need a woman to work off some of this restlessness! Manus, fetch me one immediately to my chamber." He strode to the door.

McSweeney looked outraged, bewildered, and helpless. "But, O'Neill, I—"

"Immediately! You need not be discriminating; anything female will do."

They looked at one another as his angry steps died up the stair. "Well, this is a situation," said Luke. "I never thought for how to meet this—more fool I, knowing O'Neill."

Moran forgot his misery, and, sitting up, said this was serious. "You know what McGuinness, your uncle, said, Rory. By all accounts it's true enough; all the English harlots have the French sickness. God knows it spreads fast enough at home, brought into the ports by foreign sailors. We cannot—"

"Now look," said McSweeney, "I am a soldier, not a procurer. It is no part of my duty to locate wantons, even for O'Neill."

"Nor is it ours," reminded Rory sharply. Here, indeed, was a situation. It occurred to him that some of the impatience and restlessness they all felt came from lack of female company—none of them would aproach an Englishwoman. The chief, with his stronger needs, had evidently reached a point where he could overlook that distaste. "Someone will know, Manus —maybe one of your men. Go and ask."

"I will not," said McSweeney hotly, "on two counts. First, I'll not be the man to put him in such danger. Yes, he goes back home with that accursed disease and what happens? All Ulster pouncing on Manus Mc-Sweeney as the man who picked out the woman! And second, I am a respectable man and not a whoremaster—turning in his grave, my father would be—"

"Now look, man. You see the situation for yourself. There is no help for it; he'll be like a madman if we do not somehow get him a woman."

"And look you," said Luke suddenly, "no need to bring in a woman off the street. There's that Polly in the kitchens. I have noted her eying him —no shy virgin she is, but not a professional. She might be more than willing."

McSweeney said doubtfully, "An imagination you have, O'Givney. I might get a kettleful of boiling water even to speak to her."

"I fancy not, from the looks she gives him."

"Go and try, Manus," said Rory. "You see none of us can do it."

"Oh, yes, gentlemen you are!" McSweeney's barrel chest swelled indignantly. "The McSweeneys are as old a family as McGuinnesses any day. Because I am bred outside noble stock, have I no pride? There has never yet been a McSweeney that was a wife-beater, a procurer, or an Anglophile, and it will not be I who disgraces the name!"

"I will argue genealogy with you later—you heard him."

"I refuse to have anything to do with it," said McSweeney, and Rory could not blame him.

"Oh, the devil," said Luke mildly. "I'm not so proud. I'll go and ask her and save all our lives." He went out; they waited in silence, which Moran broke to sneeze and remark that he hoped to God Luke was right about the girl, otherwise it would be awkward.

But when Luke returned, he was humming. "I had to make a little bargaining with her," he told them negligently. "It worked out to ten shillings. I would not say she's worth it myself, but under the circumstances— She is just going up to him now."

"Well," said Moran, "if she's safe, it will be handy enough with the girl in the house. Perhaps it will keep him in better temper."

Rory said he doubted it, and went up to his own chamber. They were all irritable these days, bored and anxious—a bad combination. He knew he would not sleep, but he lay down on the bed and stared at the ceiling. He thought of the queen, those absurd treaties, of Leicester, the ministers; and all to keep his mind from O'Neill and the woman. At Benburb one spoke to a manservant, and presently Ena came, or one of the others—an open, casual, good thing, like ordering a meal to stop hunger, and that was how it should be. The English, pretending hunger did not exist, making a shameful thing of it . . . He thought of Moyna, and cursed under his breath. O'Neil there, across the passage, satiating himself on a woman —what matter the woman? Christ, how long would they remain in England?

The chief's chamber door crashing open brought him off the bed in a leap. He did not hear what O'Neill was shouting about, but fear for his safety was never far from any of their minds. He drew his belt dagger and ran out to the passage. O'Neill's chamber was opposite his own; the chief was standing in the doorway, shouting furiously at a girl cowering away from him, a drab slattern of a girl, half-unclothed, her gown clutched in a bundle under one arm.

"Get out—get out of my sight—oh, Christ—oh, Christ—do you hear? Out!" With a frightened squeal, she turned and plunged down the stair, almost upsetting Luke and Moran as they ran up. The chief put a hand to his head. "Christ help me—Christ help me!" Rory followed him uncertainly as he turned back into the chamber, the others crowding up behind.

"O'Neill—what is it, what—"

O'Neill seemed not to hear; he sat down on the bed and rested his head in his hands. "Oh, my God, what is the matter with me? Never before—nothing like this—a sickness in me it is. It was not the woman—it was not Catherine—Catherine—Catherine—God aid me, I am sick for the sight of Catherine—" They had never heard that voice from O'Neill.

Moran and Rory stood helpless, bewildered, not knowing what to say or do. It was Luke who moved first. He thrust his little harp into Rory's arms and crossed to the chief, knelt beside him, and took his shoulders gently.

"My fine man, O'Neill. Easy, now. So you discover the truth at last— in the end there is only the one woman, and not a thing only of the body it is. That is good, be easy for it, do not go fighting it. This little need will pass and all the better for it you will be—"

O'Neill gave a long sigh and lay back on the bed, an arm flung across his eyes. "I am a fool—a very great fool. Sing to me, Luke. Sing me all my war songs—and take my mind from love."

CHAPTER XIV

O<small>N THE</small> morning after that O'Neill had been bidden to another meeting with the queen's ministers. His household had seen little of him since his outburst of the afternoon before; he kept to his chamber, dined alone, and did not appear that morning until the time of his departure. Rory judged his mood as dangerous because he was in unrelieved black with no jewels save his rings, which was unusual with O'Neill. He said little to the chief, lest he provoke him; McSweeney came to announce that the guard was formed, and they set off for Westminster. Rory wished O'Neill were in more amiable mood, and McSweeney voiced the same thought.

"He's spoiling for a fight, and no wonder. God help us if he loses his temper! Have you thought, one wrong word would give them the excuse to take offense and punish him, maybe with legal right? If he should curse the queen, or strike the lowest official—"

"He knows the danger, Manus. A tight hold he's keeping on himself." McSweeney said gloomily, "For how long?"

The small guard was left at ease in the street; O'Neill, with Rory behind, was ushered by a liveried page along the corridors of the immense Norman pile of Westminster, to a small council chamber. Cecil, Bacon, Pembroke, and Walsingham sat about the huge carved table, and the queen was at its head in a taller chair. The light from the window behind made a shining halo round her head. The chief inclined to her stiffly before taking the one vacant chair at the foot of the table.

Cecil opened the discussion smoothly, "It is gracious of you to join another meeting, O'Neill. Her Majesty is concerned to complete a trade agreement between England and Ulster, and since you make this journey, we assume that you also have an interest."

"Assuredly," said O'Neill noncommittally, looking at the queen. She was a different woman from the gay flirt of yesterday; she sat erect, her eyes remote and impersonal on all the men. Before her lay two documents, the pacts they offered O'Neill, with an inkstand and pens.

"That being the case," said Pembroke vaguely, "it appears strange that O'Neill should decline definite discussion. He seems to imply he does not look with favor upon the agreements we offer—both of great benefit to Ulster."

"There might be other opinions," said the chief.

"Oh, yes. Please be assured," said Cecil, leaning forward earnestly, "that we do not seek to force you in any way to sign a document you do not approve, O'Neill. If any word or phrase should require explanation or seem to you ambiguous, we should be happy to discuss it. You need have no suspicion of our motives." His overemphasis subtly made the chief out an ignorant barbarian, unsure of himself in modern usages among civilized people. O'Neill's mouth flattened, but when he answered it was in the same noncommittal tone.

"I am quite capable of reading Latin script, Sir William."

"You were given copies of the documents, I believe?" asked Bacon anxiously. "Ah, yes, of course. You have read them?"

"I have read them."

"Perhaps, if O'Neill would say which provision he finds objectionable, we could make some adjustment," murmured Walsingham.

"I find objection to all of them," said the chief bluntly. Rory felt a stab of alarm. If their suave bullying continued, it might prod him to open fury, and no telling what he would say or do. "I will not sign these documents."

Cecil gave the ghost of a shrug; Pembroke stared down at his hands; Bacon looked at the queen; Walsingham slid a hand up his jaw. The queen spoke for the first time, her voice thin and hard and dispassionate.

"O'Neill perhaps considers the agreements offered him as prejudicial to the interests of Ulster?"

"I do."

"Why?"

"Since I refuse to sign them I see little point in discussing the provisions. I did not come here to consider a contract you offer me—"

"Oh?" said the queen softly. "Then we were under a misapprehension."

"But," said O'Neill, smiling at her, "to offer you a contract of my own devising. I thought we all understood that."

"You speak of a contract."

"An unwritten alliance," said the chief, his eyes fixed on her.

"That kind of agreement I do not like. I would ask you to tell my ministers the precise fault you find in the agreements we offer."

"As you will. Ulster will admit no foreigners legally beyond the border. All the provisions in these agreements would outlaw that fundamental principle. I refuse to sign them."

Slowly the queen rose. "There is no more to say then. If O'Neill would draw up his own suggested contract, we would be pleased to read it and express an opinion."

"Yes, indeed"—Bacon, nervously genial.

"For the moment, then, we adjourn," said Walsingham.

"O'Neill will inform us when he has his own document copied"—Cecil, with more than a hint of sarcasm. The chief stood, and his voice rang bass to Cecil's soft tenor.

"I might do that, Sir William—and possibly suggest some provisions not greatly to your liking. But is there not a saying that the art of statesmanship is compromise?"

"Quite true," said Cecil. "It surprises me to hear you subscribe to it."

O'Neill's smile widened on him. "I only quote. I never compromise, Sir William—with anyone, upon any matter." He gave the queen a casual nod and made for the door. Rory could not risk a backward glance, but wondered what expression she wore; Elizabeth Tudor was not accustomed to such careless informality. To most women, even a queen, it would underline his masculinity, but Rory had a notion it annoyed this woman greatly, though she might not exhibit it.

As they emerged to the corridor the chief was muttering to himself. He was furious, not at the proposals of the ministers, but at Cecil's subtle insults. "So he thinks me a savage! By Christ, English!"

The ministers had remained in the council room; there was no sign of pages or guards, and they went unaccompanied to the turn of the passage. But the little scene was not ended.

There was a rustle of skirts behind, and the queen's voice spoke his name. Rory thought O'Neill was as startled as himself; he whirled. Elizabeth was coming up the passage after him. In the dimness she might have been a graceful young girl calling after a lover, but as she drew nearer one saw the angularity of body, the face paint, the narrow eyes. As if she donned another mask when the door of the council chamber closed after her, this was the woman of yesterday, mockingly flirtatious. Her voice was thinly metallic as always.

"O'Neill! After all your protestation, you are rude to make such haste out of my company!"

The chief recovered himself instantly. "Only because I thought you wished it, lady."

"A ready answer! Since when does any woman wish to be rid of the company of a handsome man?" She laughed, laid her hand on his arm. "Now all that nonsense of political council is ended, for the time being, let us not be so serious! I ride in the afternoon with some of my court tomorrow. Do you join us?"

"Very gladly, of course, my thanks."

"You will not forget? Oh, nonsense, you are not a man to put yourself out for a woman—even Elizabeth of England! I do well to doubt you. An hour past midday—do not keep me waiting!" She gave him a provocative smile and withdrew down the corridor, walking lightly. The chief watched until she had vanished again into the council room, drew a long breath.

"By Christ, did I not know? Did I not say it? She is but dallying, playing the ministers into belief she is cold to me! Do I need more proof?"

It was certainly auspicious. He was jubilant as they rode back to the house and related the events to Moran and Luke. "You see, doubters! I am always right—women I know!"

Luke said, "Do not go naming the foal before the stud has mounted the mare." But O'Neill laughed at him impatiently, and went up to his chamber to sort over his wardrobe for clothes to impress the queen next day.

He should, Rory thought, do that. When he came down to the hall the next midday he wore a dark green kilt and saffron tunic; the emblem of his clan, the Red Hand, was sewn on each shoulder. He was newly shaven, jeweled, and in exuberant spirits.

"You'll take escort?" asked Rory. On other occasions, when O'Neill had joined the queen's riding parties, he had taken a few guards for dignity.

"Yourself and McSweeney only—tell him the jeweled trappings on the black." With no premonition of what the day would bring, Rory relayed the order to the constable.

There was a little crowd already gathered in the courtyard when they arrived—a dozen nobles, but only two or three ladies to satisfy convention. The queen preferred men about her, conscious, perhaps, of her poor qualifications for feminine competition. Leicester was there, elegantly dressed, the plume in his velvet cap half a yard long. He watched the chief surreptitiously. O'Neill did not deign to join any group in desultory talk, but stood at a little distance waiting for the queen to appear. When she came, late by half an hour or more, he moved quickly to be first at her side.

"You see how prompt I am, lady, at your bidding!"

"Indeed—you surprise me! And what magnificent emeralds, are they not, Robert?" Leicester muttered sullen agreement and offered to lift her to the saddle at the same instant O'Neill held out his hands. "Two gallant gentlemen—which shall I allow the privilege? But I must not create jealousy in either!" She beckoned instead to her groom. O'Neill and the earl stepped back reluctantly; she let the groom settle her in the saddle.

There was some jostling for position as they rode out, but the chief managed to stay by her side, and Rory and the constable, of no mind to let him get far off, rode close behind. Leicester crowded up to her other side. In the city streets it was not possible to talk, let alone overhear the conversation ahead, but they turned soon to quieter paths, out of the city proper, along the bank of the Thames. Rory heard the queen's high laugh ring out often; from the audible snatches of talk. It was evident she played her favorite game with any two men, setting them at odds.

A trifle more than an hour after leaving the city they were in a pleasant wooded lane, the river shining dull in the near distance. The queen reined up so suddenly that in the narrow way Rory and the constable nearly rode into her.

"A pleasant spot, gentlemen. Let us dismount and walk a little." O'Neill was off his horse at once and forestalled Leicester in lifting her from the saddle. She thanked him with a glance, kept one hand on his arm as she walked up the rise under the trees. The mounted grooms came up to take the horses; Leicester tossed his bridle to one and made haste after the queen. The rest of the party dismounted obediently and scattered about the little grove.

Rory said tersely to McSweeney, "Keep the horses," and followed to fall in unobtrusively at the chief's left shoulder.

The queen halted before an ancient spreading tree whose roots had raised a grassy bank. "Shall we sit down? It is unseasonably warm for February, is it not?" There was sly mischief in her eyes for Leicester. He doffed his cloak at once and spread it for her, and she sat, inviting them to join her with a demure look. Yes, there was something about this woman: it was like watching a painted puppet imitate a lady—this sallow, angular, unbeautiful woman behaving like a famous charmer—but it held some fascination, making you wonder what trick she would be up to next. The two men seated themselves at either side.

"O'Neill has said he is enjoying his stay in England. Tell me, is it different from your own country?"

"Different, yes. But lands do not vary so much, it is the people in them."

"I stand corrected, sir!" She laughed. Leicester was scowling.

"But I am disappointed in one aspect of my visit." And the chief bent to her, smiling, inviting inquiry.

"And what is that?"

"Why, I came to England in the hope of finding myself a suitable wife, lady. One of your lovely English girls, of good breeding and substantial dower, and pleasing to the—eye." He was smiling suggestively into her own eyes. Perhaps no woman but Elizabeth Tudor could withstand that forceful charm at such close range. She only tilted her head back to meet his gaze.

"And you have found none such?"

"Oh, yes, one I desire ardently! But I hesitate to approach her."

"Ah, a tyrannical parent, perhaps? It is true, O'Neill, few well-bred Englishmen would consent to give a daughter to a foreigner—however wealthy and noble."

"All women are not under the jurisdiction of fathers."

"Fathers aside"—Leicester entered the conversation in a loud voice—"any respectable young woman might hesitate to wed a man who has reputedly peopled a province with his bastards." The queen frowned; belatedly, Leicester realized his error in using a term often applied to herself. He said hastily, more smoothly, "I understand that in your law as well as ours, O'Neill, a ruler may name his successor. I have frequently wondered how you could settle on one heir, with so phenomenally large a potential selection." That little thrust pleased her; she laughed, and was dutifully echoed by others.

O'Neill looked Leicester up and down leisurely. "I confess I do not see why the question concerns you, my lord," he said in a drawling tone, and paused before adding, "since it is scarcely a problem you will ever be called on to solve yourself." The queen's laugh was maliciously delighted; Leicester laid a hand on his sword.

"But tell me, O'Neill—you would marry an Englishwoman?"

"Indeed, the one of my choice." He bent his charm to her again. "If I can persuade her—"

"There may be difficulties," said the queen. "Aside from the fact that you are not English, a father might be reluctant to make a marriage contract with a Catholic."

O'Neill drew back a little. "What has religion to do with true love?"

The queen leaned against the tree and shut her eyes. She said in a dreamy tone, "Religion has to do with everything, my friend—like money. I, myself, for instance—you do not mind if for a moment we speak of myself?—I could not consider wedding any but a Protestant."

Leicester smiled under his hand; there was brief silence. She had told the chief in plain language that his suit was vain. She opened her eyes and looked at the chief with a slow smile.

"Of course, in the event that I desired—very ardently—to wed a man of that persuasion, if he should renounce the Roman church for the English, I could take him with good conscience."

"Not all men are so weak as to renounce God," said O'Neill stiffly.

"Then my love should have to burn in secret. Of course, it is a hypothetical problem. I should prefer to wed an Englishman." Her eyes made promises to Leicester as to what Englishman she meant.

Whether she only amused herself idly, no one could say; but O'Neill, at least, took her seriously. Rory had been watching the woman; now, looking at the chief, he saw to his alarm that O'Neill's expression was black with rage. After all the high hopes she had engendered in him, she had, in a moment, destroyed them—or so he took it. It had been the stumbling-block from the first, as all had warned him—her hatred of Catholicism.

He drew farther back from her. "Some of my countrymen told me, when

I planned to visit England, that Englishwomen are all coldhearted. I think they were right." He got up to his feet in one motion. "I also think I will be returning to my own country, where women are kinder."

The queen turned to Leicester with a lift of her brows; he rose, assisted her to her feet. She smoothed her gown leisurely, her painted lips curving in a little mirthless smile on the chief. "But O'Neill forgets," she said gently, "he cannot return to his own country—until I give him leave to do so."

There was instant dead silence over the whole scene. Rory's heart gave one leap. He thought, So here it is—we always felt there was danger—but what and how? The chief was motionless, staring at her; Rory stepped closer to him. When O'Neill spoke, all vestige of personal emotion had vanished from his tone; it was clear and cold.

"The queen forgets somewhat also—that she has afforded me a signed guarantee of safe entry and safe departure."

Elizabeth's smile widened. "It is not our habit, O'Neill, to forget anything. Indeed, there is that document. 'To pass without molestation over all borders into English territory, to return past English borders unharmed.' But"—she tilted her head, and there was dancing mischief in the green eyes—"but we did not stipulate when, O'Neill. There are no time limits set by the guarantee. We should be inhospitable not to press for a long visit from such a distinguished guest. O'Neill will stay—as long as it takes him to decide to sign the generous treaties we offer Ulster. Until then will he remain to grace our court." And on the last sentences her voice was steel unhidden by velvet.

The chief went white with shock and rage. Now she revealed to him the infamous trick she played. Rory looked at O'Neill and panic struck him. For one moment fury mastered the chief, and in that moment he took a step toward her, hands out. Then Rory moved between. He might be committing suicide, but he took the chief by the upper arms, speaking urgently in their own tongue.

"No, O'Neill! For the love of Christ! They'll be on you like a pack of wolves if you lay hand on the bitch—" He felt all that tense power straining against him, and knew he could not hold him. Then, with a violence of effort that shook his whole body, O'Neill had himself in hand.

"My thanks to the queen for the useful lesson in the art of statesmanship. It is evident that if compromise is an essential part of such craft—honor is not. I beg the queen's indulgence to intrude my presence on her no longer today. She has sufficient escorts without O'Neill." Only then did Rory dare let him go; he swung about and strode down toward the road with long steps, very erect. Rory followed on shaking legs.

But he had seen the excitement in her eyes, and in his mind was the incoherent thought: that was what she wanted, what she had hoped for.

It exhilarated her to be in danger from him—and if he had touched her he would have been dead in thirty seconds for personal attack on the queen.

He heard Leicester laughing. He took a long breath. He thought of the imminent danger he stood in himself, and felt weak again.

McSweeney was walking the horses at a little distance from the English grooms. He looked startled to see them returning alone and put a hand to his belt dagger. Perhaps he thinks we must run from attack, thought Rory dully. The chief took the bridle but did not immediately mount. He turned to Rory. His mouth was thin and straight, his nostrils dilated, his voice savagely low.

"Rory McGuinness, you have offended against the law. You have laid hands on a chief to restrain him. That is a crime punishable by death."

"I acknowledge the crime and crave pardon for it," managed Rory. McSweeney's eyes bulged, turning from him to the chief.

"I do not give it," said O'Neill instantly. "Here is your punishment." He drew back his right arm and struck Rory a terrific blow in the jaw with his clenched fist.

"McGuinness! Come back now, man—St. Patrick and all saints, is he dead entirely? McGuinness!" Something wet and cold splashed in Rory's face; he moved feebly to escape it. "Oh, God be praised, alive you are! Come now, let me help you sit up—holy angels, I was thinking he had killed you!" More water trickled into his eyes.

"Jesus and Mary, are you off to drown me?" Rory raised himself with the help of a strong arm. When he opened his eyes the landscape swam to a green-gold blur, and then he saw he was lying in the road, propped on McSweeney's shoulder, while several English grooms watched with bored interest.

"The best part of half an hour you're out. Blessed saints, I thought you were dead on me for sure!"

"Stop praying over me, Manus." He felt his jaw; it was swollen and painful. "My Christ, that was a blow."

"That was a man who struck it. But what is it about at all, McGuinness? Why is he angered at you? I did not believe my own eyes until I picked up the tooth he knocked out of you—here it is—and you lying there in the road like a corpse—"

Vague alarm stirred in him. "Manus, where's the chief?"

"He rode off alone as if the devil was at his heels—"

"Fool! He should not be alone, you should—"

"Now would I go and leave you stretched out here? Also, he ordered me to stay. He looked at you and laughed, but not meaning it mirthful, you know, and then he said to me, 'Bring him to life and fetch him back to me, Manus, it's a brave man!' And up into the saddle and off before I could close my mouth. Is it better you are now?"

"Fine." Rory staggered to his feet, groped for the bridle, still clutching his jaw. "We must find him, we must hurry, he should not be alone—later I'll explain it, Manus—now we must hurry!"

CHAPTER XV

In his nearly thirty-four years of life, Shane O'Neill had frequently been angered, but he was never so angry before or after as he was then, at Elizabeth Tudor, and he was never wholly to lose that anger all his life. She had tricked him as no woman had ever done; she had insulted his honor and his manhood; she had checkmated him as neat and cool as any master statesman. He was angered at that, but far deeper and stronger and colder was he angered because, for the first time in his life, a woman had looked at him and flirted with him and shown attraction for him, and then, with a laugh, rejected him as beneath contempt.

He was for the moment beyond cursing or any outward show of anger. He stood in the center of the room, tall and straight, and only the bright fury in his eyes betrayed the emotion in him. He said in a flat voice, "So I know where I stand. I know now. It was a trick, and she planned it that way from the first. It is only made open today."

"But—" Moran and Luke were still trying to make sense of the hurried account Rory had muttered at them—the chief would not explain his own humiliation in detail. "It is a breach of the guarantee if they restrain you any way—they cannot—"

"Spare me your imbecilities! England is an island. Look out there—" O'Neill jerked a shoulder at the window. "Disguised as hawkers and loungers, but they are the queen's men guarding me. Yes, yes, so they cannot lay a hand on me without breaking the guarantee! Can they not? One move from me to leave the country and what happens? Some excuse they'd find to keep me, and if I offer violence I am instigating a fight for no cause, with no violence offered me! 'Certainly, O'Neill, you may send any letter you wish'—and it doing duty in the guards' convenience, but who is to say it was not lost or destroyed after being carried across the border? I have two choices only. I can bring it further into the open and challenge them and get myself very courteously shut up somewhere on some excuse, or stay here at beck and call of Cecil and the rest. But they will keep me here until I have signed those treaties—or until I can persuade them, until I can trick them in return—" He stopped. Very deliberately he took up the crystal decanter of wine from the table, weighed it in his hand, and flung it across the room to smash against the stone hearth. The wine made a great crimson splatter on the stone and the floor.

"My cunning ones!" he said in a whisper. "So you think to trick O'Neill! Like that will English blood be spilled—for every insult you offer a thousand Englishmen will die!"

"What will you do?" asked Moran numbly.

The chief looked up from the splinters of glass, the splatter of wine. He smiled. "I am O'Neill. Did you think she tricked me entirely? There was always this possibility—I was gambling against it, and I knew that when I came." That was his pride speaking; he had never doubted his ability to win Elizabeth to him. "What will I do? I choose the lesser of two evils for the time being. I will remain here and argue with the ministers in long words. And you"—he looked at Rory—"will get out of England and carry this news to Ulster."

"What?" Rory shook his head to clear it; his jaw was aching still from the blow. "You want me to leave you—"

"Fool! They dare not harm me— Do I need my own guard? They'll be guarding me like fond parents; they want me quick, not dead—at the moment! Dead men do not sign treaties. They are watching the house, but I think you may get away. And a little fiction we'll make to disguise your absence here. Yes, likely the servants are bribed to spy. You'll be ill in your chamber—we might even kill you off. Why? God's love, man, can I trust a letter? The Dean and I have a code, but it may be they know it. And any letter after this may never get out of England. I will take the safe way and send you."

"But what good to carry the news?" demanded Luke. "Those at home will have masses said for us, true—"

"Fool!" said O'Neill again. "There is a plan to meet a situation like this. Was I a callow young lover making this journey, never considering failure? I knew how it might go. Look now, Rory, you get back to Benburb with this news, and your work is done. I've but to delay here until the plan is carried out."

"The plan?"

"You will see. I will never sign those treaties. And once I am out— ah, she will regret the day she thought to take O'Neill so easy! God, God, give me patience to wait and smile at them and speak soft, until I am free! They will learn the danger of meddling with O'Neill!"

Rory had a little excitement the next few days; some of it he could have done without.

Surprisingly, the chief produced English clothes for him—which showed O'Neill had more foresight than they had supposed. The clothes were damnably uncomfortable, padded diaper-trunks, hose, a stiff tunic with boned stays, a plumed hat, and leather top-boots which made Rory wonder how the English could walk. A peculiar impulse to self-scourging it must be, that made foreigners wear such clothes. Under the tunic he had a small fortune in gold: in fact, he was more fearful of being robbed than of failing to reach Ulster—it was more gold than he had ever seen in his life.

He left the house that night by the rear door, as soon as the servants were abed. It was necessary to use caution, surrounded by all these English. The chief gave him a great many orders and suggestions; he troubled to remember only one—to get out of London, since there might be spies at this port, and make west to find a ship. At the door in the dark, Moran and Luke clasped his hand in turn, wished him luck. The chief's hand closed on his shoulder.

"Mind what I have told you. I trust you not to fail me."

"I will do my best, O'Neill." The door shut behind them.

He walked out of London that night on the west road, and stopped in midmorning to bargain for a horse, judging he was far enough off by then not to be traced. He expected to be cheated on the horse, and he was not disappointed. O'Neill had not been so clever, perhaps, dressing him in the clothes of an English gentleman: his English was not good enough to pass as his own tongue, and he was unmistakably a red Gael out of Ireland. For the five days he rode through England, he was jeered at and insulted at every tavern as a foreigner aping English gentry. He held tight to his temper through Berkshire, and at Swindon in Wiltshire, when the farmer taunted him, he only swore back. He spent the third night in Bath quietly enough, but he was not in any mood to hold his peace when he came to Glastonbury in Somerset. There, where tradition said the gentle Savior had built the first church in England—which was a lie, for there were no Christians in England until Irish missionaries carried the word there—he got into an argument with a couple of insolent tradesmen, but it amounted to nothing more than emptying their ale over one another, the cowards refusing to fight him when he drew his dagger. It was not until he came to Exeter in Devon, the last night before he reached a port, that he had a real fight, with a brawny young farmer. The fellow, like all Sassenachs, carrying no knife, it was soon over, and small loss if the whoreson did not recover, though it proved necessary in consequence to get away in a hurry. Altogether, considering everything, it was a peaceful enough journey—for a McGuinness in England—and he rode into Plymouth on the coast of Devon the sixth day after leaving London.

It was drawing to dusk as he came into the town, and he went down to the waterfront to a tavern, with the dual intention of having a meal and locating a ship for Ireland. It would be pure luck if he found one heading up the north coast; but few English ships traded north in Ireland; he would be satisfied with one bound for Dublin. When the tavern keeper brought him the half-rank beef and weak ale which was all the place offered, he asked about a ship. The man gave him an incurious look —foreigners of all kinds were common in a seaport—and pointed out an elderly fellow sitting alone at another table as a shipmaster who was sailing for Dublin. Rory abandoned the unappetizing meal and went over at once.

"Your pardon, I'm told you sail for Ireland soon."

The man glanced up. "And what affair of yours?" he asked in a rough voice.

"Well, I should like passage, if—"

"I don't take passengers."

Rory said, "I'd pay you well. Ten pounds?"

"I don't take passengers."

"Fifteen," said Rory. The man reared back and looked at him.

"You must be almighty anxious to get to Dublin—or out of England. I misdoubt ye're a renegade. Irish by the look of ye." And he spat on the floor.

Rory hung to his temper. "Look now, why should you not take the gold for my passage, you going anyway? No trouble I'd be—"

"Nah!" said the man contemptuously. "Your sort I know. I'm a Treherne of Cornwall, and I don't carry renegades from justice." Perhaps he was naturally suspicious, or ale had turned him so. "Likely there's a reward posted for you. I'll see the town justices about this—a murderer you'll be maybe." He rose unsteadily and Rory, exasperated, caught his arm.

"Look now, I'm offering good money—" The man flung off his hand, and then stopped dead as another hand was pushed flat against his chest.

"The ale is talking in you, Treherne," said the newcomer in a gentle voice. "You'll give the young man a poor impression of Plymouth town. I'd advise you to beg his pardon." Treherne stepped back and muttered what was meant for an apology, and Rory looked at the other man curiously. He was of middle size, slight, with sandy-red hair, beard, and mustache, a man of perhaps forty years. He was unmistakably a gentleman, but, unlike any Englishman Rory had ever seen, he wore a belt over his tunic with two daggers thrust into it.

"Come, Treherne," he pursued, smiling. "I say the young man looks quite honest. You'd not contradict me?"

"No, sir," said Treherne sullenly.

"I scarce thought so." He turned to Rory. "I make out for Dublin myself, with the tide, in two hours. You desire passage?"

"Yes, but—" He did not look like a shipmaster.

"We can come to some arrangement." He took Rory's arm. "But not here—a dull place it is and always filled with waterfront scum. Come along." He turned to rake the old man with a glance. "Oh—Treherne."

"Yes, sir?"

"You'd best not go to the justices. 'Twould be a waste of time."

"Yes, Sir Tom." What kind of noble shipmaster was this?

Rory's new acquaintance led him out to the street. His glance slid over Rory, recognizing his doubt. "But forgive me! I am so accustomed to being known I sometimes forget that not all the men in the world know me. Allow me, sir—I am Stukeley." He made a bow. "You are surprised that so famous a mariner offers you a place in his ship! But I am subject to whims. You are the gainer. You know my name, of course."

"Of course," said Rory hastily. "Only surprised I was as you say—Sir Thomas." Had the other man said Sir Tom?

"Most certainly. I heard you offer Treherne fifteen pounds—that will do." Stukeley grinned at him. "Be easy, friend, I'll not ask your name or business. Running from justice, are you? Irish at any rate—which generally comes to the same thing. My only interest is in the color of your money. Would you care to board now? I can send a man to fetch your bags—"

"I have none, it's a hurried journey," said Rory truthfully. He was of no mind to trust this man too far, but he cared little what ship or what master, so long as he got to Ireland. He let Stukeley lead him in the darkness up the waterfront.

"Evidently. You do not know my name, do you?" He laughed. "Conceit, Thomas, conceit! Shall I tell you why you should have known it? I am a bastard, my friend. Only one kind of bastards boast of their birth —the royal ones. I am half-brother to the queen."

Rory glanced at him in the dark. Was there truth in that? Old King Henry had been a stallion in his day, he had heard. They came past the door of another tavern and in Stukeley's profile against the light was a fleeting, uncanny resemblance to Elizabeth—something in the line of the jaw, the pale-red hair. Coincidence, and he playing on it?

Farther on, Stukeley turned up one of the wharves; tangles of mast and lines showed darker against a dark sky. "Here is my *White Dove*—mind the plank." There were men on the deck who saluted him respectfully. "You may have the second cabin, friend, all to yourself. I'm sorry I cannot offer you a pretty concubine to share it, after the fashion of nobles in your own country. A friendly custom I find that." He picked his way along the deck, sure-footed, thrust open a door. "Stand a moment, I'll strike a light." A spark, and dim light flared; it was a small cabin, sparsely furnished. Stukeley had kindled the wick in a dish of oil. "Satisfactory?"

"It will do. We cast off soon?"

"With the tide. I'll see your money before we sail." But Rory had no mind to strip before him to let him see how much gold he carried.

"You'll have it," he said briefly. Stukeley cocked his head at him.

"Now I wonder—an Irishman, and likely on secret business of some sort. I wonder if you are somewhat to do with my friend, the Prince of

Ulster. He's visiting Elizabeth, and all Europe laying wagers on whether or not he'll win her. I might wish him luck—it would serve both right to be tied to one another! I'm no servant to either. A man in my profession cannot afford allegiances. But I ask no questions." He turned to the door. "I expect to make Dublin at dawn day after tomorrow. No gratitude necessary"—as Rory opened his mouth, not on thanks. "You see, my friend, I'm no plodding cross-channel merchant, not I! I am"—and he made Rory another elaborate bow before departing—"I am a pirate."

And there was a pretty situation. What had he got himself into? Or was Stukeley only a little mad? So long as the ship landed him in Ireland Rory did not care, but with all this gold on him— He got out the passage price hastily while he was alone. Stukeley returned before they cast off, to collect the gold. Looking at it, he said thoughtfully, "New-minted coin. Out of the north you are, then. No Irish in the south knows what color gold is any more. But I said no questions." And he shrugged.

Rory slept uneasily that night, and not for rough water. In the morning his vague fears were sharpened by one look at the crew of the *White Dove*. This was a pirate safe enough. Every sailor aboard looked as if he would murder his grandmother for a copper and the contrast between them and Stukeley's mincing gentility made the captain a sinister figure. Moreover, from the solicitous inquiries for his health, he had a strong notion that Stukeley guessed there was more gold where the first came from. Murder was done every day of the week for the hundredth part of what he had on him, and he could not fight a whole ship's crew. All he could do, in fact, was commend his soul to God—and keep the door bolted.

That he did, for two days, and nearly starved, pretending seasickness. He did not give a curse for the gold as gold—while money was useful to have, it weighed little against O'Neill's life and the mission he was on. But they would not stop with taking the gold, men like these; they would likely toss him overboard into the bargain. But when a dismal dawn showed through the one round window, the second morning out, he was still there to see it—and, to his enormous relief, it showed him Dublin Bay, the humped island-mound offshore, the gray line of buildings along the waterfront. By Christ, another half-hour and he could swim in! Did he misjudge Stukeley and his crew after all?

He did not. He heard the anchor chain rattle; they were tied up to one of the wharves. To hell with formality, he would be off this ship as soon as possible; he laid a hand on the door. It was bolted outside.

With escape so near, he would not be taken like a sitting bird. He considered the window, which gave on the deck. It was small, but he might squeeze through. He was on the point of trying it when he heard Stukeley cough at the door, and whirled to face him as he entered.

"Why do you bolt me in, Sir Thomas?" Put on a bold front, that was the way. "I—"

"Oh, please, friend." Stukeley raised a deprecatory hand. "Let's not start the scene there and play it out at such length! I am a busy man, I cannot waste time at this. I've a bargain to offer you. I believe you are carrying a sizable sum of gold on you. Money I like—being a Tudor, if by the left hand! Maybe you stole it yourself—at any rate, you are in no position to argue. I could easily have a few men strip you of it and dispose of you over the side, but I mislike unnecessary murder and also, if I took the crew into my confidence, I should have to give them a small percentage of the proceeds. Either way, I will have it. But if you hand it over quiet I'll let you go off free—you lose the gold but save your life. Which will you have?"

"Yours, you English robber," said Rory, and rushed him, knife out. Stukeley was not taken entirely unaware; quick as a cat, he reached for his own knife, but Rory hit him left-handed in the face, and Stukeley staggered, tripped over the stool, and went down full length. Rory fell on him and banged his head on the floor hard. He could not wait to finish him, but gained the door in a stride—the plank was down from deck to quay and he ran for it like a hare.

The prospect of sharing the gold did not deter Stukeley from making a try for it; he came staggering after, setting up a yell for the men to stop Rory, and a few sailors ran for him. Rory reached the plank, all but fell down it to the wharf, and, scattering the dockside crowds, led the pursuit up the waterfront, finally losing it—and himself, as a stranger in Dublin—among the warren of alleys and streets. Slowing his pace, catching breath, he reflected with a grin that he would take pleasure in telling O'Neill that his generous supply of money had put him in greater danger of failing his mission than any English watchdogs.

He had three immediate desires: a large meal, comfortable clothes, and a fast horse. The meal he had at a tavern. It was not alone for comfort he needed to shed his English garments—north of the border they might get him stabbed for an Anglophile. O'Neill had told him a name: one Thady O'Brien, a street-hawker. O'Brien was pointed out to him, on inquiry and after search, a little red-haired man, not young, carrying tarts on a wicker tray slung round his neck. He surveyed Rory with soulful brown eyes.

"You'll have one, my handsome gentleman? Two a penny."

"No blandishment, southron," said Rory in their own tongue, liking him at once. "Can you not see I'm no Sassenach? I was told to say to you I'm a friend of Colm McCaffrey."

"Ah, are you now!" said O'Brien, and unslung the tray. "Good luck to it and what can I do for you?"

"Get me a kilt and I'm your friend for life. It is no wonder the English are all bad-tempered and they wearing such damnable tight clothes."

O'Brien laughed. "Come along, I'll put you out of misery." He took Rory to a cubbyhole of a room in an ancient tenement building, took the English clothes and a piece of gold, and promised to fetch back other garments at once. "Could you do with a drink while you wait?"

"Could I!" said Rory feelingly. "I've had nothing but wine or beer since Christ-tide." O'Brien called on all saints, wondered he was still alive, and produced a jug of *uisgebaugh* which kept Rory excellent company until he returned with a plain cheap kilt and tunic and a pair of sandals.

Curious, Rory asked O'Brien questions, and the little man answered readily, trusting him by the password. There were a dozen or so men in positions like his, street-hawkers or beggars who collected information for O'Neill, watching and listening. O'Brien was the only one who knew the principal agent here, McCaffrey.

Rory offered to pay for the help, but O'Brien refused indignantly. It was nearly midday, and Rory wanted to get up to the border by night. He made a quick bargain for a horse, and rode out of Dublin an hour later. By dusk he was nearing the border town of Dundalk; he turned off the road to wait for full dark. The guard stations here were half a mile apart.

When it was dark he walked north between the stations, leading the horse, lest his silhouette show on a rise of ground. He walked two or three miles, until he was sure he was past the border. Was it a fallacy, the belief that air the other side of that border was cleaner? He did not think so; the very ground felt freer under his feet.

He mounted and, clapping his heels into the horse, rode north for Ulster at a gallop.

PART THREE

WAR

CHAPTER XVI

"H<small>E IS</small> dead," whispered Lady Catherine, and collapsed toward him, fainting. Rory had entered the fore-passage at Benburb to face her just coming down the stair. Hastening to support her, staggering under her increased weight, he saw Moyna hurrying down white-faced; heard the door-guards running and shouting Hugh's name. Then suddenly he was the center of a gathering crowd. He had ridden fast, only ten hours up from the Pale, and in his weariness it was all a blur of faces and voices—Hugh, the Donnellys, McArdle, Ferdoragh, O'Hagan, a dozen under-officers, servants, loud and excited.

"He is prisoned—the Tower—I knew it!"

"Where is he, what has happened—"

"I told him, we all told him—Christ, what—"

"Be quiet and let the man talk! For God's love, someone look to Catherine—"

"She has only fainted, she will be right in a moment—"

"Let him talk! What has happened, Rory?"

He collected his wits with effort. Two menservants took Lady Catherine from him, carried her off, Moyna following, dutiful, but casting him one backward glance as she went. He lifted a hand to silence the babble. "Listen, all of you—the chief is not harmed and he expects no violence, but I've a deal to tell you for all that. Let me tell it over a drink and a meal."

"Come into the hall," said Hugh tersely.

He had seldom been listened to so flatteringly. The food and drink warmed him to the tale, and he gave them all the details; they listened in silence save for an occasional question or exclamation, Hugh pacing up and down, the Donnellys grim and notionless, O'Hagan leaning forward intently, Ferdoragh stroking the hilt of his knife, McArdle grave as always. The only interruption came when Hugh struck his forehead and bellowed for guards, dispatched riders to Armagh. "No need for a letter—you, Fergus, to the Dean, and Conan to the chief justice. Tell them Rory McGuinness is here and they must come at once for discussion. Stay—another man, you—you know the house of Turlough Lynagh O'Neill, south? Just this side the border—give him the message also and tell him I bid him come at once, at once! Now go on, Rory."

Rory ended the tale temporarily with his departure from London; now was no time to intrude personal experiences on them. When he stopped, the three younger Donnellys and O'Hagan sprang up and began making impromptu plans to invade England. McArdle said, "That is a cunning woman." Hugh pressed the other four down to their chairs again.

"That little ruse of his we try first?" asked Edmund. "Is it enough to persuade them?"

"The first move," assented Hugh grimly. "If it proves insufficient, we will try something else."

"Did you have any trouble getting out of England?" asked O'Hagan of Rory, who laughed.

"The other way about—more trouble getting into Ireland," and he told them about Stukeley.

"Jesus and Mary"—Hugh was amused—"that renegade Sassenach! I know of him, yes, he has run arms to Shane from Europe. I've not thanked you, Rory. You've proved loyal and resourceful and served him well."

There was a chorus of assent to that; Rory was modest, and Dudley burst out with denunciation of Elizabeth. Hugh silenced him with a violent oath. "Cursing is no help and little satisfaction. We can make no serious discussion until those other three are here tomorrow. Meanwhile, the man wants a rest, on the run a week and more. Rory, anything in the house is yours," Rory was glad enough for the moment to get away and let them talk it over in private. But he did not go up at once to his chamber. Instead, he went to Lady Catherine's; she would be distraught, and it was only courtesy to set her mind at rest. Moyna opened the door to him.

"Oh, McGuinness—my lady just asked me to find you. You are kind to come of yourself." Her smile was surprised, warm. He was surprised himself how very good it was to see Moyna. A decent, pretty girl of his own blood after all those English, that was it. Her soft voice in their own tongue after the harsh English, that was all. If they had been private, he would have reached for her and would she come to him willing, eager, as she had once? He would find out soon. He was respectful on greeting Lady Catherine, and told her at once that the chief was safe, personally. She clung to Moyna's hand, listening, her eyes dark with distress. But as he talked, the color came back to her face and she gave a long sigh.

"It is only these treaties they want him to sign—he will come home safe, but perhaps not soon." And after a moment she smiled. "So he will not marry the queen. I am a little glad for that, though he hoped for it."

"You should rest, my lady. Are you cold? Another blanket—"

"No, no, I am quite all right." She sat up straighter. "Do not be silly,

Moyna, I have been quite well the whole time, you know." In spite of her awkward body, pregnancy became her, Rory thought. She was six months with child now—had Moyna said June? By appearances it would be a big one. "We must pray he will be brought home soon. You said there was a plan?"

"Yes, I don't know it but there is one."

"You must lie down and rest," said Moyna firmly. She shepherded Catherine over to the bed and Rory out of the chamber. She was a determined girl, even at eighteen. She followed him out and shut the door. "McGuinness, tell me the truth now. Were you trying to soften it for her? Is there danger to him?"

"Ah," said Rory, "another conquest for O'Neill! You're so anxious?"

"Men!" said Moyna. "I am anxious for her. Yes, she has been well enough, and she's very happy for the child, but it has been worrying for her. Would they dare harm him?"

"I doubt it, from all we can guess about their plans at present. It is those treaties they want. No, I believe he'll get home safe, soon or late."

Moyna bit her lip. "I hope it will be before her time."

Rory hesitated, feeling awkward. "Is there—that is—do the midwives expect difficulty? I don't know—"

"Oh, no, nothing like that, but she is twenty-three, you know, and it is a first child. Women should have the first young."

"See who's speaking." As he said it, he thought, faintly disturbed, that Moyna might be thinking to wed soon herself. It would be a little blacker sin to seduce wife than virgin. Damn, he would have her, he must.

"You are a meddlesome good-for-nothing," retorted Moyna, annoyed. "Also you are dying on your feet, the look of you. Get off to your bed."

"I'll do that," he said through a yawn, and then laughed. "You know, that woman, Elizabeth—a queer one she is. They call her the virgin queen—I am surer she is the latter than the former—but I tell you, when she rejects O'Neill she'll never marry at all. If she can resist O'Neill, she's not for any man's taking."

Moyna regarded him curiously. She said, "Well, there are women and women, McGuinness. Some of them are so peculiar as to love a man not for looks or rank or wealth or charm, but for no reason at all—and often they're sorry for it, but there it is. Now get off to bed and take some rest."

It was late the next afternoon, darkening to dusk, when the three men expected arrived within the same hour. Turlough Lynagh had farther to come, but the messenger reached him at dawn and he had set out at once. The Dean and old Fleming came ahead of him, but not by long. It was time for the evening meal, but Hugh settled them all in the council room and had the meal brought in there while Rory recited the tale again for the benefit of the Dean and Fleming; he could not include Turlough, who looked incapable of understanding a nursery tale. The Dean asked several questions; Fleming spoke no word, but sat staring down at his clasped hands. When Rory paused, he lifted his head and said thinly, expressionlessly, "You have done well, young man—my commendation."

"So they have him in a neat little trap," said Terence Daniel. "That canny woman! I'd have sworn— No violence, but he'll be kept in England until he signs those pacts. Could they actually prevent his leaving without force?"

"That's my thought," said Hugh, "and they cannot. But they needn't use force to keep him, to make the issue open. Easy enough to give out that he is ill, or some other excuse."

"He will never sign their treaties," said Dudley. "I know him—never!"

"If it proves the only way to get free, he may have to," said Hugh, "but we'll try a trick or two on them first." Rory sat back, hoping they would not ask him to leave; he wanted to know about this trick.

There was a stir, an apologetic rumble from the corner where Turlough Lynagh sat. "That first business as he instructed? If you forgive it, Hugh—"

"Well, you're not backing out now?"

"Indeed, no," said Turlough, horrified at the suggestion. "Very pleased I am to aid him—a good chief he is to me, and increased the dowries for my daughters, and gave back the land those bastardly Fitzgeralds stole. But a little idea occurred to me—"

"Yes, well, in a moment, Turlough. We must make some definite plans. Terence?"

The Dean was leaning back in his chair, stroking one soft white hand with the other. "We will produce a fine drama for them," he murmured. "A battle—there will be several battles. The greatest is nearby, and is taking place today. Hugh is leading half the army, and let us see—which are the traitors?—McArdle—O'Hagan—"

"And myself!" cried Ferdoragh gleefully.

"Very well, and the Donnellys stay by Hugh. This black traitor here" —he smiled at Turlough—"is claiming the chiefhood, and has strong support from the other half of the army. We want some trustworthy men to spread the news. You can choose them better than I, Hugh. Pick some to scatter south and tell the whole awful story."

"We have already had a half a dozen battles with the traitors," said Edmund. "We have the last today, you said?"

"Why not?" Hugh laughed. "Here they are attacking Benburb from the hills behind. We defend mightily, but at last Turlough prevails. He occupies the castle and hangs us all—a terrible destruction it is, two thousand dead and wounded. His men will be busy for days burying the corpses. He has proclaimed himself chief and announced if Shane ever dares challenge him there'll be a war the like of which Ulster never saw. A

fire-eater he is!" and he clapped Turlough on the shoulder. The big man
blinked and looked embarrassed.

"I am happy to be of assistance. But, Hugh, I had a notion what to do
next—" No one paid any attention to him and he subsided.

"They will have the news two or three days from now in the Pale,"
said Fleming thoughtfully. "Radcliffe will be greatly interested—he will
write to the ministers at once. All they know of Turlough Lynagh is that
he is Shane's blood-cousin; otherwise he is an unknown quantity to them.
They will applaud Shane's deposition in any case, and hope to win
Turlough over to them—so the next thing to do is show them definitely
that Turlough is no Anglophile."

"To make the devil they know seem preferable," grinned Edmund.
"A massed raid on the Pale?"

"Mhm, a bit indefinite," said the Dean.

"I had a little idea—" Turlough.

"Best let us make the planning, Turlough," said Hugh kindly. "At any
rate, once they know the usurper is against them, they'll be at sea. They
will say to themselves, O'Neill's rank is stolen, his army split in allegiance, his power ended once for all. What matter if he does not sign the
treaties? It is Turlough we must be rid of now! Let O'Neill come home
and busy himself at civil war with his cousin!" He chuckled. "Visions
they'll have of these two terrible warriors, like the Kilkenny cats, fighting
until they destroy each other. So—we'll hope and pray—they will let him
go."

"Yes—but, Hugh—"

"Well, well, what is it? I fear you're no strategist, Turlough."

"I acknowledge it," said Turlough humbly, "a man of peace I am entirely. I've no experience in such matters. But I would like to do something
to please Shane. The Sassenachs are so fond of Dungannon, always giving
him presents and money, urging him on to claim the chiefhood—I only
thought—" At inquiring looks, he turned red and fidgeted. "He would be
better dead."

"By Christ!" said Hugh, much struck. "That is a notion! Two blows
with one ax—we're rid of Dungannon and trick the English at once!"

"A good choice," approved McArdle.

"Indeed," seconded Edmund. "A quick attack, Hugh? Swoop down and
sack the place—"

"And let a number escape to tell the story. Let's see how it will go.
Today is Thursday. Better give this bastardly usurper a week to settle
himself at Benburb after today's battle! Say a week from today, then—all
mounted troops, six or eight hundred—"

"By night," prompted O'Hagan.

"Yes, I think so." Hugh was grinning delightedly. "It is but a short ride.
This, I am going to enjoy!"

It was a clear moonlit night; the troops made soft thunder in the half-dark. Hugh had come to watch the fun, though he could not go in with them, as supposedly he was at war with Turlough. Rory had come for the same reason, and would go in. He was riding with Hugh and Turlough; McArdle, Ferdoragh, and O'Hagan led the troops. Hugh was grumbling to himself in a low voice.

"My ax-arm aching for a fight and I must stay outside and watch! We are near enough, I think—yes, the crossroads, and a little lake round the next bend, and past it, Castle Dungannon. Call a halt." He spoke to the line leader, who relayed the command back; the troops slowed, came to a stand in the road, and the officers gathered at roadside round Hugh. "Cormac—Terence—Ferdoragh, now look, this is to be a quick affair. This hour the household should be at the meal. Make for the hall first. Aside from Dungannon, it is no matter if you kill many; let most get away to spread the news, but make a good drama of it—bloody and terrifying, you know—"

"Yes, yes, I know what we want."

"My Christ, I wish I might go in with you!"

Terence O'Hagan's deep laugh sounded. "It would never do for the chief's brother to be seen keeping company with the villain who steals the chiefhood."

Hugh turned to Turlough. "And I hope to God I am not sending the poor man to his death! Listen, Turlough, you must be the one to take Dungannon. One of the captains will point him out to you. Those in the house will be in no state to note details, but make as fierce an appearance as you can. Cormac, you'd best have a few men guard him in the fight."

"I will be all right," said Turlough unconvincingly.

Hugh grunted. "Have you ever killed a man, cousin?"

"Not that I recall," said Turlough apologetically, "but I do not like Dungannon. I'll take him."

"Mind, no hesitation—we want them to see you seven feet high and slicing heads at every blow! For God's love, man, try to look a bit more like a dangerous rebel war leader!"

Turlough said humbly, "I'll do my best, Hugh."

O'Hagan gave a command and the troops set off again at a walk. Hugh called after his cousin, "Turlough!"

"Yes?"

"Bring the head back to me. It's not that I mistrust you, but you are inexperienced—and I know your soft heart." As the first troops vanished in the dark, Hugh swore. "Or his soft head. This annoys me, Cormac. I've not seen a decent fight in a year and he is not going to enjoy it at all!"

As they dismounted in the yard and started for the house, McArdle reminded Turlough, "Don't forget to shout the clan-cry to let them know who you are," and that, at least, the big man could do, in a deep roar as they charged in. Hugh's prediction was right; the household was gathered for the meal, and most of them were trapped in the hall. It was a scene of loud confusion, men shouting, running, and fighting in surprise and fury, plates and cups from the tables flying, the hounds baying at the tops of their voices, overturned decanters making pools of wine and corpses pools of blood, the few who kept their heads defending with any weapon to hand, and a great noise of cursing in Gaelic and English—for Dungannon was entertaining some English friends, which added zest to the fight.

Dungannon was the first man dead; after that they only amused themselves a few minutes. McArdle was at Turlough's side, Rory behind—being one of those detailed to see he was not killed—as they entered the hall; and he shouted, pointing to the head of the table, "Him with the brown beard and pearls on his tunic—Dungannon!"

Turlough entered into the spirit of the affair, inexperienced as he was; he plunged up the hall, bellowing the clan-cry—"I am O'Neill! I am O'Neill!" He leaped the first table, seized Dungannon by his beard, pulled him up from where he sat petrified with surprise, and hauled off with his ax in an awkward blow that might have missed Dungannon and bit deep into his own left arm. But Rory and a couple of others dodged it and went in at Dungannon with their daggers. Dungannon staggered back with the impact, and Turlough's ax, with all his strength behind it, sliced off his head at one stroke—it could not have gone better if they had rehearsed it. Mindful to orders, Turlough retrieved the head and clung to it grimly.

Meanwhile, half the men of the house were hauling out weapons to make defense and the other half crawling under the tables to get out of danger. Some of the invaders tore down wall torches, set fire to the tapestries, brought one down blazing to fling it across the tables. Others made a tour of the ground floor in search of loot, and set alight anything that would burn. Soon enough defenders and invaders alike were more concerned with getting out of the inferno than killing one another.

When the long cry came to join retreat, Rory and the other guards hurried Turlough out, he still clutching Dungannon's head. Rory found his horse and stayed by Turlough as the troops scattered and made off at a gallop for the meeting-place, a forest clearing a couple of miles away. One of his companions shouted, "That went well—O'Neill will be pleased!" and Rory shouted and grinned in answer, and asked Turlough if he took any wound; but the big man seemed dazed.

They found Hugh waiting at the clearing; a half-hour's grace was given the troops to rest and have a drink and talk over the fight before they started home again.

"He did well, Hugh," said McArdle when he took his flask from his mouth. "The look of him, he put the fear of God in them." He offered the flask to Turlough.

"I brought the head," said Turlough in a strange voice. "I brought you the head, Hugh."

"Fine—fine, man." Hugh stretched out a hand. "Well, let go of it, dolt, let me see!" Turlough's fingers were tangled in the long brown hair. Hugh disengaged them and held the head up to the moonlight to study its features. "Yes, that is Dungannon," he affirmed in satisfaction. "Brian Kelly O'Neill, thou ingrate coward of an English-lover, may your soul burn in hell forever!" He made to toss the head away, stopped. "What shall we do with this, now? It seems a pity to throw away such a relic."

"Take it back to Benburb and spike it over the gate," suggested Mc-Ardle.

"Dungannon was not handsome in life and his head would make poor decoration," said Hugh. "He was not sufficiently important to have his head spiked over any gate. No, I tell you what we will do." He laughed. "We'll pack it up nice and neat and send it to Radcliffe with a letter from Turlough."

"My own darling man!" said O'Hagan approvingly. "That is the best idea you have had in a year."

Hugh swung the head back and forth by its hair, his eyes afire with inspired mischief. "The letter will say, My lord Sussex, herewith comes to you a gift from the new chief O'Neill, who—who—"

"Who wishes," put in McArdle helpfully, "that it had been yours originally—"

"And who will take steps in the future," continued O'Hagan, "to send that gift to your queen."

"Excellent!" said Hugh. "I want a volunteer rider to carry it to Dundalk and deliver it to the city commandant for Radcliffe. Turlough, do you not—Turlough!"

"Yes, Hugh?"

"What is the matter with you, man? Are you wounded?"

"No, I am fine. I was just thinking, it was a very short fight. Only into my stride I was. Hugh? I do not suppose there is any other Anglophile roundabout you would like taken off? It is a fine ax you gave me; I never thought an ax would be so easy to use! But I had the chance to use it only on Dungannon. A grand feeling it was, charging in there. I thought—well, there is the Maguire. He is Anglophile and lives not far off. We could—"

Hugh began to laugh with the others. Tears of mirth blinded him; he flung an arm about Turlough's shoulders. "Cousin, cousin dear! An O'Neill it is, after all!"

They rode back to Benburb and settled down to wait the news from England, that the English swallowed the tale and believed Shane O'Neill of no further importance. But they had no news of any kind for some weeks—not until Colm McCaffrey rode north from Dublin.

CHAPTER XVII

Dublin—Ulster, March 1562

THEY had been uneasy in Dublin, not knowing the truth of the rumors out of Ulster. Although Rebecca argued with him, fearful of danger if the tales about Turlough Lynagh were true, McCaffrey at last decided to ride north. After slipping across the border by dark, he went only as far as Armagh, to see the Dean and discover the truth for himself.

Daniel, knowing he was trustworthy, sent him on to Benburb to see Hugh O'Neill. There, McCaffrey met the archvillain, Turlough Lynagh, and could laugh with the captains over his former uneasiness. But he had nothing to tell them except that the ruse was believed by the deputies in the Pale.

"Did they swallow it, you ask?" He grinned. "Whole, O'Neill, whole! A good story it is. They were talking high when the news of usurpation first came, how this settled the matter once for all, no more trouble with O'Neill they'd have. Then you took off Dungannon, and they did not know what to think. By what he says, Radcliffe has got the very idea you meant—better to let the chief come home to waste his strength fighting his cousin than go on haggling over the treaty. But maybe the queen and her ministers are thinking different."

There was no way to know. They could only wait for news to drift out of England.

Dublin, April 1562

"I'll beg her pardon," said Radcliffe, "for aught I ever said of her. An astute woman—but then, she is a Tudor. That cold streak of shrewdness in all of them, maybe the Welsh blood—Celtic, after all. And with this new development, O'Neill is finished."

"I only hope," rejoined Sydney, "that we do not celebrate prematurely. Now there is this new chief, or so he names himself, to contend with. And the Dungannon affair—"

Radcliffe laughed contemptuously, pouring himself wine. "I have dealt with the Irish twenty years, my friend—I know them. They are like children—no perseverance in them. They are the greatest braggarts and liars, the most quarrelsome people on earth, and it is a fact they enjoy fighting kinsmen better than foreigners, being the savages they are. Always easy to disunite them. We need not trouble about this Turlough, once O'Neill is let free and returns to Ulster. The two of them will go to war and which- ever comes out the victor, both armies will be exhausted. I remind you, that great army we have lost sleep over this ten years is cut in half now, by all reports."

"Mhm—but by what Cecil writes—"

"Yes, and I cannot understand it. Surely the queen sees that to delay letting O'Neill out of England only gives this Turlough time to gather strength against us. She is bound to have that treaty. Still, the situation is immensely improved. I have said it before, I know the Celts—give them enough rope . . ."

London, April 1562

"My blunderers," said Elizabeth Tudor. She looked about the table at her ministers, but her smile held only a hint of contempt, for she was a woman and knew better than to show any man contempt—any man she might use. "You, at least, Sir William, should be aware it is seldom neces- sary to use a blunt sword where a bodkin will do the work. It was the first problem you presented me when I took my throne— O'Neill, this trouble- maker, this threat to peace—like a pack of children frightened by an ogre! And Radcliffe as bad as all of you together, trying to frighten me with re- ports of the Ulsterman's great army!" She lifted her shoulders in a light shrug.

They looked at her and at one another. Cecil said deferentially, but the faint rueful exasperation in his tone was clear, "If you had explained your intention, Your Majesty—"

"Oh, yes, you were quite anxious about that!" She raised her head and laughed. "He is what the Irish call a man and a half, is he not?—for women, if nothing else! Give me credit for more sense than to fall ro- mantic victim to such obvious masculinity! He was so confident he had only to reach out his hand and take Elizabeth of England! Mark, now. You gave me the facts— I saw the danger as clear as you. What did you all advise me to do about O'Neill? 'Bribe him,' said some. But he will not ac- cept bribes—too proud a man he is, and too wealthy to need them. Rad- cliffe said, 'Build an army to defeat him.' But how much gold would that take, to match the army he owned? You, Sir Francis, said, 'Assassinate him.' But assassins want high wages, and in fifteen years, how many have tried and failed, sent not only by us but by his other enemies? Hundreds! I give you a lesson in politics, gentlemen. I have captured O'Neill at the paltry cost of eight thousand pounds and a little prevarication."

Pembroke said, "And very nice too, gracious lady! Be sure we looked on with admiration. But—"

"But? I will finish him for all time. It is always easier to take advantage of an enemy's weakness. O'Neill's is his overweening pride. It made him believe every word I wrote and it brought him to my heel like a spaniel. I will not let him off the lead until he has signed that treaty."

Cecil cleared his throat, fidgeting with a pen. "If you forgive it, Your Majesty—I have had a letter from Radcliffe in Ireland. I think the treaty is no longer of first importance. That agreement naming Dungannon the heir to the Ulster princedom is naturally stalemated now. But since this kinsman usurps the chiefhood and apparently, in Radcliffe's opinion, would never be won over to deal with the Pale authorities in friendship, the sooner O'Neill is let to return, the sooner they will be at each other's throats and the Pale relieved of trouble from both."

"You have given me that argument before," said the queen. "My answer is the same. You may be right, but no caution is ever wasted and I am looking further ahead than next year or the year after. I will have that treaty signed. Perhaps O'Neill is finished because of this usurpation, perhaps not. What I am sure of is that once he signs a peace treaty with me, he is finished once for all. That treaty will turn all his allies against him, all our enemies that now are his friends, and he would never receive support from any of them. He will sign that treaty or he will stay in England the rest of his life."

Sir Francis Walsingham sighed and stirred. "I would not believe everything an Irishman says—I have too much experience with them. Politics is a chess game, with mate going to him who thinks most moves ahead. Your Gracious Majesty thought ahead of O'Neill once, but may I suggest that he might think ahead of you now? All we know of the present situation in Ulster is at second and third hand. And I remind you that there is no conception of honor in Celts. I think it not inconceivable that there may be a ruse practiced on us. Even if not, and if O'Neill signs the treaty, he may return to Ulster only to collect his army and make war on the Pale."

"You credit him—and the Irish—with too much shrewdness and too much temerity," said the queen. "Very well, say that he defeats this cousin and wins back his rank and possession, gathers his army. We have heard many reports of his strength—I discount the half. Any army of Englishmen is superior to another army twice its size. What you suggest is so narrow a chance, we may risk it."

"You do not think it would be politic," asked Cecil gloomily, "to afford Radcliffe some reinforcement? He asks more troops—"

"He is always asking more troops! To hold such a little portion, and against such little natives! No, I do not, Sir William. We shall see no more effective rebellion in Ireland for years to come, once I have dealt with O'Neill. All that remains, once he has signed the treaty, is to infiltrate Ulster with rumors against him, foment quarrels among his supporters. I will leave that to you, Sir Francis—you have a good grasp of such espionage." A complimentary smile. "Meanwhile, we give not an inch concerning that treaty, let him rave as he will!" She laughed. "This affair has amused me. A boastful savage like O'Neill, thinking to trick Elizabeth!"

Dublin, May 1562

Radcliffe had vague nightmare visions. One O'Neill or the other, he felt, would make him trouble whatever occurred. In early May the renegade Turlough Lynagh came down in force to raid the Pale, burned two country houses and a large section of planted fields. When he had finished cursing, Radcliffe wrote an urgent appeal to Sir William Cecil: "You must understand my position. I have the barest minimum of a command to maintain order here. It appears the military authority in England thinks the Pale only a convenient training ground for untried officers and recruits. Three-quarters of the men under me scarce know one end of a sword from the other. They have little chance to learn more, as my equipment is also disastrously low. For adequate defense of the Pale I must have more men, more experienced officers, more guns . . ."

Cecil had excuses and suggestions for him. "Her Majesty considers military expenditure for your command unnecessary at this present. Privately, I take your point, but I am powerless to aid you. It may be possible that you raise native troops by recruiting within the Pale . . ."

"Native troops!" said Radcliffe to the chancellor. "And what does Cecil think they are worth? To build an army on paper—a thousand footmen, a thousand troopmen—in the army lists it looks well and the queen is pleased. But in the first emergency, when we need those troops, what happens? They melt away overnight. I could recruit a thousand in the Pale tomorrow, Irish who would swear allegiance for the sixpence and uniform allotment, and the next day vanish. Native troops be damned!"

London, May 1562

"Undoubtedly," said Cecil to Walsingham, "he had arranged a code with his advisors in Ulster. You've not deciphered his letters?"

"I had men working at it, but it is of small importance."

"There was that third attendant who disappeared—it was given out that he left O'Neill's service. Which may have been true, of course."

Their voices were low on these asides before the real business of the day. The long chamber was chill despite the sun fingering in a high window. Pembroke, opposite, was listening to Bacon with an absent smile. "He should be coming soon—another hour wasted." Walsingham cast one glance at the chair heading the table where sat Elizabeth Tudor, silent, remote, erect, her gaze not on any of her ministers. He smiled under his hand; he said to Cecil, "It is a personal account between them, that is why she will never let him go without getting that treaty."

Cecil would have answered, also smiling, but at that moment the double doors at the far end of the room swung back. All the ministers looked up, but the queen sat motionless, her straight back to the door, and never turned as the Prince of Ulster entered the council room. They had met with him many times then, and as intelligent cynical Englishmen they knew that a man's worth is not always to be seen in outward features. But each of them privately knew a twinge of envy, hardly admitted, for this man as a man, for the size and color and strength of him. He was, to-day, all in dark saffron, and the inevitable jewels, finer than any the queen possessed, ablaze all over him. The silent clerk, self-effacing behind him, was a drab figure by comparison, even in the foreign kilt.

O'Neill strode up the length of the room to come round the table and take the chair set out for him at its foot, facing the queen over the polished oak. He stood, not deigning any inclination to her; his straight, lean, handsome features never changed expression on her; but the queen gave him a very small, amused smile.

Too often had they sat at this table to use formality. O'Neill drew out the chair, seated himself; the secretary stood behind. There was a general clearing of throats, resettling among the ministers, but the queen did not stir, or O'Neill. They faced each other like duelists, each waiting the first thrust.

Cecil placed a hand on the flat parchment page in the center of the table, the drawn treaty with the queen's even, tight signature at its bottom —that revealing script, penurious, but the capital letters pure arrogance— and the empty space below that. He said, "Again we meet with you, O'Neill, to offer you this written pact. It is to be hoped you are now willing to make discussion—"

"Discussion!" O'Neill's rough bass was unapologetic on interruption. "What discussion can I put my mind to at this time, when I am restrained here and a tyrant steals my rank in Ulster? All I can think of now is retribution on that man—this nonsense of treaties—"

"Her Majesty has no interest in Ulster," began Cecil.

"No, nor will she have!"

"Or in what you do there, but she is anxious to conclude a pact of friendship with your province, for the betterment of trade. If—"

"You talk and talk and say nothing!" said the chief passionately. "Long words you give me as excuses why I must remain. Discussion! Friendship! In plain language, you are keeping me here a prisoner! For the love of God, let me go—let me go to defend myself against this treachery!"

Walsingham said, "O'Neill imagines much that is not so. Prisoner? That is surely not the case. We are speaking here of this treaty . . ."

They had said it all before. They had heard before all he said in answer. They spoke and heard again now; and beyond their voices Elizabeth sat unmoving at the table head and spoke never a word. But when a little silence of defeat and suppressed anger fell about the table, she leaned a trifle forward. Her voice was quiet, but the words it uttered were small bits of ice dropped one by one.

"O'Neill, for five months my ministers and I have been urging this treaty on you, and for five months you refuse. You say we restrain you in England. I remind you that there has been no violence offered you. If you maintain there has, you lie. But this I have to say. Among us here, let us have it open. Very well, then, you are kept against your will. The hour you sign this document, you are free to leave. But until you sign, here you stay, and no argument or cajolery or threats will ever change my mind." One narrow white hand was twined in the pearls hung about her wide ruff. Now she pulled the strand tight, suggestive—a gallows' rope—and her eyes on him were hard as stones.

O'Neill looked at her; he looked at the ministers in turn: Cecil, his gaze fixed on the parchment; Bacon, smiling uncertainly at the queen; Walsingham, grave as a judge; Pembroke, staring into space, fidgeting with the ring on his finger. And again at Elizabeth, whose eyes had stayed on him. His mouth went taut, relaxed to grimness from fury. He said, cold and abrupt, "I reach the end of forbearance. I will sign."

In an instant the scene changed; warm cordiality surrounded him. The queen smiled; she leaned back in her chair. Cecil rose and carried the long parchment to the end of the table, laid it before O'Neill. Bacon came to his other side to offer a pen with a slight bow, and Walsingham brought forward the inkstand to convenient reach.

"Perhaps you would care to read over the document again—"

"I do not need to read it over," said the chief. He took the pen, thrust it impatiently into the well, and signed Elizabeth's treaty in his large, bold, black script running up crooked left to right. He stood as Cecil retrieved the document; the queen already had her hand out, and Cecil took the page to her at once.

"But O'Neill has signed only his one name here; it is not a legal signature," she said softly.

He faced her, standing; it was to be seen he leashed in rage; then he returned evenly, "That is my only name in law. Any man may be this O'Neill or that O'Neill. I am the chief, I am the O'Neill, and that is my legal signature."

The queen smiled. "O'Neill is in England and he will sign according to English law, with his full name."

A moment he looked at her. He turned and snatched up the pen; he took the parchment from Cecil, bent and scrawled his baptismal name ahead of the other. He flung the pen down to roll and drop, and none stirred to retrieve it. "There is your treaty. I wish you joy of it."

The queen took it from her minister, looked, and was satisfied. The little narrow smile might have been painted on her mouth. She said gently, "You have my leave to go."

CHAPTER XVIII

IN THE last week of May, Sorley Boy came to Benburb to see if they had news. In the absence of the chief, formality had somewhat declined at the castle, but as if the memory of his presence bade it, his captains took their appointed places at his table each night, his tall empty chair set out beside that of Lady Catherine; and of habit, Rory sat at his place behind. The Lady Catherine that evening sent word she would not join them at the meal. Sorley had spent the afternoon with her in her chamber, and he voiced his concern to Hugh.

"She is worried for him. Yes, yes, so are we all, but it is not so good for her in her state. I cannot understand this long delay."

But there was no more to be said about that than they had all said before; the talk was desultory, broken by uneasy silences.

They had lingered over liquor, and Hugh was just rising, the servants carrying off the other tables, when the hounds with the gate-guards set up a furious baying. The officers all listened, waiting tensely. The house door opened, shut with a crash, and the guards at the hall door started forward as it swung back. The man who caused all the excitement looked small and lonely between two guards in the doorway—a little flame-haired man with soulful brown eyes, in shabby garments. The captains made for him in a body.

"Thady—" Hugh reached him first. "You've news—"

O'Brien gave him the nobleman's salute respectfully, bowed to the others. "News I have, O'Neill. I did not stop in Armagh, I knew you must have it at once, you'll forgive me to come unexpected—"

Hugh shook him, terrier with rat, in his impatience. "For God's love, man, tell!"

"Yes, it is all right—the O'Neill is coming out of England." A long, concerted sigh from all who heard. "McCaffrey had it from his—Sydney's —woman; the deputies heard three days back. I am telling quick as I can! He is to leave London the twenty-second day of this month—that was two days ago—and likely land in Dublin the twenty-sixth or so. He—"

"God be thanked, God be thanked," said Hugh, echoed by many. "And you, Thady, to come so prompt—a hard ride you must have made of it. You'll be wanting food and drink." And he nodded at a listening servant, who hurried off. "Catherine must know at once—"

"I will tell her," and Sorley was out of the hall immediately.

"But—there's more—"

"Well?"

"He has signed that treaty with the queen. Very pleased they all are for it."

Hugh's mouth set grimly. "Has he now? I see—I see. An obstinate woman it is. The only way he could get free." He looked round at the officers. "Well, brothers, so the die is cast now. The hour he sets foot in Ulster we are at war."

For the first time in its history, Benburb was left virtually unguarded. A skeleton force remained there, and the rest of the army, with all the high officers, came south to camp in forest above Dundalk, waiting to welcome O'Neill when he crossed the border. They waited five days, and on the first day of June, he came.

They had men posted to watch the road, and when the party was sighted—the three mounted men ahead, the led horses, the foot-guards ranked behind—they went out to meet him. The army was all in straight ranks, the officers before each troop and line. Even old Liam Fleming had come, and the Dean, and the chief's three resident priests, and the castle musicians. The pipers blew bravely on the clan war march, the banners fluttered high. It was a scene of splendor to cheer him. But when the rider of the black horse sighted it, and flung up an arm and came on at a gallop, it all broke into confusion; they could not greet him so orderly. All the men broke ranks, a great roar went up from four thousand throats, and the army surged forth in a wave of laughing, shouting, weeping men. He was delivered safe out of the hands of the Sassenachs and they could not wait to reach him, touch him.

But he would not stop and make camp to tell them the story in detail. One arm round Turlough Lynagh, the other round Hugh, all the other captains and Sorley crowding close, he gave thanks for the welcome and in the same breath demanded to know what force was guarding Benburb. "But no matter—we must get on, we must get back and collect supplies and equipment! I will not waste an hour beginning this war!" That drew a growl of approval and anticipation. "Ah, they will regret they thought to take O'Neill! I will humble Elizabeth and England to the dust!" He ordered an immediate march north. He was looking well, if thinner and older.

They marched past darkness, made camp at last a long day's march from Benburb. O'Neill did not want to talk of his time in England; he was making plans for the war.

"Two days, that is sufficient—we come south again at once to attack,

at once! A lesson I will give them for all their insults." He named Manus
Donnelly to command the home guard to remain at Benburb, and Manus
howled protest but was forced to accept the order. "And Sorley, maybe
you would want to join the fun? Your army I do not need, but it will be a
war to enjoy—for us!"

"You never had an invitation quicker accepted," said Sorley promptly.
"I'll go on to Dunluce at once and collect my men. A pity to miss the
first attack, but we can join you in a week."

The Dean was seated on a boulder nearby, looking uncomfortable, a
civilized city man in the wilderness. "Ah—Shane. I would like to hear a
bit more about this treaty."

The chief looked at him quickly. "Are you saying I am wrong to make
war against a pact I have signed? It was signed under force, it is not legal!
Even you, cautious man, cannot expect me to swallow such insult—and
from a woman as well as a Sassenach!—with no thought of vengeance!"

"I have not said it," murmured the Dean, and added to his cup, "and
no good it would be if I did. No."

"Vengeance I will have, and a hundred times over. They thought to
give me a lesson in statesmanship, did they? Well, I will give them a
lesson in war."

He was up before any man in camp the next dawn, and stirred them to
form marching ranks before it was full light. By the falling dusk of that
day they were drawing up to the castle on the cliff.

If O'Neill had any fear in him, it was for an unmanly display of emotion. Rory thought he was not displeased that Lady Catherine came down
to the fore-passage to welcome him. He ignored the tearful servants
crowding up, the cavortings of his hounds, everything else, to make one
stride and clasp her in his arms. But he recollected himself immediately
and told her brusquely she should stay abovestairs this near her time.

The whole castle and the permanent army camp in the hills behind
became a scene of confusion as supplies were gathered, weapons sharpened, gun-horses and troop-horses brought up from pasture, all an army
in the fields must have collected: deerhide tents for the officers, cooking
pots, blankets, extra flasks, cloth for bandaging, gear for the horses, the
cannon carts, vast supplies of dried venison and beef, liquor in leather
flagons. The retinue of camp followers collected their own supplies and
made ready to trail after the army. There were two groups of women
—even in war women would be conventional: the respectable wives to the
soldiers, and the common harlots; in the field they kept apart in separate
camps. It caused much nuisance, Rory was to find—especially when a
husband strayed into the wrong camp. Father Brendan was an old man
and O'Neill would not have him make the campaign, but the two younger
priests would accompany the army.

O'Neill came to Benburb on the third of June, and announced that he would march south again on the fifth; and so he did, with three and a half thousand men behind him, all their battle equipment, and six guns which McArdle persuaded him to take. He refused to allow Turlough Lynagh to accompany them to war (although the big man pleaded to go); he said he owed his cousin something and would not see him butchered needlessly.

But as short a time as he remained at Benburb, something more happened while he was there.

The chief had little to do while his orders were carried out, nor had the captains. They held long discussions in the council room, but Rory suspected they were only talking and drinking, not planning the campaign—what was there to plan? They were only going to fall on the Sassenachs in force. Rory was hanging about the fore-passage that afternoon of the day before they were to march, hoping for a sight of Moyna; he had not seen her since they returned. Ena he had seen— "Be sure and take grand loot from them, McGuinness!"—and last year he would have laughed and kissed her, but for some reason he felt impatience with her now: a pleasant girl, but she had lost any glamour for him—he knew her too well. He did not really hope to meet Moyna, so busy with her lady, and he was surprised and pleased when he saw her descending the front stair, just as the chief and the captains came down the passage from the council room.

"Moyna—" But she paid no notice to him at all.

"O'Neill," she said hesitantly. "Your pardon—O'Neill—"

The chief halted and swung round impatiently, his hand on the door. "Well, what is it?"

She took a step down to the lowest tread. Rory thought, almost resentfully, she had no right to be so pretty when, for a maidservant, she was so haughty. But she was not looking haughty now; something had frightened her, he thought.

"I am sorry to trouble you, O'Neill. It is Lady Catherine—it is the child coming, and she is asking for you—"

"Somewhat early," said the chief noncommittally.

Moyna's hands twisted together; she came farther down toward him. "It is two weeks and more too soon—and many hours now, O'Neill! She would not have you disturbed for it, but still the child does not come, and she—they—the women, they think you would best come to her—"

"Nonsense!" said the chief. "What have I to do with it? It is Catherine's business, let her get on with it."

"Oh, but—O'Neill—she is weak now, and still it does not come, and she has been calling for you all the time, and then when the pain is not so bad she says not to trouble you, but—they said—perhaps—"

"Then why do you come troubling me?" he asked coldly. "A pack of frightened females! Catherine will be well enough, a good healthy woman to bear strong sons. It is a woman's duty in life, a thing they expect, a little pain in childbed. You should all know better than to summon me on such an occasion! A man is indecent to mingle with midwives!"

Hugh laid a hand on his arm. "Shane, you cannot make it right by saying so, if there is danger to her. Perhaps you had best—" He wore a troubled taut look. "Go to her, Shane!"

O'Neill threw off his hand. "You're an old woman yourself to believe a crowd of silly women! Catherine will be fine. I cannot drop all my responsibilities to run to a woman in childbed, it is absurd—I will hear no more of it!" He jerked open the door, and Moyna took another step toward him, hand out.

"Please, O'Neill—she has a bad time—and calling for you—if you would only come and let her see you, speak a word—"

"I will hear no more about it!" thundered the chief. "It is a woman's thing! Go away and cease nattering at me. It is indecent!"

"O'Neill—" But he strode out of the house, banging the door after him. The captains looked at one another uneasily. Hugh suddenly turned and went into the hall; they heard him pouring a cup full, and the others followed. Moyna pressed her lips together, stood a moment in indecision, turned, and ran up the stair. Rory ran after and caught her on the first landing. For the moment his lust for her was in abeyance. She was only a frightened girl. The whole household was fond of Lady Catherine, he no less than others.

"Moyna—" He took her arm. "Is it bad?" Women did die in childbed sometimes—not often, but this was a first child; they said there was danger with the first.

"Oh, McGuinness!" She leaned on his arm gratefully. "Yes, I—I am frightened for her! I wish they would let me in, but they—the midwives, the married women—they said I must stay outside because I am not wed, and it's silly—only fetching and carrying and asking how she does through a crack at the door! And she has cried out so!"

"Do you think—" Not the Lady Catherine!

"Oh, I don't know, but I wish—" She gave a little sob. "I should not be talking of it with you, but I wish he had come! I know it is not customary, but I think if she saw him—she loves him so much, and wants his child—" She stopped abruptly, clutching Rory's arm tighter.

They had come to the top of the stair and turned down the west corridor toward the chief's apartments and Lady Catherine's chamber. Unconsciously he listened for outcry, but there was only silence. When Moyna halted so suddenly he was startled, and then, following her eyes down the passage, nearly gasped himself.

Standing motionless at the closed door of the lady's chamber was the tall figure of the chief. He must have come by the rear stair at a run to be

here so quickly. A moment he stood there, one hand lifted tentatively
to the panel. Then he began to beat on it with both fists.

"Open—let me in! It is the chief—let me in!"

There was a scurry of feet inside; the bolt was drawn and the door
opened a thin crack. The pallid face of a middle-aged woman peered
out; Rory recognized her as wife to the officer McFee. "Oh, my lord
O'Neill—please not to make such a noise. You cannot come in now—"

"Before God!" roared the chief. "You send for me in all haste and
then refuse to admit me!"

"Please, my lord—the noise—you must not shout so—"

"Who says 'must' to O'Neill? Out of my way, woman!" He pushed
her aside roughly, shouldered into the room. "And my Christ, anyone
should know better than to bolt a door when a woman is in labor of a
child—of course it delays the process! Out of my way, all of you!"

"Oh—no," breathed Moyna at Rory's side. "Not like that! He should
not—" Through the half-open door Rory could see the foot of the great
bed, two or three women of the house. The first woman leaned on the
door, her hand still out as if to pull him back. "My lord O'Neill—"

And then the chief's voice again, loud and impatient. "Catherine!
Catherine! Listen to me! You are causing much annoyance by all this,
you understand? I will not have it! Catherine, open your eyes and look
at me! You are being a nuisance, making such disturbance in the house!"

A whisper from the woman at the door, "My lord O'Neill, I beg of
you—"

"Catherine, do you hear me? You are well and strong to bear children,
you are frightened for no reason! You will make the child come now, at
once, and it will be a fine, handsome son, and you will be recovered and
well afterward. I will not have it otherwise, do you hear? Catherine—"

"Oh, O'Neill, no, I beg—" Then, in a little silence, another voice, low
and weak but with still a hint of laughter in it.

"Yes, Shane—I will—try—" The woman at the door gave a wordless
moan and darted forward into the room. The sudden silence was tense,
frightening; Rory realized he was holding his breath. Moyna's fingers dug
into his arm. What was happening in that pool of silence in there?

Suddenly the chief appeared in the doorway. He blundered into the
doorpost and stood leaning against it, head bowed and shoulders sagging;
the hand he raised to wipe sweat from his forehead was shaking violently.
And with that, the little spell on Rory and Moyna was broken and impulsively both started forward. He heard their steps and straightened instantly. He gave them a defiant, haughty stare.

"Did I not say it would be all right? Women are always making a fuss
over nothing—another time I will remember it and not be so indulgent!"
He turned down the passage at a long stride, his carriage erect and proud.

And beyond the chamber door, his newborn son raised a rebellious wail to a world he found strange and cold.

That was a fine summer morning they set off for war, the dawn mist clearing to a blue sky and a warm sun. The army traveled in four sections, troops ahead, light foot-ranks and gallowglass after, then the guns and supply horses, and last, the women. The hounds, fifty of them, were with the foot-ranks, but O'Neill never trained hounds for fighting—he thought too highly of them; they were used only for carrying messages among officers in the field. The guns and heavy supply were brought down through the hills behind, the cliff path being too narrow.

Ferdoragh was grumbling to Rory as they formed loose ranks for the march. "These three years and more wasted—I should have had you trained as a useful troop leader."

"What are you meaning, wasted?" demanded Rory. "I am still the chief's bodyguard, mounted or afoot, war or peace, and my place with him."

Ferdoragh laughed. "Guarding O'Neill in battle, there is a jest for you." One of his junior officers, Diarmuid Ryan, who was by way of being a friend of Rory's, was riding at his other side. He laughed too, but said, "Don't listen to him, Rory! He's only wishing he had you in his command to swear at the way he does the rest of us."

"Do I need you to tell me! Never mind, uncle, there never was a McGuinness yet needed any training in how to fight." Rory grinned and rode on ahead along the troops to find the chief. O'Neill headed the army, with Dudley at his side. Hugh and Edmund were riding just behind and made room for Rory without demur.

Edmund was sniffing the air like a hound. "Good weather for war," he remarked. "At least the fogs are past—I don't like fighting in fog. I meant to ask, you saw the Lady Catherine? She's well?"

"Quite well, though weak, and very happy for the son," said Hugh. "A fine big one, and a double for Shane already—you should see. Shane has made a good jest over the name."

"What is it to be?" asked Rory, forestalling Donnelly.

Hugh laughed. "He has given the boy two names, mine and another. Hugh Gavelock."

"Hugh of the Chains?" repeated Edmund. "Oh, because of that absurd tale that he kept the lady chained in his dungeon! A jest indeed—" That rumor had probably been spread by Calvagh, in his disgruntlement as his wife's elopement.

"Catherine was amused. A good omen as we go to war. Not that we need good omens," added Hugh with a grin. "They've nothing to meet us with."

"It will be a good fight for all that," prophesied Edmund. "Once they're stirred up to fight, the English are stubborn warriors. They will give us a good war."

He was not wrong; that was a good war.

CHAPTER XIX

O'NEILL attacked the English Pale in the first week in June of 1562, nine years almost to the day since Radcliffe's own unprovoked and unsuccessful attack on Ulster of 1553. Both forces were better equipped than in that former war, but O'Neill's was still superior. The English military in the Pale numbered not quite three thousand, and half of those were recruits on their first duty, most of the junior officers and many of the seniors, city soldiers who had never smelled cannon smoke in their lives. But they stood; they stood firm, after the first surprise of the attack.

O'Neill attacked just west of Dundalk, and got ten miles inside the Pale before any large defending force was brought against him. But when it came, it stopped his advance dead and, when the whole English strength was out, pushed him back nearly to the border.

The subchiefs, O'Cahan, O'Dogherty, and O'Hanlon joined their men to O'Neill's, another five hundred altogether, and Sorley Boy came in with a thousand in the first fortnight of the war. That made the attacking army half again the size of the defenders', but they held stubbornly. Radcliffe had acquired seven cannon—French guns they were, the Ulstermen found on capturing one—and he used them a good deal. In all the encounters between O'Neill and Radcliffe at war, whatever the armies they led and whatever the terrain, their essential differences and individual geniuses were clear. O'Neill was a cavalryman; he relied on swiftness of attack, a changing pattern of battle, and the two traditional maneuvers of cavalry: using troops to circle at the flanks and close the enemy in, then sending the gallowglass to fight hand-to-hand while the troops held the enemy penned in with the axes. That was effective on English, for they had no weapon comparable to the deadly Irish ax.

Radcliffe, on the other hand, liked to draw a line, entrench his guns, and settle down to a steady pounding of the enemy line from a distance, making now and then a charge of troops to gain ground. And most of the Irish disliked that way of fighting. If a man must choose, Rory thought, any day he would sooner be hacked to death with axes than blown apart by gunfire. A man had the chance to hit back in a close fight, but there was no action to Radcliffe's sort of war. Small boys throwing stones at each other, as the chief described it, and he with the largest pile of stones winning the argument.

As men have different ways in war, each is master of his own. When O'Neill succeeded in chasing Radcliffe out from behind his guns and forcing a real battle, it usually ended in retreat by the English; when Radcliffe refused to be drawn and continued his cannonade, he inflicted more punishment on the Ulster army than in closer fight.

Not a week after the first attack, a diplomatic message came through the lines, a sternly formal communication from the chancellor, demanding to know why the Prince of Ulster so wantonly broke his peace agreement with England to attack the Pale. The chief, reading it, said with a laugh, "Cusack signed this but it is Radcliffe's composition. And it was written in almighty fear—"

"Of O'Neill." Sorley Boy nodded.

"No, not at all! In fear of seeming to fear O'Neill! He is at great pains to make it plain this is no plea for truce."

And that was understandable, taken unaware and poorly equipped as the English were. Rory made one in an army that fought Radcliffe's army in three wars, and by the army one knows a general. Thomas John Radcliffe, Earl of Sussex, was no rear-line general: he fought alongside his men and he was seldom caught napping. When the English were provoked to close fight Radcliffe was always to be seen in the vicinity of their standard-bearers, mounted on a tall gray horse, gesturing commands with his naked sword and often wearing bandages over wounds he had taken.

There was no point to arguing the causes of a war while it was fought; O'Neill did not trouble to outline his reasons for attack in a letter to the chancellor. He sent back the letter with the words scrawled across the margin in his own hand: "The Chancellor and all his associates are well aware it is not O'Neill who makes this war, but Elizabeth of England who played him false—ask her how high she rates her cleverness now, Radcliffe!" And that ended diplomatic exchange between them; they settled down to fight the war without needless talk.

O'Neill was hot for a fight and very bitter about the enemy's preference for long-range battle. "Guns!" he would ejaculate, staring at Radcliffe's line of cannon snugly entrenched across an open space of land from his camp. "My curse on the man who invented them! Sit and fire cannon from a mile away and call it a war—that is the English for you! Cold blood in them only." And that would start the argument again, McArdle and some of his artillery officers defending modern warfare. At times it seemed to Rory that they talked of little else that summer. They made numberless forays to drive the English out from behind their guns.

That first savage onslaught over the border the English surprisingly matched with a series of defensive charges which drove the Ulster army back. But having retaken that ground, Radcliffe made no attempt to follow up victory; he could not; he took too much loss in those charges. He concentrated on holding the Ulstermen where they were, desperately playing for time, pinning them down until reinforcement might reach him from England. At that, it must have been some satisfaction to his soul, when he had been asking reinforcement so long, to be able to say, "I told you so," to the ministers. He hung on, two incredible months, until the reinforcement came. Very cunningly he took advantage of the terrain, always choosing a rise of ground to line his cannon, deploying his troops nicely. Then O'Neill would charge his line, and the cannon fall silent as the English came out to meet him, and they had some hot fighting then. At no time in that summer did Radcliffe have more than two thousand men to send out; he had to hold some at the line to look to the cannon in the event they were overrun. But those fought well. They held desperately to every foot of ground. And when the Ulster army succeeded in routing them, they showed themselves disciplined troops, the men at the line working at top speed to move the guns from capture, and the rest fighting obstinately in retreat to gain time.

During those first two months O'Neill estimated that the English lost four or five hundred men dead, and again that number wounded seriously enough to be taken off the field. They also lost two of their guns. After capturing them, O'Neill would have overturned and left them, but McArdle prevailed on him to add them to his own cannon.

It was characteristic of O'Neill that he never minded reverses in battle; they stimulated him. Each time they routed the English, only to see them dig in their cannon and prepare for another contest of strength, he swore in pleased admiration. But sooner or later the numbers of English would dwindle too far to stand against him at all, for by the end of July he had more unexpected reinforcement to his own army.

One pleasant summer afternoon when the cannon smoke mingled with the heat haze over the hills, a large party of men was sighted approaching from the north. Alert for possible danger, the chief ordered up some troops to meet them, but as they drew near, Sorley Boy, shading his eyes with his hand to identify the banner they rode under, began to laugh. "It is safe, Shane—I might have known it! He would come on hands and knees if he must, to join a fight and have some war practice." It was the young Scot chieftain, MacArthur out of Antrim, who, on hearing of the war, had collected his three hundred men and marched south.

O'Neill told him, "I do not need any mercenaries," and MacArthur yelped in fury.

"Mercenaries! Do I want pay to fight Sassenachs? We came to share the fun with you if you can use us."

"I cannot," said O'Neill austerely. "This is my own fight, I will beat them myself. I'll have no Scots sharing this campaign."

"You have got Sorley with you," said MacArthur resentfully.

"That is a different thing, he is a close friend. I can invite friends to share entertainment, not so? But this is my fight and it will be my victory."

"You are a cursed selfish son of a whore," said MacArthur hotly, "and I demeaning myself to offer to join an Irish chief at all!"

"Scot bastard!" said O'Neill. "Go home and play with your toys, little man." And, knowing MacArthur, Sorley caught his arm as he reached for his dirk.

"Now peace, you two! Why can he not stay, Shane? Only three hundred men—"

"And every one of them worth three of yours!" said MacArthur.

In one of his lightning changes of mood, O'Neill threw back his head and laughed. "Very well, my young stallion! I'll be generous and let you stay. But under my orders!"

"Agreed—to fight English, I will even be subordinate to an Irishman," said MacArthur.

Rory took a few wounds in his first months' experience of war, but none serious. Situated as he was, he had more freedom in a fight than the regular officers or men. It was folly to speak of guarding the chief in battle, as Ferdoragh had said; a dozen men could not keep near him. He always rode into battle at the head of his troops, but in the press he was as likely to be one place as another, with the pipers and the captains looking about wildly for him, to take orders. Edmund said they might well adopt the English custom of having a standard-bearer with him, that the army might see where its general was at all times. But the chief seldom gave orders once a battle was joined, and few beforehand; his principal idea in war was to get in to the enemy and lay on the axes.

None of the captains or the chief took any significant wound in those months. The chances of a deep or mortal wound were not great in the kind of close fighting they had with the English. In a tight press of men, afoot or mounted, the worst wounds were from ax and dagger, admirable weapons for short-range use, and the English used neither. Their footmen were armed with two-edged broadswords, their troops with swords and lances. All a man need do to make a sword useless was get in close under it, to prevent its swing. The majority of O'Neill's casualties were from English gunfire. He had made the usual arrangements with nearby landholders and two monasteries, to receive his worst wounded; but few needed to be sent behind the lines. A man caught in gunfire was generally killed—which was one of the arguments McArdle put forward in defense of the big guns.

The arquebusiers of both armies were more evenly matched; O'Neill had five hundred troops armed with hand-guns; Radcliffe, by August, had a like number. But only at short range could the hand-guns be trusted for any accuracy; the only practical use for arquebusier troops was to have a hundred men fire in the same direction and hope for ten hits.

In August, Radcliffe had reinforcement from England: no more cannon, little equipment, but a thousand men, more or less. The battles went back and forth into November, the English holding stubbornly. In the close fights against the Ulster gallowglass the destruction they suffered was great. Generally they tried to carry off their wounded, but once or twice O'Neill overran the field so swiftly they were prevented; on one such occasion, the Ulster officers counted two hundred and thirty dead, and half again as many wounded who were unable to flee with the retreat. Not wanting to be burdened with prisoners, O'Neill let the English come and fetch them off, but the dead were a nuisance.

"Good Irish land burdened with Sassenach corpses!" he said after each battle, the burial detail going out to its dismal duty.

And Hugh with a grin: "Well, that is whyfor the English came to Ireland, is it not—for land!"

O'Neill had expected, with his greatly superior force, to overrun the English army in a month and bring them to plead for truce before they could have support from England. But Radcliffe hung on, and after his first replacement troops came, it developed into a longer and more boring war than any of the Ulstermen had expected. And O'Neill and Mac-Arthur, who had discovered friendship for each other, took turns complaining bitterly, "English, my Christ! Why do they not come out and fight like men?"

There were political overtones to this war, not that O'Neill cared for them now. The fact that he had signed a treaty with Elizabeth made him legally the aggressor. England's enemies, Spain and France and the Pope, cared little for the niceties of legal rights; they would be delighted to see a sound defeat administered to the English—in private. Openly Spain and France must use caution, and wait to see which way the Pope acted. That O'Neill had signed a treaty with England disturbed his former allies, as well as outlawing his legal pacts with them. They watched the war as spectators only.

When the war was four months old, O'Neill had a letter from His Holiness, chastising him severely for making alliance with a Protestant ruler. Apparently, the news of his war with England had not reached Rome when the letter was written. Relations between Ulster and Rome had not been warm the last year, owing to O'Neill's pressing demand that the See of Armagh be given to Terence Daniel. The Pope had taken his decision in this matter possibly in consequence of that.

O'Neill had no care for what the Pope said; he thought little of a de' Medici. But he dispatched letters to His Holiness and to his allies of last year, setting forth the circumstances in which he had signed the treaty and now gone to war. All that was of minor importance to him; he needed no reinforcement from abroad.

But he had confidently expected to defeat Radcliffe and be relaxing at Benburb for a little rest before the hunting season opened. Instead, on the first day of November, there he was, still in war camp nine miles southwest of Dundalk but not at war; the two armies sat in camp, only watching each other.

Before the autumn had much advanced it was evident the winter would be early and severe. By November, if they had driven the English out to fight, it was little fighting either could have done on slippery wet ground. The usual winter retirement was indicated, but Radcliffe cannily waited for O'Neill to make the first move. The chief cursed at the delay, but the war was at a standstill until the snows were past.

"There is no sense sitting here waiting for thaw," he pronounced with a shrug. "February, with luck, we can force some action." None of them was sorry for the necessity of a winter halt; it was boring work, lying in camp listening to the guns sound every few minutes. But the captains were surprised to learn he intended to leave no guard at all at the war line; ordinarily a nominal force would remain through the winter, those men being relieved at intervals. However, O'Neill ordered the entire army to prepare for march north.

"No guard at all?" exclaimed Hugh.

"Whyfor? Radcliffe is scarce planning to invade Ulster immediately! I have a little idea in my mind. Next season we will beat them well, I promise you—no more of this tiresome exchange of gunfire!" O'Neill held out his hand as a few flakes of snow fell. "Yes, it is senseless to stay here."

"And what is this little idea?" McArdle wanted to know.

The chief grinned round at them; contrarily, he was in excellent spirits. "I'll not say. You'll see it in operation—a surprise for you as well as the English!"

"But—just walk off and leave them here?"

O'Neill laughed contemptuously. "They will take the respite with prayers of gratitude. They will spend this winter desperately building an army to meet me in the spring. They will take the farmer from the field and the clerk from the desk to have a force to meet mine three months from now! Let them. In the next campaign I will defeat them utterly, it matters not how many they have. I promise you some good fighting."

So the entire army packed up supplies and withdrew north, doubtless to the surprise of Radcliffe and his instant suspicion of a trick. The English army lay there in camp, watching them go, and it was to be conjectured that Radcliffe waited a week before withdrawing to Dublin. He was a canny man, and knew O'Neill might plan to catch him disorganized in a final surprise attack.

CHAPTER XX

THE officers in general left the army harlots to the common soldiers. In consequence, after that long boring campaign, they were all hot for some love-making, Rory no less than the others. But he found that it left him vaguely dissatisfied. It was nothing in Ena or any of the other friendly girls at Benburb; perhaps he was growing old at twenty-four. For eight or nine years, like any man that age, he had taken easy women as available, and enjoyed them. It was not exactly that his taste was jaded, but—what? He did not know: only that Moyna, and his desire for her, plagued him even after a night with another woman.

How did he feel for Moyna? Only a slip of a maidservant, she had no right to disturb him so. He had seen her only once in the three days since they returned—Moyna, passing him in the corridor, stopping for a word, flashing him a smile. And that night he had no impulse to seek one of the free women; he only grunted when Diarmuid Ryan, who shared his chamber, announced that intention. The castle was a gay place these days, officers and their wives reunited, but he felt morose.

He waited for her the next midafternoon when he knew she would be free, the Lady Catherine resting. When she came out of the lady's chamber he was there to take her arm, draw her along the passage.

"Well, McGuinness it is—" with a sidelong smile. "I suppose you are wanting me to come a walk with you."

He laughed. "Not in such weather. Suspicious you sound—you've never a kind word for me, Moyna."

"And should I have? Where are you taking me now?" She tried to pull away, but he drew her with him into a chamber he knew was unoccupied, stopped her protests with his mouth, holding her tight. She struggled with him and then did not struggle; suddenly she was straining up to him desperately, and the excitement in him became exultation, and he did not stop with kissing her. She murmured more protest indistinctly, and then wrenched away and leaned on the shut door, gasping.

"You will not—no—I'll scream," she panted, "and you know the house rules—" He stopped where he was; he did know. But she did not run from him; she stood against the door, looking at him, slim and rounded in a green gown just the color of her eyes, and all that waving black hair loosened on her shoulders. "You will not," she said strangely.

"Now, girl, a minute ago it was you as well as me—" She had him hot for her now. "Let me show you now, let me—"

"Stay where you are!" She had one hand up to her heart. "You or any man will not send me the road my mother took! Are you thinking I am a silly woman like that Ena, never thinking for tomorrow?"

"Playing the prude, are you?" He knew better now, and reached for her confidently. She slapped his hand away, and something in her eyes made him pause.

"You not the only one saying that either, and all of us knowing it's not so. That's no matter. I might want to say yes to you now, this minute, McGuinness—you thought it out well, this chamber so convenient and a bolt on the door too! But I know what comes and does not come to women like that, and it's not a life I want. I stay a decent woman until I find a man to wed me proper—"

"Oh, I might have known!" He was defeated, and irritated at her. "Women all the same in that." He bit back more words; he was so inflamed for her, Christ, he almost made the offer. "If I said I would wed you, you'd turn and bolt that door yourself—"

"Maybe and maybe not," she said. "Is it an offer you make me?"

"My Christ, no!" said Rory.

"And just as well. For I'd not marry you, gentleman though you are. It's more than the vows and the ring and the marriage bed I'd have—but—"

"More?" he said, and laughed. "What more is there? Women!"

She jerked open the door. "Oh, you don't understand—maybe no man ever does, and I only a silly girl thinking it. Leave me go!" He had taken her arm again.

The lust died in him and he was ashamed. This was no way, crude as any lout of a peasant. "I ask pardon, Moyna. I should not have—"

She seemed not to hear; she ran down the passage away from him without another word.

When Rory left the hall that night Hugh's sweet tenor was rising soulfully above the harp on a love ballad. But he was feeling stale and gloomy, in no mood for either love songs or liquor. He went up to his chamber righteously early, and a manservant, just leaving it, saluted him.

"The Lady Catherine would speak with you in her chamber."

"Now?" asked Rory, surprised. Receiving an affirmative, he reflected uneasily that Moyna must have complained of him. He was a fool to feel disturbed for that: what did a woman's censure amount to? He was young then, so he thought, Nothing at all. He went into the west wing, along to the lady's chamber, tapped on the door. It was not Moyna who opened it to him, but another servantwoman, middle-aged, with a face like the side of a hatchet.

"You wished to see me, lady?"

Lady Catherine looked up. "Oh, Rory. I did, yes. Will you be seated?"

He sat down in the chair nearest the door, feeling uncomfortable. The middle-aged woman was evidently a nurse, and Lady Catherine was ensconced in a deep chair by the small hearth, several cushions at her back and a robe about her shoulders, nursing the infant. Rather surprisingly, the chief had said no other man should raise this son and the lady refused to have a wet-nurse, caring for the child herself. She paid no further notice to Rory for a bit, stroking the infant as it nursed; against the deep blue of her gown and bright crimson of the cushions, her breasts were very white and full and the child's hair shone deep auburn. The nurse looked Rory up and down and seemed to approve nothing about him.

"It is turned very cold," he said, "is it not?"

"Yes," said the lady.

"But then, of course, it is November." There did not seem to be anything more to say about the weather. For no reason he commenced to feel very nervous. "Er—the child does well? He is grown some?" He was not interested; it was a form of compliment to ask.

She murmured, "My small darling, the man cannot see how you have grown!" And she whispered endearing infant-talk, so that he was embarrassed. He felt unusually large and awkward, an intrusive male here. He looked about the room, and remembered what Hugh and others had been saying—how, if the O'Donnell were dead or a divorce could be got for her, the chief would wed the Lady Catherine tomorrow; he was regretting now he had not taken Calvagh O'Donnell's life when he had the chance.

Lady Catherine's was one of the largest chambers in the castle; it had formerly been part of the chief's apartments, and the inner door led to another chamber of like size, but not the chief's. There was the great bed in a little alcove, the hearth with two armchairs beside it, several deerskins spread on the stone floor, a lady's French dressing table with drawers and a mirror, no fewer than three carven chests. It was a palatially furnished room but not wholly a lady's. Incongruously, there were two war axes hung on one wall. Among the jars on the table was a man's gold armlet; one of the chests bore the O'Neill device, the Red Hand, carved in its top; and the chair opposite the lady's was built for a large man, the back tall, the legs high. This was a room shared by two people and that was odd; with a mistress one visited, not lived. And the odder thought came to him that this did not look like a chamber of a nobleman and his mistress; it looked like the chamber of a nobleman and his legal wife. He recalled his wits hastily; Lady Catherine was speaking.

"There, he is finished, my small love. You may take him, Shena—careful, do not wake him." She handed the child in its bundle of blankets to the nurse, who marched out with it stiffly. She settled back, fastening the gown across her breasts, and turned her attention to Rory. "I think you know why I have asked to speak with you. My maidservant, Moyna, tells me you offer insult to her."

"Well," said Rory. "Well, I asked her pardon." He looked at Lady Catherine boldly. Noblewoman or no, he thought, she was scarcely more than a girl, only his own age.

"That hardly excuses it. She is a respectable girl"—Rory repressed a retort; tell him that!—"and I always took you for a gentleman."

"Well, my Christ, so I am! I never meant any harm—" and that was a lie if he ever told one. "A pretty girl she is, but—"

"Only a maidservant?" said Lady Catherine gently. "To a true gentleman the rank makes no difference. Moyna has been with me five years, and no people she has of her own; she is under my care. I have hoped to arrange a suitable marriage for her. I'd remind you, Rory, how gossip goes—if it is said you have an eye to her and perhaps a little more, it would be difficult to find an honest husband for her."

"I never meant any harm," he said loudly. "What's a kiss or two, my lady?"

Lady Catherine was silent. At last she said, "I have great fondness for Moyna—we are friends. She was comfort to me in less happy days. She is asking something of life she will maybe never find—few of us do—but at least she has the courage to ask it. I'd not have her hurt."

"I don't mean to hurt her," said Rory, and that was nearly the first true word he spoke.

"I hope not. I have a match in mind for her, one of the home farmers. His first wife is dead and he desires another to help him on the land and give him sons. I have heard some rumor that the officer McFee offered you his eldest daughter?"

"Well, yes—some time since. No, she is not yet betrothed to any. I—do not choose to wed now, that is all."

"I see."

"Er—this man, a young man he is?"

"The farmer? Why, that is none of your affair, why do you ask? No, not precisely, if it is any matter. It is for myself and Moyna to decide."

"Of course, I ask pardon, I only—"

"I will not keep you," she said, smiling at him. "But I hope you'll remember, Rory, and not offend Moyna again. She is a good girl. She likes you, I think, and would not have spoken to me except that I discovered her still upset for it. I'd not like to speak to the chief about you."

Nor would he like it. He was respectful, and took his leave gladly. But as he went back toward his own chamber exasperation grew in him and he thought of all the subtle retorts he should have made her. A fine lady to be so nice for morals, she bearing a child to one man and wed to another!

She soon enough had forgotten all the grief she had suffered from two arranged marriages of her own, when she could consider marrying Moyna to a stolid middle-aged farmer. Wed to one like that, the girl would doubtless be fair game for any more personable man—say a tolerably good looking young McGuinness. But maybe she did not like red hair. . . . A farmer! And not precisely young, the lady said. Very probably he had a scraggly gray beard. And snored like an ancient hound.

It was none of his business. He came into his chamber and stumbled over a stool in the dark, swore and kicked it out of the way. The noise woke Diarmuid, who swore in turn and demanded, "Damn you, Rory, am I not entitled to my sleep, I spending the afternoon in Meriel's bed?"

"Do not dare mention women to me!" said Rory. "There is no sense or understanding or generosity in any single one of them!"

"Maybe not," said Diarmuid with a yawn, "but I like them."

Rory unclasped his belt, started to get out of his tunic. "Always the trouble and fuss over trifles! Nothing ever suits them, what is done or not done!" Probably that farmer kept hogs and never cleaned the stink of them from himself. And serve her right, turning down a young strong man—tolerably good looking.

"Mhmm," said Diarmuid, "but so nice and soft they are."

"Always such attention to the conventions!" said Rory, sitting on the bed to unlace his sandals. "I swear, if the angel Gabriel came down and offered a woman his gold crown, she would be putting up her nose at it because he did not bow when he offered it!" Very likely the man wanted a wife less than a farm laborer and would yoke her to a plow as some farmers did their wives. What Lady Catherine was thinking of—!

"Probably," agreed Diarmuid, "but such pleasant warm curves they have."

Rory kicked off his sandals, stood to unwind his kilt, and flung it over the stool. "Do you know what is the trouble with women? The easy ones are so Christ-damned easy, and the respectable ones are so Christ-damned respectable!"

Diarmuid laughed. "Go to bed, you've had too much of O'Neill's liquor."

It was the next evening at the table that the chief startled them with his new plan.

"We have some time on our hands," he said blandly. "I am going to build a new house."

They all stared at him. "In the middle of winter?" exclaimed Hugh.

"Why not? I'll set the army to work under the masons, it will keep the men out of mischief. The devil finds occupation for idleness," said the chief sententiously.

"But—a new house? Why and where? What will you use it for? I don't—"

"We will remove there as soon as it is finished. Yes, the whole household. We will," said the chief pleasurably, "abandon Benburb." He looked round at the dead silence, the chorus of loud protest that followed it, with a grin. Abandon Benburb! He had built it and lived in it as his personal stronghold for seventeen years.

"You've run mad," said Hugh.

"Bear with me! It is part of the plan for the English, brothers—you will see it as it happens. And enjoy your last day or so of rest. There will be plenty for you all to do!"

He was not jesting. Incredible as the scheme was, to build a house large enough for all his household and move into it in twelve or thirteen weeks, more incredibly he saw it accomplished. Short of carrying stone and mixing mortar, the officers all worked nearly as hard as the army and the master workmen brought from Armagh.

If he had set out to discover a place most difficult to erect a house, the captains said to one another in exasperation, he could not have succeeded better. The new house was built in the middle of the island in Lough Neagh, Eilean-na-Gearrssaich, the island of hares; and in the midst of the work they were forced to snare hares right and left to get them out of the way; the place was alive with them.

The house was principally of stone, and had no such fine finishing to it as Benburb, but was a solid, stout house. And that was not all they built, for the chief would also have shelters for the horses and the army on the main shore opposite, where were erected, as well, several jetties into the lake.

They made camp, and a cold one it was, on the shore of the lake, and the chief supervised the entire operation from start to finish, driving the men ruthlessly; they had to carry stone five miles in the end, to collect enough. Even the captains were beyond demanding answers to all their questions by then; the chief was always like a child for a secret, and would say only, "Wait and see!" On his orders, they stripped Benburb of everything movable, everything of any value. Lady Catherine, the infant, and her maidservants were quartered comfortably on the chief O'Hanlon while the removal was completed; every other occupant of Benburb—menservants, womenservants, officers, their wives, all the children small and large, the whole stable of horses, the whole kennel of hounds—came up to Lough Neagh and settled into the new house. It was the last day of January when Lady Catherine arrived with her retinue and the job was officially done— at the expense, as Hugh and others pointed out, of exhausting the army.

"How you expect them to keep strength for fighting the English next season, God alone knows," he told the chief.

O'Neill only laughed. "We'll have a good month or more to rest, I promise you. The roads will not be clear for marching another six weeks, if then."

"And what all this has to do with the campaign—"

"Wait and see!" said O'Neill for the hundredth time. "The one thing you have not asked, what will I name the house?"

"I cannot say I've the strength to be interested," said Hugh resignedly.

The chief cuffed him exuberantly on the shoulder. "Well, I will tell you, anyway. A fine appropriate name I give it—Fuagh-na'ngall—Hatred of the English!"

"May it stand long," said Hugh gloomily, drinking to it obediently along with the rest. "Though I doubt it, what the masons said of mortar put on in frost." It was not, certainly, the castle Benburb was.

O'Neill was unoffended at criticism. "No matter if it does or not. We may be here three months or so; after that, the house may fall in for all I care." And the captains groaned in concert.

"You expend all this labor—not to speak of what it costs in gold—for a house to live in three months? Mad you are." And O'Hagan shook his head.

"To beat the English as I will beat them this next campaign I would beggar myself. Which reminds me," said the chief thoughtfully, "I'd best send for Turlough. He can stay here throughout, just to be safe. Poor Turlough. Ruin the whole scheme it would, if Radcliffe found him at home and saw the sort of man he is."

They stared. "Radcliffe? But Turlough's house is nearby to Armagh," said Ferdoragh. "The English will never be in four days' march—"

"You think not?" said O'Neill. "Well, well, maybe not, but I'll take no chances."

The first week they occupied the new house, reinforcement for the army arrived. The old McGuinness sent a hundred men in charge of his two grandsons, Rory's brothers. Rory was pleased to see them again and hear news of home. His brother Fergus was fascinated by the guns and went to McArdle's command, to be one of the supervisors of McArdle's manufactory in the hills outside Armagh, where all the gunpowder for the army was produced.

The week after that the Scots rejoined them, Manus Donnelly riding out to intercept them at Benburb and bring them to the new house. To their astonished questions, the chief, much pleased at their mystification, refused to reply. "You will see," he repeated. "This will be a campaign to live in history forever. You are going to see the English"—he drew his knife mockingly across his bare throat—"annihilated!"

CHAPTER XXI

DAPHNE FLEMING had retired from the French Court to make her home in Ireland with her uncle. She brought in the tray to the hall, with the bottle of Jerez wine. Liam Fleming eyed her sardonically. "An honor, Terence. Served you are by a king's mistress, if a trifle long in the tooth."

His niece retorted, "Be quiet, old man! I must show proper respect for the church!"

Fleming chuckled. "If you were unhandsome as most churchmen, she would not trouble." Terence Daniel smiled at her, never averse to personal compliments.

"We will do without you, woman," said Fleming. She withdrew. The blue terrier drowsing by the fire woke and began to hunt fleas. Fleming added, "You were about to say?"

Daniel shrugged. "His Holiness is not too well pleased with either Shane or myself. I would like the See of Armagh, but not at the expense of Shane's excommunication. Which I have told him, but he has made up his mind I must have it. I don't wonder, privately, that His Holiness is incensed. Now"—he laughed—"Shane would have me press for an annulment for the Lady Catherine. The Pope would listen to almost any other man, and when her blood-uncle, Sorley Boy, cannot succeed in that endeavor—"

"Mhmm, yes. There are also the treaties. A bad business, a bad business—losing him allies. They would all have to be convinced and coaxed over again to make new pacts—and the de' Medici woman never would, though she hates England."

"Of course," said the Dean, "he is in no need of them at the moment. He is saying he will administer a great defeat to the English in the coming campaign."

Fleming poured more wine deliberately. "I should not take this," he said. "It is bad for my digestion." He sipped. "I am not thinking of this next campaign. I am thinking of five years from now, Terence. A bold man he will be, but at times shortsighted. Yes."

Dublin, February 1563

"I am not off to argue with you," said McCaffrey peaceably. "Give over, woman." He hugged Rebecca with one arm. She leaned against him a moment.

"You are too old to go soldiering."

"I am eight-and-thirty and there is pith in me still—as I trust you can testify! My brawn will be more useful behind an ax than opening doors for Sassenach gentry. And speaking of that—" The knocker banged on the door to punctuate his words. Rebecca whispered a curse in her own tongue, turned, and rustled into the parlor.

McCaffrey opened the door, bowed Radcliffe and Sydney into the parlor; he heard Rebecca being gracious. He waited at the far end of the passage, saw her come out and down the passage to the door of the next chamber. Quietly he came down to join her. When he kissed her it was not in passion, but in comfort and, oddly, friendliness; in this time he had come to know her for a courageous and lonely woman. Hebrew she might be, and Italian at that, but the same way she had of his own race, making little jests to cover fear and loneliness and sorrow.

She put her arms about him there in the dark. "Ah, Colm," she whispered, "I do not want you to go and be killed."

"There, woman." He patted her clumsily. They stood unspeaking, and the voices of the deputies came clear from beyond the hidden door.

"So that is the situation," said Radcliffe. "Excuses! I can give the queen a dozen excuses why it is almost inevitable we lose this fight—but for all that, by God, I will do my utmost to see we do not! The question of ammunition alone—it must all be sent from England, and there is too little, too slow, coming in. Where does he have his? I wish I knew."

"How long can we hold?" Sydney's voice was grim.

"Hold?" Radcliffe barked a short laugh. "We will hold until hell freezes! I will not be beaten by this wild Gael savage short of death. But you might get down on your knees, Harry, and give thanks that winter set in early. We have had a longer respite than I hoped. But by March at least the roads will be passable, and we must be on the alert for renewed attack. God, the heavens seem to conspire against us—I had a piece of news today—"

"Not more bad, I trust?"

"Those cannon I was expecting in—two heavy guns—little enough, but God knows I could use them. They were on a ship taken by pirates in the channel a week ago. And, if you please, the pirateer was the *White Dove,* Stukeley's ship—the bastard! I wager you he sells those cannon to O'Neill at a long price—O'Neill would take them only to keep them from us! That has a reason near forty years old. Tom Stukeley is bastard to the old king and jealous as the devil of the queen's legitimacy."

Sydney said, "We have a stronger force now than three months back. If—"

"I mean to use it. I will march early to give him no chance to invade past the border again. Oh, God, will I never be done with trouble from O'Neill! I never thought I was that great a fool—nor William Cecil either, for that matter! The Irish I should know after more than twenty years. Preening ourselves that we finished him with a signature on a piece of parchment!"

"We could not guess he would so wantonly break his word."

Radcliffe drank, leaned forward. "I asked to meet with you here tonight because the chancellor still refuses to sanction it. Statesmen, like women, are fools to remain perfectly honest. I have a force to meet O'Neill, but not to equal his. He may have six thousand men. But remove O'Neill and the whole army falls to pieces."

"Another assassin?" Sydney was troubled. "I don't know . . . I don't know."

McCaffrey listened, heard the name, the plan. He met Thady O'Brien the next afternoon, at a disreputable tavern; over liquor he told the information. "But no need to send it in a letter. I am going north myself tomorrow."

"Oh?" said Thady.

"To join his army. Laugh, would you? Look at all this muscle wasted on serving English! Provoking it was, hearing the guns when the wind was right."

Thady grinned and agreed. "You think the prince will take a southron?"

"He will take me. Thady, man—it's the woman I mislike to leave," he said awkwardly. "You'll be trusty for her? She will have information now and then. You are to go to the house once a week or so."

"I will," agreed Thady noncommittally.

"A queer thing it sounds to say—but she is a good woman. Ah, she may earn her living as what they call courtesan, but—a woman who is what a woman should be, warm-hearted and generous, that is a good woman. And such a talker she is," he added ruefully, "it is a wonder she does not give herself away before now. You'll see none but yourself know of her."

"I will." Thady finished his drink and looked thoughtfully at the empty cup. "Would you like to be carrying a gift to O'Neill, Colm?"

McCaffrey laughed. "It's not much I could give such a wealthy prince—"

"I promise you he'll be pleased with this. Did you come along England Street by the cathedral? Well, come with me now." He led McCaffrey out, along the gray wet narrow twisty streets of Dublin toward the English cathedral in the square, opposite the warren of English government offices. "They put it up only yesterday. I thought maybe you'd not see it."

"What?"

"Look," said Thady, and gestured.

At the corner of the church wall facing on this street seven or eight people had collected in a little crowd to stare at something fastened on the wall. An English soldier in the uniform of the light foot-ranks stood there, stiff and straight. "He is there to read it to them," said Thady, "when he has a large enough crowd or someone asks. I heard him, but I got an educated friend to confirm it—who knows when a Sassenach is speaking the truth? The jest is, probably he cannot read himself and has only memorized it."

There was a large square public notice fastened on the face of the wall. As short a time as it had been there, rain had stained it in dark streaks, but the crudely printed black letters stood out boldly. McCaffrey read it between amusement and excitement.

REWARD!
to enny laying information leading to
the capture of
JOHN ONEALE
100 crowns of gold
to enny delivering up the seevered heed of
the sayme
JOHN ONEALE
10,000 pounds of gold!*
TAKE NOTISE!

"My Christ," said McCaffrey, "I must take it to him! Would he not be pleased! That is a sum of money."

"I can help you get it down," offered Thady. "The soldier goes off duty at dusk."

"No need—I'll get it," said McCaffrey, still chuckling.

He left Dublin before dawn the next morning. Rebecca came down through the sleeping house with him, and she made her little jests—how surely he would never be able to ride the whole day after this pleasant night—telling him to fight well for O'Neill. And then, at the last minute, there in the cold dark passage, she gave a little sob and clutched him tightly. "Oh, I am silly, but I do not like farewells—not at all! In this life, who is to say when they are not forever? Colm—"

"There, woman."

"Get off quick now, pay no attention to me, I am foolish. Colm, do you take this—" She pulled off one of her rings, pressed it into his hand. "A bloodstone is a good talisman, it will protect you. Nonsense, it is worth nothing, take it!" She stood on tiptoe to return his kiss; her hands were cold and soft, clinging. "A woman like me, no man of my own I

---

* Approximately $50,000; the largest reward the Crown has offered before or since for any wanted man.

have, so all of you belong to me, all you stupid strong men that will be forever going away to fight your foolish wars! God go with you—yours and mine—and keep you safe."

He rode through the empty dark streets, a little sad. When he came along by the cathedral the square was deserted, and he climbed up on the wall to get the notice down, rolled it carefully in an extra tunic for protection. He kept feeling dispirited to leave the woman, until he got out of the city on the north road for Ulster, when his mood lifted a little. He commenced to think with pleasure of the events ahead of him and flexed his ax-hand in anticipation; he thought how pleased the O'Neill would be for the fine gift he brought him.

London, March 1563

"How dare he!" said Elizabeth Tudor. Her ministers looked at one another resignedly. It was what she had been saying for seven months. "To defy me—how dare he!"

"If Your Majesty would care to see it, I have a letter from Radcliffe—"

She whirled on Cecil. "Do I need to read it? How dare Radcliffe either, forever asking more guns, more men! Does he think England grows gold in her fields? He has the largest army ever in Ireland these forty years! To fight this barbarian, these little rebels—I cannot understand how he could fail—"

Cecil interrupted her, his deference gone thin. "Radcliffe is a more than capable general, Your Majesty. Providence usually favors the general with the larger army, which O'Neill has."

"That I have heard before, too. You know the situation as well as I, my friend. We cannot afford to send more support. We have very near stripped England now. Trouble, forever trouble in Ireland! What use to us as a colony is it? Costing twice as much to keep as we take from it!"

"You are not the first to say it," said Sir Francis Walsingham softly to his clasped hands. "Will the Tudor abandon what the Plantagenet took?"

Elizabeth's mouth drew to a thin straight line. "What England takes she holds—against a hundred O'Neills. Some man may desire that reward strongly enough to try for it."

Cecil sighed. "There have been many attempted assassinations. None has been successful yet."

A brief gloomy silence fell. The queen said in a hard voice, "It may be five years or fifty, but I will see O'Neill dead and done. I swear it by my mother's name."

CHAPTER XXII

O'NEILL was enormously pleased with McCaffrey's gift. He caused it to be hung above the hearth in the hall. Later, when they removed to Benburb, he brought it there to grace the same position, and it hung there the rest of his life, the piece of decoration he was proudest of and never failed to point out to visitors.

"She knows her mistake now! Ten thousand—she would have to pawn her jewels to pay it, and would she not do so gladly!"

"Let us trust the occasion will not arise," said Hugh.

"I do not think it! Ten thousand, is that all they think I am worth? Another little insult at that! A decent sum, but not for O'Neill alive or dead!" He laughed. "Well, among us I admit it—if my visit to England accomplished nothing else, it added to my education about women. Only two important interests to life for reasonable men—women and war. So now I will add to her education in the latter. And Radcliffe's, yes." He and the captains had been amused as well by McCaffrey's pilgrimage to join the army; he assigned him to the gallowglass under Terence O'Hagan. "But I trust Thady O'Brien will continue to get information out."

"Oh, Thady is a good man, he will do that, O'Neill," McCaffrey assured him. "He is nosing about now, trying to find the exact English strength."

"That I've no care for. All I want to know is when Radcliffe marches."

"We cannot wait for news of that," objected Edmund Donnelly when McCaffrey, expressing gratitude, had been led off by the constable, McSweeney, to start on his new duties. The captains had been pressing O'Neill for definite marching orders, and he put them off without explanation; he was still cherishing his plan for the campaign. "It is decent fighting weather now."

"It is," agreed the chief. "They will march this week or next."

"Exactly. We should be starting south to make another invasion past the border," said O'Hagan energetically.

O'Neill leaned back, yawning. "Should we? That is what Radcliffe would expect me to do."

Sorley Boy looked around the group of captains. "Has he been long in this mood?"

"Since you last saw us," said Hugh with a groan.

Fortunately for all tempers, they had not long to wait, for the second day after that a man came from Armagh on a lathered horse: the agent of the Dean, bringing news that the English marched. Thady O'Brien had sent a rider from Dublin the same day Radcliffe led his army out. The English had marched from Dublin on the first day of March, and this was the third. All the officers paid O'Neill back in his own coin by repeating, "I told you so!"

"We should have gone south two weeks ago," said Hugh violently, "as soon as the roads were clear. We can never beat him to the border now! All the advantage we have lost—"

"We can meet him as far south as possible," broke in Edmund, "if we get off today."

"Christ, he will be at the border now, even with footmen—" O'Hagan.

"Peace," said O'Neill, grinning. "So you all think I am going senile? When have I ever lost a fight?"

"My Christ, you cannot mean we do not march?" Ferdoragh was almost tearful.

O'Neill laughed. "Oh, yes, we will march. Today or tomorrow, little difference." And he added gently, "North." In the midst of dead silence every man stared at him and his smile broadened. "Look, my doubters, trust me. I have every move of this planned—I know just how it will go. For now, all you need to know is that we are going north, and split the army into groups to lie hidden in forest."

"But Radcliffe—the English—they will—"

"We may have to use a little patience." O'Neill sprawled back in his chair luxuriously, cup in hand. "Radcliffe is a cautious man. But sooner or later he will walk into the trap. He cannot resist it."

He had indeed planned well. He sent a dozen men to watch the English on their way north, so he knew from day to day where they were, what Radcliffe was doing. His own army and those of the Scots he split into small groups in scattered camps west and north of Lough Neagh, and permitted no camp-followers on this campaign to hamper swift movement, nor did he take any cannon. For ten days the captains pleaded to go south at least to the border of Ulster.

"I see you mean to make a trap," said Hugh, "but you cannot be thinking to let them cross the border! They are up to the river now!"

"Wait," said the chief.

Radcliffe came to the border of Ulster on the twelfth day of March. He must by then have been very curious that he had come this far without meeting opposition.

"I know what is in his mind," said O'Neill. "When I began this war, they believed my cousin, Turlough, was splitting the clan against me.

Then I came down on them and they knew it was a trick. Now Radcliffe is wondering if it was a trick after all. He has no reliable information out of Ulster, and he is thinking perhaps through this winter I have been deposed or assassinated."

"Are you going to let him cross the border?" asked McArdle uneasily.

"At his own convenience."

Radcliffe hesitated there a full week. He waited and watched, but all he saw was farmers and villagers going about their business. On the eighteenth day of March, the English crossed into Ulster.

"But it is mad! Shane, you must—"

"We are near the beginning of it now," promised O'Neill. "Look, fainthearts. Do you see now why I built a new house? Presently the English will come to Benburb. How do they find it? Abandoned! At once, up goes their spirit! Surely O'Neill is dead, his castle stripped, his army scattered!"

"Elaborate lengths to go for a trap," grumbled Hugh. "My Christ, we are giving them Ulster!"

O'Neill laughed. "A little present for good behavior! They will not hold it long. Wait—"

"And see," groaned all his men together, and he laughed again.

When Radcliffe reached the city of Armagh and still met no defending force, he evidently decided it was time to take advantage of this extraordinary situation. As O'Neill had prophesied, he was much stronger than he had been last year—he had received reinforcement from England during the respite of the winter. He had four thousand men, twelve heavy cannon and fourteen light, another five hundred arquebusiers. He now proceeded, and it was a foolish but a natural thing for him to do, to separate some seven hundred men from his force to occupy Armagh and hold it in the name of the Crown. He set up two guns in the central square and called on the chief justice, the Dean, and other civic leaders to capitulate formally. They all gave in meekly enough.

"My Terence," said O'Neill affectionately. "A persuasive liar he is, as a churchman must be. He is telling Radcliffe how I am assassinated by hired ruffians sent by my villainous cousin, Turlough."

"Will they believe it?" doubted James Donnelly.

"They will, when they see Benburb."

On the twenty-ninth of the month the English army came to Benburb, which they explored thoroughly. What else would Radcliffe think, finding that great castle abandoned, but that what the Dean and Fleming had told him was true? He marched on at a brisker rate, obviously more confident.

"He is led by a vision," said O'Neill. "If this terrible Turlough is Ulster's new ruler, there has been no sign of him as yet. Possession is

nine points of the law. Radcliffe thinks to separate his forces and leave
guarding troops at all strategic points."

"That is the plan?" asked Sorley. "To wait until the army is split?"

"Then we should have to separate too, and it would be a dozen small
fights instead of one big fight. No." The chief smiled. "No."

The day after that, from a vantage point in wooded hills, they saw
Radcliffe's army marching up this north road. There were advance
scouts to fore and flank, but this was the Ulstermen's own country and
they knew how to keep hidden—the English saw nothing but open land
and farms. It was a brave show they made, the standards carried
high, the general ahead on a tall bay horse whose trappings gleamed in
the watery sunlight. Wending up the road with the cannon moving behind, they would take an hour to pass one place.

O'Neill was crouched in the bracken on the hillside with most of the
captains. Those who were not swearing in low voices wore grim expressions; it was no pleasant sight, an English army moving unopposed
through Ulster. But O'Neill was smiling.

" '. . . and terrible as an army with banners,' " he said softly. "I seem
to remember that is in religious scripture somewhere. So now he is in the
trap. Now we are behind him."

All the captains asked at once, eager, "Attack?"

"Attack," confirmed the chief. "Wait, my hotheads! Listen. By dusk
they will camp, five or six miles on from here. We fall on them by dawn
from the west and east flanks. They will be"—he grinned—"shall we say, a
little surprised? But they will fight well. Soon or late they will break,
because we are the heavier force. When that happens, we will drive
them north—"

"North!"

"That is the direction they evidently desire to go," said O'Neill
amusedly. "We will keep them turned north and northwest, and they
will make stands and give battle all the way, but we will never let them
turn. We will harry them up to the border of Tyrconnell, and there we
will have one great battle, because Radcliffe will know, if he dares cross,
that red villain Hugh Ruadh will be on him like a thunderbolt for invasion, and, caught between the two of us, he would be finished. He will
make a desperate stand and try to break south—and we'll be kind to him,
and let him through, after inflicting as much injury as possible. But we'll
not let him go southeast, we chivvy him direct south to miss his supply
troops. If any of that great army gets back to the border of the Pale, it
will be in no condition to make much defense."

"My own man," said O'Hagan warmly. "A pleasure it is to fight under
you."

"And whyfor could we not be told all this in advance?" demanded

McArdle, and then shrugged and laughed. "A scheme indeed! Almost I feel sorry for the man, the shock he is going to get!"

The first attack, as ordered, came at dawn. The English were taken entirely by surprise, and, half of them being still rolled in their blankets, it was butchery for the first few minutes until they were organized. The test of an army is how well it fights against odds, and the English always gave a good account of themselves in that sort of fight, being stubborn men. They made a good battle of it and did not break until midmorning. When they showed signs of withdrawal, O'Neill bore heavily on their southern flank to drive the retreat north, and in that direction it went.

They retreated in fairly good order, taking all their cannon ahead and forced to leave only minor equipment; they also carried their wounded.

"Not for long," prophesied O'Neill grimly.

He chased after, harrying them every step of the way, and, being unburdened with guns, he could move faster. The English whipped up the gun-horses unmercifully, but cannon could be pulled only so fast, and at dusk of that day the Ulster army had already passed two poor beasts cut out of harness and left to founder by the way, having given all their strength. O'Neill never let the English stop that night or all next day, pressing after them so close that his lead troops at times could hear the voices of the English vanguard. He could have caught them up, but that he did not intend, only to keep them from rest or from slipping away east or west.

Radcliffe saw the trap he was in; there was nothing in this world he could do about it. He must have wished desperately for those seven hundred men he had left in Armagh. (But he should have known the Celts better, and had less contempt for them. There were seventeen hundred people in Armagh, and none of them particularly liked Sassenachs; a week after the rest of the English marched out, not one of those English guards was left alive.)

The English stopped and gave battle a dozen times on the way toward Tyrconnell. Their losses were fearful: the foot-ranks were cut to pieces by O'Neill's gallowglass. Battle by battle, each ending in their retreat to the northwest, they left the land strewn with abandoned equipment and their dead. It began with more foundered gun-horses—Radcliffe would sooner lose a division of foot than one cannon—then they were forced to leave blankets, many field utensils, more tents. And they had other dangers to cope with than battles. The English regular soldiers were not accustomed to the harsher Irish climate this far north; they were incurably addicted to a diet of preserved beef and beer, and not unnaturally, about this time, a virulent plague of dysentery spread through the army, so that Radcliffe was burdened with sick as well as wounded. Also, their supplies were dwindling, and the supply train, cut off by two days' march when

O'Neill brought his first attack, was out of reach, sixty miles southeast. O'Neill gave them no time to forage for food; all they could do was fight and run and fight again.

At the end of a week Radcliffe abandoned one of his light cannon— the off rear wheel of the wagon had split away from its iron shoe and would need time to repair. They made another stand the morning after that, and for the first time Radcliffe retreated and left his wounded on the field. The Ulstermen never went near them; perhaps the country folk nearby would care for them, perhaps not. And five miles on, the Ulster army came to one of the heavy English guns bogged down in a mudhole.

"Oh, do they not know now!" said O'Neill. "Elizabeth and her clever little ministers and this canny general who should have known better in the first place, and he tasting defeat at my hands once before! They know better now than to bait O'Neill! Let us drive the lesson home."

As Radcliffe drew near the border of Tyrconnell, he slowed as much as he dared and gave more stubborn battle, seeking desperately, by a number of ruses, to break through or slip round and turn back southeast. He knew well enough what danger he would risk by going on into Tyrconnell. Red Hugh O'Donnell, nominal ruler there because Calvagh, the chief, was a broken old man after his brush with O'Neill of three years ago, was no Sassenach-lover; he had a thousand or more men, and would rush to repel invasion. So it was by the border of Tyrconnell they had the most savage engagement with the English, who fought like madmen, determined not to be driven farther north. All the way Radcliffe had never been able to use his guns—he had no time to line them; they were only a burden to the army. He tried to use them now, but he had not enough men to fight a battle and entrench twenty cannon at the same time, and he lost eight guns overrun by charges. The battle went on for six hours without pause, and for three of them the English were beaten as soundly as an army could be, but they would not give in. Toward the end they trampled their own dead and wounded as they fought.

But this was the time to let them turn. When the first wavering of the English line came, O'Neill's pipers blared out the command to open ranks, and by a seeming accident of battle order, the gallowglass fell apart to each flank for one moment. Radcliffe, seeing the answer to his prayer, seized his chance with cool promptness. He sent in his heaviest troops to that thin place in the Ulster flank and hammered his way through, the Ulstermen putting up just enough resistance to make him think he won against odds. The English broke at once into full retreat south. They had to leave all but six of their guns, which must have been a blow to Radcliffe's soul—he had been begging for those guns ten years, and now had never the chance to use them. Also, they left their dead and most of their wounded.

"Let us get our breaths after that fight," said O'Neill, "and then play sheep dogs again." That was the word for it; they ran the English like dogs with sheep, strung out north and east of them to keep them headed due south for Leinster. They gave them little time to eat or sleep in a week, and were not so fresh themselves at the end of it.

It was a sorry-looking army that fled from O'Neill, a limping, bloody, hungry, sick army without supplies, without blankets or bandages, hauling its wounded along anyhow on litters and the gun-wagons. The heavy gun-horses had foundered or been killed, and the cannon left to Radcliffe was pulled by troop-horses, eight to a gun, the troopmen walking. The arquebusiers had no ammunition; some of them, showing decline of discipline, tossed away their weapons on the run. Twice the Ulster army had come on evidence that the English butchered troop-horses for food, being so near starvation.

Radcliffe had lost some fourteen hundred men, mostly in battle, some from illness. O'Neill had lost a scant three hundred in contrast, and his army was still in good fighting condition.

O'Neill chased them south and they went willingly. They would have preferred to go southeast and make liaison with their supply train which, not knowing where the army was, had stopped to await orders in south Ulster. Radcliffe bore heavily in that direction, but O'Neill kept him to the south. The English did not stop to offer battle now, but only kept ahead; again O'Neill might have caught up for attack, but he said no: "Keep them on the run. Another battle will finish them, and that we'll have closer to the border of the Pale." So the English missed seeing their supply train at all, and were harried down past the southwest border of Ulster into Leinster. Being there, Radcliffe had no choice but to turn east for the Pale, though that was the last thing he would want to do: in such a state, his army could not make much defense of the border, and he would only be leading O'Neill in to invade.

But once into Leinster, O'Neill said, "We'll take a little rest and let the Leinstermen take over. There are chiefs here, too." He sent out scouts; his prophecy was correct. The English, making east toward the border of the Pale, were not five miles down that road when they were met by a delegation of southron chiefs, Callaghan, O'More, and O'Kelly, who politely requested some explanation of the presence of a large English army on their land. O'Neill had no way of knowing what answer Radcliffe returned, but it was easy to guess his emotions. Six years back, on a thin excuse, Radcliffe had led an expedition into Leinster in an effort to widen the border of the Pale westward, and he had killed a good few Leinstermen then—if they needed any further excuse to dislike the English. If the chiefs chose to regard his entry now as invasion, he would have their men to fight as well as O'Neill's.

"I have never met those chiefs," said O'Neill pleasurably, "but if we had rehearsed this, it could not go better." The scouts reported that

Radcliffe and some of his officers had been courteously haled off to the Callaghan's house to make diplomatic talk. "As I would expect." The chief nodded. "They are not fools and can see Radcliffe's condition for themselves—they will give him leave to pass through and enter the Pale. This is one of the rare occasions when cannon is useful."

He sent McArdle to meet the guns he had captured from the English, which had been trailing the army for this very purpose. The day's respite, provided all unwittingly by the Leinster chiefs, gave the cannoneers time to take the guns northeast round the English camp, and all the Ulster army followed. They waited behind a range of little hills overlooking the road, ten miles east of the Callaghan's house. And when Radcliffe's army, in dismal order, footsore, exhausted, all but starving, came in sight down that road, the guns opened fire on them in one thunderous cannonade, and the rest of the army charged out to fall on them. It was not a fight—it was slaughter. The English believed O'Neill still behind them, and they were in no kind of spirit to put up any defense. They did not attempt to form line—they broke and ran, leaving their remaining six guns behind.

Radcliffe reached the border of the Pale on the last day of April. He had eighteen hundred men left from an army of four thousand, and most of those were starving, wounded, or sick. He had lost all his cannon and half his horses. He had no ammunition for the arquebuses he kept.

"They know now," said O'Neill. "They will think twice—and twenty times more—before ever again they tangle with O'Neill!"

The Leinstermen were an insular lot. They came to speak with O'Neill that night: Callaghan, O'More, O'Kelly, and an escort of ten smart-looking troopmen. The chief received them graciously, rising to offer Callaghan, a fine-looking, elderly man, his own seat—a flat boulder drawn to the fire and spread with a stag-hide. He introduced all his captains, Sorley and MacArthur, and had cups filled for the visitors.

"You understand, O'Neill," said Callaghan, "we have no quarrel with Ulster. But the presence of such a large army in our territory, quite unwarranted, is disturbing."

"Army?" said O'Neill in surprise. "But you are mistaken, my friend, this is no army. Only a few of my household and our retinue—we are on a little hunting expedition. Where the beast leads, we follow, that is all there is to it."

"I see," murmured Callaghan. O'More, a sharp-faced young man, was grinning openly. "A hunt, is it? A trifle late in the season, but perhaps you do not keep strict dates in the north."

"I have heard that Ulster stags are famed runners," remarked O'Kelly.

"Oh, this is not an Ulster stag," returned O'Neill blandly. "A foreign beast—but a good runner all the same, gentlemen." They exchanged slow smiles.

"I take it you do not expect to be intruding on our land long?"

"I would not think so. We certainly mean no harm to the men of Leinster."

"I trust O'Neill will remember the rules of hunting on private land," hinted O'More. "A fair share of the kill."

"I will keep it in mind," said O'Neill gravely, "though as you live nearer the lair I would have thought you might run the creature a little yourselves. I understand you put a spear or two into it a few years back, but it grows cannier with age."

When the chiefs had ridden away he sat down on the boulder by the fire and laughed until he wept. "Do we go on to invade now?" asked Hugh, smiling in sympathy.

"Tomorrow." The chief wiped his eyes, still shaking with mirth. "I need a night's sleep after the chase we have had. Radcliffe"—and he began to laugh all over again—"Radcliffe will be waiting for us, brother!"

CHAPTER XXIII

R ADCLIFFE was waiting. Somehow, in thirty hours, he had collected his army for one last concentrated effort, and it was evident that he meant to hold the border until not one man remained alive. He could not hold it, but he did. The terrain favored him, though he had no guns, but it seemed impossible that only two thousand men, in that condition, could stand against O'Neill.

Radcliffe sent riders back for the handful of troops left in Dublin as home guard. His tired, beaten men only just managed to hold their line at the border until those troops reached them. But another few days of fighting would have seen the defense broken, if they had depended on the regular military alone. The Ulstermen could not understand where all the fresh English were coming from, until Thady O'Brien slipped through the lines one moonless night, and came to O'Neill's camp.

"It is always extremes with English," he said. "It takes a calamity to stir them up to fight, and then they never know when they are beaten! They will not let you invade until every Sassenach in the Pale is dead, O'Neill. The chancellor has proclaimed a state of emergency and they are sending every Englishman who can walk to the line. Some are coming willing, and the rest are forced into it. Of course, they're not experienced soldiers—"

"Do I need you to tell me that? So that is where they have all these fresh men. Well, it makes the war a little longer, that is all. A fight they want, a fight they will get."

"Radcliffe has four cannon coming in tomorrow or next day," added Thady. "Sent from England they were, and arrived just after he marched north."

O'Neill grinned. "Has he now? That will please him. I will take those guns away—children should not be allowed to play with such dangerous weapons."

He played a diabolical jest on Radcliffe over that. He made a direct onset at each of those four cannon, and the English fought for them grimly, but, one by one, O'Neill captured them. And then he set them in a row in an open space in full sight of the English army, and deliberately blew them to pieces with his own guns. It was a gesture of vast contempt; it was saying to Radcliffe, Do I need more guns to defeat your pitiful little force? It would be a knife in Radcliffe's heart, seeing those fine new guns destroyed.

Whether it made Radcliffe squirm or not, it did that to McArdle and MacArthur. They were cannon men; they loved the big guns as a troop leader loves his horses.

But the English line held against repeated charge and gunfire. It held desperately through May, but by then it was evident to all O'Neill's army that they had no more reinforcement. There had been some troops sent from England, and, as O'Brien said, they had stripped the Pale to defend it; now there were no more fresh soldiers coming up. It was not possible that the queen refused Radcliffe aid; it was simply that England had no more aid to send.

In all the fighting Rory had taken a few wounds, but none serious enough to put him off the field. Nor had he lost any friends; the casualties among the Ulstermen had been light. That week, in one of the charges on the English line, he had taken a sword cut on his right arm—not deep, but painful and annoying. As the troops formed to make a charge this morning, he was trying to pull the bandage tighter with left hand and teeth, cursing, and Diarmuid Ryan tied it for him.

"It is not poisoned?"

"No, no, it heals well, but a damned nuisance," said Rory. "It would be my ax-arm, of course." Then the pipes quickened tempo, the yell sounded signaling that the English came out to meet the charge. It was no passion for battle brought them out at a run; the officers knew they would be driven back, and had no mind to lose a foot of ground. Rory heard Hugh somewhere on the flank call out to the chief, "Mark the captains behind!" The officers were advancing to the rear of their men, forcing them into action.

As usual, Rory lost sight of the chief in the first minute. His horse brought up chest to chest with an English troopman, who swung at him with a long sword. The Englishman was only a youngster, the beard newly sprouted on his jaw; he looked frightened but determined. Rory went in with his ax and felt the bridle-arm break under his blow; then the tide of battle took them apart. The Ulstermen were yelling like demons from hell, the Scots silent, according to their different ways in battle, and the pipes still sounding charge. He had a brief engagement with a middle-aged troopman who knew how to use a sword. Glancing up as that man was carried off in a jam of men and horses, Rory saw that he had got tangled with some of Ferdoragh's men, and Ferdoragh himself was not far off, standing in his stirrups with the battle fever on him, cursing exultantly as he hammered an opponent—and another mounted Englishman behind was aiming a lance at his back. Rory shouted, "Uncle—behind!" but his great uncle never heard in all the noise. Rory spurred to reach him, knowing he would be too late. The lance came down, Ferdoragh dropped from the saddle; then Rory rammed into the Englishman's flank, missed his first blow, and dodged the lance as it came back. That was one professional troopman left: he had the loose rein in his teeth, a long knife in his left hand; he maneuvered his horse round deftly with his knees, thrust the lance into its saddle sheath, and whipped out a sword. Rory cut at him; he swayed away and brought up the sword in a French thrust, aimed diagonally for the heart. With the shorter hand-ax Rory would have been a second ahead in striking, but for that cut weakening his arm. The sword took him full in the chest; his ax crashed down and he knew he had missed his blow—then he heard a voice cry his name. He was on the ground in a blur of horses' legs and men. He thought: This is it, then, and tried to formulate a suitable prayer, but the last conscious emotion in his mind was exasperated regret: And I never had that Moyna girl after all.

When he came to himself, he lay for a time, wondering how he came to be in a ship; there was the motion, and sickness in him too. He opened his eyes and saw above him a sweat-lathered sorrel flank and a man's hairy bare leg down it. He was, he realized, in a litter swung between two troophorses, as deep-wounded men were carried.

"Well," said Diarmuid Ryan's voice, "he is awake." He turned his head slowly. Diarmuid and McFee were riding behind the litter. "How is it, Rory, bad?"

He tried to shake his head. The pain in his chest was a dull ache, not sharp. "Don't move," said McFee. "Run near through you are and have lost a deal of blood." Rory did not try to answer that; the movement of the litter was rousing nausea in him. He swallowed determinedly and asked for Ferdoragh. "Oh, he is fine, boy, the lance took him on the skull and, thickheaded as he is, never harmed him at all. Is it sick you feel?"

"I do," said Rory, and was, over the side of the litter. They watched interestedly.

"That will weaken him," said Diarmuid. "Have we far to go?" Rory did not hear the reply, drifting into unconsciousness again.

The dreams of fever came to him, but he knew they were only dreams. In a lucid interval, he was aware of grave bearded faces over him, a hand prodding to bring alive a sharp pain in his chest, and his own voice saying irritably, "Jesus and Mary!" A deep voice said approvingly, "It is to be seen he is a pious man," and someone else said, "He is swearing, not praying!"

Then he was in a black void, and Moyna was somewhere in it, too, for he heard her despairing voice. *You do not understand—you never understand*

. . . *more than that, more.* He wanted to reach her, cried her name, but a great wind came up and carried him away to another place where there was nothing, and he knew that was a dream. But he came into a better one; he was on the hillside behind Benburb and it was summer, warm and gold, and she was there, and smiled and kissed him. The dream broke, and he tried to reach it again but could not.

He came to himself fully after that and heard voices speaking over him. "He does well, then?"

"Oh, he'll be fine. Just a little rest he needs, and meat to gain back the blood. The wound is clean. But I have had a job to keep those monks away from him, I tell you! They wanted me to wash the wound and re-bandage it every day—fancy, to open it fresh each time! It was washed once in good liquor, and that is enough until it's healed."

"Good." That was Diarmuid Ryan. Rory made an effort and opened his eyes. "Well, he's awake. How do you feel, man?"

"Fine. Where—is this?" He was in bed, and saw a rough stone wall, a small table, a chair.

"You are at the monastery of Kilfearn with some of our other wounded."

Rory said weakly, "Well, I never thought—to die in a monastery," and they both laughed. The other man, he saw, was a troopman, one Cassidy, evidently detailed as nurse.

"You are not going to die here or anywhere else at present," said Diarmuid. "Could you eat a little beef if Cassidy fetched it?"

"Half a cow," said Rory.

But Moyna had been only in the dream, surely. He blinked experimentally, but she did not vanish—Moyna sitting in the chair beside the bed, placidly sewing. He must be in fever again, though he had been convalescent several days. "Moyna," he said.

She looked up. "Oh, you are awake. Is there anything you want?" He shook his head, staring at her. She wore a blue gown, and a few yellow field daisies, essence of summer, were tucked in its bosom. She was even prettier than he remembered.

"How—when—"

"How am I here? Well, you may blame Lady Catherine," she said with a shrug. "The chief was not pleased but she came south last month, you know, and is staying at the house of a friendly landholder hereabouts, one Burke, who has the ugliest wife I ever saw but she is pleasant enough. And the chief was very angry and said she must return north at once, and Lady Catherine smiled and said she was so lonely for him, and so bored there with nothing to do, could she not stay a week, only a week, and see him sometimes? And O'Neill—"

"Chatterer," said Rory. He did remember now, how the chief had pretended to be angry, though the lady rode from Tyrone with a stout guard and it was pleasant weather.

"You asked." She looked round the room disparagingly. "It is not my own notion to be here. She has a tender heart, and you have protected O'Neill now and then. Concern she had for you, and nothing would do but I must come and see how you recover. It is disgraceful; a woman has no business in a man's sick-chamber, and a monastery too, but she would have it."

He could think of nothing more to say; he only lay and looked at her. It was indeed immoral for a woman to be in a man's chamber and he ill in bed, but oddly comforting to see her there, so pretty—Moyna. He wondered about that betrothal the lady had spoken of, to the old farmer. She was only a maidservant, but—

"Would you like a drink of milk, McGuinness?"

"Am I an infant? I would not."

"Well, that is what they have been giving you, that Cassidy said." He knew that all too well. It was some notion of the monks that liquor is not good for sick men. "I will call him," she said, rising. He wanted so much for her to stay, but could not ask it. She folded her work away tidily in a little sewing-bag and said primly, "I am glad your wound is better."

"Moyna. Moyna, I never apologized right for that time—please do not be unfriendly, now—"

"Unfriendly?" she said in surprise. "Would I be friendly or unfriendly, I, a maidservant, to a gentleman like yourself? I only obey orders from my lady."

"But—you will come—again?"

"If she tells me to," said Moyna briskly, and went out. Rory cursed at the ceiling. He was cross with Cassidy, had no appetite for a meal, and even behaved rudely to the old priest who came to see him that evening. He hoped she would not come again to upset his mind . . . perhaps she would come again tomorrow.

She did. He stayed awake all the morning, and then, despite himself, slept; when he woke she was there beside the bed. He wanted to reach out and take her hand; he did not.

"Can I fetch you anything?" she asked dutifully.

"No, my thanks."

"I think I will best call your nurse."

"But you have just come!"

"I have been here an hour."

"You will come tomorrow?"

"I have told Lady Catherine," she said with asperity, "that I will not come here again. It is immoral, the monks looking at me as if I am a wanton, and this soldier of yours grinning at me! She cannot expect me to do such things, and I will tell her so."

He tried to sit up. "Still angered at me you are—I've apologized—"

"Angered? What have you to do with me? Not that you were not wanting somewhat to do with me a while back—and that is another reason. I will fetch your man. Good day, McGuinness." And out she went.

When McFee came to see him the next morning Rory was still angry, and still not sure why. McFee said it was good to see him looking more himself.

"I am fine," said Rory. He had been at Kilfearn ten days then, and, though he was somewhat weak, the wound healed well and he had not much pain from it now. Cassidy said it would leave a grand scar. He had been allowed to sit up the last two days; tomorrow he would try out his legs. "How goes the war?"

McFee shrugged. "Every day we say they cannot hold any longer. But it begins to finish—we are five miles inside the Pale and killing them in hundreds. It is not war but massacre. You make a good recovery from the look of you; the chief will be pleased. He says he's a little fondness for you after all this time. Cassidy is an old hand at nursing wounded." He gave Rory a sidelong smile. "And I hear you have another visitor, as well."

"Oh, do you?" said Rory. "That is a nice thing. I am surprised at Lady Catherine, sending that girl here—and I naked in bed in a monastery! It's indelicate. Someone should speak to them both severely." Was that the reason he was angered?

McFee grinned. "Rather you than me, boy. I've twenty years on you— a little secret I'll tell you, Rory. We put ourselves over women in law and religion and every way, superior beings we are sure enough—according to us. Maybe we are some ways, but in truth, women, they rule us in secret ways and never a man past thirty or so but hasn't discovered that. Weapons they bring against us not steel, and hold our lives in their hands start to finish. You speak to the lady if you like, not me! And I should be getting back to the line."

After he had left, Rory stared up at the ceiling, bored and restless and sorry for himself. That Moyna. She had not wanted to come and see him; she had not cared at all. And why should she? And what matter was it one way or the other? But he knew it did matter. And so at last, lying there alone, he understood it, clear and whole. Perhaps it was not that men were stupid about it, but so concerned with other things; it was simple to know, if humbling.

He hardly heard the door open and Cassidy enter. "Are you ready for a meal, McGuinness? I think it is time I am firm with these monks and give you some liquor; it will put heart in you."

"Cassidy," he said, "you must send a message for me at once. At once! The Lady Catherine, she's staying nearby—I want to see her as soon as she may come. Send at once—"

"Very well." Cassidy looked at him curiously. "I'll see to it. Don't excite yourself now."

If Rory asked him once whether he had sent the message, he asked a dozen times. He slept little that night, and in the morning he insisted that Cassidy shave him—women had foibles, and any little thing like a two weeks' beard might put her off. Cassidy shaved him but refused firmly to bathe him. "You bathe too often, McGuinness, it is weakening." He helped Rory into some clothes, however, to give him confidence, of which a man naked has little in a social way.

But when Lady Catherine came, all Rory's well-chosen words deserted him. He had not remembered how pretty she was, too. He had not known she would have another child, in four months or so, he judged. She was friendly, in her warm manner. "It is good to see you recovering well, Rory. The chief will be pleased for it. Your man said you especially wished to see me. What may I do for you?"

"Well," said Rory. He pulled himself up a little higher on the bed; he thought, Now do not go making too much of it! It would never do to be so undignified as to bring emotion into it. "Well, it is—only a thing that occurred to me."

"Yes?" She sat in the chair beside the bed, watching him with her grave blue eyes, the hint of a smile in them.

"I am twenty-five years," he said rather loudly, "and time it is I acquired a wife. I've thought your maid, Moyna, might do well enough, and as she's in your care I'd ask permission, my lady."

"Moyna?" she repeated, sounding much surprised. "You would wed her? But she is only a maidservant, and you a gentleman of a chief's line."

"Well, yes," said Rory, "but what matter is that? My blood makes up for hers, I daresay. Of course, she is nearly twenty, a wife should be taken young to be properly biddable, but I'll overlook it. I think she would do well, if she is not betrothed elsewhere?"

"Oh, no. But I cannot credit that you mean it. She would have no dower at all."

"That cannot be helped," he said magnanimously. "And certainly I mean it. I've just said so!"

"It would be a fine match for her," said Lady Catherine seriously.

"It would. Also"—he had just thought of this—"with the difference in our ranks, she is bound to be a docile and agreeable wife."

"Mhm," said the lady. "If you are truly serious, Rory, I feel it my duty to warn you that she is often impertinent."

"Oh? Well, youth—" He gestured impatiently.

"And also she wastes time in idle talk."

"It is a thing most women do."

"And she has a hot temper."

"Well, I cannot help that. She must learn to behave respectfully, and so she will if—if you will but grant me leave."

The lady walked her fingers along the blanket in absent play. "So you do not change your mind. Do you love her, Rory?"

"That is a long word," he said stiffly, "and little to do with it."

"Sometimes a great deal. Do you?"

"My lady, I only want a plain answer—would you give me leave?" She looked up, smiling. "Do you love her, Rory?"

"Women!" he said. "Always the romance—even in a marriage contract! As you say, it would be a good match for the girl, if you—"

"Rory. Do you?" She bent over him, her red mouth curving, her eyes full of laughter.

Well, McFee was right. And if women had their subtle ways of ruling men, sometimes—he learned that minute—it was good to let them see men knew it, and give in to their knowing it. He took the lady's hand and kissed it. "Unman me and have done! Yes, my lady, I do. Does that satisfy you?"

She began to laugh. "It does, Rory. Why else would you ask such a betrothal?"

"I would not have her say yes only because it's a good match." He pulled himself up straighter, earnest. "If you would tell her, my lady—ask her—only if she wants it—"

"Yes, I understand. I will, Rory, I promise. Do not worry now, I'll see to it. You should rest."

"Please, my lady, if you would—"

"Did I not say do not worry? It will be all right." And as she went out and down the passage, he heard her laughing and laughing to herself.

He was more ill and fevered that night than when his wound was new. He thought morning would never come; when it did, he had no appetite for breakfast. And then he thought Lady Catherine would never return to bring him his answer. He had Cassidy help him dress, sent him out a dozen times to see if she had come. By midday he was in a black mood: she had forgotten the whole matter. Of what importance were his desires to anyone? No one had concern for him at all; he might better have died and been out of a cold world.

And then Cassidy came in and said the lady had come. Rory sat up in bed. "Well, fetch her in!"

"She is talking with Father Lannery, McGuinness; she will come in presently." He went out, and Rory waited impatiently, conscious of his heart thudding painfully on the wound. It seemed a long time before the door opened again, but then his heart gave a violent lurch, for it was Moyna who entered. He had never seen her looking so lovely, in a rich gown of green brocade, hair caught up with a green-and-silver ribbon.

There was color in her cheeks but her mouth was grave. She gave him one quick glance and came up to the bed, not close, looking down. He could not speak for a moment.

"Lady Catherine told me what you said to her yesterday, McGuinness. I did not believe it—or maybe that you were in fever again."

"No, I meant it, Moyna—I—"

"Did you? Good of you it is to overlook my breeding. Is it you think a low-bred wife will be more docile to you?"

"No—I—"

"Oh?" she said. She raised serious eyes. "Are you remembering the things I've said to you before? Maybe it's because you know that is the only way you might have me. Is it all you want and all you would give, McGuinness—the ring, and the vows, and the marriage bed—and a little lip service to me all the rest of our lives long, and I overlooking any little betrayal you might make because you made me a lady as your wife? Because if that is all, I will not wed you, if I had never the chance to wed another man in my life. I know it is foolish in me, not to take what I might have—if it's only a hundredth of what I want—but I will not."

He reached a hand to her, but she stepped back. "Only a hundredth part, Moyna? You do—want that—at least, of me?"

And she nodded gravely at him, her color rising a little.

"I'll tell you that, for there's no pride left in me about it. Pride is a bad thing to mix with love. Yes, I do. But not only part of it—all of it. Why did you ask, McGuinness?"

"Because I understand about it, Moyna. The rest—you said I never would know. I know it now."

"Ah, do you?" she whispered. "Then tell me what it is, for I'd be sure you truly do."

That time he got hold of her hand and held it tightly. "The first thing, my heart, is that love, it isn't taking—it's giving, only wanting to give. If there's no feeling like that, not love it is. And the second thing, it is not only the lust—good that is, but only the outward way of it. It is the being together and wanting to be together, and the little private jokes, and all the shared things. And the third thing is a thing I couldn't name, but it means even when there is quarrel and trouble, the loving stays, because it is stronger than any little quarrel between. Or if the trouble is outside, the loving cuts it in two, for that someone is there to share and help. That is all I understand about it now—and is it enough, Moyna?"

"It is enough." Suddenly she was on her knees by the bed, holding him tight, but careful of the wound. "It is what I wanted to hear. Rory, Rory, you do not know how I've wanted to say your name. Now you will tell me—it is all for me you feel those things? Always?"

"All—and always, love, I promise." A long time later he held her away a little. He said, "A suspicion is in me you women conspired against my freedom—the Lady Catherine telling me of that old farmer!"

She muffled a laugh in his shoulder. "She said—she heard the chief say a thing about women that is also true of men. Tell a man he cannot have a thing, and straightway his passion is hot to have it. Rory—is it?"

"Just you wait, girl," he whispered to her, "until they let me up out of this cursed monastery . . ."

"I am quite strong now," he said. "Senseless it is to stay any longer."

"You are strong as an infant," said Diarmuid Ryan. "One of the Sassenach bugle boys could take you at the first blow—if they had any left."

Rory denied it vigorously. "But I'll be dead in another week, of boredom."

Diarmuid grinned and filled two cups. "Not so bored you'd be if your betrothed was here? Cassidy was telling me—"

"And that is another thing." He thumped the blanket angrily. "Women! This finicking attention to all the conventions." For Lady Catherine had said that, as they were betrothed, it was obviously improper for him and Moyna to meet privately, and had whisked Moyna north again with her to the house on the island, pending the end of the war. And September, she said, was soon enough for the wedding. It was eternity. "At least," said Rory moodily, "I might be spending my time profitably, killing English."

Diarmuid drank. "No need. That's what I came to tell you. The English have surrendered and sued for peace."

CHAPTER XXIV

IT WAS the end of July when Radcliffe sent a formal surrender note across the lines. He did that on the chancellor's order, or so O'Neill guessed; left to himself, Radcliffe would have fought on until they all died. But Cusack, probably by order from the queen in England, hoped, by surrendering before the Pale was overrun, to prevent more destruction and gain more concession over the truce table.

"How the English love diplomatic discussion!" said the chief amusedly. "More interested they are in arranging for the truce talk than they were in the war!"

He was of no mind to waste time over a treaty. Rory was to hear it said later that if all great leaders make, at some time, one great blunder, that was O'Neill's, in that summer of 1563 when he failed to follow up victory over the English. He had brought England to her knees; he might have occupied the Pale. What was the reason behind the tame peace he made?

No man who knew O'Neill needed that explained. O'Neill had started the war for a personal reason: it was the insult from Elizabeth he needed to avenge, and that he had done. He had been concerned to show Elizabeth she could not rule him, and, having given the English a sound beating, he was completely satisfied.

If anything in life was certain, it was certain that the English authorities in the Pale were astonished and gratified at the peace terms they were offered after their surrender.

"Not the English, who know him, but everyone else," surmised Hugh, "will be saying it is evidence of O'Neill's great generosity, even to English! It is nothing of the kind. He's had enough war for the time being and is impatient to get home, is all."

"But what terms has he given them?" asked McArdle. Rory had just returned to the line. The captains sat about the fire in camp, talking idly, the chief having retired early. Leaning on a boulder as back-rest, Ferdoragh's shoulder touching his, while the flagons went round, Rory reflected a little sleepily he would miss war camp in a way. Good to be under a roof again, with softer beds than the ground: and there would be

Moyna. But this was good too, this male companionship, the dark studded with many other fires where men lounged, ate, drank, talked, somewhere harmonized on an old song, and on the summer night wind the various lusty odors of army camp, the horse lines down the slope, tomorrow's breakfast simmering in the cook-pots, up the hill by the stream the sanitary trenches, and everywhere the smell of four thousand unwashed, relaxing, happy army men after a long war.

"Terms?" said Hugh with a yawn. "Nothing to speak of. He will have the new west border of the Pale drawn where the battle line is, which gives the Leinstermen back scarce five miles of land. Dundalk will be an open city, free for commerce. The military strength of the Pale is to be kept to three thousand at maximum. One or two other little things—I misremember. There is only one provision will really gall them," and he laughed. "He demands ten thousand pounds in personal damages, incurred while he was restrained in England and his cousin, Turlough, tried to usurp the chiefhood. They know well that was a trick by now, and will not enjoy handing him that money as a present. But they will accept the terms."

"After some haggling, if I know English," said Edmund Donnelly.

There was some haggling, and it infuriated O'Neill. He refused bluntly to meet the deputies and make discussion. He had laid down the terms; if they would not accept them they could continue the war. The chancellor asked for time to consider the provisions of the document offered, submit them to the queen; O'Neill sent back a message allowing twenty days. But before they capitulated completely, the deputies asked again to discuss with him "according to the usual procedure of this situation," which drew a sharp note from the chief telling them he made his discussion with axes and cannon, and that was the only discussion he would join.

They had no tongues any more for that sort of talk. In the last week of August the chancellor formally accepted the treaty in his and the queen's name. Would O'Neill be pleased to name the day and place he would meet to have them sign?

O'Neill was pleased at the properly humble tone of that letter. It arrived under a truce flag, brought by a guard of stolid Sassenach troopmen and a tight-mouthed officer. The chief stood to read the message, one hand on Hugh's shoulder, reading it aloud, amused, to the group of officers about him. Terence Daniel and old Fleming had come south, only the day before, to witness the end of the war; they made two of the group. From Fleming's expression he was displeased at the remarkably easy terms of the treaty; probably if he had been present when O'Neill drew it, he would have argued for sterner measures. But the die was cast now.

"So it finishes," said the chief with a short laugh. "They know who is master now!" He tossed the page away contemptuously, and Fleming bent to pick it up, smooth out the folds, glancing at the black clerkly script and Cusack's signature.

"You do not want this, Shane? May I have it?"

"Why should you want it?" O'Neill was amused.

"It is not so often," said Fleming slowly, "that one has such subservience from English. I would keep it as a souvenir, let us say."

So the army broke camp and marched north, to find the household settling into residence again at Benburb, as ordered. The new house would be kept as a summer residence and army shelter for maneuvers. The combined armies would remain at Benburb for three weeks and then assemble at the meeting place where the English were to sign the treaty.

Lady Catherine and Moyna had decided between them—of course Rory had nothing to say about it—that the wedding should be on the last day of September. He thought it might have been sooner, but did not mean to be ungrateful; everyone had been kind. Her lady had given Moyna new gowns, and a respectable sum of money as a dower. Hugh O'Neill, telling him what a fool he was to marry, gave him an overwhelming gift, one of his Arab studs. The chief promised to provide the dowry for his first daughter, and gave him choice of the half-dozen vacant chambers in the wing of the castle allotted to married officers.

But it was provoking that he should have so little to say about his own wedding. And something more provoking than that—the conventionality of females! He was allowed to see Moyna each day, but never alone; Lady Catherine or some other was always present, as social law dictated for those betrothed. There he would be, sitting in Lady Catherine's chamber with the two of them sewing and chattering away as women will, and Moyna so entrancingly pretty and the lady keeping a watchful eye on him. "The weather is holding beautifully, I hope you'll not all have to journey in the wet next week." Moyna smiling demurely—who was never demure in her life—and murmuring agreement. "You are feeling quite yourself again, Rory?"

"Oh, yes, fine I am. It was not so bad a wound."

"But the man who nursed him said it would leave a scar, did he not, my dearest?"

"It is not quite seemly for you to mention such a matter, Moyna."

"Your pardon, my lady."

"No, do I not tell you I am no longer to be called so? You will be a lady yourself now and must call me Catherine."

"You're kind—" And as the lady's eyes went to her work, his hand reached for Moyna's, hers meeting it warmly.

"Rory"—and their hands fell apart guiltily—"would you fetch my sewing knife, please. I think I have left it on the table beside the bed." He got up, went to the alcove where the great bed stood, looked. "Oh, I am sorry, here it is after all." And not long after: "You have been here an hour; it is time you left us. We have other things to do than sit making conversation with you." Yes, it was annoying. The two of them play-acting was what it amounted to. He understood the reasons for it, but it was irritating. And the occasions when they could snatch a few minutes alone, on a dark stair or in some corner, were infrequent. Well, only an-other week—another few days—when he returned from this meeting, they would be wed.

The meeting was to be in neutral territory, but the English had far-ther to come. It was at Drum Cru, at the border of Ulster, that O'Neill met them. That September was mild and warm; the Ulster army had an uneventful journey south and made camp nearby the great field where the pact, which historians would name the Peace of Drum Cru, would be signed.

O'Neill put up a show for the English that day. He was dressed all in saffron, fresh-shaven and groomed, jewels ablaze on him; his black Arab wore all scarlet trappings, with emeralds set in rein and brow-band. All the captains were handsomely clad and mounted as well, but finest were Hugh and Dudley Donnelly as the two senior commanders. Dudley's rank was all but empty now; for the last year his body had wasted and he was scarcely strong enough to lift an ax. O'Neill had called in every learned physician in Ireland to prescribe for him, but none could do much to improve his health. He was a wraith of his former self that day, thin and deathly white except for twin spots of fever in his cheeks.

The entire army, more than four thousand strong, formed ranks to greet the English when they came. O'Neill was in the center of the field, flanked by Dudley and Hugh; immediately behind him in one line were the other three Donnellys, O'Hagan, Ferdoragh, and McArdle; and behind them, in even ranks stretching across the field, all his great army, troops, gallow-glass, light footmen, cannoneers. At right angles to the chief ranged the twenty mounted pipers and behind them, forming one side of the three-sided square MacArthur, O'Cahan, O'Dogherty, O'Hanlon, and their ranked men who had joined for this war. Facing them at the other side of the field were Sorley Boy and his army. Standing just ahead of O'Neill's horse was young John O'Hagan with a small field desk open before him.

The deputies, being English, were very concerned to comply with all the formalities, and in foreign territory they employed a neutral witness to the meeting. This was the Anglophile chief, Maguire, and the deputies stayed at his house on their way north.

When they came, they looked a pitifully small company in comparison: fifty mounted troopmen riding under a banner bearing the device of St. George. The chancellor, Sir Thomas Cusack, rode ahead, then Radcliffe, then in a row abreast the Crown-deputies, Sir Harry Sydney, Sir William

Fitzwilliam, Radcliffe's brother, Sir Henry Radcliffe, and the chief justice of the Pale, old Plunkett. The Maguire rode with Cusack. He was in an unenviable position. He was Anglophile only for favor; he disliked the English, but feared O'Neill, for his army was small and his land adjoined O'Neill's. He would be reluctant to take part in this, but had no choice.

The little company of English rode straight across the field toward O'Neill; they came in dead silence save for hoofbeats on turf, and they were greeted by dead silence. Not for English the courteous piping, the lowered banners which a victor would give a vanquished enemy who had fought bravely. Midway in the field the English guard halted in ranks, and the principals came on alone. The chancellor's horse was not a length away from O'Neill's when he drew rein.

O'Neill would not deign to speak first, and the chancellor felt the same; he glanced at Maguire, who was getting cold looks from every man in sight: from Sorley Boy because he was the first husband of Sorley's wife, from all the Ulstermen because he was Anglophile, and from all the Englishmen for a like reason—they had no respect for a traitor to his own race. The Maguire, a big dark man running to fat in middle age, stammered a few formal phrases and O'Neill nodded austerely.

"The O'Neill is pleased that the deputies have come so promptly to make the treaty between us legal," he said. He looked at them one by one and a slow smile grew on his mouth. The chancellor was expressionless, but a muscle jerked in Radcliffe's lean jaw; Sydney looked grim, old Fitzwilliam as if he might loose a torrent of curses any moment.

"The deputies are pleased to meet with O'Neill for this purpose," said Cusack shortly. "I am myself authorized to sign for Her Majesty, the queen. Let us now proceed to this business." They would not want to waste time over it, but would get away quickly to forget the taste of defeat.

O'Neill gestured at John O'Hagan, who spread the official document out on the desk. The deputies dismounted; O'Neill did not. His sprawling signature was already set to the bottom of the paper. Cusack accepted the pen first and signed twice, once in his own name, once for Elizabeth. He handed the pen to Fitzwilliam, who scrawled his name in ill grace, and Sydney followed, then Henry Radcliffe and the chief justice, Plunkett. Radcliffe himself was the last to take the pen. It seemed a physical effort for him to use it. He stared up at O'Neill for a long moment, clenching and unclenching his jaw; then he bent and signed—Sussex—in a rapid scrawl.

"There is your treaty, O'Neill," he said in a loud voice. "I wish you joy of it. It is no choice of mine that I sign it, but only as a soldier under orders."

The chancellor took his arm. "Come away—come away." Radcliffe choked back more words with obvious effort and turned to obey, but O'Neill's voice stopped him.

"That sounds remarkably like a threat." He put down a hand and the secretary gave him the signed paper.

"Make what you like of it!"

O'Neill ran a swift eye over the names. He was smiling. He said, "But you have not signed your full name. This is not a legal signature."

Radcliffe took one step toward him and halted. His voice was taut with fury. "That is my name. Under the queen's favor, I am Earl of Sussex, and that is my legal signature."

O'Neill said in a velvety tone, "The earl is not on English land now and he will sign according to Gaelic law."

For one moment it seemed Radcliffe would spring at his throat. Then the chancellor spoke to him quietly and he stepped out, took the pen and paper from the secretary, bent to the desk, and scribbled under his first signature, in large script—Thomas John Radcliffe Earl of Sussex. The pen snapped in his fingers; he flung the pieces away. Perhaps he did not trust himself to speak; he turned and mounted quickly, as the others already had. Without any further exchange of formalities, the deputies rode back toward their guard.

The Maguire all this while had been watching O'Neill uneasily; he was, for a moment, unaware of the others' departure. Now, suddenly realizing he was alone confronting O'Neill's army, he wheeled his horse and galloped after the deputies. The little cortege reversed ranks neatly and trotted off back to the road, the English banner high above. And O'Neill began to laugh, watching them go.

"And that will be the last we hear of the English for a long time to come. Don't they know now how dangerous it can be to provoke O'Neill!"

"The mark of a reasonable, likable man," said Fergus, "is the ability to take a joke on himself gracefully."

"Then I'm neither one," said Rory shortly. "A heathen custom it is if you ask me." He was still angry about it, after a week. Often enough he had joined in plaguing bridegrooms himself, but never realized how annoying it could be when one was on the receiving end of the jest. The wedding service had been solemn enough, performed by Father Brendan in the chapel of the castle; but afterward, like all weddings, it had run to much feasting and dancing and merriment, and the high point of the evening came when a dozen brawny young men carried Rory and Moyna bodily up the stair to the nuptial chamber, followed by a noisy crowd. That far he would go; a pleasant, harmless custom it was. But they all stayed until nearly dawn, dancing and singing and shrieking with mirth at the discomfiture they caused. Yes, he had made one of such groups before, but this time he did not enjoy the joke.

"Never care, Rory," put in Diarmuid slyly. "A notion I have we'll be doing the same for Fergus before the year's out." Fergus looked sheepish, aimed a playful blow at Diarmuid, laughing.

"Don't tell me!" Rory stared at his brother. "Has some cunning father got his name on a contract at last?"

"Well, I did mention it," said Fergus mildly, "before the wedding. But the state you were in, it's a wonder you remembered your own name through that. I"— He dodged Rory's fist—"peace, now! It's true enough. McFee's girl, Lileas, it is."

"Well, I congratulate you, man—a pretty girl she is." Magnanimously Rory reflected there was no need Fergus should know McFee had offered the girl to himself. And, Christ, he had hesitated a bit then! If he had taken the offer—but that was a calamity he refused to contemplate, and hastily took a drink.

"When? Oh, McFee said the last of the month—"

"Convenient," said Rory. "This all arranges itself very nice, have you noticed, Diarmuid? Maybe that was why the chief would give them no more time to think over the treaty. We end the war and come home with just a month to take a little rest—and get Fergus married—before the hunting season opens."

Diarmuid agreed. "Though at the moment a ten-tined stag would not tempt me, the rest I need after that campaign. Now the war is over, we can take our time at various occupations"—with a grin divided between the other two.

"I wouldn't be too sure," said Rory, pouring another drink, "about the war being over. If not that one, some other. O'Neill being O'Neill—I'm woolgathering, is all." He sat back, smiling to himself over his drink. Everything was fine with him these days; he felt nothing could go wrong ever again. He had Moyna and the new wonderful thing between them, his own important position, all these good friends, and he had come through a hot war unscathed. And O'Neill, the most powerful man, would never be challenged by any, would hold his place as chief and prince all the years of life to come. Life was very good these days. The words he had just spoken faded from his mind the minute after they left his tongue— but he was to remember them later.

PART FOUR

conquest

CHAPTER XXV

LADY CATHERINE'S second child was born in the last week of November, another son the chief named Art. O'Neill was openly and ardently desirous now of wedding the lady and legalizing these sons, to make his chosen heir's claim a trifle more regular; even the promise of a good hunting season did not take his mind from the temerity of Calvagh Donnell to cling so stubbornly to life.

"If O'Donnell was anywhere in reach of Shane's ax," said Hugh, "his life would not be worth an English penny."

"Less," said McArdle.

O'Neill said it himself. "My Christ, why did I let him free? O'Neill, forgiving treachery so easy! I should have taken his life then. If he ever gets in reach of me, I'll not be a fool again!"

But Calvagh, more fearful of his nephew, Hugh Ruadh, was too canny a man to risk his feeble life north of the Pale. He had turned officially Anglophile and stayed close in his new Dublin house. Red Hugh was probably adding his curses to O'Neill's that Calvagh lived.

Whether it was that or some other cause, the chief was restless; he did not settle down after the English war as all his captains did, grateful for a little rest and other amusements. Even a few hot runs after stag failed to satisfy his eternal lust for action; and his temper was touchy for all save Lady Catherine. McArdle went east across the River Bann to his land and clan-castle, to check on his factors; Edmund Donnelly took Dudley down to Fedan to consult another physician; Hugh rode north to visit his foster father. The rest of the household settled to the usual peacetime pursuits: hunting, training of horse and hound; in the evening, gathering in the hall to relax about the fire drinking, refighting old campaigns with much argument, dicing and singing. And there were days of communal sports, soldiers against officers or all joined, at riding maneuvers, wrestling, racing, knife-throwing. But the chief took little interest; where he formerly was first to join any contest, to prove his superiority, now he watched absently, as if his mind strayed elsewhere, and often shut himself away alone in the council room, drinking and brooding. A mood it was, his household said to itself easily; one day he would come roaring out to challenge the best wrestler or dicer or horseman, and prove all over again that no man could best him at anything.

Rory took Moyna to his home, the McGuinness' castle, for the Christ-tide season, to make her known to his family. Fergus and his new wife rode along, and the season was celebrated well. Fergus and Lileas remained, Fergus' time of service in O'Neill's army being done; Rory and Moyna rode again for Benburb on the second day of the new year of 1564, after the first day's feasting and merry-making. They had been wed three months then, and she was worrying that she did not yet conceive. Rory laughed at her. "Borrowing trouble you are—give it time!"

"But three months! Oh, Holy Mother, what if I should be barren!" That was the thing all women feared; she was only a trifle comforted when he pointed out how Lady Catherine had lived with the chief nearly eighteen months before conceiving.

They came to Benburb at dusk on the third day of January, and, like everyone else of the household, they expected a continued quiet winter, with the most excitement a few good runs after stag, for the weather had stayed open. They had just two peaceful days before the chief began a new campaign.

Rory saw at once that his mood had darkened; he looked like a man spoiling for a fight, and after the fight they had last season that was odd— even for O'Neill.

That morning, Rory, coming down the passage by the open door of the council chamber and glancing in casually, had seen the chief staring at the wall, absorbed, intense: nostrils dilated, one hand stroking the blade of an unsheathed knife, and a little fixed absent smile on his mouth. And all he stared at was the map fastened on that wall, an ordinary map of Ireland. Rory was still puzzling over it that evening when the household joined for the meal, and O'Neill sprang his surprise on the captains.

He had eaten unusually little; he sat playing with his knife, refilling his cup again and again. Lady Catherine gave him a few troubled looks; the others at the table were engrossed in talk of last summer's campaign, except Dudley, who watched the chief. The platters were carried away, the two main tables folded and stacked in their place against the wall, the other company dispersed. A couple of servants were hovering at the chief's elbow, awaiting orders to clear his table, when suddenly he banged his cup down on the board.

"No more talk of that war!" he ordered violently. "Liam, Terence, and now all of you. Let me, for Christ's sake, forget it, the only mistake I ever made in my life." He seemed not to see the amazement on all the faces turned to him; he said to himself, with something close to savage agony in his tone, "My life—my life! In two months I will turn six-and-thirty—Christ, the time wasted! They do not give a man enough time!"

Lady Catherine put a hand on his arm. "Shane—is it unwell you are?"

"So I do not waste any more," said the chief. He said over his shoulder, "Luke, silence!" And he spoke quickly, sharply, as if they all knew what he talked of, as if ending a long discussion with definite decision. "I will have your entire commands, Hugh, Edmund, and Cormac. Half Terence's gallowglass, half Ferdoragh's light foot—Cormac, arquebusiers only, no cannon. Full field rations and equipment, lined to march at dawn day after tomorrow. James, you and Manus in command of the home guard until I return."

In dead silence they stared. "And where do we march?" asked Hugh. "Another war you are starting? On what men?"

O'Neill laughed. He was suddenly in excellent humor, as if decision lifted his mood. "A strange thing I tell you, brother, I can't be certain. I can give a guess as to who we are not going to fight, that is all. Some fighting we will make and some talking—I think more of the first than the second. That remains to be seen. Until we see it, all you need to know is the order. We march day after tomorrow." He stood, unheeding more questions. "That is all, I said! I ride for Armagh to see Liam Fleming —I will be back tomorrow dusk." He snapped an order at the nearest servant for his horse, and the man ran. Rory stood up.

"You will want me, O'Neill?"

"I will not," said the chief, and made for the door.

O'Neill returned twenty-four hours later, and still vouchsafed them no explanation. In the next dawn they marched, not knowing their destination. But now the chief was in gay mood for action, teasing them as he had teased them over the building of the house on the island.

They rode southwest from Benburb, a day's march, forded the Blackwater, and camped on the opposite bank. The chief slept early; the five captains sat asking each other where they were bound and whom they would fight, and, no answer forthcoming, slept, in turn.

The chief scarcely gave the troops time for breakfast that morning, before calling the march. They had ridden five miles before the sun was full risen. It was good country they passed through, open, rolling, bare with winter, but promising of much pasturage in spring and summer.

Hugh at the chief's side hazarded, "We are on Maguire's land here."

"So we are," agreed O'Neill pleasurably. "So we are. And ahead of us round that pass in the hills is Maguire's castle. You remember from thirteen years back?" That would mean, thought Rory, the time they had come down on Maguire for their sister's complaint of him, only to find that Maguire had more reason for complaint.

Hugh's mouth set rather grimly. "I do."

But the chief's high spirits were undampened even for that memory.

He said, "It's a fine house Maguire keeps—in thirteen years he'll have repaired the damage we made it."

"Very well, Shane, let's have it open. Are we fighting Maguire, and whyfor?"

"Oh, brother!" said the chief. "Is Maguire a fighter any day of the year? He runs too much with English and picks up bad habits of compromising."

"Christ," said Hugh mildly to Rory, "when he is in this mood I regret I ever laid eyes on him."

Beyond the pass they came in sight of the Maguire's castle, a large stone house walled in, and the chief called a halt. "Camp," he said tersely to the officers. "Anywhere about here you fancy so long as you stay in sight of the castle. Hugh, Cormac, Terence, Edmund, with me—Ferdoragh in charge of the camp." The six of them rode on toward the house, and Edmund remarked that Maguire was not his choice of a man to visit, doubtless offering thin hospitality. The chief only laughed. At the house door he dismounted; their approach, that of the army, had been noted, and several boys came running to take the horses. The door opened and a couple of menservants appeared, then the big figure of the chief Maguire, that man Rory remembered from last September: the paunchy dark man with quick-shifting eyes. He stood in the doorway and looked at O'Neill striding up toward him, the captains after. Rory saw his throat muscles jerk once; then he took a step forward.

"It is a pleasure to welcome you on my land, O'Neill. You will enter my house and take refreshment—"

O'Neill halted five paces from him. He was smiling; he raised his arm and leveled a finger at the other chief. "Hughie Maguire," he said, "you fawner on English, you little bastardly Anglophile, you knew I would come for you one day! I have come."

Maguire wet his lips. "You will—enter," he said haltingly, "and allow me to offer you—" His voice died.

"Not the host you are, Hughie—no more. I give you six hours to be out of this house with all your household."

"I—you cannot come here to steal my land! I will not—"

"Hughie, man," said O'Neill, and he put a hand on the Maguire's fat shoulder, shook the big man playfully back and forth, "your eyesight is failing you. Out there are fifteen hundred soldiers under my order. I'm not wanting your house—houses I have—I will see it razed to the ground and every soul in it if you say the word. Including yourself. How many soldiers have you, Hughie?"

Maguire had gone dead pale. "You cannot—steal my holding with a word," he managed. For fifteen years he had gone in terror of this day; but he could not believe it came at last.

"You have five minutes to make your choice," said O'Neill. "Say yes

and gather your people and get off this land which belongs now to me
—or say no and be shut up in your fine house and roasted to death
within the hour. A sensible man you are, we all know, careful of this
well-stuffed skin of yours, and you making concessions to English for little promises of safety and the avoidance of a fight. Make up your mind,
Hughie—which?"

Maguire's loose mouth worked. "Thief—and murderer!" he gasped.

O'Neill's smile never changed. He slapped Maguire across the mouth
open-handed and the big man's head snapped back. "No man says that
to O'Neill safe, Hughie. You are not worth clenching my fist for, no more
than a woman. I'll be generous and give you another chance to change
No to Yes. Look at the soldiers, Hughie. Which shall it be?"

Maguire looked up at him a second more; he swallowed; he backed
away. O'Neill said, "Run, Hughie! Hurry!"

Maguire argued not one word more. He ran. And O'Neill sat on the
stone wall opposite the door, belt flask in hand, and watched, while the
whole household packed up gear and made off. In three hours the house
was empty of folk: sixty people riding away behind Maguire, who turned
to look back a dozen times before the cortege passed beyond hills out of
sight. The chief, surrounded by the captains, laughed long and loud
watching it go, flung down his empty flask, and got up to embrace
O'Hagan with one arm.

"Terence, my able man, you will now find the nearest home-farm and
choose us a couple of good fat sheep for dinner, to be butchered at once.
You will tell the farmer he is now a man of O'Neill of Ulster, and any
little complaint for the sheep will not be well received. But you will pay
for them all the same—always wise to make friends where possible. I
have a fancy for roast mutton tonight."

"I do not move one step," said O'Hagan, hands on thighs, "until we
hear a bit more about this."

"Bear with me. I will tell you all about it—over the roast mutton."

The sheep carcasses were stripped. O'Hagan had bribed a few farmers'
boys to act as servants; it was clumsy service, but tonight O'Neill was
not noticing. He sat at the head of Maguire's table, pushed away his
empty plate, wiped his knife on his kilt and thrust it into his belt, refilled
his cup deliberately and as deliberately spoke. All the humor was out
of his voice.

"Several things I have to tell you, and the first is that I was a fool. The
greatest fool in the world, last September." He raised his hand to quiet
denial on all tongues. "Polite you are, but that is the truth. Liam said it
and Terence said it—and a month later I was saying it myself. My Christ,
I had them on their knees! I might have occupied the Pale! Was it
destiny for me to be a fool just then? Now I will have it all to do over

again one day. But more I have to do in the meantime. Take a look at England there across the channel," and he gestured as if that were literally possible. "A wealthy land, never care by what mishonest treacherous commerce the wealth came. Look at France, another rich land. And the Low Countries. All those are nations, under one monarch. Ireland is not a nation. But look back—look back! Long ago there was a nation here, and in that time a powerful nation. In the days before Christianity, Ireland was the power in the West, with her High King's armies, the Scottish Picts and the Britons under her heel, colonies in Gaul and Germany— and whyfor? how?—because there is always power in numbers. Ireland today, what is it? The Danes and the Sassenachs came and split the monarchy, destroyed the nation. And ever since it is provinces and territories under a thousand chiefs and princes." He was dead serious, his voice shaking and hard with passionate conviction. "The English would not have been suffered to remain one year if Ireland had been a nation when they invaded! But how did we resist—how do we defend? A chief here, a chief there, and how simple to subdue them, they with so few men —and each always so ready to believe rumors of treachery told by English, ready to go fighting among themselves, while the English smile and smile so friendly and reach out a little in this direction, a little in that—until one day we will wake up to find they hold the whole country. I see it; God gives me the vision to see it now. It is the task I was created to do. Nations are better than many provinces bound together only by blood and tongue."

And now they all listened seriously too, forgetting to drink, watching him. They had never heard O'Neill speak so passionately.

"Look, you," he said. "Ulster is the largest, richest province in Ireland, and I am a strong man, a strong ruler as my sire was not. But if my heir is a weakling or a fool, most of my work is undone. A nation, with national laws, can withstand a weak ruler for a little and not fall to pieces. Unity —there must be unity!" He emptied his cup. "So I am going to make a nation here." He was not boasting; he was interested to explain all this. "Unity gained by force is not so strong as that entered into voluntarily, I know that. But much of this will have to come by force. I also know clan-chiefs. I am aware no Anglophile will listen, which is why I did not approach Maguire, and will not approach some others. A few may see sense and join under me, but I will take by force all those who refuse, and so warn them. I will take this land province by province, if it costs me twenty armies the size of mine now and the rest of my life. All Ireland I will have under my kingship and make one nation again."

While he refilled his cup, McArdle said noncommittally, "The seat of the High Kings was at Tara, and that is not too far from Dublin."

"Do not labor it," and now it was a savage whisper, savage at himself, "a fool I was—a fool! I might have banished every Sassenach out of Ireland. They had nothing. Now, even in three, four months, the tale is a little different. But I will defeat them ten times if it is needful. The whole north I will take first, and then move south and west. Give me five years, and I will hold all Ireland except the Pale, and an army twenty times this size, twenty thousand men—"

"That is a task even for O'Neill," said Hugh softly to his cup.

The chief asked quietly, "What is the one thing will always reconcile enemies?"

And McArdle answered him. "A common enemy."

"You have said it. Once I have taken this land, the most will acknowledge my kingship because I lead an army to drive out the English once for all. That I will do. I will take the Pale last as I might have had it first, and build a nation here, perhaps to rise to power in the world again, under my rule."

They were watching him strangely, almost as if he were now that great king. Then Hugh rose to his feet and lifted his cup. "Let us drink to our next High King, brothers." And only Rory saw the faint twist in his smile, and the trouble in his eyes.

CHAPTER XXVI

REBECCA sat at her dressing table, fidgeting with a bottle of scent, cosmetic jars, because she did not care to see him there behind her, getting laboriously out of his clothes. But in the mirror she saw him, paunchy, gray, fussy. She was very tired of Harry. Seven years she had been with him; he kept her only, as he had taken her only, to prove to himself and other men that he was still vigorous. She stared at a pot of rouge and thought of Colm. She wondered, had she known a man like Colm long ago, would she have walked a different road all these years? Would she have wanted to? On the whole, she was as satisfied as one might be with life. But she thought of Colm with a smile, and hoped he was safe, and that he might come to see her again, as he had once last autumn when the war was ended.

"It is worrying," said Sydney. "I hope Radcliffe returns soon. I saw Kildare this morning—I was telling you, was I not? Quite bewildering. Of course, there was old enmity between O'Neill and Kildare, but no quarrel with Maguire."

"I know little of all this," she said, and thought how typical of Harry, or any Englishman, to talk politics to a woman he would bed with in twenty minutes' time.

"No, of course not, my dear," he agreed vaguely. "A most unpredictable man in any event. Like all the Irish. I am alarmed by what Kildare said. Yes, yes. I must write to Radcliffe tomorrow—in case he delays in England."

But that letter Sir Harry never wrote. Radcliffe landed in Dublin on the noon tide next day from a two months' visit to the queen's court. In that two months, much had happened in Ireland, and nothing he liked. He had some bitter words for the chancellor that none had thought to inform him of these new developments.

"It is possible," said Cusack uneasily, "that there was personal grievance—"

"Personal grievance be damned," said Radcliffe. "I have not fought O'Neill in three wars without learning somewhat about him. He could have had both Maguire and Kildare any time this ten years. Why only now?"

His letter to Cecil was long, after some private rumination. The bare fact first: "I return to find more trouble in the north, and trouble to speculate upon. In January, O'Neill marched with half his army, occupied Maguire's land and banished that chief, who fled for shelter to the Earl of Kildare. Not a week later did O'Neill follow—neither Maguire nor Kildare keeping any standing force of defense—and stealing Kildare's holding, he chased both chief and earl south. They have taken shelter with Ormond at the border of the Pale, whence you may imagine we hear much outcry and pleas for help against this insolent thievery. Ironic to ask the chancellor's aid! O'Neill then marched west against O'Connor, which chief, by all account, repelled attack with his small force but has been subdued. There was no quarrel with O'Connor whatever, no reason. . . . O'Neill now holds and occupies near all of Connacht as well as Ulster. I am much disturbed for the circumstance, and would ask that you communicate this intelligence to Her Majesty . . ."

He added the results of his own speculation, writing quickly; read over what he had written, signed it. But he left the letter open while he poured wine, strolled over to the window of his office room. He looked down on the gray Dublin street, where a dispirited March drizzle fell. In his mind moved the thought: A shrewd man, Cecil, and the queen perhaps even shrewder; and speaking of personal grievance, she had that for O'Neill. But they lived in London, not Dublin—safe, snug London, an England inviolate of invasion four hundred and ninety-eight long years. His firm mouth twisted on the thought. He gulped the wine; he sat again at the table and wrote swiftly beneath his signature: "In Ulster there tyrannizeth the prince of pride; Lucifer was never more puffed up with pride and ambition than that O'Neill is. He is at present the only strong and rich man in Ireland—and he is the dangerousest man, and the most likely to bring the whole estate of this land to subjugation under him, that ever was in Ireland."

At the castle of Benburb the days passed slowly for the women, their men away at war. Moyna said with a sigh to Lady Catherine, "It's a queer thing to think, but I believe the servantwomen are better off. Duties they have to pass the time, where what is there for ladies? Sit and sew and chatter . . . and pray the man stays safe."

"Are you tired of being a lady so soon, then?"

"Well, I would not say that! Advantages to it, too—see, my hands are let to grow so nice and white! And, of course, there is the child to think of."

"Mhm." Lady Catherine looked fondly down at her own son nursing against her. "Some comfort it is, but not for everything."

"And not until September—such a long time. Do you think they will come home a little before?"

Lady Catherine said slowly, "I don't know, Moyna. But we must try to keep cheerful. Shane wrote that the fighting was nothing in Connacht. All this war, all this war."

"It is men," said Moyna. "The stupid bloodthirsty creatures they are, they can never be satisfied to stay quiet at home. Such fools, out killing each other. I wish they would come home. And I, another fool, hoping it is a son in September."

Lady Catherine laughed. "So we are all fools, women and men together. Have we got what once we wished for, you and I, Moyna?" But Moyna had no chance to answer, for a rush of feet sounded in the passage and Manus Donnelly burst in.

"Your pardon, Catherine, but I knew you'd want to hear at once. There are scouts come—Shane is an hour's ride off and the army with him!"

Sorley Boy MacDonnell was curious and disturbed for news he heard of war in the west. He had seen O'Neill last in October, when he left Benburb to ride home with his army after the war. He would have thought that great victory over the English would satisfy him a year or so—but with Shane, who ever knew? He discussed it idly with his officers, not with his wife, who nursed a hatred for her two brothers since their disavowal of her. But he did not discuss it with his chief when MacDonnell visited Dunluce, and something lay uneasy at the bottom of his mind for it. In the middle of March he announced his intention to ride for Tyrone to visit O'Neill; he took with him a mounted escort and three of his officers, Buchan, Swain, and MacPhail. His wife, the Lady Mary, was sullen for it, resenting his affection for her brothers, perhaps, too, his love for his niece. He told her peaceably that he would not be absent long.

He rode from Dunluce on a Friday, and came to Benburb by late afternoon of the Sunday, to meet a strange welcome. For fifteen years he had been a close friend to these men, and to the chief, like a brother. When he rode up to this castle there would be embraces, warm greeting, much shared talk and laughter. This day he rode past the gateguards into an empty courtyard; not until grooms had come to take the horses did the house door open, and then there was something like horror in Hugh O'Neill's voice as he exclaimed, "Sorley!"

Sorley stood away from his half-hearted embrace, puzzled, a little hurt. "I do not intrude, Hugh?"

"No, no, how could you, man? You're welcome—" And the others, crowding up then, added a chorus of uneasy greeting. At least there was no apparent change in O'Neill. He embraced Sorley warmly, loud on welcome; and Sorley looked at him consideringly.

"I came of curiosity, Shane, I confess. I hear you are on a new campaign."

"Oh, that!" said O'Neill with a laugh. "We can talk of that later—come in and take a drink, tell us how it is with you this six months."

Before the house gathered for the meal, Sorley went up to see Catherine, and was more puzzled and alarmed at her reception. She clung to him tightly, weeping. "Sorley, dear Sorley—"

"Catriona, what is this?" Catherine seldom wept; he turned her face up to his with one hand, searching her wet eyes. "What is it, unhappy you are? You no longer feel content here? Shane—"

"Oh, no, how could you think—! No, I am foolish, is all—I'm so happy to see you again, it has been long." He could get no more from her, and the uneasiness grew in his mind. His three officers wondered about it to him privately—with friends among the Ulster officers, they were a trifle hurt, too. But when they came down to be seated ceremoniously at the chief's table, there was nothing wrong with the hospitality they were offered. It was a false-genial note in O'Hagan's voice, the peculiar glint in Dudley Donnelly's eyes, the unwonted silence of Hugh, that was strange. O'Neill was his usual self, in good spirits, garrulous; he plied the Scot visitors with food and drink. But Catherine sat silent, pale, at his side, eating little.

When the meal drew to an end and the table flagons were refilled, the platters carried off, Sorley took advantage of a pause while O'Neill drank. "Enough of jesting, Shane. I said the news is you engage in another war lately."

O'Neill exchanged a grin with Hugh. "Oh, it was not much of a war," he said casually. "Not compared to that last campaign against the English—good fighting we had then, not so? These men had nothing to bring against me."

"A quarrel you had with Maguire?"

"Do I need an excuse to make war against an Anglophile? That was nothing. I marched in and occupied his house and Maguire fled—to Kildare, who was likewise struck by panic when I followed. So they both fled—to Ormond, and there they are now, complaining loud to the chancellor, and much good may it do them!"

"And there was mention of O'Connor," said Sorley.

"Oh, O'Connor. We had a little warmer fight there—O'Connor is a bold man."

"Your grammar is wrong," said Hugh. "He was."

"My pardon, you're right! Scarce six hundred men in his army, but they fought well. So did he."

"So you have taken the rest of Kildare and all of Connacht. That is a deal of land," remarked Sorley. O'Neill's eyes were watchful on him, but he was still smiling.

"It is."

"Why?" asked Sorley bluntly. O'Neill's smile widened very slightly. "That is what you came to find out, is it not? Well, to answer that question I must give you a little lecture, Sorley." He sat back in his chair, drank, stopped smiling; and his voice dropped to dead seriousness as he went on speaking. Sorley sat looking down at his cup and listened to him talk with passionate conviction of nations and unity; he thought all the captains had heard this before by their expressions. Glancing at his own officers, he saw them absorbed—and that their minds had not moved on to the next step.

"Ireland must be a whole nation to itself again," O'Neill was finishing, "and that is what I am making it now."

"That is a task," said Sorley noncommittally.

"It will be a task, but I am O'Neill. I will make it—I will take it. Some of the chiefs will listen, not all. Hugh Ruadh O'Donnell will not, no. We will have some hot war for Tyrconnell. I will take the north first"—he was watching Sorley again—"and then move south. Not any of the southron chiefs have a force to equal mine."

"And when do you march against Hugh Ruadh?" asked Sorley. There was a brief pause; Hugh half rose, McArdle opened his mouth to speak. Then O'Neill laughed and shrugged, but when he spoke his voice was hard.

"In the autumn, my friend. That will give me all the spring and summer to take Antrim and drive out the Scots."

It was said, what Sorley had feared and expected to hear. He sat motionless one moment, and when he looked up to meet O'Neill's eyes, there was no enmity or anger in either gaze, but something nearer sorrow. Sorley said, "So be it. There are worse ways to die than by the hand of a friend."

And O'Neill said, "I'll not offend you by asking betrayal of your chief. But this I will say. No love you have for James MacDonnell, and he is the strong ruler in Antrim. Stay out of the fight and I will not touch you or your land."

Sorley stood up from the table. "Sins on me, and my chief I do not like, but clan loyalty cannot be shirked and he is my chief. I fight for my clan." His officers stood with him, waiting for what might come.

O'Neill rose to face Sorley. He said gravely, "I should not have asked —you are the most honorable man I know. Will I show less honor to my brother? You have ten hours to leave Tyrone with your men."

Sorley let out a breath. Very well might O'Neill have prisoned him with his escort, for he knew Sorley would carry warning to the Scot chiefs. It was a gesture few military commanders would make, to throw away all advantage of surprise attack.

"My thanks, Shane." Sorley started for the door, his officers behind him; and then he looked back with the ghost of a smile. "This is once I do not wish you luck. We meet on the field."

"We meet on the field." And all the captains rose as a mark of respect for former comrades as the Scots left the hall.

The three officers exchanged some incoherent talk as they waited for their horses in the courtyard; Sorley did not open his mouth. They got away inside twenty minutes, and down the cliff path in record time. Swain was repeating in a dazed voice, "I do not believe it! Why? I cannot believe it—"

And Buchan, who had always admired O'Neill, said harshly, "You ask why? All that talk about the good of the country! He is thief and bully and desires more for himself, that is all!"

Sorley spoke for the first time since leaving the hall. "Hold your tongue, Ian! That is a great man back there, and a man I love like a brother, and he is in the right with his dream of a nation. But I will fight him because it is my duty to do so—and God help us all!" When they came to the main road he added, "We go straight north for the Red Bay to warn the chief."

Buchan subsided to sullen silence; it was MacPhail who asked, still sounding incredulous, "What have we to meet him with? Gilchrist, Mac-Arthur, Brodie—they will all join, but—"

"With all the chiefs, four thousand, five—but what matter? O'Neill does not lose wars. We are four dead men," said Sorley Boy, "riding to warn a dead man."

CHAPTER XXVII

"F OR THE love of God, James, will you listen to me!"
"No man can lie that well. I do not see O'Neill telling you of attack
and letting you go. But I know what he did say to you—"

It was a strangely calm group of men that gathered in the MacDonnell's hall to hear Sorley. They could see for themselves the condition
of those four men who had made such a swift ride to the Red Bay. The
MacDonnell had been entertaining Brodie; Gilchrist lived not far off,
and MacArthur, and messages were sent at once. The chiefs MacLachlane
and MacFarlane lived farther south.

"I will tell you what he did say," repeated MacDonnell. "He said,
'My brother, go and tell them I invade by the north road, so they will
concentrate defense there, and I will come in south for the kill.'"

"No," said Sorley. "How many times must I say it? If you want it
plain, James, yes, he asked me to stay out of the fight, and in that event
would not harm me. I told him I fought with the clan, and he is an
honorable man—he let me go. What I am telling you is this. Now he
knows we are warned—"

"And I do not see O'Neill giving away advantage like that, either."

"Before God, will you listen! Your pardon, I am overwrought. See it,
James! He cannot make surprise attack now—he knows that—and I know
Shane O'Neill. To invade Antrim by surprise, he would come south, by
the open road, for swiftness. He will not do that now—he will come by
the middle north road because he expects we will concentrate defense
south."

"O'Neill is no fool. He is too experienced at war to invade Antrim
north. It would be too easy to defend. He will come south—"

Without apology, Brodie interrupted, "And soon. A day—two days, now
he knows we are warned."

"Why so?" The MacDonnell laughed. "Are you taking Sorley's word
for gospel? He speaks with O'Neill's tongue." Sorley stood and paced
across the room, restraining himself with effort. "But I agree, we cannot
take chances, we must prepare to meet him at once. I can have my army
lined for march in eight hours. Brodie, you can join in that time? Mac-

Farlane and the others we can collect on the way. Sorley, you must go north for your men but you can join in two days. Hard by the mouth of Lough Belfast, that is the place. MacArthur—"

"MacArthur takes orders from no other chief," said MacArthur. Despite the difference in their ages he faced MacDonnell steadfastly. "A war leader you are, but I am a better one by nature and I have fought with O'Neill. Like Sorley, I know him. What Sorley says is right—he will come north."

"I believe it," added Gilchrist to that. He turned a look of dislike on MacDonnell. "Other men know Sorley Boy better than his chief—he is a long way from traitor or coward. I take his word on this."

"You are both fools," said MacDonnell tautly.

MacArthur stood. "We waste time arguing—defense must be arranged. Sorley goes north and I abide by his decision."

"And I," said Gilchrist.

"Fools! To split defense like that—we have an equal force to his if we stay together—"

"Listen, James." Sorley's tone was quiet. "I know he will come by the middle north road. I will meet him there and defend. What you do is your own affair, but remember this—Gilchrist and MacArthur with me, we are two and a half thousand strong southwest of Dunluce. We will make every effort to hold him there until you can come to support us. Expect the message telling you he is across the Bann." He turned for the door; the other two chiefs followed him.

As they mounted in the courtyard Sorley said violently, "God! Why will they not see it?"

"No use putting long words on it," said MacArthur. "Where do we gather the armies?" With that one question he showed his knowledge of war and his mettle. An army can have only one leader; MacArthur knew that, and was putting himself under command of Sorley, who had the most men in their combined forces. Gilchrist echoed him.

"My thanks," said Sorley curtly and gave orders. "We gather southwest of Knockboy. We'll be forced into retreat and can make a stand there."

"As you say," said MacArthur. "Thirty hours." Without further word he beckoned to his troop and rode off at a gallop, Gilchrist following.

Sorley took all six of his cannon from Dunluce down to the Pass of Knockboy, and left the cannoneers to entrench the guns there. He knew sure as death they would be forced back toward that place. Ten miles farther west he made liaison with MacArthur and Gilchrist.

They marched their armies westward again to Kilwarden Wood, where the road narrowed, and there they made camp and waited for O'Neill —for O'Neill and battle. The place was well suited for ambush, which Sorley hoped to make; but they waited a full day for news from their advance scouts that the Ulster army was in sight. By dusk Sorley was worried. "Is he one trick cleverer after all? He might guess I would await him here, so he might come in south. Christ, should we have stayed with James?"

"The die is cast now," said MacArthur uneasily.

That next day was unseasonably warm for spring. They waited from dawn to midday without news from the scouts down the road; then, without warning, it began. Some of the footmen had wandered a little distance into the wood in search of a stream, and returned on the run. "Axes—yonder in the wood—many axes cutting through the brush!"

"That is Shane," Sorley said almost calmly. "He knew I would lie in wait for him on the road, so he cuts his way through the forest." There was scarcely time to call up the men in ranks before the Ulstermen began to emerge from the wood. It was a disorderly fight from the first, for they had not expected to come on the Scots at once and all the footranks were ahead, making a way for the troops through the dense growth. But they came out swiftly, and, the space being narrow, it was a tight press of battle.

Before they had been fighting ten minutes, one fact was obvious to the Scots. They knew that army well. Sorley turned a gray face to Buchan, riding into the press knee to knee: "He has split his army too—and we can expect no support from James!" It was but half the Ulster army they were fighting; the rest would be south to meet MacDonnell.

That was not a pleasant fight for Sorley. As he rode into it first, ax in hand, his horse brought up with a jerk not a dagger-stroke from Terence O'Hagan. Both axes were up to strike, both hesitated in midair; both reined their horses aside and engaged other men. None of the Scots was sure how long it lasted; they were forced into retreat several times, made stands to fight again. In the first retreat past their camp into open country, they could identify O'Neill leading the pursuit, mounted on one of his black Arabs, waving a stained ax. Sorley saw O'Hagan, Ferdoragh McGuinness, Edmund Donnelly, Rory McGuinness, who was the chief's personal guard, junior officers of troops he knew —but not Hugh. He would be in command of the rest of the army, south.

When night shut down, they had been driven back ten miles. In full dark the pursuit slowed, they drew away far enough to halt for rest, and the officers discussed strategy. MacArthur was limping and swearing from a nasty ax gash in his thigh; Gilchrist, that small, red, cold-eyed man, was unwounded. "You are directing this fight," he said to Sorley; and MacArthur sat by the one small fire, his young, dark, handsome profile etched sharp in flame, silent. "Have you any useful ideas?"

"I am not a defeatist," said Sorley, "but we are against odds. Yes, I have a suggestion, but I do not make it a command—if you disagree, forget it. We are ten miles from Knockboy. I need not tell you we will be forced into more retreat tomorrow, and ten miles of running and fighting means many dead and more wounded. If we give them that ten miles and reach Knockboy by morning, we can hold them at the pass with my guns. It is losing ground for advantage—but maybe you do not see it that way?"

"The only wise course to follow," concurred MacArthur. "We lose the ground but save men for future fight. I am agreeable, but it will be a night's work to get that far."

"Let us get off now," said Gilchrist. So they rallied the men, tired as they were after the day's fight, and started northeast for Knockboy as swift as they might travel. They must reach the pass before light, for to be caught outside before they could get into position behind Sorley's guns might mean they would be driven through with no chance to stand. The sky was just lightening when they drew up to Knockboy; the cannoneers had entrenched the guns, and behind them they felt, for the moment, more secure.

"Let him come on," said Sorley. "We can make a decent defense here, odds or no. At least he will know he has been in a fight after it." Thirty minutes later they sighted O'Neill's army approaching.

They stood at Knockboy two days, two days of almost constant battle.

The pass there came down steep between rocky hills, impossible ground for horsemen and difficult for foot. It was so narrow that relatively few men might hold it against many, even without guns. Sorley's six guns were trained on the mouth of the pass and the narrow, steep road leading up to it, and inflicted much injury on the enemy. O'Neill, as usual, had no guns with him, but he made repeated charges up the hill—disastrously and to Sorley's horror.

The charges continued on the second day. By noon, cannon smoke hung like a gray curtain over the whole scene, and a wall of corpses piled at the foot of the hill. And still the charges came. "Is he gone mad, to send foot against guns?" But an hour after midday, one charge got enough men through to reach the gun nearest the mouth of the pass, and a following charge, made so swiftly the rest had no time to reload and prime for another fire, rushed in to support that attack. The Ulstermen took the gun; they worked at top speed to turn it, and even as Sorley sent in men to make more contest for it, the gun roared into the Scot ranks. More charges came up the hill, wave after wave pouring on the Scots, overrunning the other guns.

An hour later they lost the pass.

Once they retreated from Knockboy they lost any advantage they had. They were not fighting great odds, for O'Neill had taken greater losses at the pass; but the odds they fought were experience at war, intense integration of forces, and utter confidence—that was an army that had never lost a war.

They fought and ran, always retreating north, for three days; and by the third day they all knew it was but a question of time. And Sorley, in the midst of losing one fight, was concerned for MacDonnell and the rest, south. "God, when I think what a war we could make if we stayed together! But it is too late now." He put his head in his hands. "My God, tell me what to do! My land—Dunluce! We are a day's march from it. Everything in me says to fight on until death, but—if we ask for peace now, there might be an easier settlement."

"I do not surrender to any," said MacArthur.

"That is your choice, Dougal. We should stay together. I will abide by a majority decision."

Gilchrist said, "Let us fight a little longer."

The final decision was taken from Sorley's hands the next day. They made a stand at a narrow hill pass, and that was the hottest fight they had given the Ulstermen since Knockboy. When they were forced back it was swiftly, under the pounding of O'Neill's gallowglass, and the retreat was split in darkness. MacArthur and Gilchrist made liaison, but Sorley Boy was missing, and half his officers were dead, wounded, or taken by the enemy. It was a rout.

There in the darkness, still mounted, the remnants of their tired armies about them, the two chiefs talked quickly, knowing O'Neill was not far off.

"We cannot risk a search for Sorley, to take the chance of being caught by O'Neill in this state," said MacArthur. "Listen, Alasadair, we'll try a trick on him. He is likely making for Dunluce, and, by the grace of God, we're ahead of him. I will take all but a handful of our men and circle west to reach the MacDonnell southward. Do you get up to Dunluce and put up a bold front of having the castle packed with men. Stand siege as long as possible—we'll be fighting toward you. The tide may yet turn."

"I am agreeable," said Gilchrist. There was time for only a handclasp. Gilchrist took twenty troopmen and rode north at a fast trot; MacArthur, with the remainder of the armies, moved west, praying to avoid the Ulsterman as he went. And in the minds of both moved a prayer for Sorley, for Sorley Boy was a well-loved man.

CHAPTER XXVIII

O'NEILL had been in a black mood all that week; it was a week of fighting he did not enjoy. The two days at Knockboy he had been in constant fury: "Christ damn him, he cannot stand against me! Why make all this slaughter?" He was overjoyed for that last battle when so many prisoners were taken. They overran the Scots strongly. It was O'Neill's determination to capture Sorley Boy safely that led to their losing Gilchrist and MacArthur; the chief made a dead set at Sorley's troops from the first, concentrating attack there. When they collected in some order, as darkness shut down, half the Ulster army was playing guard for the great crowd of prisoners, and O'Neill, triumphant, was leading a troop-horse with Sorley Boy, bloody and unconscious, lashed face-down across the saddle. He ordered an hour's rest and march after it.

"My Christ," said O'Hagan resignedly, "after the day we've had I could do with a decent hot meal and some sleep. What is all the rush, Shane? Likely we'll come up to the others in the morning—they are worse off than we after that last fight."

"To hell with the others for the moment," said O'Neill. "I want this over and done with. We go north to take Dunluce at once." He gave orders to chain the prisoners, mount all those wounded to hasten the march; before midnight, they had made another ten miles north. The captains were uneasy about Sorley, who had not regained consciousness; O'Neill kept him in charge all the way. "Alive? Of course he is alive—some whoreson gave him an ax-cut across the brow, and if I discover what man, I will hang him on the instant, mistake or no! But it takes more than that to kill a Scot."

By the gold-rose spring dawn they came in sight of Dunluce, that great gray fortress with its back to the sea. For all their exhaustion, the promise of a little rest and comfort spurred the men to carry out orders with a semblance of energy. A rude circle of logs chained together was erected and the Scot prisoners, all chained at the wrists, were herded into it. The cannoneers set up Sorley's six cannon, which O'Neill had brought from Knockboy, in a row down the hill from the camp, lined to aim for the castle wall. Sorley was then with the rest of the prisoners, among which were many of his officers and a good three hundred men.

The chief's tent and those of the captains had been erected; but O'Neill was taking no comfort there, nor did Rory see Ferdoragh or any of the rest nearby. A troopman directed him to the prison lines, and then he saw the chief, Ferdoragh, Edmund, and O'Hagan making down the hill toward that place, and hastened to follow.

Sorley Boy had come to himself and sat on the ground between two of his officers. The wound he had taken, a glancing ax-cut across the brow dangerously close to the eye, had been tended. As the Ulster leaders came to the chained-log barrier and paused, the Scots looked up, glowering, Sorley no more amiable than the rest. The chief said nothing at all, but stood, hands on thighs, regarding Sorley with bright, pleased eyes.

"A bad cut that is, Sorley," said Ferdoragh. "What bastard so forgot himself to give it to you? Shane will have him hanged." Sorley did not answer.

Edmund Donnelly smiled round the little group of officers. "You are all offered parole, who will surrender in peace and promise no trouble."

"I do not want parole for myself or any of my men," said Sorley hardly, staring at O'Neill, who only grinned.

Edmund shrugged. "Your own choice, men. I only obey instructions to offer it. This is no very comfortable place. If you officers will take parole—"

"I refuse parole!" exclaimed Sorley. "I will stay with my men." The chief grinned at him.

"You are not offered parole—only your officers." He turned and beckoned; Rory saw that four gallowglass men were approaching down the slope. "A chance you had to stay out of this war, and did not take it. Now you will take what comes. The officers may speak for themselves." All the officers in hearing refused in one voice. O'Neill laughed. "Scots," he said, "how they will hold anger! Well, we'll not force it on you. But you will not stay here, Sorley." He prodded Sorley with one sandal; excited mischief was in his eyes. "Get up, man."

Sorley rose with a growl. "Christ damn you, Shane! Is it not enough for you to beat me at fight? Must you come here and gloat over me?"

"Scot bastard," said O'Neill, grinning. "The time is not come for you to lie out of this war. A lucky thing I take you prisoner—you can be useful. I have a fancy to enter that fine castle down there," and he gestured largely at Dunluce. "Would you care to assist me in the project?"

"Overhopeful you are," and Sorley laughed at him. "If I know them, Gilchrist and MacArthur are holding Dunluce with a thousand men, and if you think you can persuade either of those two to surrender in a hurry, you can think twice."

"Maybe and maybe not," said O'Neill. "We shall see." The gallowglass men had come up now, and Rory saw that two of them bore a long pole, the trunk of a young sapling ten feet long, the bark stripped rudely from it. "Bring him along," ordered the chief, and without more talk started down the slope toward Dunluce. Two of the soldiers took Sorley by the arms and marched after him.

"God's help," muttered Ferdoragh, "will he do that? I did not believe—"

"You know him as well as I," returned Edmund cryptically. All the Scots were standing, staring after their leader, curious and angered.

O'Neill strode out onto the flat open space before the castle gate, where the road led along the coast. Since dawn and the army's approach, there had been a crowd of watchers on the wall, and these observed the little procession, as interested as the prisoners and the Ulstermen up the hill. After the chief came the two soldiers with Sorley, then the two with the pole, and chains, and implements. With growing horrified understanding, Rory watched with the others.

In the center of the open space before the house, opposite the gate, O'Neill halted and gestured at the men with the pole. They commenced to dig and in a few minutes had embedded it firm in the ground. O'Neill tested its strength, nodded, and pointed at Sorley. The other two led him up, stripped from him all his garments, and chained him upright against the pole, facing the castle. O'Neill surveyed him and spoke again, and all the watchers saw Sorley fling up his head defiantly as he answered. The chief laughed and turned to the castle gate; his deep voice carried up the hill as well as to those over the wall.

"Here is your leader, Sorley Boy—and here he stays until you surrender the castle!" He turned then and came back toward his camp at a leisurely pace.

MacCowie, who had been eying him grimly, here intervened with a first-class exhibition of cursing, but the chief showed no anger for it, listening with detached interest until the Scot's vocabulary was exhausted. "A tongue you have, but little imagination," he commented. His eyes were on the plain before the castle, on Sorley Boy chained to the post. "A bloodless victory it will be. I have killed enough of you former friends. That is a man beloved by his people—they will suffer with him. He will hunger and thirst and burn in the sun, and they will see it—and tomorrow they will surrender the castle."

"An inhuman cold-blooded thing—" burst out MacCowie hotly.

"Is it not?" agreed O'Neill. "If it were James MacDonnell out there he might stay until he rotted. Not Sorley. He is too well loved by all who know him."

"And yourself one of those men," said O'Hagan noncommittally. The chief nodded slowly, his eyes still on Sorley.

"Myself one of them. The man O'Neill. This is the chief O'Neill, who

never lets sentiment interfere with battle advantage." A moment more
he stood silent, looking at Sorley; shrugged, turned to the prisoners, told
them. "If you change your minds about parole the offer is still open,"
and started back for the main camp.

The Scot prisoners scarcely took their eyes from the scene below that
day; among the Ulster officers it was little different. Over the wall the
crowds of watching heads increased. And all who watched suffered with
the man chained to the post. It would be an early year; even at the end of
March the sun was warm and would burn tender skin usually covered.
By the end of the afternoon, though the distance was too great to see,
Sorley was probably feeling the effects of that burning, but he gave no
sign. The naked white body was still upright against its support. He would
be thirsting too, and all who loved him watching helpless. When night
shut down he was still standing erect, but that would be mostly pride.

When dawn broke the next morning, again a silent crowd of watchers
over the wall gathered; and they all saw that in the night Sorley had
struggled against the chains. The ax-cut on his brow had opened to stain
his face with blood, and blood had flowed from a wound on one arm to
darken the stripped post and the ground. But he was still upright. The
crowd on the wall thickened; those in camp could hear the thin mutter
of their voices. Toward midday there came a movement on the wall to the
banner staff over the gate.

"Look there!" Ferdoragh was on his feet. "They are making to lower
the flag. It will be Sorley's men, and the others arguing for it—"

They all saw; and so did Sorley. Thirst had hoarsened his voice, but it
carried far enough. "Damn the first man who calls surrender! Hold the
house and never care for me!"

His banner stayed over the gate. The captains did not like that at all,
nor did the chief, who was in a rage. "Just like that thickheaded Scot
it is, to kill himself to spite me!"

"Now what did you expect?" asked Edmund reasonably. "That Sorley
would kneel and offer you the castle at a mere threat?"

"He has offered token resistance, all that's needful," said O'Neill angrily. Rory, who slept by custom before the door of his tent, got little
sleep that night: the chief lay wakeful, thrashing about in his blanket,
swearing to himself. But he would never recant on his word, and he had
sworn to get surrender of Dunluce.

The sun was warm that morning; to a naked man with no escape from
its full glare, it must be torture, but Sorley never moved. The hundreds
watching from camp and castle could guess what agonies of thirst and
blistered flesh he suffered, and suffered with him. And again toward dusk
there came movement on the wall, and men with a white flag stood below
the banner staff; again Sorley raised his head to refuse defeat. When he

managed to make a sound from his dry throat it was a harsh croak of defiance.

"Hold—the house! I—never—surrender!"

The dark shut down on the third day with his clan-flag still raised high.

Rory had seldom seen the chief so irritated. "Christ damn that bull-headed Scot! He will kill himself only trying to get the best of me!"

"I said it was a wrong notion," Edmund repeated. "I am not sure it is altogether honorable either. But no, you would do it."

"Honorable!" roared O'Neill. "What could be less honorable than murdering my friends? I only try to avoid more of that! It is his damned stubbornness—"

Rory slept sound that night; the chief never came to his tent at all but sat brooding by the central fire. When Rory woke it was past dawn, and, his first thought being of Sorley, he put aside the tent-flap and looked down the hill. The white body on the post had sagged forward into its supporting chains, head hanging. Good Christ, he is dead, thought Rory, scrambling up, and heard O'Hagan echo him nearby.

"He is dead, I tell you." The chief and the captains stood staring down into the clearing.

O'Neill directed a few rich curses at Sorley Boy. "Damned obstinate Scot, he is not so easy to kill! They must surrender soon—now, today!"

But all morning nothing moved at Dunluce or in the camp. It was a warm spring day, the sky cloudless blue, a pleasant breeze off the sea; the smoke from the army's cook fires drifted lazily upward, a few birds chattered from the trees, and the line of men along the wall steadily watched the camp and Sorley. O'Neill never left his place halfway down the hill near the prisoners, where he had a good view of the clearing. He paced back and forth restlessly, swearing to himself. Sorley never stirred, and they all began to fear he was indeed dead, of thirst or his wounds.

After midday all the captains came down to the chief and argued with him to release Sorley. "Never! I said it, I will not take it back! They must surrender! Oh, Christ, these obstinate Scots! Must they see him dead before they give in?"

But not long after that the men on the wall began to haul down Sorley's banner, and now he was helpless to stop them. Edmund said, "There, it comes now," but O'Neill was not placated.

"Christ, must they be so slow? The fool might die while they bring down his flag—" But it was done; and slowly, jerkily, the white banner was raised over the castle gate. Dunluce had fallen.

In a moment all was confusion; there was nothing of the usual dignified formality about accepting capitulation. A troop-guard formed hastily; men ran up with the officers' horses. The prisoners, fired by activity, commenced climbing over the barrier chains and tangling with the guards, in a fair way to start the fight over again, until O'Neill, just swinging up to the saddle, shouted, "Fools! This war is over—they are free! Follow me down!" O'Hagan added a hasty order to strike off their chains. The chief had waited to lead only a hundred or so troops, as token formality; he rode down the hill at a canter ahead of them, Rory with the captains behind.

The gate was already opening, and as they swarmed down toward it, the released prisoners in a ragged crowd after the Ulster troops, Gilchrist and a dozen troopmen rode out to meet O'Neill. The two groups met at one side of the clearing.

Gilchrist leaned from the saddle to proffer his ax, handle first, to O'Neill. "I surrender to you"—and his agate eyes were coldly bitter, but the hint of a wintry smile twisted his mouth. "But the jest is on you this time, O'Neill. Dunluce you could have had any time for a little loss. There are thirty men in the house."

No one ever saw O'Neill taken aback for long. He laughed. "Do you tell me! I will never believe Dougal MacArthur turned tail and fled."

Gilchrist showed his teeth. "The rest of your army is wishing he had. And much joy may you take of this traitorous victory—killing a man ten times your worth to avoid a fight!"

O'Neill's mouth went flat. "Watch your tongue, Gilchrist! No man worth more than O'Neill!" He turned to look over the heads of the collecting crowd to the place Sorley hung in his chains; he grinned. "But it's a good one, I grant you!"

He wheeled his horse and charged through the crowd, dismounted almost before he drew rein, pushed past those worrying at the chains about Sorley. "Get back, fools—give me room! Edmund, fetch me a saw!" But he could not wait for that; he swung Gilchrist's ax and began to strike the chains apart. At the sixth blow, Sorley collapsed toward him, released, and, after flinging down the ax, he caught up the limp body and hoisted it over his saddle.

They all started for the castle gate in a clamorous crowd—it was a farcical ending to a war, Rory thought later—Scots and Ulstermen mingled about the chief, who led his horse, steadying Sorley with one hand. At the house door he took Sorley in his arms as he might lift a child and thrust past the crowd of women and servants inside. Ferdoragh and Rory close after him, he strode down the fore-passage to the nearest door, that of the council room, and laid Sorley flat on the table. Turning, he pushed all the excited followers out into the corridor with a variety of oaths. Only two, a tearful manservant and a tall dark woman, eluded him.

"You have killed him—my love, my darling, speak to me! Shane, you devil, you have killed him—"

The chief turned back with a roar, seized his sister by the shoulders, and pushed her out the door by main force. "Out, you damned wanton! You that cannot stay faithful to a man whose one finger is worth more than your whole easy body! I do not want to lay eyes on you again while I am here!" He pushed Ferdoragh and Rory aside to bend over Sorley. "For the love of Christ, let him breathe!" Sorley lay still, gray of face, his body much blistered from the sun, his cheeks sunken, looking like death. "Come now, man, you'll be fine, not bad you are, come now, *avic—*" The manservant was snuffling and gulping; the chief swung on him in irritation. "Here, be of some use, idiot—fetch water, and make haste!" He hung over Sorley, swearing, while the man ran for it; when it was brought he tore a strip from his short cloak and began to bathe Sorley's face, washing away the caked dust and blood. "Come back now, *avic—*you'll be right enough! Not bad you are at all—"

Sorley's eyes opened slowly and focused on him. Gratified, the chief said, "There, you see, it needs more than that to kill a damned thick-skulled Scot like this one! Let me give you a drink, man." He held the flagon to Sorley's mouth. "Easy now, not too much or you will be sick."

"May God damn you," said Sorley in a hoarse whisper, "you treacherous Ulsterman, and all your clan, for twenty generations to come! My curse on you for a coward and traitor—"

"God be praised," said Ferdoragh emotionally, "he yet lives!"

O'Neill laughed and straightened. "Lives, do you say? He is still strong while he can swear at me! Here, man, fetch some other servants, get him to bed, feed him! Edmund—Terence!" He pulled open the door to face the anxious crowd in the passage. "What in the name of God are you all doing, wasting time so? Two hundred to occupy, the rest in camp—all the Scots within walls. Ferdoragh, do you collect the servants and have them prepare a meal. Starving I am. And set a man to watch that they do not water the liquor—I know the devious ways of Scots!"

CHAPTER XXIX

To THE victor belongs the spoil, said the proverb; and though they knew that Sorley would recover, that their part in this war was ended, the Scots who gathered in the hall of Dunluce that evening were gloom-ridden. Like every large house, Dunluce sheltered dozens of families—those of Sorley's kinsmen and officers, as well as servants. With O'Neill in possession, the castle might be handed to any man in his favor if he did not keep it himself, and all of them left homeless. But before the meal was served, O'Neill rose at the head of the main board and called for silence.

"I make an announcement I have already made to your master, that all you Scots may enjoy your meal better! Dunluce I have taken by default, but to show my strength only. I now formally return this castle and land to Sorley Boy, under my favor." He paused to let the relieved cheering die. "As for all you army men here, nominal prisoners within these walls you are, and I will leave a few guards to insure that, while I fight the rest of the war. But you'll be deprived of nothing and have nought to fear. My congratulations on a good defense, and God take the men we have killed in this fight. Now let us forget it and eat together in friendship."

Another outburst of cheers and thanks greeted that, and, on the whole, it was a merry party set to on the meal. None had enjoyed this fighting of the last ten days; but while no Scot could look with favor on the invasion of Scot land by Ulstermen, few men in Antrim would regret the death or deposition of James MacDonnell.

O'Neill did not sit at the table over liquor as was his custom, but, having eaten, rose, cup in hand, and wandered out to the passage. He did not say no when Rory followed; in spite of everything there might be a Scot or two who would think O'Neill improved with a dagger between his shoulders. O'Neill climbed the curving stone stair to the east wing of the castle and the chamber of its master. They had seen no more of the Lady Mary; from the glimpse he had of her Rory thought she scarcely feared O'Neill, but was probably sulking in her own chamber. The chief walked in without announcing himself and stood over the bed, looking at Sorley Boy.

Sorley was much recovered with a few hours of rest, meat and drink, if still weak; he lay propped up in the bed on a couple of cushions, flagon and cup to hand, and looked back at O'Neill. His officer, MacCowie, sat by the bed; he glowered at O'Neill and kept silent.

"Well, brother, how goes it?"

"Better than you intended, you bastard," said Sorley amiably, and O'Neill laughed.

"Not so! By God, Sorley, if you took permanent injury I would do penance the rest of my life! I did not want to kill more of your men. Listen, man. I have some fighting still to make and I want you out of the way. When you are rested enough, you are going to Benburb, nominally my prisoner—but," as Sorley started to protest, "only until I finish this war. I will want your help then. You are well known to all the landholders here. I will meet with them to discuss peace terms, and I promise you now, I deprive no man of aught who will listen to me and take oath not to rise against my rule. You can help—"

"That is generous."

O'Neill shrugged. "See it clear. I am out to unify a nation, not increase dissension. I want no more land for myself, why should I? At the least, you can tell the other Scots I am a fairer ruler than MacDonnell."

"No lie that is. I will agree to that."

"Good." The chief would have spoken further but at that moment one of the Ulster footmen peered in the door.

"My lord—they said you were here. The commander, your brother, arrives with the rest of the army."

"Ah! I thought we should be seeing Hugh today or tomorrow. Have him come up at once to me here." A few minutes later Hugh entered unceremoniously to embrace the chief.

"Well met, Shane! How goes it? Sorley, brother—wounded? What bastard did that to you? Rory, man, good to see you! For the love of God, give me that flagon, I am dry!" He sprawled in a chair and beamed round at them. By all evidence, he had ridden long and hard; his clothing was dusty and stained; it was a good two weeks since he had shaved, and he wore bandages about one leg and one forearm. But he was in tearing high spirits, as usual after a fight.

"Well?" demanded O'Neill impatiently. "What news? How has it gone, what is the military situation now? I take it you've not just rid off and left MacDonnell to his own devices?"

"In an opposite sort of way, yes," said Hugh. "Give me a chance to take a drink, will you? I don't know how you have fared, but we have had a war—have we not! Especially since that young devil, MacArthur, came in"—he let out a groan—"just at the wrong time! But you want it from the beginning. When did you take Dunluce, by the way?"

"Tell your story first. You came in by the south road—"

"Ten days ago yesterday. MacDonnell was waiting just where you said he would be, a bit north of Lough Belfast, and we had a fine fight there. But I was mindful of your orders—of course he had men primed to set signal fires and call in support from Cantyre and the islands. A nice thing, all the western clans down on us! I sent a force up the coast behind him to destroy the signals, while we played hide-and-seek round Kilultagh Wood a few days. Six days back we started to chase him north, and I swear, Shane, MacDonnell is growing old! The last stand he made I could have destroyed him; a child would know better than to pick such a place for a battle! The slope of a hill, loose stones all down it, and us above him! But in the middle of the fight, my Christ, down comes MacArthur and a good thousand men at us—I said a prayer, I tell you! Maybe Mac-Donnell planned it so, though we'd not seen MacArthur up to then—"

"No, he was with me," interrupted Sorley, chuckling. "Trust him to run fifty miles to a fight! What happened?"

"Well, it was a good fight. We got them started north again eventually and two days ago we took the Red Bay. We never let MacDonnell turn south or east, so on he came willy-nilly toward Dunseverick, and we had another fight there, and I was thinking the war was about over, for you'd said we should meet at Dunluce, and between the two of us— Well, we took Dunseverick, but—I'm sorry, Shane, such a short distance, too, but the fact is—"

"The fact is you have lost MacDonnell?" O'Neill was amused. "He was running too fast?"

"Like hare from hound," said Hugh in satisfaction.

"Well, he'll be somewhere about licking his wounds—never care, we shall find him. Are there many losses?"

"In round numbers, a hundred and a half dead, thrice that wounded. I left the worst wounded in the monastery by Carrick-fergus."

"An exciting few days you've had—like ourselves," said Sorley. "It is unfortunate you lost James."

O'Neill said smoothly, "It would, of course, be helpful to know where MacDonnell is, and you can likely make a shrewd guess. But I know your clan loyalty too well even to consider asking that you give me any aid you might. Even though you have never owned great friendship for your chief—"

Sorley was turning his empty cup round and round in his fingers abstractedly. "Exactly. It would be very wrong in me to tell you anything I might guess—however I feel personally, as you say." He ruminated; they all watched him, MacCowie suspiciously. He could not openly give O'Neill any information; that would be treachery to his clan. But there is—as Rory's mother was fond of saying—always a way to beat the devil round a gate. Sorley held out his cup to Hugh, who promptly refilled it. "Is it not queer," he remarked conversationally, "how men differ in battle? My-self, I always prefer to retreat onto low ground."

"I agree." O'Neill nodded. "A downhill course often encourages the pursuit to run by while one waits hidden in cover. MacDonnell thinks dif-ferent?"

"He thinks different. He likes high ground." Sorley drank. O'Neill and Hugh exchanged glances, and Rory could nearly hear them thinking: Mac-Donnell is probably somewhere between Dunseverick and Dunluce—what high ground lies there?

"If he is in hills," said O'Neill, "easy enough to coax him down to fight. Show him a few troops, ostensibly alone, in an open space, and down he comes at them, and the rest of us falling on him from the flanks."

"Always a good maneuver," agreed Sorley. "It would be the very place for it, too."

"Oh?" murmured O'Neill. Between Dunseverick and Dunluce, in hills above an open plain.

MacCowie opened his mouth and shut it, looking at Sorley.

"MacFarlane has a summer residence up Glen Maol Mor," said Sorley inconsequentially, and left it at that. Hugh grinned and sat back; O'Neill smiled up at the ceiling. In hills to the east and south, somewhere in Glen Maol Mor above the great open plain of Glentaisi.

"So what now?" asked Hugh. "Do we go out to find him tomorrow?"

"I think," said O'Neill gravely, "that we discuss the battle plan in more privacy."

Hugh turned a grin on Sorley. "Listen at me, I forget we are among enemies! Right you are."

"Sorley will excuse us. He understands how it is. I have much to do." O'Neill stood. "I've yet half a war to fight, and cannot waste time here in idle talk."

"Indeed," said Sorley as gravely. O'Neill and Hugh turned to the door. Rory followed; but as they came out to the passage, he heard MacCowie's voice for the first time in that little scene.

"Speak of treachery! As barefaced a betrayal as I ever expect to hear—"

And Sorley's reply, amused: "Betrayal? I was but making conversation. The writing on the wall I can read—there is only one end to this war, better have it over and done with. James' hands are none too clean—he deserves all Shane will give him. And would I not like to see that fight!"

O'Neill was hot for that battle and lost no time getting to it. He left a half-division as guard at Dunluce to hold the house and its occupants, and took the rest of the army, three and a half thousand strong, southeast for the place he was sure MacDonnell, with the major Scot forces, lurked. In the first sun of that next day, before they marched from field camp, he split the army into a dozen small groups, which separated with orders to rendezvous at a place not far from the plain of Glentaisi.

"MacDonnell is a canny one," he said to his captains, "and canny men with him. They know we have joined by now and outnumber them by a thousand or more, so they are not going to invite a battle army to army. They are lying low, playing for time until support comes in from Cantyre and the west Highlands. MacDonnell will have sent warning by now and those clans will be readying to bring help. So we will entice MacDonnell out of hiding and destroy him—then the rest will give us no trouble."

He sent advance scouts on foot to have a look for the enemy. They brought back gratifying news. As Sorley had surmised, MacDonnell, with the other chiefs, was up at the head of the glen with their combined armies.

"Good," said O'Neill. "We'll lure them down." Ferdoragh and a small force of men were the lure. They came up toward Glentaisi plain without attempt at concealment, seemingly unaware that the enemy watched them. The bait was too tempting for the MacDonnell to resist. Whether this was a scouting party hunting for him, or had got separated from the rest of the army and was trying to make liaison, it was a small force. He came down himself with a few hundred men to destroy it. Thus far he had had only defeat from the Ulstermen, and wanted a little retribution.

He collected his force at the glen-mouth, and came charging out onto the plain, shouting his clan war-cry, less pious than savage—"God and St. Andrew!"

In the next thirty seconds he had a surprise. The little party of Ulstermen fled modestly toward the east side of the plain; and out from the cover of wood burst O'Neill and two thousand troops in full charge. It was too late for MacDonnell to attempt retreat, and the surprise only added to his rage. He was at full gallop twenty lengths ahead of his men, and O'Neill ahead of his; they came charging down at each other, two axes up to strike, both forgetting their formal war shouts and yelling curses. It seemed they would ride into each other at full speed; at the last moment, O'Neill reined just slightly to the left and as they passed within inches, their stirrup irons all but touching, both struck. O'Neill had the advantage of a longer reach. The blade of his ax cleaved through the top of MacDonnell's left shoulder down to open a deep gash across the breast; MacDonnell's blow was deflected and plowed a little cut on O'Neill's right arm.

Then they were twenty yards past each other, the Scot chief's bridle-arm hanging limp. But he wheeled his horse by knee pressure as O'Neill reined sharp round, and they came on again; this time, O'Neill stood in the stirrups and struck backhanded, a vicious, powerful blow that opened MacDonnell's breast right to left, across the first gash. MacDonnell never got in a second hit; the horses clashed, and MacDonnell's went down. The force of O'Neill's blow drove him back and he fell behind, but, with one foot still in the stirrup, he was dragged when the horse scrambled up and ran. Then the armies came together with a crash—that swiftly it had happened—and O'Neill was bellowing to O'Hagan, "Get him off the field!"

O'Hagan and two of his troopmen swooped down on the panicked horse, swept up the broken body that was MacDonnell, and carried him off behind the battle under guard. Once too often he had met O'Neill and would never swing an ax again.

But the men on the hill were watching; at first sight of O'Neill's army, the other chiefs called out every man they had and came down the glen, not stopping to form ranks, with no choice now but to give battle, no matter the odds. There was a war leader left to them, and a good one. MacArthur deployed all the troops to right and left as they charged, circled the battle and pushed the Ulster troops into their own gallowglass. It grew into a major battle, for thirty bloody minutes, before MacArthur's losses and the weight of O'Neill's numbers drove the Scots into retreat. As they broke, O'Neill's powerful voice rose over the pipes: "Take MacArthur alive! I will hang the man who harms him!" The Ulstermen chased the retreat ten miles and took more than three hundred prisoners.

The day did much to soothe the chief after the campaign against Sorley Boy; this fight he had enjoyed. If the MacDonnell still lived, it would not be for long; O'Neill had promised himself those blows for fifteen years. The back of the Scot defense was broken.

They made camp where they were, found a stream, staked the horses, and built fires, while the chained prisoners were herded in a circle of post-and-chain. As the chief rode in from the last foray and dismounted, the first question he asked was, "Is MacArthur captured?"

Ferdoragh ambled up to answer, the original color of his kilt invisible under bloodstains, the day's dust caked with sweat all over him; he was already gnawing a bone. "I took him, Shane. He is in the prison lines loaded with chains after the fight he made. Hurt? My Christ, no! Would I harm a hair of the young cockerel's head? I took the handle of my ax to him—maybe he is awake by now."

The chief laughed and strode for the prison lines without stopping for a drink—and that was a day that left a man with a dry throat. He shouted MacArthur's name down the lines, and the young chief came up, glowering at him in the light of the prisoners' fire. "Dougal, brother," said O'Neill, and reached out his hand. "The best defense you made any general could make—you are a great one, as I always knew! You will take my hand and share my tent as paroled prisoner."

But Scots are hard and strange men, and MacArthur was still in a red haze of temper; he cursed O'Neill richly, and at that, O'Neill's own temper flared and if MacArthur had not been chained the two would have gone for each other all over again. MacArthur was still cursing when Hugh came up and, with no wasted word, dragged him out of the lines, took him off privately and gave him a full flagon. The combined efforts of Rory, Ferdoragh, and O'Hagan got the chief calmed down at last, and, all of them being weary after that day's work, the camp settled into its blankets early, only the posted guards alert on all sides.

Fighting Scots was not like fighting English, but almost like fighting among friends; moreover, MacArthur, besides being friend to Sorley Boy, had fought alongside the Ulstermen against the English last year, been friend to the chief and liked and admired by the captains. A pity it was, they felt, he continued to hold anger. But as they broke camp the next morning, the outposted guards came in with a terrified lone Scot who stammered that he sought MacArthur. It was one of the young chief's menservants from his home, looking for the Scot army to give MacArthur the welcome intelligence that his lady-wife was delivered of a son.

Since his wife had already presented him with five daughters to find dowries for and only two other sons, MacArthur's delight at the news smoothed away his anger entirely. When Hugh and O'Hagan had primed him with several drinks, he was more than ready to take O'Neill's hand and swear renewed friendship. So they were reconciled, and the Ulstermen could go on to subdue the rest of the Scots with lighter hearts.

CHAPTER XXX

Rory had hoped to get home to Benburb—after this long while it seemed home, with Moyna there—at least for a visit, but not until the end of June was the chief sufficiently sure of tenure to leave Antrim. All that summer, small raiding parties of Scots and Ulstermen ranged Antrim, and had frequent skirmishes.

O'Neill made a quick ride to Benburb the last week in June, staying only three days. Ostensibly, he went home to see if Sorley was fully recovered, but Rory thought actually it was to see the Lady Catherine. Had he no sympathy for that? It was good to be with Moyna again. She would have the child soon, now—September. Maybe it was that, for Moyna was no nervous female, but she confessed that she had been fearful for him in this war. "We knew there would be some terrible battles. I was so frightened! Of course, I did not say so to anyone, that is no use, but I prayed for you all the while."

"We had need of it, my heart." He did not add that they would probably need more prayers when O'Neill went against Red Hugh O'Donnell. He was just drifting into sleep that night when, in the dark, she said, "Rory."

"My love?"

"A queer thought I kept having while you were away fighting. We women are forever complaining about men, how they are always going off to fight and kill each other, and desire love with many wantons, and are altogether uncouth and rude and annoying. And yet, not one of us has any use for a man who is otherwise."

Rory drew her closer. "Women have no sense—that only proves it. Think how much more contented you'd be with a meek, acquiescent husband who did not know sword from ax, and never argued with any man, and never looked at a female before his wedding day, so he scarce knew how—" He was interrupted by a yawn and Moyna laughed soft.

"God knows there are few enough like that."

"Well, we've little more sense for it. What does a man seek when he goes looking? Good breeding, wealth, fertility, mildness of disposition? My Christ, no! He wants a slender figure and a pretty face and a bright eye. Of course, I was more reasonable. It's no matter at all, I said, if she is dull and plain, so long as she will be a dutiful wife—" Moyna slapped him smartly and he caught her hand to kiss it.

"That is what I get to marry a red McGuinness."

"Well," said Rory through another yawn, "it looks that you'll be keeping this red McGruiness awhile longer at least—there was a time or two I had my doubts of that."

On the first evening of O'Neill's return to Dunluce, Terence O'Hagan came riding in from Dunseverick with the news that the MacDonnell was dead.

"He died hard, Shane. The broken leg never healed, and the wounds in his body were poisoned; a sorry state he was in. But he would not see a priest until the last, though I offered it. When we saw he was dying I brought Father Owen in to him and he made the last rites, but all for nothing. Even while the father was blessing him he rose on one elbow and said, 'All my enemies I forgive—except O'Neill! May the whoreson burn in eternal hellfire!' And his voice failed, but he managed to sit up more and say it— 'Tell him I meet him in hell and renew the fight!' And then he died."

"And the devil took him with open arms," said O'Neill. "I trust you put a heavy stone over him, Terence." He swore to himself. "There is going to be a fight for that chiefhood. A dozen men have equal claims. I wish to God Sorley was nearer kin."

"It may go to Queen Mary to decide."

Brodie was on parole with MacArthur and most of Sorley's captains, and sat at the same table with O'Neill's men; now he laughed, hearing that. "Then him with most political favor will be chosen." There was voluble agreement among the Scot officers.

"I'm no fonder of Stuarts than you," said Buchan, "but do not go blaming the queen; only a girl she is."

O'Hagan laughed. "Were Hugh here, something he'd have to say to that."

O'Neill laughed with him. "Whether or no I succeed in chasing the English from Ireland, England is a ruined nation if Elizabeth does not produce an heir. A son of Mary Stuart could take her throne, and a Stuart on England's throne would finish what I begin."

MacArthur had been thinking of the first subject. "I know one who will claim the chiefhood—Aspuke MacDonnell. He was hoping that Mac-Donnell would name him legal heir, but you notice he's very prudently stayed out of this fight, waiting to see which way the cat jumps. Aspuke might be a Sassenach the way he has of sitting on the fence. Ten to one he'll come fawning on you for favor. I would not advise that you trust him in any measure."

"Aspuke?" repeated O'Neill. "Yes, I have heard Sorley mention the name. If it goes to the queen to decide, it may be in abeyance years."

With MacDonnell's death, O'Neill came into possession of that chief's vast holdings in Antrim. He desired no more land personally; the Mac-Donnell's he used to insure his tenure. He gave new land to Sorley, Mac-Arthur, Brodie, the Scot clansmen who would support him, and to those of his own men who were landless and, holding Antrim land, could over-see his rule here. The great fortresses of Dundrum and Dunseverick he gave to James and Manus Donnelly, and Terence O'Hagan also was in-vested with house and land.

The entire army had been amused at O'Hagan that summer. He was the chief's age, a confirmed bachelor and something of a rake with women, but destiny will overtake every man, and when O'Hagan fell, it was a great fall. He was hopeless victim to a pretty farm girl half his age and size, and married her almost before his friends had time to savor the jest. She had him as securely bridled as ever married man was, and even pre-vailed on him to shave off the great red mustache he had worn for years. When Hugh heard about that, he said gloomily it was a sign the Ulster captains were growing old and weak.

By the beginning of August the conquest of Antrim was complete, all the chiefs and leaders dead or captured. The island chiefs who escaped fled back to the islands to lick their wounds and complain to the queen for this outraging of Scotland's Irish holding. O'Neill had arranged formal meeting with the Scot chiefs and landholders, for discussion of terms, at the Red Bay House. A week before that meeting was to be held, Sorley Boy, now quite himself, rode from Benburb to take part. He brought the chief a letter from Lady Catherine which appeared greatly to delight him; the rest of that day O'Neill was in high spirits.

"Somewhat the lady wrote him he was glad to hear," hazarded Fer-doragh as they gathered for the meal that evening.

"I wonder now what under the heavens it could be," said McArdle innocently.

"It was June we rode into Tyrone," counted Rory. "Likely March it will be. I wonder if it's to be another son or a daughter this time?"

Whether it was for news of the lady's new pregnancy or not, the chief was merry over the meal, calling on O'Givney, who, of course, had accom-panied him all this campaign, for one ballad after another. As they sat talking over liquor, the tables cleared away, he looked round suddenly at Rory.

"I have just remembered a small matter I meant to speak of. A little debt I am owing you I should repay."

"Debt, O'Neill?" Rory was surprised. "If you're meaning that Scot foot-man came on you behind at Glentaisi—"

"Oh, that and one or two other things. Ferdoragh reminds me, you

have served me well a matter of five years and a bit, and let's hope will
continue to do so. A little reward you might appreciate?"

"Reward be damned," said Rory, returning his smile. "No encourage-
ment of that kind I need to serve you, O'Neill."

"Good man, but I shall give you some nonetheless. What do you say to
a little land?"

Rory found himself on his feet, incredulous. Land! Only chiefs and
high clansmen could own land—land was worth more than gold, more
than life. O'Neill did not mean it. He stammered, "Land—but, O'Neill, I
don't—"

"There is a small property called Kilclain in south Antrim—just north
of Monynimrock—part of MacDonnell's holding it was. You may have it
and welcome. I will see the deed transferred to you tomorrow."

"My Christ," said Rory excitedly, "no words to thank you, O'Neill!"
Land! Land to leave his sons, a house of his own, a place of his own!
Would he not have something to tell Moyna when he got back to her!

"Nothing," said O'Neill largely. "Welcome you are. It is one for you, two
for me. I want loyal men in Antrim now. This house is but a day's ride
from your chief's castle. You may ride down to have a look at it if you
like." In the midst of his excitement Rory realized it was not indeed pure
generosity on O'Neill's part; on two counts it would serve him: as he said,
another loyal man here, and also the chief, McGuinness, had always been
a trifle lukewarm to O'Neill of Ulster and largesse distributed to a McGuinness of the chief's line would do no harm in that direction. But it was a
great thing all the same; already Rory was making plans about it as he
uttered more thanks, accepted congratulations.

The chief gave him leave, and he rode down to inspect the property,
taking Diarmuid Ryan with him for company. He found it a fine place,
a good solid stone house and forty acres about it; an overwhelming present. They rode on to the McGuinness' house and he made some boasting
about it—he had a right to. There was enough affection between him and
his brothers that they showed no resentment at his favoring.

"But I'm not wanting to leave O'Neill's service—why should I? And while
I'm with him my wife and family I'll keep at Benburb. I will need a responsible factor at Kilclain." Even a good name to the property, he
thought—the monastery of the pleasant meadows: maybe long ago there
had been a religious house there, and it was hallowed ground; that was a
good omen. His father nodded, his grandfather, the chief, wheezed and
regarded him approvingly.

"You turn out better than I expected after all, young one. Feared I
was you'd follow Ferdoragh's feckless way, and he wandering about fighting for foreigners, no steadiness to him at all. But your wife will keep your
nose to the grindstone." In the end it was decided that Fergus and his
wife should go to live at Kilclain to manage the property, the McGuinness

donating an appropriate staff of servants. Even in the event, Rory thought, that some future day he left O'Neill's service, there would be plenty for both families there; he and Fergus got on well. So it was arranged, and Fergus rode north with them as far as Kilclain to look it over, decide with Rory what they should acquire of furnishing and stock. MacDonnell had left the house empty for long; there were no disgruntled Scots to deal with, and the tenant farmers, this near the border of Ulster, were half Irish and amenable to a new overlord. Rory's only discontent those days was impatience to get back to Benburb and tell Moyna his great news.

At the formal parley with the Scot chiefs O'Neill was unusually impersonal with them; he argued his great plan with vigor. He had Sorley Boy, MacArthur, and Brodie, all respected men of proven honor, to swear fealty and help persuade the others, but the response was cautious.

MacFarlane put the prevailing view when he said, "The O'Neill speaks of unifying to make a nation and drive out the English. That sounds very well, but nations have rulers and the O'Neill is proposing to make himself High King with full right over his kingdom. No man here will accuse me of being Anglophile, but I would say, one ruler can be as autocratic as another. The English have no authority in Antrim and have never had. Should we accept a ruler where there was none before?"

"I do not accuse you of being Anglophile, but of shortsightedness," said O'Neill. "You will remember my father letting them into Ulster. How long are you thinking they would have stayed west of the river if I did not chase them out entirely? English we all know. I say to you, unless we unify against them, they will take the whole country. Speaking of rulers, what else was MacDonnell here, holding five times as much land as any other chief?" His persuasive smile was on them. "The political tide is toward unification. You will have to walk in step with some neighbor eventually—would you rather walk with me or Elizabeth of England?"

"There is only one answer to that," said Aspuke MacDonnell, "but I am not convinced of what you say. The Pale authorities have made no move toward Antrim."

"God give me patience," said O'Neill. "Did I say shortsighted? I should have said blind. My friends, there is a fox coming down on your neighbor's barns to steal poultry. Will you refuse to join a hunt because he has not raided your own hen-roost? Enough!" He slapped a hand down on the council table. "I have laid out the terms. I name Sorley Boy, MacArthur, and Brodie my deputies here. I take no land from any of you, but I will have a pledge that on request you send me half your forces of men to serve in my army, for which I will pay the usual mercenary rate. What do you say?"

There was nothing they could say but yes. The Scottish queen would not approve that Scot land was invaded, but she had domestic difficulties and little military force; it was unlikely that she would do more than protest formally. The chiefs submitted to O'Neill and signed his treaty. In the first week of September O'Neill marched out of Antrim, the war officially won.

The army arrived at Benburb the day after Moyna's child was born. That was the first news to greet Rory; he was up the stair and down the passage to their chamber in record time, to find her as excited as he and eager to exhibit their fine new son to him.

"Now are you not glad you wed me? See what I've done for you! Oh, Rory, do tell me quick! The name, stupid! You never would say—"

"Well, I've not given it much thought, a little thing like that."

"Oooh, liar! You must have! Dying to know I've been, nothing to call him by at all—tell me, Rory!"

"Give me a chance to consider it!" But he relented, kissing her again. "He will be Michael for my grandfather, does that satisfy you?"

She sank back, smiling. "Mhm, yes, a good name it is, and besides your grandfather might be giving a namesake a little present."

"Mercenary! But I can't say I'm as pleased as all that." And he contrived to frown at the infant.

"Why, what do you mean, what is it?"

"Well, my Christ, all your black hair he has! Every man I know will be jeering at me that my wife's bloodline is stronger than mine!"

Moyna giggled pleasedly. "I'm sorry indeed, my love, but only in the nature of things it is. Maybe some of the girls will have red hair," she added condescendingly.

"Another word and I disown him! But I come back with news for you, too—wait until you hear—" It was a question if they were more excited for the son or the tremendous gift O'Neill gave Rory. She was quite amenable to his plan that she remain here, though she might have more authority as mistress of Kilclain.

"All these wars the chief makes—" Moyna sighed, looking at him a little wistfully. "It seems I've scarce seen you this year. Are you to be at Benburb long now, do you know? I have hoped—"

He held her close, turning his face to her shoulder to hide the trouble in his eyes. "Maybe a month—six weeks. I am not sure."

That was almost a lie. The chief had said to a similar question, "Until the hunting season? Well, we'll take a little rest, but not that long. Yes, it will be a good season, brothers—but we go hunting fatter game than stag."

CHAPTER XXXI

O'NEILL had stronger reasons than tradition of enmity for a war against Red Hugh, who had coveted Catherine and more than a few times offered her annoyance while she lived at Rath O'Donnell. What was the truth about O'Neill's dream of a nation? Even the men who knew him best could never be sure of that. Some said it was impartial patriotism, the strong desire of a strong man to restore Ireland to all her former greatness as a nation; some said he thought once for Ireland and twice for Shane the Proud, and if he benefited the former it was more to see himself High King. The English were sneering that as he fell short of making himself King of England, his wounded pride demanded he be king somewhere. His other enemies accused him of wanton thievery, saying O'Neill of Ulster could never stay content at home but was driven by boredom to make war unjustified if there was none justified to join. Rory was inclined to think it was a little of all those reasons.

Now, though O'Neill needed Tyrconnell to complete his conquest of the north, it was not primarily a political campaign. He had a good hard hatred for Red Hugh and was well pleased at the excuse to face him over an ax.

He had said he would give any ruler but Anglophiles the chance to join under him before making war. But Red Hugh was a different matter. "No Anglophile he," said the chief, "but do you see him listening to a word I say? If O'Neill of Ulster said the sun rises in the east, Red Hugh would deny it to his confessor." He would not approach this enemy with soft words.

On the other hand, as he made plain to his captains, he did not want Hugh Ruadh dead. In that event, old Calvagh in Dublin would name a new heir to the chiefhood, and probably an Anglophile. "I would rather have Hugh Ruadh holding in Tyrconnell for me," said O'Neill, "than another man who would let the English in the minute my back was turned. But he has got to be whipped hot and heavy, so that never again will he even entertain the thought of challenging O'Neill. And that I'll see to."

So he never parleyed with Red Hugh at all. He took his entire army to

Tyrconnell in a quick two days' march, and over the border he fired every field and house of any size, laying waste the land all the way up to Rath O'Donnell. Ten miles this side, Red Hugh met him. The nominal O'Donnell had little to defend with, only a thousand men, but they had a fight, as O'Neill had expected.

The first battle drove the O'Donnell men past Rath O'Donnell, and O'Neill halted his pursuit to ravish that. He had all the furnishing carried out and built of it a great bonfire. He prisoned all the servants, took the several professional concubines Red Hugh kept and added them to his own camp-followers. He took the stableful of horses for his troops, and burned every home field a mile in each direction. By the time the Ulstermen caught up to have another engagement, Red Hugh had heard of that, if he needed another reason to spur him on against O'Neill. He was not slow to join battle again and again. After two weeks of slash-and-run back and forth across Tyrconnell barely half his men were left, the rest dead or taken, and in the last fight, he himself was taken prisoner.

O'Neill would not deign to walk down to the prison lines for O'Donnell; he had him fetched up by two gallowglass men—McCaffrey and the constable, McSweeney. On a boulder covered with a stag hide before his tent he sat, legs wide, leaning negligently on one arm, watching as the two big men led that third big man toward him. About him stood and sat all his captains, Rory to the left behind. Hugh Ruadh O'Donnell, Rory had never seen at close quarters, and he was a man to see: a man much like Turlough Lynagh without Turlough's amiable temperament. He lacked an inch or so of O'Neill's height but was twice as broad, a hard-muscled red bull of a man. No, thought Rory: a boar. The vicious wild mountain boar, the wanton killer: even the red bristles round his jaw the same, the thick, muscular neck, the little shrewd eyes with the look of the killer in them. But he was not a weak man. That was the last coherent thought Rory had for some moments, for Hugh Ruadh, his mouth drawn in a snarl, wrenched away from his guards and flung himself at O'Neill, head down. His wrists were chained and he was disarmed, but he could make destruction, and Rory plunged between, knife out, hearing O'Neill's loud command, "Don't aim to kill!" He was half the size of O'Donnell and that big red hairy body struck him like a cannon ball; they went down, Rory beneath, stabbing blind, feeling teeth in his arm. Then hands hauled O'Donnell off him and he stumbled to his feet, rubbing his arm ruefully, all the breath knocked from him. Colm McCaffrey hit O'Donnell hard with clenched fist and O'Neill ordered, "None of that —yet. Are you right, Rory?"

"I am—when I get some air," he panted. O'Donnell grinned, feeling the gash in his side, his eyes saying were it not for the chains, Rory would have more to recall him by.

"It has not changed," said O'Neill. He had not altered his position for the little attack; the captains had moved with Rory, and now, at his gesture, stepped back. He stood slowly, slowly unslung the short riding-cloak from about his shoulders, took two strides to stand a pace from O'Donnell and look him in the eye. O'Donnell spat at him and cursed. Edmund Donnelly plucked grass and wiped the spittle from O'Neill's tunic; the chief gave that no notice. "The same O'Donnell," he said, smiling faintly. "Now hold him where he is, men, and if he opens his mouth, shut it for him. I have somewhat to say to you, my red stallion. I'll say it slow and more than once so you can take it in, for a thick skull you have. Listen. I have come to take Tyrconnell. Not for myself I take it, but in the process of building a nation here. If you will acknowledge my rule, I make you no more damage and take nothing more from you. The chief, O'Donnell, is subchief to me as you will be in your time. Are you listening, Hugh Ruadh?"

"I would not listen to you, and yours the only voice I could hear." Even his voice was like the boar's—rough and sullen.

"No choice you have," said O'Neill. "You will listen and you will hear. Now I will say it all over again, and again after that, to make certain you understand. Tyrconnell is mine. Listen, Hugh Ruadh. From Lough Swilly to the River Finn it is mine, from the west sea to Salmon Castle it is mine. Henceforth you will mind that. I will build a nation here if a thousand men like you stand in my way. Listen, Hugh Ruadh." He was deliberately calling O'Donnell a lack-brained fool; he said it over four times, his eyes holding O'Donnell's steady. O'Donnell stared back as steadily. "Now I have got it past the bone of your skull," O'Neill said, "but I must drive it home to your small brain. Continue to hold him." He loosened the throat fastening of his tunic, measured the distance and with that little smile still fixed on his mouth, he took both fists to O'Donnell. McCaffrey and McSweeney were both powerful men but they had work to hold O'Donnell under the chief's hammering. Perhaps it was the only time in his life O'Neill so far forgot honor as to strike a bound man. His blows were measured, deliberate, every one with all his force behind it. In three minutes O'Donnell's face was a mask of blood, blood streaming down to clot in the coarse red mat on his chest. When a blow caught the guards off balance and O'Donnell went down, O'Neill bent and hauled him up to strike him down again. And when he had hit O'Donnell two dozen or thirty times, he stopped, took a breath, and asked, "Do you learn the lesson, Hugh Ruadh? Repeat it to me."

O'Donnell spat teeth and blood. "Christ-damned cowardly whoreson of an O'Neill!" he said thickly. "That lesson I don't learn any day."

"You will learn it," said O'Neill. He began on him again; the men about all watched impassively, but Rory felt they shared some of his own disgust for the sight. Not so much for the brutality of it—when he chose, O'Neill was ruthless, and they had all known that before. It was the literal sight. Rory had seen some grisly things on battlefields, but none had ever affected him like the look of O'Donnell under O'Neill's fists that day. When the chief stepped back a second time O'Donnell's face was a red pulp, his nose flat on one cheek. "Repeat the lesson to me, Hugh Ruadh" —and he was breathing hard.

And again O'Donnell spat. "Too stupid—I am—learn that lesson, you bastard—"

"You will learn it." O'Neill's silk tunic had ripped open as he struck; in quick impatience he ripped it the rest of the way, flung it off behind. And again, and again—how many blows had he struck now? They lost count. Edmund turned suddenly away; O'Hagan was staring across McCaffrey's head to a soaring hawk; even Ferdoragh, the stolid, looked unhappy. And Rory was not the only man there who thought those blows were delivered not for a nation, but for a woman.

The last time O'Neill struck, O'Donnell was driven again from the guards' hands and went down backward and stayed, and from the shoulders up he did not look like a man any more; the marks of this hour he would carry to his grave. O'Neill stood, letting him lie, getting his own breath. He said to McSweeney, "Bring him alive." The constable fetched a leather bag of water and flung the contents over O'Donnell. After a moment O'Donnell moved; he sat up, and O'Neill nodded at the guards; they hauled him to his feet.

"Repeat the lesson to me, Hugh Ruadh."

O'Donnell raised his bloody head with effort. His eyes could not focus any longer on O'Neill. He made two attempts at speech before he got it out in a harsh whisper: "Tyrconnell—is—yours. I acknowledge—fealty."

"You are a slow learner," said O'Neill through his teeth. "See you are a retentive student." But that O'Donnell never heard; he slumped between the guards again, unconscious.

O'Neill sent O'Donnell back to his stripped castle; O'Donnell's men he released without weapons. He rode for Tyrone through the first snows, having got O'Donnell's signature to a treaty substantially the same as that he pressed on the Scots.

In winter he could make no effective war, and must delay going against Burke and Sullivan in Galway, or the Leinstermen, until spring; he settled the army into permanent camp. But if he could not make any fighting, there were still men he might make discussion with.

Before Christ-tide he rode south to visit O'Reilly. That chief was no Anglophile; but he had reason for caution, with the English just over his south fields. O'Neill talked seriously to him, and O'Reilly listened. At the end, the subchief said, "I need not tell you it's on the sidelines I've sat and not the fence. A man's first duty is to himself and his people.

But I am a reasonable man, and I see the time is come when I must say a definite yes or no."

"And which is it, Eoghan?" O'Neill gave him his charming smile.

"I say more than yes, O'Neill. I put myself and my holding at your disposition, because this is a great work you do. But I am wondering if you can accomplish it—even O'Neill of Ulster."

The replies O'Neill had from the Leinster chiefs were noncommittal. But O'Rourke acquiesced out of fear, pledging a hundred men. McMahon did the same. Altogether the chief was pleased at his success thus far. He had said, if it takes twenty years; but it appeared that might be an overestimation.

"Say five. On the whole, it goes well. I hold the whole north now. Next year," said O'Neill, "or the year after, I will hold all of Ireland. And then, brothers, what a mighty beating will I give the English!"

CHAPTER XXXII

ASPUKE MACDONNELL made a pilgrimage round Antrim that late winter, visiting chiefs and clansmen. On the last day of February he came to Dunluce.

"The first matter," he said to Sorley, "is that a majority of those who signed the pact with O'Neill last year are now dissatisfied and draw a petition to reconsider its provisions."

Sorley Boy regarded him grimly. "If the chiefs think to wriggle out of that treaty now they are mistaken."

"It might be argued that to make a treaty with a foreign ruler the chiefs show disloyalty to our queen."

"They signed it," said Sorley, "and they will keep it. Have you presented this petition to MacArthur and Brodie as the other representatives of O'Neill in Antrim?"

"We have not. The petition we will send direct to the Ulsterman."

"More fools you. I will hear no more talk of that, and I will take steps to inform O'Neill that this is no plotting of mine. There was another matter?"

Aspuke talked about that in his soft blank voice; presently Sorley cut him off. "In plain language, you seek to enlist support of enough clansmen in a petition that the queen approves you as the new chief. You get no pledge from me. Aside from any other consideration, your first act as chief would be to outlaw the treaty with O'Neill, and my honor is pledged to maintain that to the extent of my power."

Aspuke looked at him with hooded eyes. "There are changes coming. Sooner than you think, you may be wishing you had never allied yourself with O'Neill. He will be finished and done before either of us is much older."

Sorley laughed. "A poor soothsayer you are. Have you heard no news this year?"

"Oh, he rides high now. Not forever. He made a little mistake two years back when he defeated the English and failed to follow up victory. They have smarted from that defeat ever since, and they are out to bring him down. If they need another reason, it is his conquest of this year. They know if they allow him to grow much stronger they will lose their hold on Ireland."

Sorley was silent, for that confirmed a secret fear of his own. The English would hold a grudge forever.

"Once they finish him," said Aspuke, "his power is ended to protect his friends, and all of you who stood by him may wish you had used more sense. They will not retain much charity for his allies."

Sorley said harshly, "I am not a Lowlander or an Englishman to choose allegiances by the favors to be had. I listen to no more talk like this, and I will ask you to leave my house."

Aspuke departed as quietly as he had come, which somehow made Sorley feel him to be the more sinister.

Armagh—Amsterdam, February 1565

Liam Fleming amused himself, over several months, with delicate intrigue designed to sow suspicion among O'Neill's enemies. Among acquaintances on the Continent, he numbered a Dutch Jew, Van Leyden who was a moneylender to royalty; and, knowing Fleming's interest, Van Leyden informed him when Elizabeth of England requested a loan. The money was meant for arms for Radcliffe in Ireland.

Fleming conveyed a suggestion to the moneylender which amused them both. Through her emissary, the Queen of England was informed that rumor of corruption and mismanagement within the Pale government, intended recipient of the gold, made Van Leyden reluctant to grant the loan at reasonable interest. If Her Majesty could make some investigation, to be assured of the honesty of her deputies, the loan would be made gladly.

As Fleming had hoped, Elizabeth took the bait. Politicians being what they were, the investigation was bound to uncover some depredations. Perhaps she would be so incensed that Radcliffe would not receive his reinforcement.

Dublin, March 1565

Radcliffe was caught between fury and fright when he read Sir William Cecil's letter; but also, he was devoutly grateful that a man like Cecil was close to the queen. Cecil understood the ins and outs of management of government offices . . . "Her Majesty appears determined upon an investigation of the disposition of funds allotted to the Pale. I realize the inconvenience this will lay upon you, and thought you should have private intelligence of the imminent arrival in Dublin of the two appointed delegates. Not, I hasten to add, that I have any remote suspicion you have aught to conceal. I attempted to dissuade Her Majesty, but you will understand that I could not show overvehemence. The delegates, Sir

Nicholas Arnold and Sir Nicholas Bagenal, I believe you know. The former is a charming fellow, perhaps a little unworldly . . ."

Radcliffe read between the lines; he did some cursing, more thinking. Awkward was a mild word for it. He made no pretense to himself about it: how many government officials took no advantage of position to line their left-hand pockets? Essentially, he cared not a half-penny whether any other man stayed free of accusation or not, under this investigation, so long as he kept his own hands clean. He was the one strong man in Her Majesty's government here, and were he removed from his appointment because of some finicking little financial maneuvers, there would be none to replace him. With events shaping as they did, it was more important that he remain in office than that the queen be sure to a penny where her gold went in Ireland. The principal requirement, he thought, was a scapegoat for himself, for certain machinations which might be discovered—a man to push the responsibility on, all neatly documented. He did not think far before he found the man.

The queen's investigators arrived in Dublin in April and spent three months prying into every office in the government, with a corps of assistants to search all the records. They uncovered a shocking amount of corruption at once, and the deeper they delved, the more they found. Retribution cleaved a wide swathe among the great and small of that government. The investigators were somewhat horrified to be obliged to arrest Sir Henry Radcliffe, brother of the military commander who, by voluminous evidence, had robbed the Crown of some eighteen thousand pounds. His vigorous denial and bewilderment when confronted with the evidence were convincing, but that evidence was clear.

In consequence of all the furor raised, every man of any remote connection with the government turned wary, and by May, as Radcliffe complained to Sydney, a man could not ask the time of day and get a straight answer from anyone.

"Just at this time, God, it is devilish! How in Christ's name dare I ask for more equipment, after this?" But there was no hint of his exasperation in the letter he wrote to the queen. He was both shocked and grieved to learn of his brother's astonishing venality; he could not but feel that Her Majesty might suspect—but no, of course, the investigation had proven him personally innocent of the villainous crimes so appallingly found to be rife. Nonetheless, he trusted Her Majesty would . . . and would not . . . and would bear in mind . . . and he was pleased to sign himself, as he hoped he might for long, Her Majesty's humble servant, et cetera.

In his letter to Sir William Cecil he vented some more genuine emotions.

"It is diabolical chance brought this on. . . . After the business at Drum Cru, I should have thought it apparent the danger we face. And now! O'Neill ravages the land. He has taken Tyrconnell, he has made confederacy with the Scots, he has appropriated the entire north and calls himself king. My friend, he spent last winter in Tyrconnell, the spring in Sligo; this summer he is in Galway—and next winter in the Pale. The situation is thus desperate, unless I am afforded the aid you pledged . . ."

London, May 1565

But Radcliffe underestimated Elizabeth Tudor, and at least one of her ministers.

"I am always pleased when such a long chance comes off," murmured Sir Francis Walsingham, rereading the letter just received from one of his European agents. "The Jesuit priests."

"What Jesuit priests?" asked Cecil.

"Why, I thought it would be useful to drive another wedge between O'Neill and the Pope. And amusing. Of course, it meant the loss of several agents, but I took care they were all expendable men—very new, untried spies, all sent into Ulster and all disguised as Jesuit fathers. O'Neill had caught and hanged four of them up to two months ago. He grew very suspicious of all Jesuits. Now I learn, as I say, the long chance comes off. He hanged another a month back—"

"Yes?"

"But the fifth was a genuine priest." Walsingham laughed. "The Pope is—um—justifiably furious. A pleasing little *coup*."

"My congratulations," said Cecil amusedly. "That is indeed useful." He was more gratified that same afternoon when he met with Her Majesty in private council. They understood one another well now; he could look back to his fears for her female instability over O'Neill with a smile. Still, she was unpredictable, and she had reason for anger over the corruption discovered in the Pale government. "I would hesitate to say it is of minor importance," he began smoothly.

"Why, my dear Sir William? If you imagine it came as any surprise to me, you rate my naïveté too high. I trust I have a grasp of essential facts. We have given those officials a great fright and they will cease their depredations for a little in any event—and use caution if they dare recommence them. I have no care for whether Lord Radcliffe is venal that way —he is a strong general, and him we need in Ireland."

"Just so. I am glad to hear this from you."

She smiled without mirth. "I thought we were finished with O'Neill of Ulster. It appears we are not."

Cecil coughed, produced some documents. "Sir Francis has sent a good many agents into Ulster. There is little surety of what they accomplish, of course—"

The queen laughed, pushed the proffered papers aside. "No, no, that

is the slow way to go about it. What did Radcliffe write? 'Next winter in
the Pale—' yes. Unless something is done to stop him."

"You will pardon if I seem hesitant, Majesty. I'd remind you of the
military clause in the Drum Cru treaty. There are twenty-two hundred
troops in the Pale now, and if there is any violence, any—"

"My friend," said Elizabeth harshly, "treaties signed under duress are
made to be broken. If O'Neill intends invasion of the Pale in any case,
need we be so timid as to fear provoking him? Something must be done
at once, the situation as it is. If we could know definitely that he hangs
back from attack on the Pale, it would be no matter. A year, two years,
would see him finished anyway. He can never hold all he has conquered.
If he leaves part of his army to keep each parcel of land he takes, he'll
soon be without an army—if he relies on treaties and oaths of loyalty
and leaves no guard, rebellion will spread behind him and he will lose
the old while he gains the new. No man and no army of men will ever
unite the Gaels into a nation. The point is, we cannot be sure he will not
attack the Pale again when he finishes his present campaigns. We cannot
afford to take the chance. Twenty-two hundred troops, you said. Sir William, six months from now I want to see an army of seven thousand in
the Pale under Radcliffe. And as soon as practical then we will attack
Ulster and finish O'Neill."

"Seven—! Walsingham had thought—I told you—"

"That is the slow way, infiltrating and fomenting dissension from
within. Listen, my friend. We will no longer try to influence Ulstermen
against him, but Englishmen. The direct way—in this case, the only way.
We may have little time. . . ."

April–June, 1565

In Tyrconnell, Hugh Ruadh smoldered in silence, but paid the clan-
tribute when it fell due. In Antrim, the Scot chiefs met and argued, and
Sorley Boy and MacArthur felt them slipping from under control; the
bloody memory of Glentaisi field had faded and O'Neill was away south
with his army. In Galway, Burke regretted his signature on a treaty, had
visions of the Ulsterman marching in and taking possession; but if it came
to a choice between O'Neill and the English? He could not see that happening. Just over the border of the Pale, O'Reilly was approached by
the deputies, and courteously consigned them to hell.

In Leinster, chafing at delay, O'Neill parleyed long with a dozen doubt-
ful chiefs. He would not make war against them unless they refused him
definitely, and that, these men had not done as yet. He might have been
more content could he have had Lady Catherine with him, but her new
son, Brian, was but a few months old and she would not leave Benburb.
To waste this good summer fighting-weather over long talks! But until the
southrons gave him a definite answer, he had no choice.

In Rome, His Holiness at last lost patience with the arrogant O'Neill of Ulster, who so cavalierly apologized for hanging a holy priest—mistaking him for a spy, he said: a mistake! His Holiness issued a proclamation excommunicating the Prince of Ulster and threatening excommunication to any Catholic who afforded him any aid whatsoever.

In Dublin, Radcliffe waited with some anxiety for replies from Cecil and the queen. Time might be short. He waited with no less anxiety for news out of Leinster. If the Leinster chiefs defied O'Neill and he went to war there, it would give the Pale a breathing space. But war in Leinster, for those chiefs had little to pit against O'Neill, would mean only more conquest. God, where would it end? Radcliffe was of two minds what to pray for, aside from the death and damnation of Shane O'Neill.

PART FIVE

destiny

CHAPTER XXXIII

In August the Leinster chiefs made treaty with O'Neill, and he marched home. It was too late in the season to begin a campaign farther south this year; he must possess patience until the spring, but he was ready to take a little rest, having met such success in this short while. Success in Ireland he enjoyed, but elsewhere— The excommunication did not worry him, though it troubled Lady Catherine and the captains; he demanded heretically who said the Pope spoke for God: it was spite, that was all. There were also the English; that first night he returned to Benburb and found a letter from Fleming waiting, he said thoughtfully, reading it, "It may be I'll take the Pale next after all."

But for the moment they took holiday. Rory took the longest leave he had had from O'Neill's service in nearly six years, and rode to Kilclain to see how Fergus did at the property. He would have taken Moyna, for she had never seen the house, but she would bear another child in November and could not ride so far. He found Kilclain prosperous; Fergus was proud of the crops they harvested, and no less to show his new son, named for Rory, who accused his brother indignantly of toad-eating him. "I suppose now you are expecting some fine present for it."

"I would not say no," said Fergus, winking at his wife, Lileas, who looked demure. "But you cannot complain—what else did you do to Grandfather last year?"

Rory capitulated with a laugh. He would look about in Armagh, on his way home, for a christening present, and a present also for Moyna, now he had some gold to spend.

O'Neill was not precisely in jovial mood these days, what with the news that came from his agents in the Pale. The night of Rory's return to Benburb, the chief sat silent by the hearth and did not join much talk.

About the middle of the evening there were sounds of arrival in the courtyard. When the hall door swung back, O'Neill rose at once; it was the Dean entering, and at his side, Thady O'Brien. Neither would be here at this hour, or O'Brien north at all, if not with important news.

And by their expressions, it was not good news. The seven captains followed the chief down the hall to clasp Daniel's hand.

"Well, Terence, what brings you here?"

"The council hall," said the Dean tersely. They all gathered there, servants scurrying ahead to kindle wall torches and fetch liquor. Daniel accepted the cup the chief offered him, and that showed his agitation, for he seldom drank anything but wine.

"Well?" repeated the chief impatiently. "What brings you here, O'Brien at your heels?"

"I at his," said Daniel. "I thought we should make discussion at once for what he has to tell you."

The chief turned to O'Brien, who was waiting to be offered a drink. Hugh filled a cup and thrust it at him, and he nodded thanks.

"Some of it you know already, O'Neill. The English will hold a grudge —they have never forgot Drum Cru. That minister, Walsingham, he has underhand tricks to play—"

"Those Jesuit priests," said O'Neill, looking savage. "And that damned bigoted Italian in Rome will not hear a word I say—"

"Softly," said the Dean. "Whatever the rights and wrongs, he is still the Pope. It looked bad, Shane. His Holiness could not know—"

"Damn His Holiness!" said O'Neill. "I apologized for the mistake, did I not?" The Dean made a gesture of resignation and signed to O'Brien to continue.

"For the last half-year there is all this rumor in England against you, stirring the common folk up to believe O'Neill is the devil himself—tales of how you capture and torture innocent Englishmen and mistreat women. And all of them believing every word, such a hate worked up against you so that last month there was a great meeting of Londoners and your effigy hanged and burned—"

"Did you ride north to tell me what I already know?"

"It is disturbing," said the Dean.

"It is. At the moment, there is nothing I can do about it. What did you come to tell me, Thady?"

O'Brien eyed him nervously. All the captains were crowded about the chief, listening; Rory thought some of this was news to them, as to himself. O'Brien wet his lips, looking from one to another as if gathering courage to give the chief bad news: to reinforce himself, he took a gulp of liquor. "On a ship from England three days ago, there came these bills to be put up all over the Pale, with soldiers to read them. Madam—that woman of Sydney's, she told me they are also scattered over England and great public notice made of it. A proclamation from the queen. I could not get one to bring you, O'Neill, sorry I am, but I got an educated friend to copy down what it says." He looked at the Dean, who produced a folded paper from his tunic. O'Neill stretched out a hand but, instead of giving him the note, Daniel cleared his throat and read it aloud in his resonant creamy churchman's voice:

" 'The public anger is so righteously roused for the threat to our Irish colony from the savage rebel-leader, O'Neill, it is our desire and intention to raise a large volunteer army to serve in Ireland protecting our holding and putting down rebellion. To all volunteers who will join our especial military force gathered for this purpose, we hereby promise at the end of their service to give every man' "—the Dean's voice hesitated only briefly—" 'a farm in Ulster. In addition—' "

They never heard the rest of the queen's proclamation. O'Neill sprang to his feet, flinging down his cup. His voice was shaking with anger. "A farm in Ulster! Ulster she will take to parcel out my land to a motley crew of Sassenach soldiers! This insolence—this arrgoance—"

Hugh was on his feet also. "A farm in Ulster! Farms in Ulster we will give them—six feet by three and worms for oxen!"

The Dean was still staring at the paper in his hand. Very quietly he said, "Listen to me, Shane."

"I will make Elizabeth listen to my war pipes!"

"Be quiet and hear me. A volunteer army is a different thing from the regular military. That promise of land the queen would never keep, but it sounds well. The common English roused against you, she might raise an army of six, seven thousand—more."

"Raw recruits," said O'Neill contemptuously. "If she had twenty thousand I would still beat them! Ulster she will never take."

The Dean sighed and folded the note. "Listen further, Shane. We have discussed it since your return from Leinster. The facts you must face. Five years ago you had many friends and supporters abroad—today, from one cause and another, you have none. In consequence of your quarrel with Pope Pius—"

"My quarrel? It was his making, the hypocritical bastard!"

"Silence! He is vicar of the church. If your excommunication does not worry you, it does myself. And that he forbids any Catholic to have dealings with you should set you thinking. France was lost to you before, but now Philip of Spain—"

"I know, I know, I know! You need not keep on as if you lectured a child!" The chief had been pacing up and down the chamber. Now he halted and bent over the Dean almost threateningly. "Are you so fearful as you sound, Terence? Since when have I needed outside support to win wars? A farm in Ulster, she says! We would burn the earth before it felt a Sassenach plow! And the Italian with his empty silly little threats! So you are thinking with them, maybe O'Neill is for a fall!"

"Never say it," and Daniel smiled charmingly at him. "I say only it is a situation you should devote some thought to."

"And what else am I doing?" O'Neill began to pace again. "A fool I was—it is clearer year by year. Well, for mistakes one must pay. It appears I will need to postpone my conquest of the west and south until I have beaten the Sassenachs again. And this time I will not call a halt until they are all dead or driven out!"

Edmund Donnelly said into the little silence, "If she can raise that large a volunteer army—" Instantly O'Neill whirled on him. His voice shook with passion.

"Doubters, cowards, all of you! Am I not O'Neill? I say if they send fifty thousand against us, they can never beat me! Cry off all of you and desert me, I will fight them alone! I will fight them in Ulster, I will fight them in the Pale, I will fight them with cannon and ax and dagger and bare fists if need be. I will fight them until I die, and if death comes to me before victory I will borrow Saint Michael's sword and return to fight them again! They will never defeat O'Neill!"

McArdle said soberly, "We are behind you in that, Shane. We would help you do that. No one is criticizing or crying off. All the Dean says, it might be an easier situation."

"Exactly. I—"

"Quiet, in God's name, Terence!" said Hugh violently. "Talk is not steel. Win or lose, we have plenty of time to talk it over afterward—at Benburb or in hell. For myself, I will be pleased to meet Radcliffe again. We never gave him all the beating he deserves."

"Rory." Moyna was sitting on the edge of the bed; she had been brushing her hair, but the brush lay idle now in her hands.

"My love?"

"Does O'Neill think this war will come soon?"

He had been talking of it from his own concern, with no thought for her feeling. "It will come, by what the Dean thinks. Spring, the chief said. By that time, when the roads are clear again, they will likely have that army gathered. But you must not worry for it. How many wars have we all come through before?" He was belatedly sorry he had troubled her.

"I don't care about any other man in Ireland—it's you. Rory—" Her hands twisted tight around the brush. "Come here—a moment. I want to say— I want to ask—"

"What is it, my heart?" He sat beside her, held her close.

"I should not say it." And so she whispered it. "There is Kilclain. You could say—it needs your managing. We could live there quiet—and safe you'd be—all of us."

He raised her face to his. A year ago he might have been angered, unthinking. But he knew more now, about women and about Moyna, and how life is laid out. Women had small understanding of the honor that would send men to fight: how should they? The personal, always for them only the personal. As if to emphasize the thought in his mind she said, "Nothing to do with you—with us. You could—"

"Moyna, love," he said. "Suppose I take an English sword in the heart this coming fight—bad for you it would be, and for the son, and this new child. But suppose I do as you say and back away out of it? Yes, the chief would let me go, a free man I am. Could I be looking my son in the eye ten years from now—win or lose?"

She whispered remotely, "It would not be that red McGuinness I wed. I should not have asked. It is not a woman's business, war—except that we bear the sons to make soldiers."

"I've another thing to say, too. Nothing to do with us, is it? Kilclain is not in Ulster and, win or lose, you and I might settle there and be content. I don't see it happening, but if O'Neill is defeated by the English and they come into Ulster, how long are you thinking they'd stay west of the river? And with the English in the north, how long are you thinking any self-respecting man who refused to bow down to them would hold to his own land? In fighting for O'Neill I fight for Kilclain."

"Yes—I see. Ah, Rory, you men forever at your stupid wars!" She clung tightly to him a moment. Over her head he looked at the son peacefully asleep in the cot beside the bed. Kilclain, yes, but the son too, Moyna, and the child in her body; it came back dimly from his lessons—hostages to fortune. Half-guilty, he knew he would be all too pleased to settle at Kilclain, a leisured gentleman-landholder, all his excitements hunting and horse-breeding. Old he was growing indeed. He tightened his hold on his wife angrily; he laughed.

"Listen, love, all your worry for nothing. Only the virtuous die young, don't you know that much? And I'm not an outsize target like Ferdoragh."

Her laugh was half sob. "That I never thought of—you're right."

Moyna smiled up at him tiredly from the pillow. "You are not pleased for it?"

"Well," he said, contriving a scowl. "One is right enough, or even two. But see you don't go producing a dozen girls with dowries needing to be found for all of them. Ruin me, it would."

"I don't believe you are displeased a bit," said Moyna.

"Well, need I be? One can see she'll be a beautiful woman and any man happy to get her, dowry or no." He prodded the infant with one finger. "See, smiling she is—"

"She is red and almost bald," said Moyna, wrinkling her nose distastefully, "and not near so big as Michael was."

"I'll not have you miscalling her. At least you choose a good name—just any one would not do."

"What else would she be but Catherine?" Moyna smiled.

"See," said Rory, "she knows me already. Clever she'll be as well as beautiful."

"Men," said Moyna with a giggle. "Go away now and let us both sleep."

He met Lady Catherine at the door. "Your new daughter is beautiful, Rory—"

"Just what I've been telling Moyna, my lady, and she saying no."

She laughed. "Maybe because she has your red hair? I'm envious—a daughter I would love."

Rory said boldly, "Well, time brings all things," and she smiled and went in to Moyna.

He wandered down the stair to the hall, found Diarmuid and a few other young officers lounging close to the hearth this chill November day; he hailed them and Diarmuid groaned. "My Christ, now we will have to listen to more rhapsodies about that insignificant female infant! Go away, Rory."

"Never mind," said Rory with dignity, pouring himself a drink. "Wait until you acquire a wife, I'll be complaining of you the same."

"You'll wait long," retorted Diarmuid with a grin. "Hugh O'Neill was just looking for you."

"Oh? Where is he?"

"Somewhere about."

Rory went back down the passage, looking for Hugh. At the foot of the rear stair he found him. "Ah, Rory, there you are. I was just about to have a hunt for you abovestairs. Come back to the council room with me, man, I've somewhat to talk over with you." He linked an arm through Rory's, led him down the passage; in the council room he filled cups. "Trouble, trouble. I have been afraid of it. The matter is, you've been lent to me for a bit, Rory. We are going a little journey together . . ."

CHAPTER XXXIV

IN LITTLE more than three months the structure of the political situation had entirely changed. Since August the treaty of Drum Cru was broken in the Pale, with the arrival of more than a thousand English troops; more had been coming in every week, and under Radcliffe now were five thousand men, twenty guns. If the English believed O'Neill had no agents to tell him that, they were fools: it was the gage flung before him. They meant to challenge him soon or late; this time the plan was theirs and whether they went to war now or next year, they would go to war fully prepared with a force they were confident could defeat him.

O'Neill would not be justified in beginning war only for that treaty-breaking. He might, with justice, issue formal complaint to the chancellor and the queen, open renewed discussion for the treaty's provisions—as he said, make more long talk for nothing. He took another second thought for the coming war, and that was, let the English begin it. He had renewed his military pact with Philip of Spain two years ago; all the other pacts he had once had with Continental rulers had been lost when Elizabeth forced him to sign with her, and it remained to be seen whether Philip would care to risk the displeasure of the Pope in honoring his agreement. But if a patient Ulster, suffering the dishonor of English, was wantonly attacked with no provocation, that would put a better complexion on it. The English being Protestant, the Pope might change his mind. And as it was unlikely the English would attack before spring, O'Neill had several months to collect his own forces and prepare for war.

With dissension over his rule in Antrim and in Connacht, he was not too sure of support from the chiefs there; and King Philip was too far off to influence directly. But Mary Stuart—it might be, despite all, he would find an ally there. He had been in correspondence with her for half a year over the conquest of Antrim; for that she had not been pleased. But there was the common enemy—England. At worst, he could hope that an ambassador would reconcile their differences over Antrim; at best, he might obtain promise of military support.

"But it will not be quite the same as your first journey," he said to Hugh. "If you get there at all." Hugh agreed thoughtfully. The channel was thick with English shipping, and scarcely a craft put out from Ireland, except English ships from Dublin, that was not stopped and searched by English patrols, the ostensible excuse being that they hunted contraband and criminals escaped from the Pale.

"And once you are there, the danger is not past either. There is intrigue at the Scot court, one cannot tell how they would receive you. I think you had best borrow my personal guard for the journey—and carry your own knife loose in the sheath."

"I'd not say no to that," returned Hugh.

This time Hugh took no escort at all: it would be difficult enough to get safe passage for two men, let alone a guard of troops. They made a cold two days' ride to the Antrim coast, and found a shipmaster to carry them to Scotland for a high fee.

But at the castle of Holyrood in Edinburgh, Hugh had not the reception he expected. It was evident that James Stuart still ruled his sister, and, through her, Scotland. Press as he might for a private audience, Hugh was given only bare hospitality and no glimpse of the queen for nearly a week, the excuse being that she was unwell. But he was determined to remain until he saw her personally.

On the eighth day of his visit, he was at last bidden to meet the queen; but he was absent from his and Rory's quarters only half an hour. When he returned, his expression was as grim as Rory had ever seen it.

"Well, you're not gone long. Did you not see her after all?"

"See her?" ejaculated Hugh. "Oh, I saw her! I have very near precipitated war between Scotland and Ulster."

"Why, what occurred?"

"Augh!" Hugh flung himself down in a chair. "Intrigue! They thrive on it, all these foreigners! The queen is no more ill than I am. She is bored and unhappy and Stuart tells her she is unwell—physicians can always find somewhat to cure for a fee. How long is she wed to Darnley now, four months? No wonder she's unhappy!" Now he was up, pacing. "All very formal it was, she talked polite commonplaces, and Stuart kept an eye on both of us. I am just about to ask private audience, when she announces she is tired. What can I do but make apologies and withdraw? But before I do so, this other comes in. I saw it was Sassenach, but how would I know who? A long young weakling it was, and drunken. I'll not repeat what he said to her—you're too young and innocent. I waited for Stuart to reprimand him, as he's the woman's brother, but he said never a word. So I told the man what I thought of him—by the grace of God, in our own tongue. And then Stuart had me by the arm and I knew it was Darnley."

"That is a pleasant story," said Rory.

"Whatever else one can say, she is a lady. She paid him no notice, but walked out on Stuart's arm. So I came away too, lest I do the man an injury. I find it in me to be sorry for her. A silly, vain, selfish woman, but not deserving of that."

"Well," said Rory, "no matter how she felt for the war in Antrim, she might be eager enough to make a pact against the English—being married to one of them, or next to it."

"Something in that," agreed Hugh with a grin. "I'll stay a bit longer and try to approach her again."

The day after that he was granted formal audience with the queen, in the presence of James Stuart. He stated the facts to them frankly, and offered a military pact with Ulster; the queen, he told Rory later, appeared scarcely to listen. It was Stuart who answered for her, suave but negative —and definite. And it would probably be of little use to stay and argue with them; Stuart's hand was still on the rein in Scotland, and perhaps the hand of John Knox over his. Scotland wanted no foreign commitments.

That night Rory lay awake long. He thought of Moyna and the children, changes he wanted to make at Kilclain, the political situation, this new war. A full moon moved up and across the sky, lighting the one narrow window in this chamber. He was at last drifting into sleep when there came a sound at the outer door, a scratching and rustling as if some animal sought entrance.

He slid out of bed, caught up his cloak to cover his nakedness, and, dagger in hand, moved across the room to the second bedstead. Hugh was deeply asleep; Rory laid a hand on his shoulder and he woke at once, quietly, as years of campaigning had taught him.

"Rory?"

"Someone at the outer door."

Hugh rose in one motion, flung his cloak round him, and reached for his knife on the bed table. Tensely they waited. For a long moment there was no sound, and Rory began to wonder if his senses played tricks on him; then there was a stir at the open door and a shadowy figure slipped into the room.

Hugh let out an expletive of surprise and stepped forward. In the shaft of silver moonlight from the slit of window they were staring at a disheveled Mary Stuart, wrapped in a long velvet robe, hair loose down her back, and clutching in both hands before her a leather bag.

"Your Grace—"

She took a step toward him; her voice was soft and breathless. "I should ask pardon—to intrude—and also to seem—impolite, today, O'Neill. I had to see you—private—it was not possible to speak openly. You will understand. I have bribed the footmen in the corridor—but it may be that they would betray, I do not know. You should leave here at once, tomorrow!

I—" She made an effort to control herself; she was trembling violently.

Hugh put his hand on her shoulder; it was impossible not to feel sympathy for this frightened, desperate lady. "You are cold, cousin," he said gently. "You should not have come, but sent a servant—be easy now, it is all right."

"Oh—" She made a confused gesture. "A servant!—which of them can I trust? You do not understand—but I had to come, I—O'Neill, you said today—you said there will be a war, that the English will attack—" She was shaking his arm.

"Yes. And soon, we think."

"What do I care about Rome?" she whispered a little wildly. "Oh, God, I try to be a good Catholic, but that I see—it is a personal thing between them—no reason the prince should be so damned by His Holiness. But I could never—Jamie said—I could not risk—and there is nothing to give in any event! O'Neill—" She thrust the bag at him. "Take it, please. It is all I have to give—I would give more, but there are—things they would miss. For your brother—to help in the war—I wish I might give more—"

"Do not disturb yourself now." She was shaking and incoherent. "Yes, I understand, I will give it to him."

"Take the letter to Argyll. He will do as I ask. And tell the prince, your brother—tell him to beat the English well! I will pray for that, to have them defeated and destroyed. I—must—go." She turned away to the door, but Hugh caught her arm.

"My thanks, cousin—and my wishes for your future happiness."

"Happiness?" She made a small sound, half laugh, half sob. "It is so long since I have even heard the word . . . Thank you, Hugh." In a moment she had vanished; they heard the light rustle of her passing across the room, a slight sound at the door—she was gone.

Hugh drew a long breath. "A light," he said as if waking from a spell. Rory's own hand shook as he fumbled to make a spark, kindle a wall torch. In the sputtering light they looked at each other; then Hugh came to set down the bag on the table beside the bed. He unknotted the strings, reached into it. The first thing he brought out was a small folded letter sealed on three sides. He put that down and upended the bag over it. A few rings, a brooch or two, a little pile of gold pieces—some French and some Spanish—a gold necklet, a lady's silver-handled mirror, two gold armlets—it was a poor motley hoard. They stared at it.

Hugh said softly, "Gift from a queen. Yes, despite Stuart, she has learned somewhat these five years." He took up a handful of the gold and let it slide through his fingers. "What might this buy? The tenth part of an arquebus—twenty troop-saddles—one round of ammunition for a cannon. Yet a royal gift, for it comes from the heart. I am sorry for that woman. Bribing her own footmen!"

"And I'm thinking she is right, we had best get away before James Stuart hears of this," said Rory.

"Yes—I daresay." Hugh took up the letter then. It was addressed in agitated script to the Earl of Argyll in Cantyre. "I daresay," said Hugh, looking at it speculatively.

They got away from Edinburgh on a cold day within a week of Christ-tide, and met snows riding down to Cantyre. Neither of them had any great opinion of Scots—always excepting Sorley Boy and MacArthur—and the welcome they had from the Earl of Argyll cheered them.

There was no Continental nonsense about the young earl: he wore the kilt and tunic, gave them decent liquor, and made no ambiguous talk. He scanned the queen's letter, thrust it into his tunic, and gestured hospitably at the flagon.

"A Highlander I am, and therefore a man of reason. No business you Ulstermen had in Antrim, but all Celts are cousins and, if we enjoy fighting each other, will forget our differences to fight English together any day. Stuarts I don't like, but the honor I've had to meet our queen—a charming lady, and a lady"—he eyed Hugh shrewdly—"in an unenviable position."

"As you say"—and Hugh met his eye with a shrug.

"She knows she can trust me, and though she dare not dispatch any of her own soldiers since Stuart is negotiating with the English, asks me to make up a force to lend O'Neill. That I'll do. It will not be much, but all good, stout men, who know how to handle the claymore. And I'll come myself to lead them."

"Argyll," said Hugh, "you restore my faith in Scots. I was thinking all of them were corrupted with living so close to English."

Argyll grinned and said he was thinking of Lowlanders. He found a fisher captain to ferry them back to Ireland across the narrow channel, which was helpful.

They did not ride straight for Tyrone, but along the north coast up to Dunluce, where they had another cordial welcome from Sorley Boy.

"I daresay you've heard from Shane," said Hugh.

"I have, and what I had to write him in reply I did not like." There was a grim set to Sorley's mouth. "These little chiefs here have short memories. Their defeats they forget, and say to me and MacArthur, 'Why should we honor that pledge of military assistance? While O'Neill is busy at war with the English he cannot come and punish us!' And what can we say in return, except to curse them?"

Hugh nodded. He said, "It is what we have feared. The Leinster chiefs are going to say the same, I would stake my life on it. And in spite of his hatred for the English, maybe Hugh Ruadh will too, out of spite and disinclination to acknowledge Shane his superior—again." His mouth twisted. "None of these men have much to offer individually, but together— Of course, you and MacArthur will be of great aid. What have you?"

"Fifteen hundred, give or take a little," said Sorley, and added sardonically, "You killed a good few of us at Knockboy. Six guns. MacArthur can contribute three hundred and two more cannon. Brodie has a bare hundred, but he'll bring them in."

"And what more force we'll collect from this two years of conquest and treaty-making we shall soon see. I think not much."

"You said the English will have maybe seven thousand. It's not great odds, Hugh. It may be a longer war than the last one, but we can beat them."

"Oh, yes—we'll beat them," said Hugh. "Will we think any other way? But maybe not all of us will be here to celebrate the victory."

"You have a premonition, to say that?" asked Sorley sharply.

"No—" Hugh laughed. "It's only that men will get themselves killed in a fight. Until March, then." He was silent as they rode out from Dunluce in a cold sea wind.

CHAPTER XXXV

T<small>HEY</small> came into the hall at Benburb in evening, after a cold, wet ride, to a chorus of welcome and two surprises. The first was Dudley Donnelly, up, dressed, and joining the company for the first time in a year. He looked deathly thin and pale, but seemed somewhat stronger. As usual, he was mostly silent and watched O'Neill. Rory was about to go abovestairs and seek out Moyna, when the chief entered and, behind him, another man. After a glance at that one, Rory slid quickly behind Hugh with a mutter.

"My Christ, that pirate it is—Stukeley, the Englishman! What is he doing here?"

Hugh had no time to exclaim; the chief came to embrace him, held him off to read his expression, and shrugged slightly. "Well, it was a gamble. We'll talk it over later." He turned, drew Stukeley forward, and introduced him casually to all the nearby men, by which Rory gathered the Englishman had just come, and been closeted with the chief. His tone held faint contempt on the name, and, from the look in Stukeley's eyes, he liked O'Neill no better than any other Englishman, but their words were polite.

"And my thanks," O'Neill was saying satirically.

"Not at all." Stukeley's tone was suave. "I go wherever there is gold to be had." He made his way out leisurely, seeming unaware that every eye was on him.

Before he was out of earshot, O'Neill said amusedly, "I thought you would all like to have a look at him. A ladylike fellow, is it not? But a sense of humor he has—I hope Radcliffe and the queen know about this."

"What is your business with that pirate?" demanded Hugh. "Rory here recognized him."

"And good to have you back—both of you." O'Neill grinned at Rory. "I'd forgot you had a little brush with him. It is his business with me, brother! Can you keep a secret from His Holiness in Rome? Philip of Spain sends me some equipment, and Stukeley is running it through the English patrol in the channel. Six cannon, and some French arquebuses as well—more to come."

"Do you tell me!" said Hugh. "He will not heed the Pope's proclamation?"

"Oh, a good churchman Philip is," said O'Neill. "He only obeys scriptural advice—that about letting not the right hand know what the left doeth. He'd be embarrassed if the Pope proved it on him, but if the rumor gets out to Rome, he can always say that the supplies were stolen from his ships by pirates."

"Well," said Hugh, "a good omen it is. Have you more news from the Pale?"

"I have. They will march as soon as the roads are clear—late March. Radcliffe has six and a half thousand, a thousand arquebusiers—a third of all ranks mounted, and twenty-four guns. A brave, bold force it is," said O'Neill, smiling grimly, "and every man in it dreaming of owning land in Ulster when the fighting is done. We'll give them land a bit farther south—to sleep in for all eternity." And they all drank to that sentiment.

The one disadvantage to letting Radcliffe begin this war was that it might begin dangerously close to the border of Ulster, since O'Neill would not march until Radcliffe did so. There might be lines drawn across Ulster at first, with the force Radcliffe had. O'Neill decided, as a safeguard, to remove the whole household again to the house on the island.

But Rory took some thought for that himself, when the chief announced that decision. He went to find Moyna in the communal children's room. She was sitting over sewing with the Lady Catherine, a few other women of the house, with young Michael playing at her feet and the infant sleeping in its blanketed basket beside her. In a year or two, Michael would be of age to live here with all the children of the house. It was the only practical arrangement to follow in a large household, all but infants together in one large apartment, cared for by the officers' wives and servantwomen—whose children also lived here. Threading his way through children of all sizes from still-tottering infants to boisterous twelve-year-olds almost men and women, Rory reflected that it was not precisely where he would want his son. He came to where Moyna and Lady Catherine sat apart, was invited to sit, and drew up a stool.

"You are looking serious, Rory—what is it?"

He told them what the chief had decided. Lady Catherine said in a troubled voice, "He thinks they would come in as far as here? I did not—Hugh! Now give the ball back to Conan, it is his."

"No, that's not likely," he said quickly. "It is only that he wants to prepare for anything that might come, that's all, my lady."

She put down her sewing. "All this war! I have been frightened—oh, don't tell me cheerful lies as if I were a child! I know this may be a desperate fight, the English as strong as they are. Art, leave your brother be now." She turned a worried look to him. "All his old enemies gathering strength. Nothing we can do—but continue to pray for him."

"Well, my lady, I do not think it is as desperate as all that, the odds are not so great." He had to raise his voice over the noise of children. Something cannoned into his chair and set up a lusty wailing; he plucked it off his leg. "Young Hugh Gavelock is it? Now, lad—"

Lady Catherine smiled, took the child from him to comfort. "Not Hugh—my Hugh never wastes time weeping like that. And another reason that is. I—well, there is to be another child in September. I never thought my—my husband would live so long. Shane is very impatient for it, he wants to legalize his heir."

"Of course, my lady," he agreed awkwardly. "What I wanted to say— Moyna, I've thought instead of going to Lough Neagh, you and the children should go to Kilclain and settle there."

"Well, I don't know, Rory. One way I'd like it, but I would not leave Catherine—"

"That is your home, Moyna, though you've never seen it, and I think it would be best as Rory says."

"Well, I'll think about it," said Moyna.

In the end he prevailed, and the week the household removed to the house called Hatred-of-the-English, he took Moyna and the children to Kilclain. They stopped at the McGuinness' house, where his mother pressed Moyna to stay on a bit, being in love with the two grandchildren never seen before; but Rory was anxious to see them settled at Kilclain. Moyna's interest and excitement at seeing the property for the first time reconciled her to leaving the familiar household at Benburb; fortunately, she and Lileas got on well, being much the same age. Fergus had managed the place excellently, Rory thought.

He would like to stay here, make a settled place for himself. Damn! Growing old and disinclined to fight, was he? Well, not that—but it seemed he and Moyna had so little time together since they were wed. He stayed two weeks into March; he did not want to leave then, but must. The night before he would ride for Tyrone, Moyna wept and clung to him.

"I wish you need not go! Oh, I know, it is no use, you must. But all this war, all this war. Rory, I am so frightened—"

"Now, woman. You know what a fast runner I am. No Englishman could catch me! A secret I'll tell you. I wish I needn't go either. Listen, Moyna, love. When this war is over and I can in honor ask, I will ask to be free of O'Neill's service and come home for good. That pleases you?"

"Mhmm . . . But a war in between."

There was nothing to say to that; he only held her closer, remembering all the time he had known and loved Moyna. "Listen, love," he whispered. "Are you remembering what we said to each other in the monastery at Kilfearn? I do not ever leave you, all of me, Moyna—in the heart I am here with you always."

"That's a fine sentimental thing to say. Not the same it is."

In the courtyard that early morning he clasped Fergus' hand, inclined to Lileas, bade his son be good, kissed Moyna for the last time. She said, "Do not look back, Rory—it is bad luck." But he did look back, unable to help it, as he reached the gate, and they had all turned away, mindful that it was also bad luck to watch a traveler out of sight. His heart was heavy as he rode from Kilclain, maybe never to see it again—who knew? If he should not come home from this war, Fergus would look to the property until the son was grown. . . . Woolgathering he was—him, a McGuinness, only eight-and-twenty, to die while all the rest of life waited for him to enjoy? Maybe other men—many others—not himself. The odds were not great. They would have another good fight with the English and beat them again, that was all.

After his wars of conquest of these two years, O'Neill's army was somewhat depleted; since the first hint of English strength gathering in the Pale he had rebuilt it to an extent, with recruits from the sept-clans. It stood now at forty-four hundreds of men, and this last three months he had outfitted his army with much new miscellaneous equipment. Impulsive, impatient, careless O'Neill might be, but as an old campaigner he knew that attention to details often wins or loses a war.

The Earl of Argyll came with the men he had promised, and Sorley Boy, MacArthur, and Brodie arrived in late March, to bring the army up to six thousand and add eight guns to O'Neill's twenty-two. Of all mounted ranks some fifteen hundred were supplied with arquebuses.

But of all the other men who had signed treaties of military support with O'Neill, only Eoghan O'Reilly kept his word. He came with two hundred men to serve in the Ulster army. O'Neill had letters from Burke, the new O'Connor, O'Rourke, McMahon, setting out reasons why they might not fulfill their pledges. In a month, three months, they would be pleased to do so. "It is a play for time," said O'Neill. "They think to make excuses until I am occupied at war and cannot punish them. Now they slide out of it, but when I have the leisure, them I'll bring retribution on!"

From Hugh Ruadh O'Donnell he had no word at all, or from the Scot chiefs in Antrim.

And that week came more information out of the Pale, from Rebecca Isham by way of O'Brien's messenger. The English strength was seven thousand men, thirty guns; and they would march on the last day of the month.

O'Neill said, "We'll meet him south, on O'Reilly's land." The army was alerted to march the next dawn.

Father Brendan celebrated mass that evening for the benefit of the men who would depart. It was a silent crowd that gathered in the chapel. How many of these men would have masses said for their souls before another month was out? Rory chanced to be one of the last to leave; as he came out and turned up the path toward the house, something made him glance back. The priest stood in the open door, his face to the night sky, and his lips were moving, but not in Latin. He was murmuring no prayer, but the words, *They that live by the sword, they that live by the sword.* Rory tried to remember how the quotation went on, but it was not important. The next minute he forgot it.

They first met the enemy thirty miles south of the Ulster border. There were scouts ahead, and when, about midday, they reported the English army in sight, the chief had a look about the terrain. He sent most of his own troops to wait in cover while the Scots circled to approach the English on their left flank.

The English had time to prepare for a charge, warned by their own scouts. They would not be sure at first of the identity of the attackers, who rode under the new banner of Ulster, which O'Neill had recently designed: The Red Hand on a background of white, and the motto below: *Lamh Dearg Erin Abu.**

They came on to take the charge, and it grew to a lively fight. After two hours or so, the English, aware now whom they fought, drew away east, and in the dark were lost by the pursuit. Radcliffe's cannoneers must have labored all night, but when the Ulster army came on them in midmorning the English had entrenched their guns and made a battle line.

"Him and his eternal guns!" swore O'Neill. "Well, we can fight his kind of war, too." The Ulster artillerymen worked under fire to line their own guns, and, after that, one day was much like another.

The guns pounded steadily at regular intervals, and however clear each succeeding dawn, by midmorning there would be a gray haze of gunsmoke obscuring the sun. Then the English guns would fall silent, and the Ulstermen would hastily prepare for a charge. The English troops would come out at the double from behind their cannon, and the Ulster troops to meet them on the ground between the guns. On some occasions, one army would be driven back, and their troops would hold desperately while the cannoneers readied the guns to move; they would retreat, to line their guns again. Oftener, they only had a hot fight, one army retreating but not in such disorder as to lose ground. That was how the war went all through April and May.

In the last week of May a sudden heavy charge of English one dawn overran the Ulster guns and forced the Ulstermen into retreat. O'Neill

* The Red Hand of Ireland to Victory.

lost six guns, and none destroyed, which meant they would be used against him. The Ulster army was driven back nine miles before they could collect their strength to turn and entrench their remaining guns. It was evident in that engagement, almost for the first time, that they fought odds—not great odds, but enough to make some difference. Radcliffe had nearly seven thousand men; reinforcement reaching him at the end of April brought up his strength to that number. He had at least partly learned a lesson O'Neill had taught him four years ago about the essential differences in their weapons. He had a larger number of heavy foot-ranks to correspond with the Ulster gallowglass, and he had equipped those foot-ranks with old-fashioned blunt-ended maces. These clumsy-looking weapons, besides being unfamiliar to their handlers, were still not a match for the long axes of the gallowglass, but better than swords. In the close fights the English foot-ranks took less and inflicted more punishment than in that war of four years ago.

The chief was soon swearing and impatient for closer battle to bring more definite victory. Just as before, except on rare occasions, the English refused to be drawn from behind their guns, and it infuriated him. He wanted hotter fight not only for its own sake, but to finish this war—by which he meant to win it—sooner.

"Christ damn them! I cannot spend the rest of my life fighting them! I want this settled! One utter defeat I will give them again and then perhaps they will leave me in peace to finish my real task—the making of a nation. This lying here in camp firing at each other, we'll never settle it this way!" And again: "June! My Christ, I could have beaten the Galway chiefs and be discussing terms by now!"

Most of the army sympathized with him. After the relative suddenness with which this war had developed, the threat of that large English army, they all felt somewhat deflated at the tameness of the fight. Since the retreat in May, they had gained back ground, but after that for some weeks neither army accomplished much.

In July, Rory had a letter from Moyna, brought by a farmer's boy from Kilclain. In the round, not ungraceful script Lady Catherine had taught her, Moyna wrote that there would be another child in December, but he was not to worry, for she was strong and well; that Michael and small Catherine were growing apace but Michael at the moment in disgrace because he had pulled all the tail feathers from Fergus' prize cock, for which he had been punished. "But I had to comfort him afterward, a little thing it was and you never saw anything so silly as that cock, his pride insulted that the hens seemed no longer to know him for a cock!" Fergus said she must tell him the heifers were doing well, and that the bay mare's foal was a chestnut colt, very large and promising. And she missed Rory greatly, prayed each day for his safety, and hoped soon to hear that the war was at an end and he would come home.

That both raised and lowered his spirits, though he was happy to have the letter. They seemed to have been at this war years instead of months, and nothing much was settled either way. But ten days after that they had a little more excitement.

Rory was thinking of his bed, early as it was, and came past the central fire toward the chief's tent where O'Neill and the captains sat talking. As he approached, several soldiers in a crowd were making for the fire, loud and angry, and from their midst came a woman's protesting voice. Curious, he lengthened his stride to join the group.

"It is a spy, O'Neill, coming up to the lines bold as you please—"

"And swearing at us, too. The English I don't know, but swearing I do in any tongue—"

"I demand to be brought before the Lord O'Neill!" That was the woman, in English. "You stupid louts, remove your hands from me!"

"For God's love!" said the chief. "Quiet, all of you!" He motioned the guards back, and the woman was revealed: a dark, vitally attractive woman, though not young, even in her drab gray hooded cloak. Her eyes found the chief at once, with no doubt of his identity, and she smiled, shaking off the soldiers' touch, stepping forward to him. "And who might you be, lady?"

"O'Neill, such a pleasure to meet you after so long!" Her throaty voice was warm. "I am Madam Rebecca Isham, in your service, my lord."

O'Neill gave an exclamation. "Do you say! What do you here alone? You've ridden from Dublin?"

"At the expense of several years from my life! What with that abominable horse, and becoming lost, and your louts of soldiers! Do not be so polite to ask me to sit, my lord—the saddle I am not accustomed to! And I regret, I've no document to prove I speak truth—"

O'Neill grinned. "I daresay Colm McCaffrey could identify you." Those who did not understand English listened, not comprehending this exchange. "And I regret, lady, we've no wine to offer you, which doubtless you'd be glad of. Come, take my seat, there's a deerskin to pad it for you." She obeyed, grimacing comically; the chief sat beside her, the captains crowding up. "This is a dangerous thing you do. You came round the English line? Why?"

"Ah, O'Neill, I had to come." She sobered. "It is Thady O'Brien—they have taken him, and eight of those who worked with him. Harry told me of it yesterday. Some man betrayed, and they are all in Dublin gaol. They are to hang soon."

"Do you tell me," said O'Neill. He spoke abstractedly, seeming more interested in the woman. The captains muttered a few perfunctory curses.

"Such a nice little man, O'Brien. He was careful to me at first," and she laughed, "because I am Hebrew. But I talked to him, and we became friends. I would not like to see him hanged, you comprehend. I had to come to let you know. Of course, I am also curious to meet this great chieftain, O'Neill," and she gave him a slow smile.

"My thanks for coming." O'Neill grinned. "I'll see they are rescued—a good man Thady has been to me."

Terence O'Hagan said, "We can't go breaking into Dublin gaol."

"A little more finesse we'll use. Gael betrays Gael to put those men in prison. We'll have Sassenach betray Sassenach to get them out."

"Bribe the guards," translated Edmund Donnelly.

"Who said anything about the guards? We'll go to the gaol warden and be sure. Meanwhile, we are remiss. Madam Isham will be tired and hungry?" He bent his charm to her again. This arrival of a lovely lady in their midst had fired him with interest. After these months of male society, he was ready for a little flirtation—or something more—and, as usual, it never troubled him to have witnesses. He smiled into Rebecca Isham's eyes, took her hand. "A brave thing you have done, lady. But perhaps this relieves your boredom with old Sydney? McCaffrey has told me this and that about you—"

"Would he not!" said Rebecca. "That I am a mercenary woman who suffers an uncongenial lover for his wealth." She met the chief's eyes with mischief in her own.

"Other things," said O'Neill with a laugh.

Hugh, beside Rory, moved restlessly; Rory thought he suppressed impulsive words. This attractive and sophisticated woman was no more reluctant than O'Neill to enjoy a passing flirtation: so much was obvious. The chief had always been interested in this woman, and now, meeting her for the first time, was putting all his persuasive charm on her.

Rebecca widened her eyes on him, demure. "After such an exhausting journey, my lord, would you have me engage in word-play with you? My wits are dull at the moment."

"My lovely liar," drawled the chief, "your wits any sharper, I'd not dare draw mine at you. I am thinking McCaffrey did not tell me the half." He rose, bent over her. "But unkind I am, not to offer you rest and refreshment. Tired you'll be indeed. Look you—I'll send McCaffrey back to Dublin with you, to rescue Thady and his men. But you'll take some rest first, and I'll offer you seclusion in my own tent."

"You are kind, my lord."

"And my escort there." O'Neill took her arm and led her off. The others watched as they vanished beyond the circle of firelight. Edmund said mildly, "Well, he might have introduced us. That is a handsome woman, foreigner or no."

"And if he had, would any of us stand a chance against him?" asked Terence O'Hagan with a laugh. There were smiles and shrugs.

Hugh did not laugh. He said something to himself in a low voice, turned, and strode away in the opposite direction.

And McArdle said to Rory, "I'd advise you not to seek your bed just yet, boy—not that Shane will be wanting two."

What the truth of that was no one could say for certain. Rory sat talking with them, dropped off to sleep on the ground by the fire. A few hours before dawn the chief reappeared, calling for guards to fetch McCaffrey and horses. Rebecca Isham strolled up from his tent, fresh and calm, to await their arrival; she greeted McCaffrey smilingly, and the big man's eyes were eager on her.

When O'Neill took her hand in farewell, they spoke only formal words, but their eyes on each other were knowing, humorous. The chief lifted her to the saddle, gave the rein into her hand, and stood watching them ride out of camp. There was a half-smile on his mouth. He said, "And isn't that poor fool Sydney the lucky man! But I'll wager he doesn't know the half of his luck."

CHAPTER XXXVI

Dublin, August 1566

THE man had come furtively to the military office, often looking behind. He had lived in the Pale all his life, so the English came easy on his tongue, but the Gaelic flavored it sharply and the officers smiled as they questioned. He told the names, and asked the reward, but they only asked more questions; he began to think it an English trick, that they would not pay the reward. Five pounds a head, it was. He told the names again, but still they did not give him the money.

"Eight of them," he said, "and that's forty pounds—"

"You can count, Irish," said the officer with a sneer. They put him in a room by himself and he was frightened. With English, always a trick. Then another man came to ask questions, a gentleman, and he had to tell it all over again.

"It is only by chance you know what these men are doing?"

"Yes, sir, yes—I never did aught wrong against you, I swear it." There was a clerk to write down all the names, but they did not give him the money. He said to the gentleman, "About the forty pounds," and the gentleman laughed and said to an officer, "See he has his blood money." The officer counted it out to him—forty golden pounds—and said he might go.

It was very heavy in the bag at his hip as he came out to the rainy dark. He got away from there quickly; but the bag was heavier at every step and he walked faster and faster. The breath came harsh in his throat. A man must live. The wife was ill since last summer, the youngest child ailing, and another to come, and now, because of the war, the English stopped building and no workmen were hired at all, and what was a man to do? Forty pounds, forty pounds. He crossed the square, almost running, up the steps of the tall old cathedral, and leaned on the pillar. He ran into the ageless quiet of it. He would confess and get penance, but a man must live—a man must live.

Antrim, September 1566

The decision upon the chiefhood of clan MacDonnell was still pending.

Perhaps the queen in Scotland and her advisors had more important matters to discuss. But there was no more important matter to Aspuke Mac-Donnell. He had busied himself for nearly a year making a try for that rank, the rank he had always coveted. The way the Antrim chiefs felt for it now, save MacArthur, who was unimportant politically, O'Neill's conquest was on paper only; whatever the queen and her ministers thought of O'Neill they would never have approved that invasion of Scot land. It was possible that when a new chief MacDonnell was chosen he might claim back all those houses and all that land O'Neill had stolen. That was worth a gamble.

He needed supporters among the high clansmen, and he had worked on all those he could reach. But persuasive talk and a little fiction built about his legitimate claim was not enough. Many of the clansmen were impecunious men. He had a notion that gold offered—nothing direct, it must all be very subtle—would get more names signed to his formal petition to the queen. Gold: he swore. Not so easy to come by these days. He owned land but not much; he had no great sums of gold to give away, not enough to buy men.

But there were ways to have gold. He was a clever man; if he thought long enough, surely some plan would occur to him. While the queen delayed, Aspuke sat at home and thought long and earnestly.

Rath O'Donnell, September 1566

Hugh Ruadh O'Donnell watched the war with interest. He had known something of the English strength and hoped to see O'Neill beaten quick, hard, and once for all; but that did not happen. The bastard was too Christ-damned lucky. Would he never be brought down?

The winter was coming on, when the war would halt temporarily for the weather; O'Neill would come home, in easier reach. Red Hugh fingered his scarred face and thought pleasurably of retribution on O'Neill. Whatever happened, if O'Neill was still alive, when he had time, he would punish Hugh Ruadh for that broken treaty. Handing Tyrconnell to O'Neill as a free gift! Maybe he would come this winter, or maybe not until after the war.

Red Hugh rode down to visit Burke over the River Finn. He talked round it, never coming out directly, but had no response from Burke or O'Rourke, whom he also visited. They dared not take the gamble. He was different, Red Hugh: a man strong as O'Neill any day. Any coward could do what O'Neill had done.

But O'Rourke said to him slyly, "Thinking about that ten thousand pounds of gold the English are offering for his head, are you?"

Hugh Ruadh swore at him. "Listen, coward, I've not all the gold in the world and well enough I'd like more than I have, but blood money I don't touch, and, in particular, English blood money! When I take O'Neill it won't be for gold, not by the hell of a long way, but for retribution and I owing him that twice over!" He went home to Tyrconnell and thought long on that retribution, and waited for O'Neill to come in reach so he might deliver it.

Rome, September 1566

The new Pope, His Holiness Pius V, unlike his immediate predecessors, was a man with some humor. He had not until now had any dealing with that recalcitrant son of the church, O'Neill of Ulster, and he regarded the letter before him with an expression between incredulity and exasperation. He said to his secretary, "But he is mad. Or possessed of a devil, which comes to the same thing. Excommunicate he is—but does he plead with me, offer some great penance, or even a bribe, as one would expect? He threatens me—most Catholic majesty of the church! I'd not believe such arrogance exists but that I see it in black and white!"

The secretary, who had served Pius IV, said resignedly and respectfully, "There has always been much trouble with that man, Your Holiness. Of course, there is usually trouble within the Irish church."

"True," agreed His Holiness. He leaned back, scanning the letter again; he laughed.

"Your Holiness?"

"I am only thinking, what a war there is going to be in hell when this O'Neill arrives there. . . ."

Dublin, September 1566

"It was all most unfortunate, my lord—"

"You never spoke a truer word," said Radcliffe coldly. "I should have thought you, at least"—looking at an unhappy Sydney—"would have had the common sense to question those men while you had them. We have always known information went out to O'Neill from the Pale, but all of it was scarcely such that men like these beggars might pick it up in the street. Very probably there is at least one, perhaps many, higher agents, about whom one or more of those men could have given information."

"Well, I knew you returned to the city today," said Sydney. "I waited that you might first question them yourself. How could I know there would be a gaol-delivery?"

"Most unfortunate," repeated the warden of Dublin gaol, mopping his brow agitatedly.

"Will you tell me how in God's name such a thing could occur?" demanded Radcliffe. "A stout prison in the heart of a city—"

"Oh, it was quite unprecedented, I do assure you, my lord, never before— I will take steps to insure that never again—! It was late, there were few guards on duty, and, by some diabolical mischance, no men at all in that particular wing. You understand, these things will happen, even in the most orderly— I, myself, was here, working late—"

"I believe your devotion to duty, you may omit that."

"Yes, my lord. There were a dozen of them came on me behind—none small, and all with daggers. They were all masked; it was most alarming, I assure you! I had not been informed these were important political prisoners"—with a reproachful look at Sydney. "Had I known that, I might have—but as it was, under the circumstances, I thought it the wiser course—I have a wife and family, my lord—in short, I—"

"In short, you went meek as a lamb and unlocked the prisoners. Oh, God, no, I am not blaming you—it is done now, no help for it." Radcliffe shrugged and rose. "No good weeping over what might have been."

The prison warden bowed out the two deputies, obsequious, still muttering apologies. The door shut, he sat down at his table and mopped his brow again. He opened the lower drawer and fumbled at the catch unlocking the false bottom, stared at the gold. He should find a safer place for it. No, he had not known they were such important prisoners. Maybe he should have guessed when this much gold was offered. But the deputies had believed him; it would all smooth itself over. He put out a hand and touched the gold, very hard, very bright. He shut the drawer hastily and poured himself a glass of wine, lifted it with a shaking hand. . . . A man must live.

CHAPTER XXXVII

H E MADE a good many excuses for himself," said McCaffrey amusedly, "but in the end he took the money. But Thady had the last word."

"How so?" asked O'Neill.

"He got me to write a note to leave in his cell, complaining about the food and accommodation."

O'Neill roared with mirth. "My own man! But the English have no sense of humor, they'll not appreciate it."

Even the satisfaction of tricking the English over that relieved the boredom of the war only a day. There were frequent skirmishes when one of the armies charged to try the strength of the opposite line, but they were brief fights and little was won or lost. It went like that all through August and September.

The war was nearly seven months old, and neither force could claim much gain. The chief was in a rage at Radcliffe; but his temper was somewhat calmed at the end of September when he had the news that Lady Catherine was delivered of her fourth child and first daughter, named Ailis for the chief's mother.

Every man at the line was frankly wishing for an early and hard winter, so that Radcliffe would withdraw until spring and they might do the same and get home for a little comfort. By the end of October it was impossible for an army to move in offense; already snow had come. But the English gave no sign of crying quarter for the cold season; they lay there in camp, full strength.

"Well, by God," said O'Neill, "if they choose to sit here and aim their guns at us all winter, we'll not be the first to withdraw!" But for this kind of fighting the only men necessary at the line were those to fire the guns. He arranged that the officers at least should take turns to have leave, throughout the next three or four months.

"And as soon as we can move in the spring, we will take them! Eight months, nine, my Christ! I want to finish this once for all and get back to more important things!"

Rory was looking forward to a leave from the line as ardently as any other, but knew it was not likely he would get one until the chief took leisure himself. He wondered if he would manage to get to Kilclain by the time the new child came—December, Moyna had said. O'Neill would not take personal leave until all the captains, in turn, had had that. It might be the end of the Christ-tide season—that seemed eternity away.

During the first two weeks of December it turned warmer, the snow melted off, and there was rain, so the ground became hard and packed; once more they could get in a little closer fighting. They had four or five skirmishes with the enemy that week.

That was a clear cold morning, the eleventh day of December; rain had fallen in the night and the space between the lines was marshy; it was not likely there would be a charge today from either line. Toward midday a rider came into camp from the north. Rory and several officers, all the captains and the chief, were sitting about the chief's fire, having just finished a noon meal. As the message rider came up, Rory recognized him as a troopman from one of the divisions left as home guard, under the command of James Donnelly. He halted before O'Neill and bowed, proffering a sealed letter. The chief took it, glancing at it incuriously, and then sat up.

"The O'Donnell seal. Now what is Hugh Ruadh writing me letters about?" He split the seal and unfolded the page. The next moment he uttered a great joyful shout and sprang to his feet. "Oh, God be thanked —God be thanked! The man is dead, the whoreson is dead at last, may he burn in hell forever! O'Donnell is dead!" He flung his arms about those nearest him, Hugh and O'Hagan, in exuberant embrace.

"Calvagh?" Hugh retrieved the letter the chief let fall. "By God, it is —formal announcement from the heir! Good news indeed!"

"I thought he meant to live forever!" O'Neill raised his voice in peremptory command. "Fetch me a horse at once! I ride immediately! Oh, God be thanked—a new man I feel for this—I have prayed for it four years and more! In God's name, hurry, you fools! I must get off at once—"

"You'll go to make the marriage? Good," and Hugh gripped his arm. "Happy I am for both of you." And all those in hearing added more congratulation. The chief gave little notice; he was striding up and down impatiently. One of his army servants hurried up with a cloak; Rory scrambled to his feet hastily.

"I'll be with you in a minute, O'Neill—"

"No need—you could not keep up with me! I'll not delay a minute while your horse is saddled!" He looked five years younger, laughing with genuine mirth for the first time in weeks. "Friendly territory all the way —I'll be absent only a few days. A good omen this is! Hugh, you are in command until I return." A troopman came up at a run, leading his horse; he seized the rein and vaulted into the saddle. "Until next week—

good fighting, brothers!" and, lifting an arm in triumphant farewell, he galloped out of camp toward the north road.

"But I should—" began Rory, watching him go. "I'll catch him up—" and he turned. Hugh's hand on his shoulder stayed him.

"No need, as he said. Thinking of missing a leave at home?" He laughed. "I don't blame you. Wait a few days until Shane is back and you may ride north with me. Good news this is indeed. Catherine will be happy for it. Did you ever see a man so anxious to tie himself down!" But his tone held affectionate sympathy, and there were murmurs of agreement. The Lady Catherine had endeared herself to all the chief's household and they knew how impatient he had been to wed her. They had been together a long time, nearly seven years. Rory remembered all the private speculation as to how long the chief might keep her as mistress, and smiled. Well, good luck and long life to them as a wedded couple!

It gave them something to talk about the rest of that day. Sorley Boy was nearly as pleased as the chief; the irregular situation had worried him. Rory was thinking that it would be a piece of news to interest Moyna also—please God, he would be seeing her soon! He felt he had been away from her for years.

The Lady Catherine that late afternoon reread her letter from her former maidservant, Moyna, smiling to herself as she read. It gave her pleasure that Moyna had found happiness in life. Laying the letter aside, she took up her new small daughter, and her two womenservants helped her to settle comfortably in the armchair while the infant nursed.

She was still sitting there when a clatter of hooves sounded in the courtyard below and, a few moments later, heavy running steps down the passage. The door crashed open and the chief burst in.

"Catherine, love! Great news I bring!" He enveloped her in a powerful hug, chair, infant, and all. "He is dead, that bastard of a husband of yours, he's dead at last!"

"Shane," she said gently, "you'll be waking the child. Quiet, now—just dropping off to sleep she was, see?"

He drew back with a frown. "Aren't you hearing what I say, woman? Calvagh is dead and you're free! We will be wed at once!"

"I told you," said Catherine. "Waked her you have." The infant began to cry. "Now, my small love, quiet, it is all right."

The chief straightened and ordered imperiously. "Here, woman, take this noisy brat away—I want to speak with the lady! Catherine, pay attention to me!"

"No, you may not take the infant," said Catherine calmly to the nurse. "I will quiet her. Shane, be still. It is most unkind of you to burst in and disturb the child so. Also, you have mud on your sandals and the floor has just been swept." O'Neill glared at her, astonished and angry. She gave him a warm smile. "But it is very good to see you at home. Do you sit down now, while I attend to the child."

Frowning and impatient, he flung himself into a chair and sat, arms folded, while she soothed the infant to quiet, the two servants looking on.

"Catherine—!"

"Yes, my dear, in a moment. There, Shena, you may take her. Be sure there is an extra blanket."

"Yes, my lady." The nurse marched out with the infant.

"Catherine! Did you not hear me? Your husband is dead—"

"Well, an old man he was," she murmured. She rose and went to the mirror, straightening her gown, smoothing her hair. He took a stride across the room and caught her close against him, hard and tight.

"We will make the marriage at once—tonight! Ah, Catherine, I've prayed long for it—God be thanked it comes at last!"

"You may go Ailsa," she said without moving, and the maidservant went out giggling, shut the door with exaggerated care. "Will we indeed?" said Catherine to their images in the mirror. She sounded surprised. "I was thinking you had changed your mind about it, Shane."

He pulled her round roughly to face him. "Now what is all this? Four years I've been waiting to wed you—"

"Yes, it is a long time. Longer than you have been with any other woman. It was not surprising that you tired of me a little—perhaps. And," she said remotely, drawing away from his grasp, "you are O'Neill, so you thought it was no matter, I would forgive you if I knew about it."

"What in the name of God are you talking about? I never—"

"Manus Donnelly has been on leave," she said. "He told me of that foreign woman who came from Dublin to see you. And how you—"

"Before God! What affair was it of his? It was nothing! Women! It was nothing, I tell you!"

"Is she very beautiful, Shane?"

"What does it signify?"

Turning, she saw his expression in the mirror: outraged, amazed, half-guilty, furious. She bit her lip, hiding the sudden laughter in her voice. She schooled her tone to sorrow and a hint of anger. "Perhaps it is the first time any woman has showed you displeasure over betrayal. Is it, Shane? They took you as you are, grateful for your attentions, and never expected faithfulness of you."

"I—!"

"That is what everyone says of the O'Neills—one cannot expect faithfulness of them. After all your protestation, it has grieved me greatly." She put a hand to her eyes, half-turned from him. "But I am not so weak or meek a woman. Perhaps you forget I am a MacLean of the chief's line, a Highland Scot, not one of your soft Irish. I will not be betrayed twice."

He got hold of her then and shook her angrily. "Haven't I told you there was nothing? Polite I was to the woman, that is all! Christ damn Manus, whyfor must he go telling you? It was nothing, I swear it, Catherine!"

"Of course," she said softly, "you had been long away from me. It was understandable—for an O'Neill."

"Now for the love of God! I swear to you I never laid a hand on the woman! I had to show her politeness!"

"Not in your tent," said Catherine.

"I never did so! I swear—"

"Would you swear before Father Brendan?"

He let her go and drew himself up, compressing his lips. "You are a damned suspicious insubordinate woman," he said coldly. "It's not for me to justify myself to you and I'll not discuss it further. We will be wed this evening in the chapel."

"I will think about it first," said Catherine.

"By God, you will do as I say!"

"It is a serious matter, marriage. I do not want an unfaithful husband." She sat down before the mirror and took up her ivory comb. "Now do you go away and let me tidy myself for the meal. I will think about what you have said."

"By Christ, you're not saying you will not wed me! You will so! The sons I must legalize—"

"Perhaps, and perhaps not," she said tranquilly. She put the comb down because her hand was shaking.

"Catherine!" And she heard the little panic in his voice; she relaxed, and the laughter rose again in her throat. "Catherine, you'd not leave me—only for that? I swear it meant nothing, believe me! Catherine, I—"

"Mhm?" His hands were hard on her shoulders; she looked up to meet his eyes in the mirror. "But you could easily find another mistress, Shane."

"Ah, damn you and Manus and the foreign woman too," he said. "I'm not wanting another woman! You damned hard Scots, putting morals before love."

"But that," she said, "you never spoke to me—love."

"You knew it!" he barked at her desperately. "No need to—abase myself—talk soft—"

"But we like to hear it, Shane, we silly women. Perhaps, if you would tell me now—?"

"Christ damn Manus! You know there's no other to matter, Catherine." He shifted uneasily behind her.

"Then tell me why, my dear."

"Ah, damn Manus to hell for eternity!" shouted the chief. "Because I love you, woman, and God knows why that is! And, by God, I will wed you if I must bind your arms and drag you before the priest!"

She leaned back against him, and she could not keep the laughter from her voice. "Perhaps I'll give you a second chance, Shane."

He jerked her upright to his arms. "Damn all women. Teasing me you've been—"

"Only a little . . . and I was displeased for that woman . . . and I wanted to hear you say it, if only the once."

"It might be easier to say after the first time," said O'Neill in a whisper, and set his mouth down on hers.

The next day after the chief had left the war line the dawn broke clear and cold. The guns began with the first light, and within an hour the sky was hazed with smoke. Rory was sitting over breakfast at the central fire with the captains; McArdle had just come up, yawning, remarking, "We're likely to have a little hotter fighting today or tomorrow, when it is clear like this—" when abruptly the English guns fell silent.

In a moment every man was on his feet. That meant a charge of the line, and soon: they never stopped the guns, to give warning, until just before a charge. There was much to do at once, but they all knew their jobs and scattered without wasted words, officers running for the horse lines, yelling orders to the troopmen, into the main camp, calling on the foot-ranks, and men rushing to fetch the captains' mounts. As his horse was brought up and he tumbled into the saddle, it flashed through Rory's mind that it would be like an ironic destiny to see him killed in this skirmish, when, in a few days' time, he would be leaving the line. The Ulster guns were still thundering to hold back the charge a few precious minutes; in record time the men were formed behind the line to meet the enemy.

Hugh was at the head of the troops, on a tall gray Arab, and Rory fell into place at his left shoulder. As he came up Hugh was cursing mildly. "The inconsistent bastards, they might give us time to finish breakfast—"

"One round?" shouted McArdle from farther down the line. Hugh shook his head—there was no time. The guns had been silent only long enough to miss one or two fires. Then the English charge came out from behind their breastworks; Hugh lifted his arm and the Ulstermen went out to meet them at a run.

They met with a crash in the center of the field and had a warm time for a little, the fighting close and hard. They got the English neatly boxed in on three sides; the only way they could flee was across their own lines—and the next half-hour saw some butchery, until the enemy broke and began to retreat, but not in great disorder. The English line would not be overrun this time.

The Ulstermen followed up the retreat. The English foot-ranks had fallen back first and their arquebusier troops were in the vanguard, firing steadily at short range as the battle moved across the field toward the English line. Still hopeful of breaking through the line, all the officers were urging the men to a more rapid pace. The pipes were blaring full charge, and battle cries sounded from every quarter to spur the action.

Rory was a little way behind the front line of charge. He heard, above all others, Hugh's voice defiant in the clan-cry; snatching a look round he saw Hugh not far off, standing in his stirrups, ax brandished high, urging his horse on after the enemy. Then his own horse stumbled in avoiding a body on the ground; he pulled it up, veered to miss another tangle of corpses. When he looked across the field again, he saw the gray horse rearing, just ahead—rein flying and saddle empty.

He never remembered halting and dismounting; he was kneeling on the ground, lifting Hugh, fumbling at his tunic to lay bare the place that slow stain came on his left breast. It would be an arquebus ball, striking square, by unlucky chance— And he was crying his name, foolish as a woman. "Hugh—Hugh!"

The blue eyes opened, already hazed, and the ghost of the familiar grin curved Hugh's mouth. In all the noise, Rory could not hear him; he only saw his lips move. "A damned—silly way—to be ending," he whispered; and then suddenly, in a great gasp, he said, "Catherine!" and turned his face into Rory's shoulder. Rory felt the life go out between his arms, and it was no longer Hugh he held, but only a dead man.

He never knew how long he crouched there motionless, feeling that weight cold on his chest, while his mind repeated, Not Hugh—not Hugh. At last it came to him that the sounds of battle were dying; the enemy had reached its line and soon the cannon would begin to roar across this space. He got up stiffly and lifted Hugh across the saddle of his horse, and took him back to the camp. And as he came in he might have been Death personified, for men talking and laughing excitedly on all sides fell silent on recognizing the Arab, and crossed themselves, and many began to weep.

It was a stricken group of men gathered to look at Hugh where he was laid—the smiling handsome face unmarred by death, the long, lithe body that had been so quick to love or war. There was nothing to say. But every man there, when he heard, had said the one thing, perhaps the only epitaph needful: "Not Hugh, no, not Hugh!" Any man but Hugh, the well-beloved.

Edmund Donnelly went on his knees to lift the brown head. "Not our Hugh—the best of us all! More grief than I can withstand—"

And McArdle said in a somber voice, "A fine wedding gift for Shane."

"Who will tell him?" asked Sorley. No man wanted that task. But Rory thought, I was with Hugh when he died; it is for me to go.

He heard himself say, "I will—tell him. I will go to the chief."

There was another silence while Edmund smoothed the brown hair stirred by the wind; then he lifted Hugh's hand and drew off the emerald ring, never from Hugh's finger in twenty years, and gave it to Rory. "Go now. We will send men after with the body—for the burial will be at Benburb."

"What is the burial?" asked Terence O'Hagan harshly. "It is not Hugh. I would rather it had been myself."

"I will go now," said Rory, and did not trust himself to speak further. A troopman brought him a fresh horse; he mounted and rode blindly, hardly aware when it began to rain or, later, of deathly fatigue. He stopped only twice to ease the horse, that sixty-mile journey. His mind was filled with nothing but Hugh—a thousand memories of him grave and gay, his ready laugh and warm handclasp, the timbre of his voice and the way he sang in liquor: a thousand things—the times they had shared. But sometime during that ride he remembered something else, how Hugh had spoken Catherine's name as he died. Catherine! So perhaps that was the real reason there was left no widow to console. Well, it would be kept a secret as Hugh had kept it.

It was just past dusk when he came to Lough Neagh. His legs were stiff; he staggered as he dismounted. A silent boatman on duty ferried him to the island. He walked slowly up to the house, mounted the three shallow steps; the door opened under his hand and he came into the fore-passage on uncertain feet.

The chief was just entering the hall, with Lady Catherine on his arm; he turned at Rory's step. He had been laughing at some jest and Catherine's eyes were alight with mirth and happiness; their hands were clasped. "Well, Rory! You decided to follow me after all—" And then as he saw Rory's expression, he dropped the lady's hand and took a step forward. "What is it, man?" he asked quietly.

Rory could not speak. If he opened his mouth, he would begin to weep like a child. He held out his hand and let the chief see Hugh's ring on the outstretched palm.

For a moment O'Neill's expression did not alter. He looked at the ring and then took it in his own hand. "Hugh," he said in a whisper. "Hugh, my brother." Lady Catherine clutched his arm, staring at Rory, a hand to her throat.

"Oh, no, Rory—not Hugh! I could not bear it to be Hugh!"

"When and how?" asked the chief, his eyes still on the ring. Rory made an effort to answer him.

"This morning—there was a charge. An arquebus ball—to the breast. He was—gone—almost at once. They are sending—they thought—for the burial—" He could not finish.

"Yes. Yes," said the chief. "Hugh. A few men I have loved, but none so deep as that one."

"Oh, no!" gasped Lady Catherine again. The tears started to her eyes. "Not Hugh, Shane—you cannot mean he is—"

O'Neill turned slowly and looked down at her as if she was a stranger. He said in a remote cold voice, "Go away, Catherine, and make your own grieving where you will. This is not a thing for women. This is beyond the love of women."

They brought Hugh home on the second day and held the burial service in the chapel at Benburb, the grave made on the near hillside. It was a strange burial, for the chief would have no keening; they put Hugh to rest in dead silence. O'Neill said, "A man buried with great wailing, it is over when the echoes die. This man, we cannot put grief for him into sound—our mourning will never end." He threw Hugh's ring into the waters of Lough Neagh—he was superstitious for the pagan gods, for all his lip service to religion, and said the water spirits which ruled his and Hugh's birth sign would give him safe journey to paradise. The day after the burial he rode back to the war line with the captains who had brought the body. He said in a very quiet voice, as he waited for the escort rank to form that morning, "This will be avenged—now, or next spring, or ten years from now if I must wait that long—revenge I will have for this."

So it was later than Rory had intended when he got home to Kilclain that time—it was in the last week of the year. There had been no more snow and he made the ride in two days, stopping at the McGuinness' house a night. It was good to see the shape of the hills round his land, the solid bulk of Kilclain, his red-and-white cattle in the fields this dry clear weather, and again to ride into his own courtyard and dismount before the door. But he was not so light of heart as he had thought, two weeks ago, to be.

The manservant, Murdock, opened the door to him; his face lit with welcome. "McGuinness—good to see you home again!"

"And good to be here. Your mistress—my brother—"

"In the hall McGuinness." But Fergus had heard his voice and came running.

"Rory! God be thanked, good to see you alive and well! On leave are you or is the war over? I was but this minute sitting down to write you a letter. The child has come, Rory, two days since—a fine son. Moyna is quite well, yes—"

Good news; his spirits raised a trifle to hear it. He went up to her, and for a little forgot all else but how good it was to be home, at peace awhile, and with Moyna. And then she was showing the new son, very proud and pleased with herself.

"See how big and strong, Rory! Even larger than Michael was—and your hair, too! Please, Rory—if you would—"

"Yes, what is it, my heart?"

"This one I'd like named for you. It's silly to say that is bad luck, and he's much like you already, see—"

"No," said Rory. "No, Moyna. Not this son. Maybe the next. This son will be Hugh—for a man I loved."

CHAPTER XXXVIII

I T WAS the second week of the new year of 1567 when Rory left Kilclain and returned to the war line. That month there were heavy rains, which left the armies helpless to move, bogged down as surely as if by snow and ice. None of them remembered ever experiencing such discomfort in the field. The weather was killing cold, the food monotonous, and the state of the war annoying; as they all agreed, it was senseless that they stay at the line at all. They could only match gunfire with the English, and that was little use. When the enemy found their range to inflict any damage on the Ulster camp or the line, the Ulstermen moved forward or back a way and then the English needed two days to break loose their guns from the frozen mud and alter the range. The same was true for the Ulster cannon. It gave them all something to do, but it was like the play of a child who builds a town with sticks only to destroy it to have sticks for another. But so long as the English seemed determined to stay out the winter, O'Neill would not withdraw.

"Spring," he said. "As soon as the weather is clear we will take them." He was not angry or impatient now, but very quiet and grim as he had been since Hugh's death.

Any man might be killed in battle, and none of them ever went into action without wondering if he would die or lose friends in the fight. But Hugh, almost like O'Neill himself, had seemed inviolate: immortal. And ever afterward, when Rory thought of him, he was forever young, gay, laughing. Rory attended mass and paid service to God, but always, secretly, he felt that Hugh did not go to the heaven the priests told of: he would not be happy in a place like that. No, he went to the place the old pagan Gaels called Tir nan Og, the Land of the Young, the land of heart's desire, where there was eternal feasting and music and dancing and lovemaking, and fighting too—there Hugh would be content. And since he was gone, it was as if they had been thinking themselves at casual play and suddenly found the point of the knife sharp where it had been fancied a blunt stick.

All of them but the chief would speak of him now, with grief and nostalgia; O'Neill never spoke his name; Rory was to hear it from him only once more in his lifetime, a time he was much moved and scarcely knew what he said.

So they sat there in camp and exchanged occasional gunfire with the enemy until March, when they might reasonably have expected the weather to be better; but it continued wet and any more decisive action remained impossible.

Upon the death of a chief, there would generally be a period of a few months allowed for decent mourning before a new chief was formally accepted. Calvagh O'Donnell had died, at four-and-eight years, in the last week of November. But Hugh Ruadh could not wait so long to assume his new duties. Some allowance might be made, for he had been chief in all but name for years, and none was likely to question his right to the chiefhood.

On the third day of April a rider from the north brought O'Neill another letter from Hugh Ruadh. A crowd of officers and the captains huddled about the chief's fire there, in idle talk, as the messenger arrived. O'Neill read the letter in silence and thrust it at Edmund Donnelly, sitting next to him.

"The new O'Donnell," said Edmund, glancing at the signature. "Now what is he after?"

"Nothing good," said O'Hagan lazily. "You can wager on that."

"I wonder," said O'Neill. "What does he want? Well, he asks me to a meeting, a formal discussion concerning the pact I have with him and that I had with Calvagh as subchief. I will need to have a renewal of that in any case, when another man succeeds to the chiefhood. Hugh Ruadh does not like the idea overmuch, but he is subchief—that he knows well! But there is something else in his mind, too, and I think I know what it is."

"Well?" Edmund tossed the letter to O'Hagan, who did not look at it but gave it to McArdle.

The chief smiled. "Hugh Ruadh has no love for me, but even less for the English. It irks him like the devil to pay me a yearly tribute, and he might be thinking to have some of it back by hiring his army to me as he pledged in our pact. He has thought twice, too, and knows if he fails to keep that agreement, I'll come down on him when I've finished the English. You see what he says—'matters of mutual interest in regard to this latest war.'"

"Y-e-s," said McArdle, "that might just be in his mind."

"I could use six or seven hundred men." O'Neill was stroking the hilt of one of four daggers in his belt. "By Christ, I could. As soon as we can move I'll end this senseless business definite. If I had that many more men I could invade the Pale by spring."

Edmund grunted. "Take the Tyrconnell men in, and share the camp with O'Donnell?"

"Why not? And he might only hire the men and stay home himself. It is my war."

"Listen, brother," said O'Hagan amusedly, "Hugh Ruadh O'Donnell never stayed home from a fight in his life. He's never lost anger at you for the times you've foiled him. I would not trust him too far, Shane."

O'Neill made an impatient gesture. "Have the sense God gave you! He's no fool. He dares not challenge me now, after I beat him to submission last year, and he with an army one-sixth the size of mine!" He took the letter again, looked at it reflectively. "I'll make this meeting with him. God knows there is little to keep me here," and he directed a brooding look at the enemy line.

"When does he ask it?"

"Next week—six days from now, at Rath O'Donnell."

"Making you ride to him!"

"What difference? I'll be glad of the exercise"—and the chief laughed. "I'll take some of you with me to make a good showing, and a guard from the home force. Who wants to come?" Since they were all bored in camp and eager for any action, all the captains volunteered, but he would take only Edmund, Ferdoragh, and O'Hagan. "We ride in the morning and stop at home a night."

"I'll ride that far with you," said Sorley Boy. "My turn for a visit at home it is, and I'll stop by Lough Neagh to see Catherine."

It was those men rode from the camp in the next dawn: the chief, Rory with him, Edmund Donnelly, O'Hagan and Ferdoragh, and Sorley. They had royal welcome at Lough Neagh; it was the first time the chief had been home since his marriage with Lady Catherine. O'Hagan's wife was staying there also, to be closer to him than on his land in Antrim.

Dudley Donnelly was near tears to be with O'Neill again after so long. Up to a few months back he had been gradually weakening, and then, for no apparent reason, began to gain strength; now he looked better than any of them had seen him in several years. He had taken on weight, his color was less deathly, and he was in good spirits; but he was still far from being a well man, and the chief laughed at his plea to accompany them on the ride to Tyrconnell.

"I'm quite strong to ride with you, Shane—and near mad after this long time shut up here with servants and women! I beg you, let me come!"

"You are strong as a newborn kitten," said O'Neill. "It's out of the question."

"But you can see for yourself how much better I am! Exercise and fresh air will be good for me. Shane, I beg, for any concern you have for me, let me ride with you!"

O'Neill looked down at the thin white hand gripping his own brown arm. He said almost gently, "It means so much to you?"

"Yes—yes! Let me come."

"Very well, then. We have plenty of time to travel slow, and if you are tired at any time—"

"I will not be—I will be fine," said Dudley on a long sigh.

Certainly he seemed so, that morning as they gathered in the courtyard; he mounted without aid and looked nearly his old self. The chief was in better spirits than for some time, and Rory thought it might be from having Dudley at his side. The two men always closest to him were Dudley and Hugh; this was the first time in two years and more the eldest Donnelly had ridden with him as of old.

Rory remarked to Edmund that his brother seemed in much improved health. "He is that," agreed Edmund. "I only hope it continues. A mysterious thing, that sickness. No physician knows the cause or cure, though I daresay the latest one treating him will claim the credit for the improvement. Our mother died with it, and I have wondered if it is something in the blood, but the rest of us are healthy enough, God grant we remain so."

Whatever the cause, Dudley seemed not to tire for the day's ride, and was in continuing high spirits to be with O'Neill on the march again. Even a night's camp did not appear to tire him, cold as it was. They stopped the night near the border of Tyrconnell; they had traveled slowly on Dudley's account and were slowed, too, by the foot-ranks. O'Neill had with him an escort of one hundred gallowglass men, no more, for this was to be formal meeting.

It was only another twenty miles or so up to Rath O'Donnell, and they made a leisurely start that morning. The day was chill and gray, but Dudley was still cheerful, more talkative than Rory had ever heard him. Rory rode behind with Edmund, Ferdoragh, and O'Hagan, the gallowglass men marching at the rear.

"You see how much stronger I am, Shane. It was all that rest and staying indoors the physicians prescribed that weakened me—if I made the last few campaigns with you, I'd be strong and well as ever! Exercise and fresh air and an interest in life, that is what I need!"

"You are yourself again now," lied O'Neill. "You may be right. Put on your cloak, man, it's a chill morning—"

"Oh, I'm fine, I'm not needing a cloak! Do you remember how we rode this way before, Shane, the night you took Calvagh O'Donnell? It was I carried him on my saddle, remember? That was a good raid—"

"I remember, Dudley." Rory wondered if, remembering, it seemed as long ago to O'Neill as it did to him. Seven years—how much had happened in that time!

"And do you remember that last great fair at Fedan? Only the summer before it was. I won the longest race that day, with the black mare you gave me—remember? A grand day that was—"

"Yes."

"And I could ride another race this minute, so well I feel—yes, and win it, too, even against you! I challenge you, Shane—a race!"

The chief laughed. "Well, if you must prove yourself, bold man!" He looked ahead. They were approaching a thick stand of wood, and the road curved west around it. "To the bend of the road!" said O'Neill, and lifted his horse to a run. The two horses, black and bay, fled down the road; the black began to drop behind, and Rory guessed that O'Neill would let Dudley win the little challenge. The others were all smiling.

"He's certainly much better," said Edmund, and added curiously, "Well, and who would those be? Huntsmen?"

A party of mounted men had appeared at the edge of the wood, above the road. Dudley reached the bend a few paces ahead of O'Neill; they heard his shout: "You see, Shane, I've won again!" But O'Neill's reply was drowned by the sudden long yell from the wood.

"O'Donnell! O'Donnell! Death to the Ulstermen!" And out from the trees charged a great unordered pack of soldiers brandishing weapons—O'Donnell's army—and at their head that red giant O'Donnell himself, ax lifted high.

It was an ambush attack; there were at least seven hundred; and the chief was alone with Dudley, two hundred paces from even the small guard he had with him, and armed only with his belt knives. Before a man could count ten they would be on him. The captains behind spurred madly, crying to the footmen to charge.

Only one move might save O'Neill, and he made it. Shouting to Dudley to follow, he reined about and came back at a gallop, to snatch a weapon and turn again to defend himself. But the distance between was too short; his horse started from a stand, and O'Donnell was not twenty paces from him, leaning forward to strike. He could never make it—but for the first and last time in his life Dudley disobeyed O'Neill.

Dudley sent his horse like arrow from bow straight for O'Donnell. Like the chief, he had only his knife, but he had that out, poised. The two horses met chest to chest at a gallop, and both staggered and reared; Dudley drove the knife for O'Donnell's breast. With his greatly impaired strength, he no more than grazed the flesh, but it was enough to halt O'Donnell and give O'Neill his chance. O'Donnell rose in the saddle with a roar of rage and brought the ax down.

And then O'Neill had reached his men behind, and stretched a hand to take the ax a panting, running gallowglass man held to him. He whirled his horse again, and saw Dudley's horse down, struggling, a twisted body under it. A great cry of grief and fury burst from him and he charged back down the road to meet the enemy.

That was not a battle: it was a massacre. They were five mounted men and a hundred gallowglass; in O'Donnell's force were at least three hundred troopmen and four hundred foot. They were not fighting three minutes before it turned to a rout. Afterward, it seemed a miracle that any of them escaped at all, footmen retreating from horsemen. The first thing Rory clearly remembered after they engaged was the chief shouting, "Back—back—try for the wood!" A moment after that he had a glimpse of O'Neill, very close. The chief had met O'Donnell, but only wounded him; and somehow in the confusion he had got Dudley Donnelly's bloody corpse across the front of his saddle and lashed it there. Rein in his teeth, ax in one hand, dagger in the other, he was engaging two mounted men at once.

They broke into retreat almost as soon as they met the charge, and streamed wildly into the wood, the one hope of cover. It was not possible to arrange the retreat or convey any orders—they only ran. The wounded tried to keep up, but if a man fell out he was gone; they could not stop to aid those less lucky. Hotly pursued, fighting as they fled, they ran southeast for the border; there was no time for talk, but every man prayed the chase would end there. The hunt scattered in the wood as they had hoped.

The next moment Rory remembered with any clarity was when he came up with O'Neill in a little clearing. O'Neill's horse was flank to flank with Edmund Donnelly's; the chief had his arm about Edmund, who sagged forward in the saddle. Then there was another blur in his mind when he galloped, and fought, and took a terrific blow on his ax-arm from some man, losing his knife, feeling the pain like fire, and galloped again. It was like that all the way, run and slash. His arm was all pain, but he could not stop to look at it. Then his horse nearly unseated him, sidestepping to avoid a horse thrashing on the ground; it was Ferdoragh's. Rory pulled up. Ferdoragh was swearing and bloody; he held a dagger with half the blade broken off, and was scarcely recognizable under all the blood. Rory tried to help him mount behind, but he could not move his arm and Ferdoragh hauled himself up astride.

"Thanks—young one." He was gasping in a queer, thick voice unlike his own. "Bastard—had on steel plate, my dirk is broke—" They were galloping again; he laid an arm around Rory to steady himself. "A good dirk it was," he muttered. "A pity it is—a great pity—" Rory was aware of hot wetness pressed on his back, and asked, "Are you bad wounded, Ferdoragh?"

"Only—a scratch, boy," and with that, he collapsed on Rory. Rory looked and saw he was dead, of a great gaping wound in the chest. So with much labor, able to use only one hand, Rory got him across the saddle-bow and lashed him there with the thongs, and went on alone.

The pursuit did not cease even at the border, but followed on into Ulster; the chase was strung out by then. O'Neill's men had drawn ahead into the hills, gaining time, but it was a desperate retreat. The first time they dared halt was in midafternoon, for only a few minutes, to try to make some tally of those lost and give the men more coherent orders. O'Donnell was not half an hour behind.

The chief laid Edmund down beside the stream where they halted, and held his flask to Edmund's mouth. Donnelly's breath came slow and shallow; Rory could not tell about the wounds under all the blood and dirt. O'Neill was talking to him, and then to Rory, the constables who came up: "If they catch us up, scatter! Make for Lough Neagh, but scatter the pursuit—now we must stay together, but remember. God, God, I will punish—I will visit such a destruction—Edmund, Edmund, man, can you hear me?" But Donnelly's eyes stayed shut.

Then a horse came up close, and the chief raised his head; it was Terence O'Hagan's horse, but a gallowglass man was astride the saddle and a body face-down across the pommel. "I thought you would want him brought out, O'Neill—"

After that, Rory did not remember anything more clearly at all, only flashes. All the rest of that day, until darkness shut down, and they were safe ahead at last, and lost the pursuit, but still did not dare slow their pace toward Lough Neagh.

CHAPTER XXXIX

I**T WAS** very dark in the wood, though the moon had risen; this was an ancient growth of oak, and thick. Except for the low mutter of men all about and an occasional moan from one of the wounded, it was silent; and they had not dared build a fire. Nor could they stop here long, for O'Donnell might be coming. Even in the dark he might be following, knowing them so few and so hard-pressed.

Rory had got his arm tended after a fashion; it was broken and useless, the constable who contrived a sling said. Later it could be set and splinted. He was used to the pain now; it was only another pain among so many. He sat against a tree and tried to rest, but it was all pain and he could not.

Beside him the chief stirred and spoke in a tired, dead voice. "Dudley. Edmund. O'Hagan. Ferdoragh. No—they cannot all be gone—not all. I do not believe it."

"O'Neill," he said, "won't you lie down now, get some rest? We cannot stop long—"

"No—no. Dudley," said O'Neill, "Edmund, O'Hagan, Ferdoragh. Not all, not all. Oh, Christ, give me your hand—let me feel a living man beside me! All my men, all my good men . . ."

There was nothing to say to him. Rory offered him his flask, but he did not take it.

"Dudley. Edmund. O'Hagan. Ferdoragh. Twenty years—more. With me—since we are children. And Hugh, and Hugh! The best of us all, as Edmund said! What have I done to be punished so? All my good men—"

"O'Neill." The chief seemed not to hear.

"More than I can withstand, it is—all gone at once—Dudley, Edmund, O'Hagan, Ferdoragh! My men—my brothers." The chief drew a long shuddering breath and slowly got to his feet. "We should—move on. We must not stay too long. Tell—the men." All who had got out were lying about there: twenty men and one of the constables. Rory went to untether the horses. They were still nervous for the smell of death lashed to their backs.

"O'Neill—your pardon." In the dimness a man came up to the chief.

"I would not ask, but he's a good man, a friend, and it will not be long. Dying he is now. If I might just see him out, O'Neill."

"McSweeney," said the chief dully. "You got out with us, Manus."

"I did." He was the one constable who had escaped; Rory identified him there, a bandage about his brow, his voice flat with exhaustion. "I'd not want him to die alone, O'Neill—"

They stepped beside him. The moonlight penetrated a gap in the trees here, and shone pure silver, unearthly, on the chief and the burly constable and a long shape stretched on the ground.

"I am surprised he lasted this long and managed to keep up, wounded so deep. But he is a very strong man. It is Colm McCaffrey, O'Neill."

"McCaffrey," said the chief; and the shape on the ground stirred and tried to raise itself. McSweeney bent over it.

"O'Neill—you must move on—they will be coming—never care for us, get on—save yourself—" McCaffrey fell back and McSweeney crossed himself.

"God with you, Colm."

O'Neill said in a whisper, "That was a good man to me. Manus, I know it is a difficulty—but we will bring this body also—for burial at home."

What would stay sharp forever in Rory's mind was their coming to Lough Neagh in midafternoon of that next day. They were a sorry procession, exhausted, limping, caked with dirt and blood. O'Neill's horse was wounded and he walked, refusing to take Rory's because Rory was wounded himself; the men led the other horses with the corpses. When they came to the jetty the boatmen started forward, loud on questions, but O'Neill spoke never a word. Under Rory's tired order, they got the bodies into one boat, the soldiers dispersing into the home camp on the mainland. In another boat he and the chief were ferried across to the island. O'Neill strode straight into the house, but halted in the fore-passage and looked about vaguely as if surprised to find himself home.

Sorley Boy appeared in the door of the hall. He smiled welcome and was about to speak, but the lady's voice cut across his from halfway down the stair.

"Shane—we did not expect you home so soon—my dearest—"

O'Neill gave a great sigh and went to meet her; he put his arms about her tightly, holding her there motionless. Rory had never seen him display emotion so openly, and even then, his impulse was to turn away. He came past Sorley into the hall, beginning to realize how very tired he was.

"My Christ," he heard Sorley say, "what is it? What has happened? You're wounded—where are the others? What—"

Rory tried to tell him. "O'Donnell. It was ambush—on the road. Seven hundred, more. I don't know how we got out."

"Christ—Christ!" whispered Sorley. "Dead on your feet you are—sit down." He filled a cup, spilling half the liquor, thrust it at Rory. "The others—"

"Look in the yard. Look there. Dudley. Edmund. O'Hagan. Ferdoragh."

"No," said Sorley. "No—not all!"

Rory told him in tired short phrases, the liquor putting a little strength in him but making him lightheaded as well. "Dudley—it was the way he would choose to die. A brave thing it was. I do not know how any of us escaped. Formal meeting it was—the chief had no ax with him—such rank betrayal—and all the guard unmounted. It was massacre, MacDonnell, it was butchery."

Sorley was beyond questioning; he only repeated, "Christ," in incredulity and horror. Rory finished the liquor and sat holding the cup, too numb and lax to set it down. Sorley said, "Wounded you are—it should be seen to," but made no move to call a servant; he sounded as dazed as Rory. "Christ, I can't believe it—"

All that while there had been silence, save for the subdued noise and voices from the courtyard. There was silence for a little after Sorley said that, and they sat quiet, Rory so deathly tired and Sorley so stricken with shock, until, from the passage outside, sounded a woman's loud scream.

"No, no—not Terence! Mother of God, not my Terence!"

Sorley Boy got up without a word and refilled both their cups.

Those two days, even after it was all past and they were safe at home, left those who had lived through them shaken and dazed for some time. Rory remembered someone guiding him up the stair, undressing him, bathing and bandaging his several wounds, and then more pain like fire in the arm, but after that, oblivion. He slept like the dead for many hours, without bad dreams or any dreams. When he woke he still felt like death, his mind slow, his body unrested. His arm had been set and strapped to splints. After lying there a little, he rose and called a servant who helped him dress, bringing him fresh clothes. He went down to the hall, where he found Sorley Boy and the lady. Sorley had a meal set before him but had not touched it; Rory was suddenly ravenous, and disposed of that, and more, too. He asked for the chief. It was Lady Catherine who answered.

"He will be all right, Rory. He is still sleeping; exhausted he was every way." Her eyes were troubled and dark with sorrow; she had owned affection for those men dead. "A dreadful thing—that is a wicked man, Red Hugh, I always knew it. A savage, and vindictive as Satan. I cannot help feeling it is all my fault—because he—"

"Now, Catherine. Do not be dwelling on that," admonished Sorley heavily. "God—the perfidy of it! Well, it was shortsighted of him—he will be punished." He rested his head in one hand. "I cannot believe it yet—such destruction. Those four good men, all at once—"

Rory said, "Some message should be sent to the line, to the others."

There was Manus Donnelly, who would want to be present for the burial —all the captains had been comrades most of their lives.

"I have sent one, Shane was in no state to think of it. You're not looking so well yourself, Rory."

He said he would be fine. "I'm still trying to believe I am alive. I never was in a fight like that."

"Neither was Shane," said Sorley.

Most of the day Rory slept again; he did not see the chief until that evening, and then O'Neill looked himself. He was grim, preoccupied, tired, but—O'Neill. He said little to anyone, and left the hall directly after the meal. And Sorley said to Rory quietly, "You saw the look in his eyes. O'Donnell will regret this—and he will regret it in hell."

"How did he hope to escape retribution? I can't understand how he dared—"

"Did you not say it was a miracle you got out? He never thought Shane would get away with nothing but a few ax cuts. With Shane dead, he'd expect no retaliation. Force is all he knows; he has no conception of the strong bonds among Shane and his men. And he came near doing what he plotted, too. If Dudley had not been there—"

"Yes." Rory thought again, if Dudley Donnelly could have chosen his way to die—as in a sense he had—that would have been his choice, giving his life for O'Neill's. A strange thing, destiny. And a strange man Dudley; peace to his soul wherever it wandered or rested.

"Vindictive, Catherine said. Yes, this goes back a long way. It was not only the war last year, though it was that too. O'Donnell will regret it," repeated Sorley.

The afternoon of the following day the captains came from the line. MacArthur, Brodie, and O'Reilly had said both McArdle and Manus Donnelly might come; they could hold the line alone a few days, with the war as it was. The burial was in the next dawn; the high keening nearly drowned Father Brendan's shaking old voice. According to Gaelic custom, the women did not attend rites for the dead, but they were not far off and the muffled weeping of those who had lost men in this battle sounded below the keens and the priest's chanting. After the ceremony, the graves were made behind the chapel, up the island shore.

That afternoon the chief shut himself up alone in the council room. Several letters had arrived for him since he had been at home; stopping only the night on his way into Tyrconnell, he had not troubled to examine them then. Perhaps it gave his mind welcome occupation now. They saw no more of him that day. Cormac McArdle and the two Donnellys went off together; James and Manus were like two men walking in sleep for the shock of losing their brothers. Rory sat with Sorley and some of the home-guard officers, who exuded silent sympathy; there was no more to say than they had said. And it was a silent, gloom-ridden company that sat down to the meal that evening. The chief's table seemed oddly empty, the five vacant places conspicuous, for the chief had the servants put out the chairs where dead men had sat. Often enough before only two or three of the captains had sat with him as now, the others being off on a hunt or at the war line of the latest campaign; but those five absent tonight were gone farther than a war line and would never join talk or laughter here again. And Luke O'Givney fingered his harp softly on a lament or stilled the strings to silence through the meal.

But the chief was himself, the decisive, autocratic O'Neill they all knew. He ate swiftly, refilling his cup several times, and before the rest had finished he sat back in his chair, looked round the table.

"And now it is time I issue some orders," he said. "We have work ahead of us." From his tunic he brought out a folded letter and turned it about in his fingers as he spoke. "Listen to me, my brothers. Comrades we have lost, and God rest them, but mourning is not revenge—and revenge I will have. Such a destruction I will bring on the clan O'Donnell it will be wiped from the earth! Punishment! It is a slight word for what they deserve!"

"Amen to that," said James and Manus Donnelly in one voice.

"And no delay taking that revenge—no quarter in the war O'Donnell asks for! But the spring is on us. In a week, two weeks, the weather will be clear for fighting—and the English will move. We will meet them and hold them, yes, by God, and drive them back and invade the Pale just as I promised—"

"Two wars at once?" asked Sorley quietly.

The chief's fist crashed on the table. "O'Neill will fight six wars at once if it is needful, and win them all! Do you doubt me? Is that what you are thinking—yes, and Radcliffe too, and the queen—as well as this whoreson O'Donnell! God knows they have thought it before, but never my own men! So O'Neill is finished! A little age coming on him—half his captains lost—his power failing him! By Christ and all the holy apostles, they will learn they are wrong! They will learn O'Neill is still O'Neill!"

"We are not doubting," said McArdle in a low voice.

"Then keep your mouths closed and listen. I will march on Hugh Ruadh at once, but I must have sufficient force at the war line to hold the English until I finish the clan O'Donnell and can come down to finish the Sassenachs. They will not stop me in this work—ten wars, a hundred, and every single man dead behind me, I will go on and make a nation here!" He paused a moment, controlling the passion of temper possessing him; when he went on his voice was more even. "I need more men than I have. A thousand, two thousand. I will take two thousand against Hugh Ruadh and that leaves not enough at the line to meet and hold Radcliffe. But I am offered a thousand men for hire." He tapped the letter lying before him on the table.

"Who offers that?" asked McArdle.

"One Aspuke MacDonnell of Antrim. One thousand men—a third mounted—two hundred arquebusiers. The price is high, but it is worth it."

"Aspuke," said Sorley. "And where does Aspuke have a thousand men? Never a war leader he's been. But, yes, I see. He has been trying for the chiefhood, and likely thinks to bribe his way to it—this is one way of having gold. Most of the soldiers he offers will be cowherds and stableboys."

"But men. Any man can be trained—and what matter is it if we lose them all in a few battles? It saves my better men. It would be enough to give the English a good solid defense while I deal with Hugh Ruadh— and I will not waste time at that either." His hand clenched on the letter.

"I mislike it," said Sorley uneasily. "Aspuke is a tricky one. Why should he offer to hire soldiers to you—why does he think you need them? Not second-sighted, he is, he could not know when he wrote that letter you would be remotely interested in adding to your army."

"He is a Scot, not so?" parried O'Neill impatiently. "It is the gold that interests him. Do not interrupt—listen. Today is what? Monday. I will go myself to make the arrangement and hire the soldiers from this Mac-Donnell, as he asks—and bring back the mercenaries with me, that will be quicker. Cormac, you ride with me. James and Manus, you return to the line. I will be back here with those men by Friday, and James, you will be here to meet me with two thousand of ours—half troops, half gallowglass. You—"

"But Shane—"

"Be quiet and listen! You will take the Scots back to the line—I will teach Hugh Ruadh with Ulstermen to keep respect for O'Neill! And Cormac makes the Tyrconnell campaign with me, the rest of you against the English. Give me a month, and Tyrconnell will be laid waste—by Christ, I will teach him a lesson he will not forget—and he reciting it in hell! And then I come south to join you and teach the Sassenachs another. Have you that in your minds?"

"Yes. Say six thousand at the line now," said James Donnelly thoughtfully, "about the English strength. Take away two and add one. We can hold them with that a couple of months if needful."

"It will not be. Hugh Ruadh I will finish quick and hard," promised O'Neill. "Will I not!"

"You ride for Antrim tomorrow, then. If—"

"I do. A day and a half to go—Ban Clough it is, not far north. Half a day for discussion, and the price I do not haggle over. Two days to return, with foot-ranks. Friday I will be back here. Saturday we march on Tyrconnell."

Lady Catherine had not risen from the table, and now she laid a hand on his arm. "Shane," she said in a troubled voice, "frightened I am—all this, it is—too much, all at once. Please, my dear, use care—there are enemies all about you, the old and the new."

"Since when am I not surrounded by enemies? And time and again they think to see me dead and done, but always I make fools of them—fools and dead men," said O'Neill tautly. "This time is no different. I am only begun to take history in my hands and shape it! They will learn! Ireland and I will have a nation under my kingship, and the power of England I will destroy—these little jealous children of men will never halt or hurt me! I have said it—they should know me now! How can they dare suppose they can bring down O'Neill?"

Her hand tightened on his arm. "Please hear me, Shane—please listen. I—there is something that frightens me—please may I ride with you to Antrim? I want to be with you."

Surprised, he stared at her with a frown. "You? But it is a hurried journey—on business among men. You would not find it comfortable—"

"Please, Shane. I will be quite all right, the weather is opening. I want to come. Only a few days, you said." She was trying to smile at him, coaxing. "You're away so much, this last two years. Please, Shane."

He shrugged, put his hand over hers briefly. "Very well, if you will."

Sorley was still looking uneasy. "You'll do well to use caution, Shane. Aspuke is tricky—"

"Listen, faintheart, a thousand men are a thousand men and I am in no mood to argue about money. If half of them are senile and the other half unbreeched youngsters, they are still something to fill up the line for the English to use as targets. It is only makeshift for a month or six weeks while I take Hugh Ruadh. And that I am going to enjoy," he added softly.

"Well." Sorley sighed and shrugged. "It is your planning. You can rely on me for what you will. And I'll ride with you tomorrow, go on to Dunluce for a few days at home, and join the rest at the English line in two weeks."

"Good enough." The chief's mind was still on his enemies and the retribution he would exact. He would have revenge not alone for the injury Hugh Raudh dealt him, the losses the English made him, but for the insult to his pride that either of them should think him such easy game. He stroked one clenched fist softly, slowly. "The little men," he said, "they never learn it is dangerous to challenge O'Neill . . ."

CHAPTER XL

Tнат next morning they rode for Antrim, a sizable party: the chief, Lady Catherine, McArdle, Sorley Boy, and Rory, with a guard of fifty troopmen. Rory would not go on with them to the meeting with Aspuke—as the chief said, he was little use as a bodyguard with his best arm in a sling. He would stop at Kilclain for a few weeks' rest at home until his arm was healed and he could fight again.

Often before he had seen O'Neill's ability to shelve completely all things of the past, either good or bad, for the planning to be made for the future. Perhaps it had been difficult that the chief do that this time, he had taken such a blow to the heart, following so close on the death of Hugh. But he had put it behind, not to be forgotten but not brooded over. Those men he had loved, and he would avenge them with a terrible vengeance: now his mind was set on the means of that, and he was full of purpose, eager for action.

The last few days had been wet and windy, and now it turned cold; but it was clear, and with a mounted guard they made a good day's ride. Lady Catherine was an excellent horsewoman and did not seem to tire, but she was silent for the most part and watched the chief much. They made camp that night on the opposite shore of the Bann; the chief's tent was erected for the lady.

It was approaching midmorning of the second day's ride when they came to the crossroads where Rory would turn off for Kilclain. And Sorley with him, for his horse had gone lame and it was a favorite; he would delay at Kilclain to see it tended, or perhaps borrow another to ride on for Dunluce. There in the road, they halted to make temporary farewells, and the chief clasped their hands. "Don't delay long, Sorley—we'll need every man at the line. Rory, see that arm mends soon and come back to me! A guard I may be needing now more than before, enemies thinking I am in my dotage to be taken like a child!"

"A week," said Sorley, "or ten days. Good fortune with Aspuke." He kissed Catherine, took McArdle's hand.

The chief smiled. "He thinks to trick me over the price—let him. I'm in a hurry to have this business done and get into Tyrconnell. The men will not be worth it"—he laughed—"Scot hirelings! Farewell, then—I see you next month, when the first vengeance is taken and I come to punish the English again. They will learn that O'Neill is still O'Neill!" He lifted an arm to the guard and reined up the north road.

Sorley called after him in forcedly jocular tone: "If you think so poor of Scot soldiers why do you go to hire more?"

O'Neill turned in his saddle with a mirthless grin. "It's only for effect, brother—to frighten the English with numbers! The Ulstermen will do all the fighting!"

They delayed to watch the little cavalcade pass: O'Neill ahead on his black Arab, his back very straight; Lady Catherine riding at his left hand, McArdle at his right, and the fifty troopmen in even ranks after. The watery sun glinted on the axes, the burnished coats of the horses, and O'Neill's banner carried by the troop constable.

"He is still O'Neill, God keep him," said Sorley, "but all of us older and troubles we never expected come on us. . . . Never tell him, Rory, but I find some of my youthful enthusiasm for war deserting me." He laughed ruefully. "Old, I am growing."

"For that among other things O'Neill will never grow old," said Rory. They reined west for the road to Kilclain.

Armagh

It was Daphne Fleming admitted the Dean to the house; but the smile on her lips froze at the look in his eyes. He went slowly into the little hall, putting off his cloak. Liam Fleming looked up from where he sat, staring into the fire.

"Terence. You'll forgive me not to rise, I am poor company tonight. Foolish in me to grieve—only a beast—my blue terrier is dead. You will take a glass of wine?"

"Old man," said Daniel softly, "we are all dead. Dead and done. Since two nights ago . . ."

London

Elizabeth Tudor smiled at her chief minister over wine. "It was but a question of time—I always said that."

"And yet none of our doing," said Cecil.

"You're wrong. It was my doing, my friend. Gold and the promise of gold."

"We must make a few plans for that, too."

The queen laughed. "But so naïve, my dear Sir William! I've no intent to pay out that much gold! So all our troubles are done."

Cecil looked at her. He sighed; he sipped wine. He said, "Until the next time, my lady—until the next time."

Rath O'Donnell

The new O'Donnell was very pleased, and if he admitted it to none, very relieved. He had never conceived that that bastard would escape the ambush; having done so, he would not have delayed exacting vengeance. Now— And there was the woman. Always the woman. Many as he'd had, somehow, that one he had coveted most, the other thing Calvagh had had he wanted. And O'Neill. Damn O'Neill. No, that was taken care of. The woman . . . He began to think how he might have the woman.

In Spain, Philip was angry and disappointed. English, always the damned underhand English. This throw of the dice was lost, but there might come another. One could only wait and watch for advantage.

In Rome, the secretary said, "You will not want the letter dispatched, then."

"I scarce think so, my clever man." The secretary would have spoken again, but His Holiness lifted one narrow white hand.

"My lord?"

"I only thought I might catch a reverberation from hell."

Dublin

"You are not looking happy," said Radcliffe.

Sir Harry Sydney passed a hand across his balding head. "Forgive me, I am out of sorts, I fear. My mistress has left me." In fact, it was as much his doing as hers, and he held no great grief. He had been fond of Rebecca, no more, and it was a relief to know he need not call on fading powers, just to maintain appearances.

"I always said you were a fool to take a mistress at your age. And such a one to choose, a silly, middle-aged French Jewess."

"Italian," corrected Sydney mechanically. Radcliffe had been right. He would not be such a fool again.

"What does it signify?" Radcliffe strolled to the window of his office room, stared down at the gray wet Dublin street. There was a crowd of people gathered in the street, all looking up at one place, beside the foregate of Dublin gaol. Some of the crowd knelt on the wet cobblestoned roadway.

"You don't seem in high spirits yourself."

For a long moment Radcliffe said nothing to that. He turned to the table, poured a glass of the amber Jerez wine. Then he said, without drinking, "It is not the way. I have learned that after nearly thirty years. I would not know what is the right way, if there is one—but it is not fight, Sydney. And I am a soldier. You know all we accomplish? Like dropping a pebble in a pool, and the rings widen out, and we drop another stone and those rings spread into the first, and the third into the second. Only muddying the water. These Irish, these Irish . . . I am tired, and I want to go home to rest in England."

And after a moment, Sydney said nervously, "I would have thought—"

"You would have thought." Radcliffe gave him a twisted smile. "So would I, friend." He went back to the window. He said, "My dearest enemy." And that was perspicacious even for Radcliffe, Earl of Sussex.

Kilclain

Sorley Boy had delayed at Kilclain; though his horse was fit after the stone was out of the hoof and a poultice applied overnight, that next day was very wet. He was an easy guest, and the household like him well.

Rory was still so tired of mind and body, after the events of that week, that he had not realized fully how very good it was to be home, save that already he was wishing he need not ever again go away. And Moyna pressing him about that until he snapped at her, and was sorry, and tried to explain. "Oh, I know, Rory, I know. Men. As touchy for their kind of honor as women for ours. Only I wish, that's all—can't I say it? One day—"

"One day," he nodded, holding her close with a sigh.

But that following morning the sky was clear steel, and Sorley said he would ride. "If I'm to have any time at home at all, I must not delay. And I believe," he added thoughtfully, "I'll stop an hour on the way to see Aspuke and find out the details of his dealing with Shane. It goes against all my instinct to have that man think he could trick O'Neill."

Rory remembered that morning so clearly—the morning the world fell apart. Sorley had ordered his horse brought round in an hour; they were all sitting at the table in the hall over breakfast. He had just offered Sorley another slice of beef. "And take another cup, MacDonnell, it's a chill morning." He took up the flagon to pour more liquor. And at that moment, Murdock, the houseman, spoke from the door in an uncertain voice.

"McGuinness—there are some arrived to visit you."

They looked up. Moyna gave a sharp gasp; Sorley sprang to his feet; the flagon fell from Rory's hand to crash on the stone floor.

Lady Catherine was standing in the doorway—a Catherine they had never seen before. She was wrapped in a torn, stained cloak, her youngest child clasped in her arms, and her eyes were lost and wild. They saw that she wore bandages about her arms. Beside her stood James Donnelly, and he was carrying the two younger boys; his person bore evidence of hard travel, and he was deathly pale and grim. Then the servant stepped back and Cormac McArdle appeared to come slowly into the hall. Cradled carefully in his arms was the eldest son, Hugh Gavelock; the child was sleeping deeply, auburn head against the man's shoulder. McArdle was obviously exhausted, his step halting, his clothes dirt-stained, sweat-stained, blood-stained, wounds on his arms and legs unbandaged, a long cut down one side of his jaw. In dead silence he came in a few steps and halted, and stood looking at them dully.

Rory found his voice and heard himself crying stupidly, "Where is the chief? Where is O'Neill?"

McArdle came farther into the room to a chair and sat down, holding the child across his lap. He said in a tone which held no particular emotion, "This—is the chief. This—is O'Neill."

"No," said Sorley. "No."

"This—is—O'Neill."

Lady Catherine spoke, and it was not her voice, that high, flat tone. "They cut off his head. They cut off his head, I saw it, his eyes were wide open and he looked at me."

James Donnelly said unsteadily, "Do not be thinking of it any more, Catherine. Come and sit down now, tired you are." He put the children down in a chair and guided her to another; she let him seat her docilely.

"Cormac—in God's name—"

McArdle looked up. "At Ban Clough it was," he said almost conversationally. "You know—we met with that MacDonnell there, as arranged. Late afternoon it was we came, and the man very cordial. The troopmen —left in camp—outside the house, only formality to bring them. I did not trust the man when I first saw him—another James MacDonnell he looked. But I did not know how it would come. Only the four of us at the table for the meal—the man, Aspuke—and the lady—and myself—and Shane. And Shane . . ."

"They cut off his head," said Catherine. James spoke to her in a low voice.

"Who would have thought—? But I should have! I should have! I knew it was a signal when he raised his hand, but there was no time—no time. Fifty of them—Scot ax-men—pouring in the door. Unarmed we were, both of us—only our belt knives. And they falling on him all at once—I could not get in to him"—and McArdle pounded one fist on the arm of his chair in remembered agony. "I could not reach him—the lady trying to protect him, and wounded—"

"The axes were very sharp," Catherine said dreamily. "I felt them striking into his body." Moyna gave a little moan and went to her.

"He fought them a long time—only his knives and his fists. And I trying to get in to him—and he was shouting as he fought. 'But they cannot kill O'Neill!'—that was what he shouted—'They cannot defeat O'Neill!' There were too many, we couldn't withstand—I tried, I tried to reach him and die by his side! And still he was shouting, even as they brought him down—I will hear it until I die—'They cannot kill O'Neill!' But then I knew—then I saw. It was not my time to die. There was still a service—I must make him." He bowed his head and was silent.

"Cormac brought Catherine out," said Donnelly. "I do not know how, against that horde. To Lough Neagh—but it was not safe, even there. Hugh Ruadh has invaded with the new O'Connor; they have near three thousand men. The English have broken past our line—only four thousand to their six, to hold them, but the Scot chiefs and O'Reilly are fighting desperate. And the children, the sons, the heir—we thought—it was needful—"

"Yes," whispered Sorley. "Yes, I see. We will—guard them."

"They cut off his head," said Lady Catherine. "They will have put it on a spike over the gate to Dublin gaol."

Moyna put one arm about her, and her voice trembled. "Come away, my dear, come away and rest—very tired you are, you must sleep."

McArdle raised his head. "It was the reward, you see," he explained painfully. "The ten thousand pounds of gold—they offered for him. The English. Elizabeth. It was the gold."

"Yes—yes." Sorley went to help Moyna support Catherine. "Catriona, my poor love, what have they done to you! Christ, what have they done to us all! She must rest, she needs care—"

"The gold," said McArdle. "The English gold that has bought so many men's lives."

Sorley turned at the door from watching Moyna lead Catherine away. "The gold," he repeated in a dull voice. James Donnelly dropped suddenly into a chair and buried his face in his hands. "Yes. So Elizabeth has the last word. But she needed to hire a Judas to beat him, she could not do it fair. And has she the last word—after all? Has she?" His eyes were on the boy, Hugh Gavelock, in McArdle's arms.

Aroused now by all the voices speaking over him, the boy stirred and sat up. McArdle smoothed the tangled hair with a gentle hand. "Do not be frightened now—"

"I am not frightened," said the boy. "Put me down, Cormac—I want to get down."

"Did we not know him?" said Sorley somberly. "He was always right—he always knew. He was right at the last. They cannot kill O'Neill."

McArdle was setting the boy on his feet, smoothing down the rumpled kilt. "That is right, lad—my good lad, go with the mother now—"

"I will not!" The boy stared up at him defiantly, small hands going to his belt, head thrown back, and the morning sun, streaming in, touched his hair to flame. "I will not go with the women—I am a man and I will stay with the men!"

"Yes—man," said McArdle in a whisper. "Yes—O'Neill." And with that a cloud came suddenly over the sun, and the day darkened, and the hall darkened, as if night fell over the whole land.

epilogue

Rory stood in the doorway of Kilclain House, looking over his land to the road, and a little worry was eating at his heart, but he looked at his fields with pride. Twenty years of time moved across his mind and he was deeply content. He had prospered here, life had gone well for him— he had much to be thankful for. Because this day marked the beginning of his forty-ninth year, he took his mind off his worry resolutely and thought instead of all he had to thank God for.

He had survived the wars; he had thus far, and God keep it true henceforth, a good life here at Kilclain. The English were in Ulster, yes, but by no means uncontested; it would be a long time before they had the leisure to try crossing the Bann into Antrim.

And he was fortunate above all in his children: to raise safely nine from sixteen was great good luck. All of them were worthy of pride, from the eldest son, Michael, to little Aidan still playing with toys in the nursery. And the girls, Catherine wed to a son of Brodie's and two grandsons there, Caristiona to be wed this year to a MacArthur. He must be giving thought to suitable matches for the others soon. His household was increased indeed, for Michael was wed to Fergus' daughter, Bridie, and there were three grandchildren, two boys and a girl, for him now. His daughter, Catherine, would be having another soon. It was a pity her godmother did not live to see those children, but that other Catherine had not wanted to live afterward, and had existed only, one might put it, a few years alone. Perhaps it was the only way for her; others had felt not much different, then. But life moved on and one must move with it.

Into war, always into war, he thought with a rueful smile and a sigh. How many men from twenty years back had fallen! Diarmuid Ryan was dead of English gunfire, God rest him, he was a good friend; McFee, Burke, O'Hanlon—but he had come through. Only the virtuous die young, as he had once said. That wound he took in the campaign of 1569, leaving him with a short leg, put him out of action and he had been content enough to settle at Kilclain here—let Fergus take his place in the army.

A lucky man, he was. . . . And for Moyna too. A bit more of her maybe than twenty years back! But still his darling and his strength and his love.

But it was all empty comfort and whistling in the dark. There was that between a man and his eldest son—well, any son, but—Michael, Michael, said his mind, and he told himself angrily, A fool you are to worry; one of the clever McGuinnesses he is; no harm will come. All the same he went on thinking about it. It was always worrying to have Michael inside the Pale south, and, his commander trusting him as messenger, he was there often enough. Michael had said today or tomorrow he would be back, and stop at home a night before going on to make his report, for his wife, Bridie, would have another child soon and, this time, had not been well . . . that was a little worrying also. He was so absorbed in thought he never heard Moyna come up behind him. "I daresay you're looking out to see how the corn grows. Do you think he'll come today, Rory? He said a week—it is a week today."

"Oh, a day is little difference," said Rory bluffly. "Michael's a clever one, they'd not catch him." And Hugh, his second son, joining them from the hall, agreed to that.

"Your eyes are getting bad, old man," he said, an arm about Rory. "Don't you see him on the road now? No, I'm not jesting at all, look there." Rory strained his eyes down toward the gate, saw the horseman, and in a moment identified him.

"God be thanked—it is Michael," said Moyna. He echoed that. They went out to meet him as he dismounted in the yard, overwhelmed him with simultaneous questions.

"Did you have any trouble in the Pale?"

"Did you meet the Spaniard safe?"

"When are they coming?"

"Oh, you've torn your tunic—" Moyna, exclaiming in dismay. Michael laughed, hugging her.

"Nothing that is, soon mended and worth it! I had to climb up on the wall—give me a chance to answer one question at a time! Bridie is well?"

"Yes—resting." They urged him in, but he turned back to unfasten something from his saddle, a long bundle wrapped in his cloak.

"This I must show you. My Christ, I'm dry; it was a cold ride up from the border! Let me have a drink before I talk." Supplied with a cup and a chair in the hall, he went on: "Yes, I saw the Spaniard as arranged—a poor, womanish fellow, and his English comical, you should have heard! But the news is good, the chief will be pleased. Spain is to send the Armada next year, as the plan goes now. He kept repeating what a great fleet it will be, the greatest ever seen in the history of the world! Well, it may be, at that."

"But the gold from the Spanish king?" asked Rory.

"Oh, that is arranged too. It's to be sent secretly from France to Scotland, and the chief will take delivery of it there. Hiring ourselves out as mercenaries to Spain, fancy! But it's only a means to an end. When the

Armada has struck England we are to invade north; they hope to send some French mercenaries as well—and I mislike the notion of fighting alongside those foreigners, but it cannot be helped." Michael shrugged, finished his liquor, rose. "But I bring more than good news. I've a fine present for the chief."

"From the Spanish?" asked Hugh interestedly.

"From the English, brother! Wait until you see—" Michael was unrolling the bundle of his cloak swiftly. "As soon as I saw it, I knew I must have it. I waited four hours to get it down in safety. That was how I tore my tunic, getting up on the wall. Look!" He was spreading it out flat on the table, pushing aside cups and flagon to make room. They bent over it curiously.

It was a large public notice, meant to be fastened up on a wall; its message was crudely printed in large black letters. Rain had stained it in dark streaks, but it was still legible.

REWARD!

to enny man laying information leeding to
the capture of
the daingerrous rebel-leeder
HUGH ONEALE
100 crowns of gold
to enny man delivering up the severed heed of
the sayme
HUGH ONEALE
5000 pounds of gold!
TAKE NOTISE!

"Is it not a fine gift?" demanded Michael proudly. "He'll be amused. The price has gone up again, you notice. I thought when I saw it— What is it, Father?" Rory was laughing.

"Nothing," he said, "nothing much. I was only remembering another day, a very long time ago." He read the notice over again, between excitement and amusement. And he was thinking to himself, Thou wise man, Sorley Boy! You knew—you were right. The line breeds true. They can never kill O'Neill from this land.

note

For the documentary-minded, Shane O'Neill was born in March 1528, at Castle Dungannon in Tyrone, Ulster. He was assassinated, as described here, in May 1567. Besides an estimated seventy-odd illegitimate offspring, he left eight legitimate children: Eanruig (Henry), Con, and Turlough (by Catherine MacDonnell); Shane Oge (by Mary O'Donnell); Hugh Gavelock, Art, Brian, and Ailis (by Catherine MacLean). His eldest son by his third wife, Hugh, succeeded to his chiefhood and, among other rebellions, led the great rebellion of 1595, which English victory, resulting in the flight and exile of the Ulster leaders in Spain, broke the spirit of the north temporarily and gave England her first firm hold on the whole country. While he doubtless fathered many sons, Hugh Gavelock died without a legitimate heir; but Eanruig, Shane O'Neill's eldest legitimate son, was the father of the famous Eoghan Ruadh (Owen Roe) who fought Cromwell. Each of these three men—Shane, Hugh, and Eoghan—was known in his own time as the Great O'Neill; which had the juster claim to the title is a matter history has not decided—and history has a way of leveling greatnesses.

The house on the island in Lough Neagh has long since vanished, but the ruins of Benburb—more lately known as Shane's Castle—still stand, as does Dunluce in Antrim. It may be imagined that it is a haunted place; that on certain moonless nights the grass bends to no wind and the bare turf where stretched the long hall of the castle echoes to no human voice, as the ghosts gather again to talk the campaigns and argue and join old mirth. And surely in the midst of them, even in death a little larger than life, strides and curses the shade of that first, and greatest, of the great O'Neills of Ulster.